A Contented Mind

a novel

Love, hope and the complicated mess of
redefining one's life.

Samantha Hoffman

Two Dog Press

TO THOSE WHO BELIEVED IN ME

This book is affectionately dedicated

Mama Gump was right after all: life *is* like a box of chocolates. But Meg's heart-shaped box was filled with the bittersweet variety, or so she believed. Yet for the moment, while gazing at her new Southern California beachfront home, Meg savored only sweetness, even if she couldn't ignore the bitterness that had brought her there.

"This looks good," Meg said, standing in the driveway.

"Is this really what you want?" Devon asked, eyeing the two-story house skeptically.

"Mandalay Bay is such a beautiful place. Smell that fresh ocean air, Dev, " Meg said, taking a soulful breath while glancing up at Devon. "This will work out. I know. Somehow, I just know."

Turning to get a better view of her surroundings, Meg surveyed the neighborhood. The street was quiet enough, with only the occasional car passing by. Most of the traffic, from what she could gather, came from those walking their dogs. The peaceful images brought an immediate smile.

She also liked the old trees bordering the street. Standing tall above everything else, their age gave them the appearance of authority and grandeur. But most of all, she loved the warm air that held the scent of desert willow and California white sage, mixed with the salt from the ocean. For a moment, Meg felt like bathing in the aroma.

"Well, I for one don't care for your being so bloody close to people, Meg," Devon whispered. "That run-in you had on Martha's Vineyard nearly scared the life out of me."

Devon was many things to Meg. Beyond being her publisher, he was her friend. She liked their rhythm, and they worked well together. Although Meg could easily question the sincerity of her own shadow, she never thought to question Devon's. She never needed to.

Even though Meg was already in the midst of writing her latest novel, Devon was still busy managing the affairs from her last novel. Calling it a "real steamer" after turning the last page, he knew instantly it would climb its way to the top of the bestseller list, just as Meg's previous novels had. And it did.

"I need this change, Dev. I need to clear my head. Heck . . .I don't know why that nut job broke into my house and tried to hurt me. But here I know I'll have peace and quiet. Maybe even chip away at the writer's block that's found a new home in my head," Meg said, giving Bob a rub behind the ear.

Always the faithful Irish setter, Bob believed his dutiful place was within inches of wherever Meg was. By Meg's choice, Bob had been her writing partner and best friend for the past ten years. Not much impressed with people, Meg never had a hard time with Bob or any other animal, for that matter. She felt blessed by Bob's innately nonjudgmental nature. His love was unconditional, without one string attached to it.

"Peace and quiet. Are you serious?" Devon asked in disbelief. "When do you ever get peace and quiet for very long? Look at you. You're such a beautiful woman, Meg. God, men . . they start sniffing around . . ."

"Let 'em sniff all they want. I don't care." Meg waved a dismissive hand in the air. "I don't intend to waste my time with a *guy.*"

As soon as Meg heard these words exit her mouth, she wanted to pull them back inside. The look on Devon's face revealed that her choice of words was a painful one. Devon, for reasons that he himself hardly understood, loved Meg ever since their first meeting ten years ago, when they were introduced by a mutual friend who recommended his publishing house represent her work.

Devon felt he saw past Meg's complexities. He knew why she held herself so distant from others. Meg had a great deal of pain, pain she said fueled her creative writing; a truth Devon couldn't argue with.

The night they spent together only added to his feelings. Struggling with two scenes from her last novel, Meg wanted to find a way to make sure the lovemaking she wanted to describe was true to life or even feasible for that matter. After a bottle of red wine and a loss of inhibition, Meg confided her struggles to Devon. Without flinching, he gladly offered his services. *Research*, he happily termed it. And in Meg's wine-enlightened mind, it made perfect sense. Ultimately, though, it was a night that forever changed Devon. He was never able to look at Meg quite the same again. Meg, however, gained the much needed insight into her love scenes she needed, and was satisfied with the thought of keeping it strictly at that.

Meg often wondered why she didn't pursue things further with Devon. His English accent alone drove the women insane, a situation that amused her constantly. When given the chance she would sit idly by just to watch the women fall over themselves striving to get his attention. He was six feet two and had a body most women dreamt of having in their bed. His dark brown hair was always neatly trimmed and slicked back, except for the occasional lock that fell carelessly across his brow. His high cheek bones gracefully gave way to his slender rose-colored lips, which were usually turned in the shape of a sly, confident grin. His eyes were a decadent shade of chocolate and, considering their darkness, remarkable was their ability to sparkle when a brilliant smile swept across his face. *He's a magnificent creature, no question about it,* Meg mused.

He was wealthy, too. Not that it mattered to Meg. She never understood the allure of money. Instead, she always felt an undeniable need to feed her restless soul, and to one day find someone who didn't want to tame it but instead wanted to explore it.

"Do you need any help getting settled?" Devon offered, raising his right eyebrow.

"We're good. The movers brought everything, and remember — I bought the home already furnished. Things should look pretty much as they did when I did the walk-through. Bob and I just need to go in and start this next chapter of our lives. Anyway, you need to get going. I'm not your only client." Meg jokingly pushed Devon's arm, offering him a gentle reminder. She needed to be alone, and Devon had other obligations that often suffered due to his affection for her.

Meg was eager for the new beginning that sat before her like a gift waiting to be opened. Life was changing once again, whether she prompted it or not. Due to the break-in on Martha's Vineyard, she no longer felt safe in her own home. She couldn't write, she couldn't sleep, and her thoughts raced relentlessly, until finally she felt forced to leave her secluded home. An obsessed fan making his way into her home and attacking her wasn't something she wanted to think about ever again, and hopefully by moving completely across the country, she wouldn't have to anymore.

Normally, Meg never had to worry about fans because she never wrote under her real name. For all anyone knew, she was an ordinary woman who lived alone with her dog. Meg was unyieldingly private; she simply never divulged any more than that.

Meg had a bright personality that sat on top of a very complex and oftentimes dark and restless soul. She didn't have a great deal of faith in people. The thoughts streaming through their minds were of little interest to her. Instead, it usually took all the effort she had to keep a firm grasp on her own. She never meant to be dark. Dark found her.

Meg found great release in writing and, to her surprise, wrote novels that were wildly popular. She always tried to give the same spirit to her characters that she felt within herself. And by doing so, she created people who led lives her readers only dared to dream about. Her last novel, *Safe People,* was still on *The New York Times* Best Sellers list, and had been for some while.

Oprah featured it on her show, using it as a sounding board to discuss women who love more than one man at a time. Because Meg's book was written with such eloquence, it also attracted attention from many well known novelists and critics.

Even *Rolling Stone* magazine wanted to interview the author, which was surprising, considering that Devon had declared that the author chose to write under an assumed name and would never give interviews. Still, *Rolling Stone* gave her novel a rave review, stating:

"Kathleen Kelley's attention to the details of *the balls to the walls* rock world was astonishing. Ms. Kelley took us on a journey that at times left us speechless but, with every paged turned, ultimately left us longing for more."

Meg was proud of this particular review, knowing that of all publications *Rolling Stone* would scrutinize her novel with a critical eye, ready to criticize anything that shouldn't be there.

Set around a rock band, *Safe People* required more research and travel than Meg was accustomed to. She was thankful for the help from the bands and musicians who put up with her shadowing them while out on tour; she hadn't, however, bargained for their romantic interest in her. Meg forgot to see herself as others often saw her, a simple side effect of spending much of her time consumed with her thoughts and stories.

But to the outside world, Meg was beautiful. Her dainty frame held her proportions as well as nature had intended. Her wavy, auburn hair hung midway down her back and flowed gracefully around her face. Her skin was delicate and fair, with a dewy glow that gave her a subtle radiance. But what nearly everyone noticed were Meg's eyes. Their large, soft shape held vibrant flints of green and gold that changed color depending on her mood.

It was no surprise to Devon when some of the musicians who met Meg became enamored with her. Devon had worked hard creating a cover story for Meg that allowed her to be entrenched in the lifestyle of the bands without telling them about the book she was writing. He was pleased with himself when he crafted the nice, little lie that Meg was a student at the University of New York, doing a thesis on the behavioral challenges of being in a rock band. As long as no names were given, the bands seemed more than happy to oblige.

After a long silent pause while standing in Meg's driveway, Devon finally acquiesced. Giving Meg a longer than normal embrace, stopping for a moment with his mouth resting on her ear, he wanted to say *something*. Hidden within his silence were the words he wanted to say but couldn't. Sighing, he gently kissed her cheek and knelt down to give Bob a rub before turning and walking away.

Watching Devon drive off, Meg tried to breathe out her nervousness, hoping in the process to breathe out her writer's block as well. Turning around, she stood in awe of her new home. She had walked through it only once. Immediately taken by its beauty, she bought it on the spot, asking only that she could purchase the furniture as well, never stopping to ask about the community, her neighbors, or the weather for that matter.

The narrow driveway led to a single white garage door with a series of square windows spanning its width. From this view, the home looked as if it had been plucked from Edgartown in Martha's Vineyard. It was a craftsman style home, with charcoal gray shake siding and white trim; a stone stairway led to a welcoming front porch and a dark mahogany entry door.

Even though Meg was a complete transplant, this home made the transition easier. It was as if someone designed the home knowing soon there would be a lonely soul coming from the eastern United States in need of a familiar place to hang her hat.

To the left of her home, hidden behind a thick row of tall bushes, was a contemporary split-level house, also on the beach. That home, Meg concluded, was typical of what she would expect for a California beach house. Because of the green wall of privacy surrounding it, she had no idea who lived there. But Meg expected, whether she wanted to or not, she would be meeting her neighbors soon enough.

"Hope they keep to themselves. I don't need any nosey neighbors wondering why I don't pull my trash can back into the garage two minutes after the garbage truck rolls away." She mumbled, stretching her neck to get a better look at the beach house that hugged hers.

The hum of the garage door closing behind her gave Meg the feeling that she and Bob were finally alone. Quietly the two stood in the entranceway of their new home. It was just as Meg had remembered it. The main room was a large open space with hardwood flooring that reminded her of her old Cape Cod. The kitchen and sitting area were situated off to the left and had a magnificent view of the ocean, as did the bedroom that sat off to the right.

White was the predominant color throughout the house. *Good for clear thinking,* Meg thought. Looking out from where she stood, past the white overstuffed furniture, was the balcony: the part of the house that smiled.

Meg and Bob walked out onto the balcony, and she leaned against the thick white railing. Folding her arms across her chest, Meg gazed at the ocean sitting in front of her.

"So beautiful, so big. Dangerous and inviting all at the same time . . .but isn't that how the most beautiful things in life are?" Meg wondered with sadness, looking down at Bob, whose eyes were held steady on the ocean.

Turning to walk back into the house, Meg stared at the boxes stacked by the entrance way and easily decided to leave them for later. Instead of starting the daunting task of unpacking, she rummaged for one very important box. The one labeled *Handle with Care VIOLIN.*

"Aha, there it is, Bob. Now all we need is a pair of scissors so we can open this damn thing." Turning in circles, Meg wondered if a pair had been left behind. "Success," she said, carefully cutting the tape on the box.

Pulling back the flaps, she slowly pulled out the violin. Meg's eyes began to water as she stared at it. It wasn't the world's prettiest violin, but it had been hers for as long as she could remember. Her parents had given it to her on the last Christmas she shared with them, when she was only ten. Because of that, it held a special meaning. After their death, she used the violin to help heal her soul.

Cradling the violin on her shoulder, Meg softly brushed the strings with her bow. Recognizing the scene before him, Bob followed her onto the balcony and curled his large body next to her feet. Beginning to play, Meg filled the air with sounds reminiscent of a soul crying and rejoicing, bouncing melodically between the two extremes. The tepid ocean air blew through her hair leaving its salty residue on her skin. So engrossed was she in her private moment, if it started raining she wouldn't have noticed.

Jadon stopped dead in his tracks — a half eaten salami on rye in one hand, a cold Dos Equis in the other, and the feeling of having just been hit in the chest by a bullet. At first he wasn't sure what he was hearing, as it didn't readily take the shape of a song; but it was beautiful and melodic. And as soon as he stopped to listen, he felt a longing stir from someplace deep inside, bringing forth feelings completely foreign to him.

Music came naturally to Jadon, for even as a young boy he was a gifted musician. But what Jadon was listening to was more than music. It was as if someone were speaking to him. He just wasn't sure what they were trying to say. Walking onto his balcony, he could easily hear the music coming from the house next door.

"Well, hello," Jadon said to himself.

Trying to peer around the wall of his balcony, the same wall he built for the purpose of gaining privacy from his neighbors, Jadon couldn't catch sight of anyone. Turning to return indoors, he couldn't fight the urge to be near the music. Sinking into one of the lounge chairs lining his balcony, he closed his eyes and listened.

Bolted awake by the sound of a horn blaring from the street, Jadon quickly realized that not only had he fallen asleep but the music had stopped as well. Startled and angered, he jumped to his feet, and thundered toward the door.

"What the hell . . ." Jadon wondered, straining his eyes to see further out his front door, before finally walking out onto his driveway.

"Thanks for coming back, Ned. Bob would've missed his things tonight when bedtime rolled around. He's an old guy, he needs his things," Meg said with a smile directed toward the gentle-faced delivery driver standing in her driveway. "I can hardly believe you turned around and drove all the way back."

"Nah, it wasn't such a big deal. Anyways, it's your stuff Ms. Scott, and we're under contract to deliver it *all*. Hate to have been further up the road and found it then. I'm just glad we saw your stuff when we did," Ned said.

"I'm pretty sure someone else would've just kept driving. So again, thank you very much," Meg said, turning to head back into the house with Bob in tow.

His view blocked by the dense row of tall shrubs lining his driveway, Jadon cut around the bushes that held the two homes in seclusion from one another. Squinting through the shrubbery, he was able to see only what appeared to be a very happy, very large dog. Managing to squeeze further between the bushes, Jadon pushed his head out for a better view, hoping in the process no one would be staring back at him. Watching the moving van driver turn and wave, Jadon quickly looked to see who was at the other end of the wave, but it was too late. Whoever it was, was already gone. Feeling foolish by his stalker-like attempt to catch sight of his new neighbors, Jadon started to take a step back when he heard the young woman's voice again.

"Ned! Wait!" Meg yelled, running back from her garage, waving a piece of pink paper in her hand. "You forgot your manifest! It's all signed, here you go. Have a great day."

Like a stone Jadon didn't move, overcome by the sudden wave that poured over his body once his eyes locked onto Meg. Having no way of blending naturally with a row of shrubs, Jadon quickly threw himself onto the grass behind the bushes.

"Holy Christ, I wonder what Bob looks like," Jadon whispered, stunned by the sight of his new neighbor.

After Meg was out of sight, Jadon pulled himself up, and walked back into his house.

Throwing back his comforter and stumbling out of bed, Jadon couldn't ignore the new day that arrived while he was sound asleep. It announced itself in a startling ring tone, one that he currently regretted downloading. After finding his cell phone hidden under his bed, he flipped it open, regardless of not being particularly eager to talk to anyone.

"Dude, where are you?" the voice on the other end asked.

"Where the hell do you think I am? I just rolled out of bed," Jadon grumbled.

"Thought we were going to meet at the studio."

"Christ...I forgot."

"Uh...that's obvious. You sound like shit."

"I've got new neighbors."

"So..."

"I heard this music. It was ...creepy and magical," Jadon said, trying to put words to his feelings.

"Okay. Got some creepy music. This sounds like a bad movie, Jay."

"Then Ned woke me up."

"Who's Ned?"

"Ned is the guy from White Glove Movers. He was bringing Bob's stuff back," Jadon shot off rapidly.

"Bob's got stuff?"

"Yeah. Bedtime stuff."

"Okay. Continue," Chick said, snapping his gum.

"I don't know what came over me . . . I sort of went into this . . . stalker mode. I was buried between the bushes, listening to Ned. Suddenly, all I could hear was this woman talking about Bob . . . and how he needs his stuff for bedtime."

"Bedtime?" Chick repeated.

"Bedtime. Yeah, that's what I was thinkin' too. Who the hell has bedtime stuff? Then I saw her."

"Her? Dude . . . you okay?"

"I don't know," Jadon said, trying to shake off his uneasiness with a feigned laugh.

Chapter 2

Meg rubbed her hands over her face. Reaching across the bed she gave Bob a thorough rub down, and watched his red, furry body turn to butter beneath her hands.

"Guess it's time to get to business, Bobby. We need to get this place livable. And we need some food. Not that either of us show signs of starving anytime soon," she said.

Opening the passenger door of her silver Mercedes SLR convertible, Bob hopped inside. Sliding onto the plush leather seat, Meg brought the engine to life. Within moments, and without much effort on her part, Meg had the two of them down the street and roaring into town.

Wanting the luxury of not thinking about anything, Meg brought the stereo to near deafening levels. Rocking her head to the music, she felt every beat buried within each song she had downloaded onto her iPod for the road trip from Massachusetts to Southern California. As road trips go, it was a good one. The trip gave Meg the chance to think thoughts unobstructed by deadlines or demands. Thoughts discovered only from behind the wheel.

Driving to the store, Meg began to think again about the movie based on her fourth novel, which now was in theaters across the country. Regardless of how many times she thought about it, or saw the movie, she never felt the director was able to bring to life her characters or the passion flowing between them. The movie was a great success, but Hollywood missed the mark as to the real fire burning within her characters.

As the ocean air filled their lungs with the telltale signs of living life beside the water, Meg soon felt invigorated. Not over her writer's block, but invigorated just the same. As she rolled out of the parking lot of the specialty foods store, she felt pleased with the small bag of odds and ends she managed to find, and even more pleased with the bottle of Spanish red wine she stumbled upon.

By late in the day the last box was almost unpacked. Because the house was already furnished, all she had to do was place her personal belongings around, christening the new space as her own. Noticing the late hour, Meg felt good with her day, having accomplished a great deal — especially for someone who spends most of the day watching her thoughts dance inside her head. Meg made her way into the kitchen and grabbed the Rioja she picked up earlier at the store.

"Well, hello, how are you this evening? Me? Good, good. Bob? Oh, he's good too. Thanks for asking." Meg chuckled, enjoying the entertaining dialogue she was having with herself.

To Meg, every bottle of wine was like a person waiting to be introduced. What rested inside the bottle, similar to what rested inside every person, was their soul, waiting to be experienced.

"Those grapes gave their lives for me, Bob, and I'm damn well going to enjoy them."

Taking her glass onto the balcony, Meg sat down and listened to the waves roll in and slap upon the beach before making their hasty retreat. *It's like listening to time tick away*, Meg thought to herself. *God's timepiece, if ever he needed one.*

Feeling the right mixture of melancholy and vulnerability, Meg set down her glass and went indoors to get her violin. She returned and, with Bob at her feet, held her violin, absorbing the energy of the wood before starting to play softly.

As she played, Meg heard the sound of a piano, played equally softly. Amused that she now lived in a place where musicians live, she quickly noticed that the piano was blending its notes with hers. Astonishing, she thought, considering she wasn't playing a song anyone would know. Somehow this pianist was tapping into her melody, matching it with a beautiful harmony. Not exactly note for note, but blending with hers just the same. Suddenly Meg felt a pang of intrusion.

While traveling with various rock bands, gathering research for her last novel, Meg had ample time alone, time that gave her the chance to take each band's music and adapt it for the violin. Sometimes it didn't work at all, while at other times it was like creating magic. In an attempt to stifle her uninvited guest, Meg shifted into one of her favorites, rocketing her playing into a fiery kaleidoscope of sound.

Within seconds, and with the same amount of determination, the pianist matched her note for note. Not trying to take away her lead; instead, he kept in perfect step with her. Trying to elude the unexpected accompanist, Meg took the song and her playing to her highest level, thrusting both of them through verse and chorus. But both violin and piano remained perfectly intertwined and ended the song at exactly the same time, on exactly the same note, as if they'd been practicing for years.

Startled, Meg grabbed her wine glass and hurried into the house. Standing silent and stunned, her body was wrapped half with the intensity of having just made passionate love with a stranger, the other half scared to death that someone could be so easily and intricately in tune with her.

"What on earth just happened? Who the hell was that?" Meg whispered breathlessly, staring wide-eyed around the room.

Cautiously walking back onto her balcony, Meg sat down. She stared at the dark ocean that moved in front of her, curled her knees tight to her chest, and wondered how something so peculiar could happen. But, she had to admit to herself, the experience captivated her heart, even if it lasted for only a moment. The intensity of that moment, and the sudden unexpected emptiness remaining once it ended, filled Meg with sadness.

Getting up, she tried to look into her neighbor's balcony. Seeing nothing, she then tried peering into their windows. The lights were out. She couldn't see a thing.

Jadon decided to keep the piano-violin interlude he had last night to himself. The entire event would sound strange, and he wasn't in the mood for anyone to ask obvious questions. Such as, "Did you go over and introduce yourself?" "Who are your neighbors?" and the most obvious question, and the one he struggled with the most, "What the hell were you thinking?" All valid questions, none of which he had an answer for.

His playing was off all day. He knew it. The band knew it. Although this didn't affect anything, it still bothered him. He couldn't get her off his mind. The fact that she was married only added to his confused thoughts. Another, more troubling thought, was that it might have been Bob who was playing the violin, not Meg.

"Just didn't sound like a guy to me," Jadon whispered, driving into his garage, tired from a long, unproductive day at the studio. "It was too sensual. God. Listen to me. I sound like a fuckin' nut case."

Even so, Jadon couldn't help but wonder if there might be a chance to meet his violinist neighbor again that night.

"It isn't too late right now," he mumbled to himself. "A normal person would just go over and introduce himself."

The thought wasn't all that bad, but the prospect of being face to face with Meg overwhelmed him.

"Something about her," Jadon sighed, stepping out of his car.

With one foot out, he realized he forgot to stop at the store on his way home. Minutes after backing out of his garage, Jadon pulled into the wine shop located only a few blocks away.

Wrangling his way around the small store, Jadon grabbed a few scant items. *This oughtta do it,* he said to himself after the checkout girl rang up his order. Turning to leave, Jadon looked through the glass door and watched as Meg walked directly toward him. Out of sheer panic he quickly stepped to the side, placing his bag high on his left arm in an attempt to block his face. *What difference does it make if she sees me,* he thought quickly, trying to make sense of his own reaction. Still in shock, Jadon stood motionless staring blankly at the various items posted on the bulletin board for sale.

1997 MerCruiser Outboard Motor for sale. "Who the hell needs one of those?" he softly muttered, while using his peripheral vision to see where Meg had gone.

"Will that be it?" the young cashier asked Meg.

"Yup. We're good," Meg replied, waving her hand in the air. "By the way, I just loved that wine I picked up the other night. It was wonderful."

"How's Bob? I was so happy I got a chance to meet him," the cashier asked.

"Oh, he's good. The move was hard. He's just now getting settled. The nights have been rough. He hasn't slept well. It's a lot adjusting to a new place. Doesn't help he wants to meet our neighbor. He keeps hanging around their house. Hey, speaking of neighbors," Meg tried to sound natural, "Um . . .you wouldn't happen to know who lives at 3318 Mandalay Bay Drive?"

The hair on Jadon's neck stood on end.

"Ya' know, I just don't know. No clue. I don't live around here."

"Oh, well. Thanks anyway. Have a nice day."

Meg grabbed her grocery bag, turned, and took only a few steps toward the door when she stopped and stared at the man standing quietly scrutinizing the bulletin board. He was about her height, roughly five foot eight. He was in good shape, with a delicate frame. His unruly blonde hair hung down to his shoulders. And from what Meg could tell, he was totally engrossed in the bulletin board. Especially when he suddenly started pulling off numerous tabs from the various pieces of paper thumbed tacked to the board.

Meg didn't know why but there was something familiar about him, something that caused every fiber in her body to stir as she continued to stare at him. Feeling her body flush, and without thinking, she moved closer, stopping once she noticed she was standing too close to someone who was a complete stranger. But, for reasons she couldn't explain, she wanted to be near him.

Feeling her overwhelming presence directly behind him, Jadon started to panic. He increased his rate of ripping tabs from the bulletin board announcements, at one point accidentally pulling off an entire index card.

"Christ," Jadon whispered, kicking the five-by-seven card toward the wall with his toe.

Realizing she'd been cemented in place for too long, Meg quickly stepped out of the store and into her roadster. Bob greeted her with his customary kiss. Backing out of the parking spot, Meg bolted onto the street.

"Why the hell is my heart racing? For Christ's sake, Meg, slow down," she yelled at herself.

Within minutes Bob and Meg were safely inside their garage. Before closing the door, Meg looked back onto the driveway, half wondering if the man from the store had followed her.

It was already nearly 9:30 p.m., and Meg felt her heart speed up. She was wondering if she played her violin, would her neighbor again join her? *Was it a onetime fluke? Did it mean something? What the hell could it mean, for Christ's sake?* Meg's mind began to spin, but she couldn't help but wonder just the same.

Grabbing her glass of wine, Meg walked out onto the balcony and gazed at the water. The surf's dramatic swooshing sounds reminded her of a large auditorium, crowded with people all hushing each other in preparation for the show. Taking the cue nature gave her, Meg picked up her violin. She cradled it in her arms, as if embracing an old friend. Taking a deep breath, she moved the violin out onto her left shoulder. Tilting her head, she rested her chin softly on its cradle, and closed her eyes. She could feel the presence of her parents tonight. She could feel their love in the air.

Within minutes the ocean harnessed the anxious crowd of waves, causing a stillness to fall across the air. Meg took the moment to become one with her violin, with her inner demons, her hopes, and her dreams. She no longer wondered if her neighbor would join, instead she felt her heart beating in rhythm to the delicate song played on her violin.

Once her thoughts were carried away, she heard the soft sounds of the piano shyly joining in. Meg smiled. Taking a deep breath, she suddenly felt connected to this stranger once again. Filling the air with a sensual sound, she hoped her new friend would know that his company was welcomed.

Jadon had waited for this moment ever since it ended the night before. He wanted it to last forever but knew it, like most spectacular moments, would soon be over. He noticed the intensity of the violin strings humming louder and stronger. Taking that as his signal, he worked to match Meg note for note.

Meg didn't have a clue what she was playing, she just stood and swayed to the beautiful music. From deep within her soul, she knew that this new friend, and his piano, were her perfect partners, as if he could see into her heart. As his playing grew more dramatic, and as the pace quickened, Meg dove fully into her notes. Her breathing grew faster as she tried to keep up. She didn't think about who this person was. She thought only of how perfect the moment felt.

Instinctively, Jadon knew Meg wanted to allow them more time. Stretching his notes he tried to give them both a moment longer with one another. Just as soon as their stillness graced the air around them, it quickly built back up. Pounding harder onto the keys, Jadon hardly knew where his fingers were landing. He only knew it sounded right. Closing his eyes, he deeply prayed the one playing the violin was Meg.

"Meg," he said softly, while the floor beneath his feet vibrated from his thundering keystrokes. Throwing his head back, Jadon closed his eyes.

Meg swayed back and forth to the steady beat they were creating. Her skin tingled with excitement as the sweat dripped steadily down her back. Tilting her head back, she felt the cool ocean breeze brush against her damp skin. And in one quick moment, they were done.

Chapter 3

"Now, darling . . .I think I've found a brilliant way to get rid of your writer's block." Devon's voice said calmly over the phone line.

"It's not another writer's retreat, is it?" Meg grumbled. "You know how much I hate those things. Just knowing I'm there for the purpose of igniting my writer's fire, snuffs out my writer's fire."

"Listen," Devon said, "although I'm slightly hesitant about this, I think you'll get quite a kick out of it. Daniel was talking with one of his friends at A & E Records in Los Angeles, and he mentioned that Equinox is searching for a violinist for an acoustic album they're toying around with. Well, naturally he thought of you. The band's studio is in Bay City, just a few miles from your home, and so Daniel already arranged an audition for you. I know, I know, it was a bit presumptuous of him. Trust me. I already told him so. But as I was thinking about it, I realized this might be just what you need. Now Meg, he did tell them you're a writer. What you decide to tell them from there is completely up to you, darling. What do you say?"

Even as Devon spoke those words he was half rethinking the idea. Meg was in a real funk, and although he originally saw this as the perfect opportunity for her to shake things up, he was also concerned about her doing exactly that.

"God, Dev, did Daniel tell them I'm not a *classically trained* violinist? What if I'm a flop?"

"Well, Daniel doesn't think it matters. You know he adores how well you play."

The phone grew silent as Meg remembered how Devon's older brother Daniel had enjoyed her violin playing during their last get-together. They had been laughing and enjoying drinks when Devon piped up about her talents. Daniel begged her to play, and, much to Meg's surprise, he was enthralled by it. But this chance would be the real test. The band Equinox was very good, and known worldwide. Even she enjoyed their music. Being a flop in front of a few judges at a high school music show was one thing, but being a flop in front of a world renowned rock band was quite another. Then again, the chance to just be herself was a hard thing to pass up. That was one thing Meg always admired about musicians: some of them had a gift for settling into their own skin. Regardless of what that skin was exactly, they had discovered the trick of just being themselves.

"I'll do it," Meg said with certainty. "When and where?"

"Tomorrow at 3 p.m.," Devon said, bracing himself for what he felt certain would be an outburst of panic.

"Oh, my God. Tomorrow? Are you serious? Holy Mother of Christ."

"Yes, that is right. Tomorrow."

"I better get some of their music. How does someone prepare for something like this? Oh, Christ, I don't even know where the music stores are around here," Meg said, quickly ending her call with Devon.

Pushing her chair back, Meg went into the kitchen with hopes of finding a telephone book left behind by the previous owners. Two drawers into her search she sighed with relief, pulling the mountainous directory from the drawer. With hurried fingers she thumbed through the Yellow Pages, finding the music section.

Ripping out the entire page, Meg squinted, struggling to picture the crossroads they were located on. Satisfied she could get there with no problem, she grabbed her keys, and told Bob to jump in the car.

Area 51 Studios was situated in the old warehouse district in a forgotten part of Bay City. It was a private space purchased by Equinox after they decided they no longer wanted to be at the mercy of someone else's timetable when it came to practicing and recording their albums. Area 51 signified a turning point in the band's career. It allowed them the creative freedom they felt was taken out of their lives once they became well known and under the guidance of their latest manager, Vince McGee. Vince was good, but as with all cases dealing with artists, there was a paper-thin line separating the band from doing their own thing and moving them forward into stardom. Although, if asked, the band would unanimously agree that stardom was much over rated.

The ring leader for Equinox was its lead singer, songwriter and guitarist, Kurt Holschick or Chick for short. Chick had a vision he felt could be expressed only through a full acoustic, instrumental version of his band. Equinox was known for their stripped down style of rock, but Chick had built a stockpile of songs needing a different approach. It was an approach Chick discovered as a small boy, when one of his favorite bands performed at Rugby Auditorium in Toronto accompanied by a violin and piano. Ever since, he had a desire to record an album doing the same.

"We got two more people coming to audition. Christ, I hope one of them hits the mark," Chick said in tired disgust, giving a quick thought to the seven auditions the band had sat through that day alone.

Each one, although talented, didn't have a clue how to blend their style with the style of the band. Moreover, none — not one —

had the charisma Chick felt would give the songs the added vibe he was looking for. Chick felt fortunate to have his band mates and the added pianist he handpicked. Each was a phenomenal musician but, more than that, they were characters. Chick liked characters. And, he felt by adding a little piss and vinegar to the band it would give the music a raw quality that wouldn't be achieved otherwise.

"This one oughtta be interesting. She's a writer. Better not be a waste of time. How the hell could a writer be right for this gig?" Chick looked around the room at everyone, as they stared back at him with equal doubt.

"Hello? I'm Meg Scott. Here for the three o'clock interview," Meg said, holding down the button on the intercom located next to the entry gate.

"Yup, here ya' go," Stu said into the microphone located inside the studio. He pushed a button, opening the black wrought iron gates outside.

"Well, she's here now guys," Stu said to Chick and the others. "Might as well get this show on the road."

Driving into the alley next to the studio, Meg's thoughts began to pop nervously like corn kernels over a hot flame. Flustered, she took a deep breath to center herself, in doing so noticed her lungs had decided to protest her natural attempt to expand them. Meg suddenly realized that life was imitating art. In her latest book *Safe People*, Beatrice — or Bertie as she was called — had a similar audition. Except it was for lead vocalist, and the band was still in its infancy. Eerily, the nervousness that Meg had attributed to Bertie was the exact same nervousness Meg felt within her entire body.

"Hell, if Bertie can do it, I can do it. I'll just go in, kick ass, and get the hell out," she said with forced determination.

Reaching over to grab her violin case, Meg walked to the door of the studio, and gave it a resounding knock. "Breathe," she whispered to herself, "just breathe."

Chick opened the door almost immediately but then was taken aback by the sight of Meg. Having put more thought into practicing the night before and all that morning, Meg hadn't given any thought to how she looked. Wanting to be as comfortable as possible, she threw on her favorite worn Levi's, a blue t-shirt that read *smile; it confuses people*, and her well traveled Vans, which were adorned with hula dancers. Smiling a gracious smile Meg quickly stuck her hand out toward Chick, who gave her a heartfelt handshake in return, before turning to his friends with the wave of his hand.

"Well, this is the band, Meg. Glad you could run down here. Let me introduce you to everyone. This is Stu . . .he's on bass," Chick pointed behind himself toward the short, stocky guy with a mop of curly brown and gold hair.

"Hey," Stu nodded.

"This is Kofi. He's our new pianist for this whole acoustic deal," Chick continued, motioning behind Meg to the tall, surprisingly thin, man leaning against the desk.

"Where's Bob?" Chick asked, as he scratched his slick, black beard and walked toward the back room. "Come and meet Meg, Bob."

Breaking away from the discussion he was just having, Bob quickly made his way over to Meg with an outstretched hand and a smile that lit up his well tanned face.

"Hi, Bob. I'm pretty fond of that name. My . . ." Meg began.

"And this is Jadon. He's our drummer," Chick interrupted, tapping Jadon on the back.

Taking his eyes away from the computer screen he and Bob were looking at, Jadon turned around. With less than two feet between them, he stood speechless in front of Meg, his neighbor.

For reasons she wasn't sure of, the same startling, almost immobilizing emotions she felt while staring at the man in the store the other day engulfed her once again. His height was the same, and the hair, same. She wouldn't forget that hair for anything. Even though all she saw was the back of him, Meg was certain it was the same man. *I'd be willing to roll dice with God on this one*, Meg said to herself.

Continuing to stand motionless in front of Meg, Jadon felt his knees struggle to support his weight, a reaction that didn't help to mask his shock.

Within seconds the air between the two was palpable to the point of being felt by all. Not knowing what they were feeling, it was undeniable to everyone standing in the room, something exhilarating and equally alarming was happening.

"Hey," Jadon said after an awkwardly long pause.

Startled by Meg's unexpected appearance at the studio, Jadon forced himself to look away. It was a simple movement, but one that without his knowing gave the abrupt impression of indifference.

Meg watched Jadon look away, as if too troubled to officially introduce himself. Feeling the sting of his disregard her smile faded.

"Hello, Jadon," Meg said politely, but as if filled with molasses, her mind felt too heavy to offer anymore than that. Quickly straightening her stance, Meg tried to shake off her urge to run for the hills. Dropping her hand, she grabbed the handle on her violin case, and tried to erase the last few moments from her mind.

Chick was baffled. Why, he wondered, had Jadon looked as if he had seen a ghost then, just as quick, looked as though he couldn't stand the sight of Meg. But sensing Meg's uneasiness, Chick tried, as he always did, to make light of the situation.

"Don't mind him, he's just being weird." Chick waved a dismissive hand toward Jadon. "Let's get this show on the road. In here is where we make magic, Meg." Chick chuckled at himself and motioned for Meg to follow him into the back room. "Show us whatcha got sister," Chick said, plopping himself down on his chair, while the other band members took their places.

Holding his arms tightly across his chest, Jadon walked behind his drums, then grabbed his sticks and quickly sat down. Now that he no longer had a firm grasp on his arms, he could feel himself visibly shake. Taking a deep breath, Jadon tried to get a handle on the unexpected turn his life had just taken. But instead, staring at Meg while she carefully took her violin from its case, all he could do was wonder how such a thing could happen.

"This is fuckin' unreal," Jadon mumbled, "It's *her* . . ."

"What's that, Jay?" Chick asked quickly.

"Nothin'," Jadon answered, glancing down at his shoes, then back up at Meg.

Chick could tell something was in the air, although he didn't have a clue what it was. Turning his head away from Jadon, Chick watched Meg walk over to the stool that was situated prominently in front of the entire band for the auditions.

Taking her bow, Meg gently swept it across the strings of her violin. Pulling her shoulder blades back and down to ease her tension, she turned to Chick, and nodded.

"Well, what we had in mind was just listening to *you*. To start. Ya' know, get a feel for how you play before we put our stuff into the mix. How's that sound?" Chick said with an easily offered smile.

"Sounds good," Meg answered, looking over toward Jadon.

Upon doing so Meg couldn't help but notice Jadon's stare, mainly because it was boring a hole through her body. Looking at the other band members who were pleasantly smiling and waiting for her to begin, Meg wondered why Jadon was giving her the death glare. Trying to view his obvious dislike as a challenge, Meg pulled her right arm up and hit her first note. Closing her eyes she tilted her head, and decided to throw caution to the wind. If she were going to bomb, she would put on an explosive show.

Playing her violin as if she had to fight to keep it under control, Meg allowed her body to arch forward and back, constantly keeping rhythm with the song playing in her head. Her right foot tapping in rapid succession, while her head kept time with the shifting riffs that gave the song its unique quality. Her notes hitting perfectly, pitched exactly as she intended them, she was in full prime.

Jadon didn't move. Watching the scene before him, Jadon now knew exactly what Meg looked liked while she made music with him on her balcony.

Wondering if she should slow things down, Meg reined in her volume. In one long pull of her bow, she poured effortlessly through a series of notes she had put together early as a child. Within those few simple chords, Meg felt as though the heavens always stopped and took notice. And with that she dropped her bow, and finished.

"What the hell?" Chick said, staring dumbfounded at Meg.

With Chick's words, Meg felt her heart crash against her feet. She blew it. She went overboard. *Damn*, Meg cursed herself silently. Smiling graciously at Chick, Meg looked around at Stu, Bob and Kofi. Not daring to make eye contact with Jadon, she anticipated a smug grin resting comfortably on his attractive face.

"Whoa, sister, you got spunk, goddamn." Chick turned to look at the others, who were nodding their heads in agreement. "That was fuckin' awesome. Where they been hidin' you? Holy Christ, look at the goose bumps on my arm. Let's see if this drink will mix," Chick twirled his fingers around mixing an imaginary cocktail. "How 'bout we play *Blue,* you come in where *you* think it sounds right. I'm curious what your musical instincts are," Chick said, reaching over and picking up his guitar, nestling it comfortably onto his lap.

"Holy Mother of Christ, they liked it," Meg whispered, taking a deep breath to reload her lungs with air. *Instincts,* she thought, *okay, I think I have those.*

The band dropped into the song as if it had been sitting on their fingertips waiting to be played. Moving his shoulders subtly back and forth to the rhythm, Chick began to sing. And although Meg could hear the drums enter in, she made a deliberate decision not to turn and look at Jadon. Stubbornly, she wasn't going to give him the satisfaction of her attention. Bracing herself for what she felt was the perfect time to join, Meg brought herself into the song with a long purposeful note that gave the song instant fullness and grace. Drawing off that feeling, Meg arched her shoulders forward, and began to match Chick's playing. Turning his head, Chick gave Meg a sly smile, watching as she flawlessly kept up with his playing. To see how well Meg could adjust, Chick broke into a solo. Meg hardly noticed that everyone except the two of them had stopped playing; instead she moved her hands with his, trying to feel what he was going to strum next. In an almost hypnotic state she followed Chick note for note until they both came to an end.

"*Whoa!!!*" Chick shouted, throwing his fist in the air. "Fuck, *yeah!* See! Now *that's* what I'm talking about. Shit, yeah!"

Sitting back on her stool, Meg tried to gather her breath — and her mind, which she discovered was currently unraveled.

As quickly as he had burst into laughter Chick turned to Jadon, "So whatda' think of them apples, Jay?

As if shot with an air gun, Jadon jumped when hit by Chick's sudden question, dropping his drumstick. Busying himself by searching for the drumstick that now rolled under his bass drum, Jadon looked up at Chick briefly. "I never fuckin' drop my sticks. Uh...it was uh...It was fine."

"*Fine?!* You serious? It was awesome." Chick looked back at Meg. "He's nuts. I think he was abducted by aliens or somethin'. Don't worry 'bout him, he's been acting fruity lately. I think we found ourselves a *weiner!*" Chick declared, shooting his body off his chair. "I mean *winner.* I better remember my manners. When can you start?"

"When do you want me?" Meg said, still trembling inside.

"Uh . . .tomorrow work for you? We're eager to get this ball rolling," Chick glanced back at the guys.

"That works for me." Meg nodded her head at the guys who were standing behind Chick and avoided eye contact with Jadon, who remained perched behind his drums, playing a solo, as if alone in a different world. "Thank you. Really. Thank you for this chance. I'm thrilled to death," Meg said, turning to walk out the door.

Rushing into her house to let Bob out for his walk, Meg played and replayed the scenes from the last couple of hours. One moment she felt thrill and exhilaration, and in the next pain and uneasiness as she stewed upon Jadon. *What WAS his issue with me?* Meg wondered.

As quickly as she was able to force Jadon out of her thoughts, he swiftly walked right back in. The mere image of him caused Meg's heart to jump. *God, he's wildly attractive*, she pondered. *Too attractive, that's it. It's just not right to be that damn attractive.* Standing next to Bob as he sniffed a tree, Meg thought about how Jadon had looked during his strange drum solo. His body moved like white water rapids. All his movements — the fast, the slow, the demonstrative, and the calm — were connected by a motion that made his body appear fluid.

"Wow, he's damn sexy." Meg shook her head, looking down at Bob.

Struck with the realization that Jadon would make the ideal romantic lead for her current novel, Meg's eyes widened with excitement. As of yet, she still hadn't come up with the perfect man. Of course she would need to dramatically tweak his personality, but as for looks, he fit the bill. As the familiar writer's fire began to well, Meg ushered Bob back into the house, and quickly threw together his dinner. *No wine tonight,* Meg concluded, sitting down at her desk and throwing open her laptop. Opening the file folder containing her novel, her story instantly took its place on her screen, right at page 33 where she had hit a roadblock two months earlier. Meg began typing furiously, chuckling out loud when she decided to use not just his physical appearance but his name as well.

As the hours melted into one another, Meg's left wrist screamed in angry protest from typing too fast. Finally the floodgates had been opened, and she was able to bridge together what she had previously written with thoughts that had been scampering in her mind.

Taking a moment to ease her aching wrist, Meg hit *Save* on the laptop, then pushed her chair from her desk to gain some clarity.

With the events of the day, she couldn't help but think about Bertie. The thought of Bertie always made Meg smile. Of all of her characters, she liked her the best. The last place she left Bertie, she was running on the seashore in Biarritz in the south of France with her young daughter and her two lovers. Bertie was happy, and Meg felt good knowing she was able to give her a peaceful ending. Meg wasn't always happy with how her characters lives turned out, but she didn't feel responsible for their fate. Once Meg gave her characters the chance to express themselves, they often seemed to develop autonomously, as if Meg were merely recording rather than creating their experiences. *As it should be*, she thought.

Only once did Meg struggle mercilessly over a character, Caterina Bennett. From the moment Meg released Cat onto the keyboard, her fate was written. Meg knew how it needed to end, regardless of how badly it tore her apart to write it.

"Oh," Meg sighed, remembering the pain she felt when Cat ended her own life. In an oddly twisted way, Meg felt herself die along with Cat that day. The movie based on the book did quite well however. *People feed off of pain*, Meg thought, looking blankly at the wall in front of her.

Jadon sat on his balcony staring at the sky, thinking. After Meg had left the studio, he tried without success to release his frustrated energy onto his drums. Adding to his troubles was the obvious fact that Chick had taken an interest in his odd behavior.

First, Jadon thought, *if I DID have the courage to confront Meg about my feelings, and that is a BIG if, what about Bob? She's married, for God's sake. Second, Chick was over the top about no relationships between anyone in the band. Hardly matters, since I'm scared to death of how she makes me feel.*

For now though, Jadon realized, Meg didn't know he was the one living beside her, playing the piano. Not wanting to miss the opportunity to be with her again, he walked over to his piano. Taking a cautious sigh, he placed his hands on the keys.

Meg's eyes were closed, her mind busy reflecting on Cat and Bertie when the soft sounds of the piano made their way through the air and gracefully into her thoughts, breaking her trance. Rushing to her violin, Meg threw the case open, pulled her violin out, and ran to her balcony.

"I'm here. I'm here . . . don't go away. I'm here," Meg whispered.

Playing slower this time, the two deliberately allowed each chord to fully develop before moving into the next. In some unexplainable way they felt they knew one another. With every stroke of the keys, Jadon ventured further into uncharted territory with Meg. He didn't want to stop, and he didn't want to turn back. He had never loved before. He had never felt someone deep inside his soul, but Meg was everywhere. Jadon felt time stand still, suspending itself briefly so he could feel Meg's energy. Keeping his hands glued to the keys, he caressed each one slowly and delicately, trying to give Meg what he knew he couldn't, his touch.

"Oh, who are you?" Meg whispered, with a sublime smile resting comfortably on her face.

Unable to prolong their time together any further, the music came to a close. Saddened by its end, Meg dropped her bow onto the balcony.

Jadon sat motionless behind his piano, with his head in his hands he tried to rub away the steadfast realization that he was falling apart.

Chapter 4

It had only been days since Devon's return to his office in Westminster, London, but he missed Meg considerably. Sitting behind his desk, he stared out onto the street and watched the people move about in all directions. His fingers tapped slowly on his desk, while his eyes showed the discomfort of not doing what his heart urged him to do. He knew, though, if pushed too hard, Meg would run. He tried to be content keeping his feelings buried deep within himself, buried under work, buried under meetings and obligations. But for every moment his mind wasn't completely engulfed in something pressing, it was consumed with thoughts of Meg.

Reclining comfortably into his chair, Devon began thumbing through his calendar. If he had a few days open, he would fly back to California to see how things were going. Tossing his calendar back onto his desk, Devon shook his head. He just left California days ago, and right now Meg needed time to work on her book, not to mention that he was the one who arranged her audition with Equinox. And from what she wrote in an email he received that morning, it worked out wonderfully. Meg sounded full of life — just what he wanted. However, he didn't like how often she mentioned the name Jadon, even though she didn't have anything good to say about him. A simple fact that brought Devon much relief. Still, he couldn't help but notice how within every other sentence Jadon's name would reappear. In all the years Devon knew Meg, he couldn't recall her being so bothered by anyone.

Wanting a more pleasant thought, Devon's mind drifted to the night he shared with Meg. His mind reflected upon that event frequently. He could still taste their lovemaking on his lips. To this day the images were clear and vibrant in his mind. Taking a deep breath, he could smell Meg, just as she smelled that evening. And within a few seconds he was able to transcend time, and be in that moment again.

Remembering how Meg looked, and the way she moved her body, Devon's face began to soften. How at first Meg was so fixated on trying to master the technical end of the scene she was working on for her novel that he felt as though he were on a movie set. But then Meg shifted her focus onto him, and those were the memories he savored the longest. He could see her slender body as she pulled him behind her, bringing his arms around her waist, her hand on his moving it slowly and steadily down her stomach, driving his fingers beneath her lace panties.

The image of Meg, as she pulled her head back in pleasure, was the vista that rested permanently in his mind.

"Damn it," Devon said, emerging from his moment alone with Meg. "I know there was something dynamic that happened that night, Meg; you just won't admit it. No, no . . . If you love something, set it free."

Frustrated on many levels, Devon grabbed his briefcase and tried to convince himself that, if left alone, Meg would do just that.

"Somethin's definitely up," Chick said, looking over his coffee cup at Erin, his wife and best friend for the past seven years. "I . . . just can't get a handle on it."

"What makes you think that, babe?" Erin asked, grabbing an orange off the counter. "Want some?"

"Nah . . . It's just, Jadon's playing is usually never off. I'm not sayin' I'm worried, I know when he needs to . . . he'll get focused. But, something has him spinning around. I swear to God it must be his new neighbors. Ever since they moved in he's been screwy," Chick said, pouring his second cup of coffee before leaning against the counter next to Erin.

"Must be *quite* the neighbors."

"No. See, I don't think that's it either."

"Okay, what is it?"

"That's the problem. I don't know."

"Want me to swing by the studio and check him out? I won't tell him you're wondering. I'll just hang out. Say I want to see how the new acoustic thing is pulling together. It'll be your first full day playing together so me poking around won't seem unusual. Then I can see firsthand if there's any *screwy* business going on." Erin popped another orange wedge into her mouth.

Chick stared at her, cocked an eyebrow, and then looked off into the distance.

"Ya know, that might not be a bad idea. You go. Scope it out. Then give me your thoughts." Chick nodded his head with approval as he made his way out of the kitchen.

Erin was relieved to see Chick lighten up. She knew the weight of the band usually rested completely on his shoulders, a weight that often worried her. She also knew Chick was very observant. If he thought something was going on, it most likely was.

Meg's eyes met Jadon's as soon as she walked into the rehearsal room of the studio. Taking purposeful steps forward, she didn't want him to unravel her the same way she felt herself unravel the day before during her audition.

Despite his many attempts, Jadon couldn't take his eyes off of Meg. He felt her presence as soon as she walked into the building. Every fiber in his body wanted to go to her, to continue where they had left off the night before, even though she didn't know it was he with whom she was playing. Unable to sleep, he kept rolling over to check the clock, anxious to see Meg again. More than anything, he wanted to watch her play the violin, hear her music, and feel her energy fill the room. There wasn't one thing he didn't want to experience about Meg.

During this, their first day of practice, or any day of practice for that matter, Jadon wanted to keep his head on straight. Unnerved that he dropped his sticks the other day, he didn't want it to happen again. Jadon loved playing the drums; he loved being so engrossed in keeping the beat he couldn't think of anything else. And for the most part that was how it worked, every time. But the other day, he had to force himself to concentrate, and it showed.

Meg pushed past the exhilarating yet disturbing feeling that she was about to shake her skin loose, a feeling she experienced whenever Jadon was near. In need of a distraction she began to get her violin ready. Within seconds, much to Meg's relief, Chick, Kofi, Bob and Stu strolled in.

"You ready to do this thing?" Chick gave Meg a fake jab to the arm.

"I was born ready," Meg shot back in a smooth voice.

"That's what I like to hear. That's what I like to hear," Chick nodded his head in satisfaction while messing with the strings on his guitar.

The others were ready within seconds, something Meg became aware of at once. *They must have already been rehearsing,* Meg thought to herself. Trying to warm up at home before getting ready, Meg couldn't seem to find the right groove, abandoning the effort she chose to stand mindlessly in the shower instead. Now she began to regret that decision. Meg also wondered if anyone knew she wasn't an actual musician — in the sense of a musician who plays in front of people and records albums sort of way. In fact, short of the few music shows she participated in during her high school years, she played only in front of friends, a far cry from the thousands of screaming fans the guys in Equinox were familiar with.

Since when did I care so much what other people think of me? Meg wondered. Yet here she stood, hoping she would not only impress the hell out of each and every one of them, but also fit in. This was something she never, not once, was able to do in all of her forty years.

Chick began smacking his gum, giving the impression small firecrackers were going off inside his mouth. "Okay . . . let's start with *Mercy Awakening*. Were you able to look over the music I gave you yesterday, Meg?"

"Um . . . sure did. I'm good. Let's do this."

"You're sayin' what I like to hear, Ms. Scott. You ready, Jay?" Chick looked at the ceiling, as if somehow he would be able to see Jadon, who was seated behind him, by simply looking up.

"Born ready," Jadon replied, looking down at his shoes.

Meg felt a sudden bolt. Looking over at Jadon, she couldn't help but wonder if he had said what he said in response to what she had said earlier.

As if sensing her stare, Jadon looked up, and deliberately stared back at Meg. Flustered by the sight of his eyes, Meg looked quickly at Chick for a cue to start playing, even though her part wasn't until after the first verse.

"Let's go," Chick said.

Tapping his foot on the floor, the band softly began to play, and Meg watched as Chick closed his eyes and began singing. And with that, she came to the instant conclusion that, instead of air, Chick breathed music and rhythm.

Have you turned a blind eye to my plea?

Why can't you come and rescue me?

Is there no hope for the hopeless, no home for the homeless?

Are you there

Hiding in the night

Behind the shadows, just out of sight?

Opening his eyes, Chick looked over toward Meg. Her chin rested on her violin, her bow was poised and ready for her first note. She felt the beats softly flowing by as she counted, then entered into the song, and played with the sense of freedom the song gave her. Meg liked the song, the melody and the words. She felt certain it was written from a place of pain and searching. A place she knew too well.

Isn't the pain in my cries enough for you to realize,

I'm not certain anymore?

I feel lost and alone, no one to guide me home.

Isn't there something you want to say?

Words that'll keep me from walking away?

Are you there?

Pulling at my soul, until my breath is gone.

Am I that close to being done?

Is there no hope for the hopeless, no home for the homeless?"

Meg understood each line of the song: wondering if you're done, done with life, done with the game, done with the bitter lows that hang on to the loose ends of joy.

Chick's voice had an earthy raw quality. It wasn't pretentious. It was a real person singing real words that represented real feelings. Meg was in awe of Chick's skill and the masterful way he expressed each song. She noticed the extraordinary talent of the other musicians as well, including Jadon. Who, she reminded herself not to notice as much as she had been noticing him.

Meg's arms hummed with a dull ache from a long day of playing. She had hardly noticed the time had crept past six o'clock. The last time she looked at the clock it was only mid-afternoon.

"Whoa, break time!" Chick said bolting up quickly, leaning his guitar on its stand. "What do you guys think? You wanna wrap it up or keep playing?" Chick looked at Bob, Stu, Kofi and Jadon, then turned to look at Meg.

Meg hardly knew what to say. She wanted to keep playing all night, but wasn't sure if her arms would let her. Then there was Bob; she was worried about how he was handling his outings with the new dog walker she had arranged for him.

"Whatever you guys want to do, I'm game," Meg answered, not knowing which answer she wanted to hear back from the rest of them.

"How's about we grab a drink, then play for a bit more, then close shop?" Bob said, stretching his well-tattooed arms above his head.

"Sounds good to me, B. Meg's in. Jay?" Chick looked at Jadon who was still sitting behind his drums. "You joinin' us, bud?"

"Yeah, I'm in."

The lounge located at the front of the studio was filled with a mix of traditional overstuffed chairs and avant-garde funky chairs. Meg opted to sit in the neon green chair molded into the shape of a large hand.

"Aha! I see you went for the *hand*," Chick said, smiling as he watched Meg try to get comfortable in a very uncomfortable chair. "It's not the most comfy, but it's cool, so we had to get it. What's your poison, Meg?"

"Uh, what do you have?" Meg asked, not realizing when they said drink, they meant drink, *drink*.

"Beer, beer, and more beer. You like beer?" Chick furrowed his brow into a question.

"Well, sure, when in Rome . . ."

Each guy, every single one, lit a cigarette and began to pace. Meg wondered what all the chairs were for if not for plopping one's body down. Then it occurred to her that they'd been sitting for over six hours, where she'd been mainly standing.

"Well, hey there, darlin," Chick beamed as he watched Erin walk into the studio.

"Hey, there. Hey, Bob, Stu . . . ," Erin said, looking around the room.

"How's it goin', Erin?" Bob offered, giving Erin a warm hug.

"Good. Busy. Things get busy, but busy is good," Erin said lightly, while her warm face glowed with natural ease, and her long brown hair cascaded over her shoulders like melted chocolate.

Grabbing Erin, Chick gave her a bear hug, lifting her off the floor before letting her go. "So . . . what brings a pretty lady like you over to the dirtier side of town?"

Erin looked at Chick for a moment, "Well you can't keep blathering on about this acoustic sound you've got going on without me wanting to check it out. What'd you expect?"

Chick was pleased with his wife's smooth answer. "Hey, Kofi is here. This acoustic deal finally gave us an excuse to haul his ass into the studio."

Smiling at Kofi, Erin looked around the room, searching out Jadon and Meg, finding Meg first.

"So this is Meg," Erin said, making her way over with an extended hand.

"Oh, yeah, she kicks serious ass on the violin," Chick said. "Gives ya beaucoup chills." He wiggled his arms as if he was spooked.

"Well, I've heard a great deal about you. You've impressed the impossible to impress," Erin said, staring into Meg's eyes trying to get a feel for her.

Meg felt Erin's sincerity; she liked her immediately. Everything about Erin exuded calm, balanced warmth. "Thank you. That means a great deal. It's been quite an experience so far."

"Well, it's a long way from being over. Chick says you're a writer?"

"Yes, yes, I am. I, uh . . . I write under an assumed name, though."

"How intriguing. Well then, I won't ask, lest I blow your anonymity," Erin said with a flare. "Just tell me this, would I know of any of your books?"

"Most likely," Meg shifted in the hand-shaped seat.

"Hmm, give me something good to chew on, some morsel."

Lightening up, Meg smiled, "Okay. Um . . . each of my novels . . . all five, have made *The New York Times* Best Sellers list . . ."

"That's too cool. Okay, now I'm on the hunt," Erin said playfully.

Remembering why she was there in the first place, Erin looked around the room, finding Jadon nestled by the window.

"So, what do you think of this whole gig?" Erin asked, twirling her finger around the room.

"It's odd, Erin, but in a weird way I feel like I'm home," Meg answered in a low whisper. "I know that sounds strange. It sounds strange to me too."

Erin liked the answer; she liked Meg. But still, she could tell something was making Meg uncomfortable, and it wasn't the hand-shaped chair.

"That doesn't sound strange to me at all. You're all storytellers. Where else should you be?" Erin gave Meg a look of approval. "So . . . what about the guys?"

"Oh God, they're great," Meg looked around the room. "Chick, he's — he's an amazingly talented person. Bob, he's so damn sweet he almost makes my teeth hurt. Kofi's funny. He's been trying to make me laugh all afternoon. It works, too. Stu, he looks like he knows something. Something I should know, but don't know as of yet."

Erin waited after Meg finished, "And Jadon, you didn't mention him."

Looking over at Jadon, Meg stared for a moment, as she often did when he wasn't glaring at her. He was sitting on the counter next to the window, smoking a cigarette, his left knee bouncing; his eyes looked tired, beautiful like pale blue water, but tired water. His blonde hair was blowing gently from the breeze of the open window. Meg's head began to turn toward Erin well before her eyes broke their gaze from Jadon.

"Oh . . . uh, well. I'm not sure what I think of him. But I know he doesn't care for me."

Erin looked over at Jadon, then back at Meg, "Well, I can't imagine that. Looks like he's stewing on something. I think I'm going to go and see what's percolating in that pretty little head of his."

Meg watched as Erin made her way over to Jadon. For a moment, in a small way, she envied Erin. Not because of Chick, although he would be reason enough to envy Erin. But that wasn't it. She envied Erin's ability not to be disliked by Jadon.

"Your head is smoking from all that serious thinking, Jay," Erin said, pushing on Jadon's arm.

Cracking a smile, Jadon tilted his head back and looked at Erin. Chick, Erin and Jadon had history. Chick was with Erin when he first started the band. Jadon was the first one Chick chose when he formed the band, ten years ago. Erin had been there through all the ups and downs. Jadon liked Erin; she helped to keep balance among the unbalanced.

"A smile doesn't tell me anything," Erin said. "What's going on? Not liking the acoustic sound?"

"It's great," Jadon replied. "You'll love it." He stubbed out his cigarette, then tucked his knees up to his chest.

Erin gave Jadon a flat look, "I know you, Jay."

"I fuckin' know you do."

Erin stared at Jadon while he stared out the window. "How's it going with Kofi? Is he turning out like you guys had hoped?"

"He's awesome. Perfect."

Erin looked over at Meg. "And Meg?"

Jadon winced slightly looking over at Meg, then back out the window, "She's . . .awesome, too."

"You guys getting along?"

"What the fuck. This isn't high school."

Changing her approach, Erin looked out the window just past Jadon's head, where she was able to get a clear view of his vision, without having to look directly at him.

Jadon kept picking at his shoe but looked up at Meg while nodding and agreeing with Erin, not paying attention to what she was saying. The casual conversation and Erin's preoccupation with something outside allowed him to hold his eyes on Meg. Jadon watched as Meg struggled to get comfortable in the giant hand chair; he also watched as a lock of her long hair fell between her breasts and gently swayed when she moved her head. Looking up, Jadon caught Erin's eyes staring directly at him.

"Well, anyway, that's what they say the weather will be like tomorrow, although I hardly believe them," Erin said quickly, taking her hand and tossing Jadon's hair between her fingers before making her way over to Chick.

"I'm ready!" Chick yelled, much to Meg's surprise. Grabbing her beer, Meg finished it in one long overwhelming drink. She didn't want to dilly-dally; it was obvious that the rest of them were already in sync. They instinctually timed everything to fall in place with one another, something Meg wasn't aware of until they all simultaneously threw their empty bottles into the recycling bin as soon as Chick declared he was ready. Meg wasn't ready when Chick was ready, but she was now, and two steps behind the rest of them heading back into the rehearsal room.

Taking a seat directly in front of the band, Erin had a complete view of everyone, including Meg, as the band picked up exactly where it had left off.

In a million years Meg never would have imagined doing what she was doing. She felt a surge of excitement travel through her when she realized how Bertie must have felt. Meg wasn't the front man as Bertie was; she wasn't a charismatic lead singer and song writer. But for the moment she was part of Equinox, and she was able to experience the energy formed when talented musicians create music together.

After a few more rounds, Jadon noticed the time. Although it was only nine o'clock, he was eager for the clock to reach 10 p.m., which was when he would be able to be alone with Meg — if alone was the word that could describe their encounters. But Jadon felt strongly that they were alone, and it was their time even though she didn't have a clue with whom she was playing music, and he did.

"Boy, I'm beat!" Jadon blurted, startling Chick who was silently off in his own thoughts after gently finishing the song.

"Oh! Okay. Uh . . . Hot date?" Chick spun around to face Jadon.

"Uh, no . . . No," he shook his head, staring down at the floor. "It's just gettin' late, that's all. I'm tired. Aren't you tired?" Jadon said, pointing at the clock on the wall with his drum stick.

Chick spun back around and looked at the clock. "It's a little after nine. No, I'm not especially tired, and, no, it's not especially late. You okay?" Chick turned to look at Jadon again.

"I'm good, man. Like I said, I'm just tired."

When Meg saw Jadon point at the time, it was the first she realized that it was after nine o'clock. Instantly she thought of her neighbor.

"Well, Meg, you're probably tired," Chick said. "It's been a long day, I suppose." He was still visibly puzzled by Jadon's abrupt announcement.

"Ya know," Meg replied, "I'm beginning to feel it in my shoulders. I'm not used to playing so much for so long. I'm loving it, though." She stretched her shoulders.

"You don't have a hot date, too, do ya?" Chick teased, snapping his gum.

"I *don't* have a date," Jadon interjected, wanting to make certain it was known.

"I, ah . . . no, no, I don't have a date," Meg stammered.

"You *do* have a date, don't you!" Chick responded. "All right, then. That clinches it. We gotta wrap this up guys. Meg's got some *guy* she has to hook up with." He began singing, amused with his newly crafted story.

"No, no, that isn't it. I do have to get home to Bob . . ."

"*Bob!* Well, he's a guy," Chick said, thrilled with the new piece of information.

Jadon's eyes darted over to Meg, startled to hear her mention Bob. He knew Bob existed, but so far he kept trying to make believe he didn't.

Meg opened her mouth to explain further, but Chick was more delighted with his fictional story than hearing about her trusty setter. Deciding it wasn't worth the trouble of explaining, Meg closed her violin case and called it a night.

Bob was thrilled. Meg was finally home, and tonight she took the extra time to make his dinner just the way he liked it. She seemed happy, excited actually. And this made Bob excited, even though he didn't know why they both were excited. Excitement is, if nothing else, exciting.

It was already nearing ten o'clock, and Meg hoped her neighbor would be coming home soon. The lights still weren't on next door. She checked. Within what seemed like minutes, Bob was already finished with his dinner and was sitting at the door staring at Meg.

"Oh, my God, now? You have to go outside, now?" Meg said, checking the time once again before opening the door.

The moon worked as a floodlight in the sky, allowing Meg to see every tree Bob casually bypassed along the street in front of their house, making it obvious that he had more on his mind than a two-minute bathroom break.

"Aw, come on. For crying out loud, Bob," Meg groaned.

Meg stood helplessly, watching her faithful friend take his leisurely time strolling around each bush lining the sidewalk. Lifting his head Bob gave a soft bark that made Meg spin around just in time to see her neighbor's lights turn on.

Quickly dragging Bob back in the house, Meg tossed his leash onto its peg, and hurried into the living room. Throwing open the French doors leading to her balcony, she pushed one ear outward, and listened for the piano.

"Nothing, okay," Meg said relieved. "Of course, he might not want to play tonight. I mean . . . it's entirely possible that he might be busy or tired. God knows I'm tired."

Walking into his living room, Jadon felt a familiar ache settle over his body, an ache from playing the drums too long and too hard. A feeling he loved. Darting into the kitchen, he peered out his kitchen window toward Meg's house.

"Lights are on," he smiled.

Sitting down at the piano, Jadon rested his fingers on the keys. Taking a deep breath he softly began to play their melody.

Chapter 5

"God damn it," Chick said, rubbing his face.

"What's wrong, hon?" Erin asked, turning over in bed to get a better look at him.

"Ah, crud. I forgot to power down the soundboard." Kicking his legs up and over, Chick launched himself out of bed.

"Do you really have to do that now? I mean, what harm would happen if you left it on all night? It's already 2 a.m." Erin reached her arm out to catch Chick before he made his way completely out from under the sheets.

"Roach said it was *imperative* that it's turned *off* after we're done, and it was on all day. It was on for like . . . twelve hours already, and it's still on. We just put that new board in. Shit. I don't want it to fry," Chick grumbled, pulling on his jeans. "I'll just run over there, turn the fucker off and be back in a minute."

"Oh, yeah, right," Erin groaned. "Unless you get an *idea* you want to try out." She turned and pulled the down comforter over her head.

"I don't have an *idea* in my head right now other than sleeping. I'll be back, unless I fall asleep on the floor at the studio," he said, walking out the door.

"Christ, I'm tired," Chick mumbled to himself, exiting the 405 Freeway.

It had been a powerful day but a good one, and he couldn't ignore it. He knew the band was making history, and if he shaped it just right, the new album would be one of their best pieces of work to date.

Pulling up to the studio, Chick jumped out of his black BMW, and stopped suddenly when his eyes fell upon the lights still on inside. But more startling was the noise emanating from the building.

"What the . . . ," Chick mumbled, putting his key in the lock. Shutting the door quietly behind him, he crept toward the noise in the rehearsal room. Normally he would charge in, but he didn't want to interrupt what sounded like Jadon hammering out a new song on the drums.

Sitting down in the lounge room, Chick crossed his legs, pulled a pack of Lucky Strikes from his shirt pocket, and lit up. Taking a long thoughtful drag, he kept his ears locked on to the music Jadon was playing. Chick could tell it was a song in its rough stages but one needing to be released.

Chick listened while his friend worked through the song, singing verse to verse, repeating some words, stopping, then coming back to do them over again. Taking another drag from his cigarette, he listened patiently. Unable to ignore the emotion that thundered throughout the song, Chick couldn't help but wonder what was going on inside of Jadon's mind. Something was tearing him apart, and by the sound of the song he was writing, it wasn't something: it was *someone*.

The song was good. It was amazing, actually. Chick liked it as soon as he heard it. Normally songs have to settle into someone. Occasionally, though, a song comes around that bowls over a person within seconds of the first beat. Having written a few songs like that, Chick quickly recognized Jadon's work as one of those remarkable songs. Relaxing into his chair, he allowed the song to slam into him, the words piercing his mind, demanding that he feel the intense emotion Jadon was feeling. Chick had no clue where the intensity was coming from, but it was undeniably there.

Feeling some level of relief as he poured himself out onto the drums, Jadon was finally able to put into words what he wasn't able to say otherwise. Although the words were cryptic, each one made perfect sense to him. Meg was the voice in his head, and the breath that moved in and out of his body. In many ways his world felt as though it were coming apart, and yet at the same time his view of the world was becoming vividly clear. Everything was brighter, even the air smelled different. He was saturated with thoughts of Meg, and he hated it. He hated that he couldn't take her into his arms. He hated the way his entire world had turned completely upside down. Turning his love for Meg into music gave him a way to work through things. He wasn't sure if it sounded good, but that didn't matter.

Realizing it was silent for a longer stretch of time than before, Chick decided to make his entrance. Normally he wouldn't have thought anything of barging in while Jadon practiced, but this was different. Something about the song felt intensely personal. Chick couldn't kick the awkward feeling he was intruding on a private moment.

"Hey, Jay," Chick said casually, not wanting to startle Jadon who was busy scribbling something down on a sheet of paper behind his drum kit.

Startled by the unexpected sound of a voice, Jadon dropped his pen. "Hey, Chick. What's up? What are you doing here in the middle of the night?"

"I forgot to turn off the board, man. I would've had you do it if I knew you were here . . . heard your song."

Jadon looked up at Chick with apprehension. He wasn't prepared for anyone to hear it yet. "Uh, oh, yeah. Um . . . well, I was just working it out, trying to get the pieces to fit. It's been bugging me lately so I thought I should just get it down and see what happens."

"Shit. It sounds good, Jay." Chick looked intently at Jadon. It was apparent Jadon was uncomfortable, almost as if he were hiding something. But more than anything he looked like he was struggling with something bigger than himself. "Want some help with it?"

Jadon stared at Chick, not completely sure how to answer. "Yeah . . . yeah, I could . . ."

Grabbing his sheet music, Jadon started searching for his pen. Darting out from behind the drums he swiftly made his way to Chick. Shoving the pages toward Chick, Jadon pointed at the scribbled notes and words.

"You see . . . right here, this is where you need to come in. I have it down, I have it somewhere . . ."

Chick patiently held the sheets Jadon stuffed into his hands, and easily concluded that Jadon needed him a lot more than he was letting on. Never having seen Jadon act anything even remotely close to how he was acting, Chick couldn't ignore the unsettling feeling that snaked through his stomach.

"Okay, dude, take your time. I'm not goin' anywhere. Show me what you got. I've been listening, and it sounds phenomenal. Just relax. Let's take this slow." Chick looked at Jadon, who still had his head down, his eyes scanning the various pages.

A sheet flew to the floor. Reaching down, Chick grabbed it and noticed Meg's name boldly marked on it.

"That. That's . . . uh . . . where Meg comes in. She *has* to play it just like that. I know that's how it has to sound. You need to tell her that. Tell her that's how she needs to play it."

"What do you mean, *me?* Dude, this is your baby through and through. You're the one who should run this one."

"*No.* Uh, no. I need you to do this for me. I need you to deal with Meg. Deal with everyone," Jadon said, praying he wouldn't have to offer any more information than that.

Chick stared at Jadon, who was still staring back at him, "You sure? All right, whatever you want, dude."

"Good, good." Jadon looked back at the sheet music. "Okay, right here, I need help with this . . ."

"Let's work it out and see what we can do with it." Chick reached for his guitar and sat down next to Jadon, who was already back behind his drums. "How long you been workin' on this?"

"Huh?"

"How long . . . ya know . . . have you been working . . ."

"Oh, not long. I mean, it just sort of came flying out of my head just before midnight, but I guess I've been working on parts of it for a couple days."

Chick had a million questions whizzing through his mind but knew better than to give sound to any of them. More than his curiosity, he had compassion for his friend. Deciding for now to ignore his questions, Chick focused on the music. If any sort of explanation was going to arrive, it would show up in its own time.

Chapter 6

Within each blissful wag of his tail, Bob showed his appreciation for the relaxing walk the two of them were taking along the beach that morning. Meg appreciated it, too. Her mind was still filled with her storyline, a byproduct of spending much of the night working on her novel. Before heading to the studio, she hoped a leisurely walk would help silence her thoughts. Ever since she decided to use Jadon as her heroine's love interest, she couldn't wait to write. She was able to take Jadon and spin him around in whichever direction she chose. By using the passion she felt during her moments with her neighbor and giving them to Elle, the lead in her latest novel, Meg was able to give the scenes life and direction. However, combining those moments with the face of Jadon was almost more than Meg could handle. Although she couldn't make sense out of Jadon's dislike for her, that didn't stop her from being drawn to him. It was a maddening fact but a fact nonetheless. And even though she made sure not to look at him, or at least not look at him as often, everything about her controlled, natural demeanor became unhinged when she was around him.

Pausing to pick up a stone from the beach, Meg shifted her thoughts to Devon. He called every day just to "check in." Meg wasn't sure what to tell him. She couldn't share with him all the thoughts bouncing around in her mind. She couldn't discuss her moments with her neighbor. She didn't even feel quite comfortable telling him about Jadon. As soon as she tried to open up about

Jadon's dislike for her, Meg could hear her attraction for Jadon reveal itself within the tone of her voice, requiring her to quickly change the subject.

Strolling back to the house, Meg glanced at the home of her mysterious neighbor. She tried not to think about him, except for the thoughts that were directly involved in their moments together. For all she knew he was just having fun, a good time playing with a fellow musician, nothing romantic, nothing sexual, nothing intimate.

Meg was aware that the possibilities for what he could look like were endless, and so she didn't want to think about it. He could be married. *He* could be a *she*. She didn't want to think about it. She didn't want to question any of it. All she wanted was to take from their moments together what she wanted. And she wanted him: the person who made love to her through music.

"Hey there, Meggie," Chick said, watching Meg walk into the studio. "We got something we're working on, so we're going to shift gears today and put all our attention on it. We gotta hammer it out," Chick pointed at the others already relaxing after having played all morning.

"Oh God, am I late?" Meg asked.

"Nope. You're good. We just wanted to work this through to get the other pieces in place before you came in. Your part is kinda pivotal, so we needed to have the rest sorta set and in place so you could get a clear picture of the sound and vision we have for the song."

"Oh . . . ," Meg said slowly.

Bending down to open her violin case, Meg looked over at Bob, Kofi and Stu, and noticed they were all taking advantage of the moment to light up a cigarette. She gave them a warm smile and then glanced over to find Jadon staring directly at her. *Damn,* she thought as she quickly looked back down, *why the hell is he always glaring at me?*

Jadon had worked all night on his song, the song that put all his feelings for Meg out onto the table. Relieved that Chick didn't try to dig into him about the subject of his song, Jadon felt it was probably obvious. Still, Chick didn't seem to realize the object of his feelings, and for now Jadon wanted it left that way. Everyone was on the same page with their part in it, and Jadon was pleased with how the song had come together. The guys, each one, fell right in to place.

I wonder what she's going to think... Jadon thought. He had worked for hours putting together her piece. It was reminiscent of the music they made together on their balconies, and he was eager to see if she would feel the same passion when she played it in the studio.

"Odee kay dee, Megaroo," Chick said, trying to lighten things up the best he could before handing Meg a piece of paper with handwritten music scrawled on it. "I know . . . it looks a bit rough," he said apologetically, "But this is your part . . . um, we're hopin' you'll feel what we're trying to express with this. It's quite different from the acoustic stuff we've been workin' on. Okay, let's do this."

Chick spun around, having given the moment all the attention he could; now he just wanted to get on with the process. The song was very hard in-your-face rock that also happened to be an exceptionally passionate love song. He hardly knew what he thought of it except that it was overwhelming. Chick had even less of an idea how Meg would receive it.

Reviewing the sheet of music, Meg tried to put sound to it inside her head, feeling a little uncomfortable once she found the melody and noticed its similarities to the music she played during her nights with her neighbor.

The room fell silent. Jadon sat motionless. This was the moment he had been waiting for ever since he put his feelings down on paper. Trying to push his emotions aside and focus himself, he dropped the first beat, then the next. The song began, with three small beats, then the full force of the song emerged as Jadon began to sing in a raspy voice.

The music can't get loud enough to drown out your voice inside my head.

You're all I hear, all I feel. You're the breath that dwells behind every word that's said.

The soft whisper that hides in my dreams, giving comfort to a mind that only screams.

The band kicked in together, creating a tidal wave of volume, causing Meg to sit straight up on her stool. She watched as Jadon poured himself into the microphone, never realizing before how amazing he sounded. His voice swirled inside her mind as he gave life to every passionate word.

I can't breathe. I can't think. I want to drink your soul and taste your dreams.

The song was both hypnotic and beautiful with its honesty, and she couldn't help but notice how emotionally Jadon sang each word. His body moved violently, commanding the driving force through the song. Watching him, Meg felt her eyes well with tears but didn't know why.

Drawing her first long note, Meg held it in place, asking the sound to stay in the air a little longer before dropping down into the next succession of notes. When she began to give the notes the sound she felt was intended, she heard the drums galloping along side of her. She had never heard the drums and violin moving together in that way; it gave her sound a speed and momentum she wasn't prepared for.

As she sunk into the music, she thought of the moments spent on the balcony playing almost exactly the same sounds, strung together in almost exactly the same way. The song was beautiful beyond comprehension; she wanted to do it justice. Without thinking Meg, stood and caught the speed Jadon was pushing her into, throwing the notes around in an unparalleled mixture of pleasure and soul piercing sadness. Then in a sudden burst, the band brought the song to an abrupt end.

Finding it hard to hide how powerfully the song had moved her, Meg quickly sat back onto her stool and tried to collect herself.

Behind his drums, Jadon sat frozen in exactly the same position as when he ended the song with a dramatic crash that quickly filled the room with silence. Holding the cymbals, keeping them from making the faintest noise, he kept his tired eyes fixed on Meg.

Sitting up straighter, Meg couldn't keep down the intense emotions welling up inside of her. The song had touched her in a way she wasn't sure how to handle.

Chick watched myriad emotions work their way over Meg. Then glancing at Jadon, Chick noticed Jadon's eyes were set on Meg. Still breathing heavily from putting his whole self into the song, Jadon's eyes showed the emotion he couldn't help but feel. Shooting a glance back at Meg, Chick began to put the pieces together.

"Meg?" Chick offered slowly.

"I, uh . . . I . . ." Meg struggled to gather her composure. "I, I'm . . . that was . . ." Meg felt her eyes fill with tears that began rolling down her cheeks. "I need to excuse myself," she said, turning quickly to head to the lounge.

"What the hell is wrong with me?" Meg yelled quietly at herself, dislodging multiple tissues from their box. "Who the hell cries when they play a song? Real cool. Real brilliant, Meg. I looked like an idiot in front of everyone."

Looking out the window and trying to clear her mind, Meg still felt the song wrapped around her like a heavy blanket, stirring the feelings she had been trying to handle lately. Her desire for Jadon, and how it sat right behind her eyes, behind everything she tried to look at. Also her desire for her neighbor, a man she didn't even know. She was angry. Angry for not knowing what to do, and how to control all she was feeling.

Meg examined her reflection in the microwave door and wiped her eyes once more. "What am I doing? Get a fuckin' backbone, Meg."

Bob looked at Meg with concern as she walked back into the rehearsal room but didn't say anything. He wasn't even sure what to say.

Jadon sat up when he saw her walk back in the room. He desperately wanted to know what was going through Meg's mind. He wanted to grab her in his arms and kiss her tears.

"Hey, Meggie," Kofi smiled, tapping at his piano, also not sure how to help.

"Okay . . . ," Meg said, standing directly in front of Chick, taking a deep breath. "Well, that was really embarrassing. I don't normally ever feel . . . um . . . that sort of emotion. Or at least in front of others. That was, well it was . . . it was the most beautiful thing I've ever heard. The sound, the words . . . were . . . Who wrote it?"

"Oh, uh." Startled by the question Chick looked back at Jadon, to discover Jadon was staring at his drums. "Jadon...and me. Me and Jadon," Chick lied, not feeling good with his answer. But what he knew for certain was, Jadon didn't want Meg to know it was his words and emotions that gave birth to the song.

"Well, you should be very proud of yourselves. It was, well, I'm a writer and I can't find the words to describe how it made me feel," Meg said sincerely, trying to laugh at herself while walking back to her stool.

"Hey, Cam!" Chick waved his hand after spotting the unexpected visitor walking into the room.

Startled at someone's presence during what felt like a very private moment, Meg wiped her eyes once more before grabbing her violin.

"Hey, Chick, Bob, Stu… how are ya'? Kofi . . . heard you were hanging out here. Hey Jay, how the hell ya doing? You look like hell. What's Chick doin' to ya?" Cameron said with a menacing grin and an English accent that made his words fall rhythmically into place.

"What the fuck you doin' here?" Chick asked with a broad smile. "We're a long way from cutting a video. So what's your British ass doing in So Cal?"

Cameron flopped down on a chair and reached for a cigarette. "I was just in town finishing up a project for Bingham. Christ. Bloody ass thing took two fuckin' months to shoot," he said in disgust, looking around the room casually until his eyes caught Meg.

Shooting up like a rocket, Cameron headed in her direction. Rolling his eyes, Chick wondered if the moment could get any more complex. It was bad enough things felt like a scene from a romantic movie, now Cameron was locked on to Meg, right in front of Jadon, who it was now obvious to Chick was consumed with love and just poured his heart out to her.

"Cam, that's, uh, Meg. She's joining us on our acoustic odyssey," Chick said, his eyes following Cameron. "Meg, this is Cameron Berkshire. He's done a few of our videos, and has managed to ingratiate himself to us. Playing upon our graces and kindness. He's a nut job though, so don't be fooled." Chick let out an unsettled laugh.

Bob and Stu also gave a chuckle, wanting to break the heavy cloud still hanging throughout the room.

"Hello, my name is Cameron," Cameron said, shaking Meg's hand.

"Hello, Cameron," Meg said slowly, taking note that Cameron appeared to be oblivious to everyone else.

Cameron stared at Meg for a long moment. Breaking Cameron's gaze, Jadon thumped his bass drum, sending a boom throughout the room and causing Cameron to turn back around toward Chick.

Chick wasn't sure if he should offer it or not, but was wildly curious as to what someone else thought of Jadon's song. Worried Meg wouldn't be ready, Chick decided to chance it.

"Hey, sit down, Cam. Listen, and tell me what you think. Meg, how about another round?"

"Let's do it," Meg said straightening her back, looking over at Jadon. Noticing his head was tilted back, and his eyes closed, his left knee hopping even though the rest of his body was completely still. Meg wanted to watch him. She wanted to watch him sing the song again, the entire song right up to her part.

Jadon hit the downbeat. Meg watched Jadon's body move while his eyes remained closed. Moving his head closer to his mike, Jadon began to sing. Opening his eyes, he looked directly at Meg. This time she wasn't going to be bullied into looking away. She stared back. Every move of his body hypnotized her. Wondering what he would be like in bed, Meg cringed at herself for thinking such a cheap thought. *Damn, why not,* she wondered. *God. Look at him.*

The immense sound filled the room and everything in it. There was no escaping its dramatic pull. The song crashed over Meg, and engulfed her like a violent ocean wave.

Meg braced herself for her part. The song felt wickedly good and wickedly sad all at the same time. It made her want to scream as much as it made her want to cry. Taking a deep breath, Meg hit her first note and threw her head back. Feeling the chord resonate deep within her, she hung on to it, nursing the sound she stretched it out as long as it would allow. Then suddenly dropping down, she hit the three lower notes in succession, the last of which was joined by Jadon, who hit it precisely in unison with her.

Meg didn't want to think about Cameron sitting and watching. Instead she kept thinking about the drums. Swinging into a flurry of complex notes, the drums running along next to her, Meg felt things speed up. Every chord was an emotion begging to be set free. As she felt the drums fade, she reached out and boldly grabbed the amazingly difficult chord that was written for her. It sounded perfect. It was a masterful mixture. It added balance and complexity to the song. It howled into the air. With a climactic ending, she dropped her arm with exhaustion. And again, timed perfectly, the band brought the song to an almost violent close.

Meg felt the tears trickle slowly down her face. Putting her head down she tried to wipe them away without anyone noticing.

Jadon held his cymbals, his head hanging down. Chick glanced at Meg to see if she was all right, then looked at Cameron, who was sitting in silence. Chick wasn't sure how Cameron was going to respond. But Chick knew a good thing, and this was better than that. As Cameron stood and began pacing back and forth,

Chick set his guitar aside and grabbed a cigarette.

Cameron turned and looked at Jadon, then back at Meg, then down at the floor before pacing again.

"When will you release it?" Cameron asked, not lifting his head.

"Dude, we just played it for the first time today," Chick said, amused by the simple fact.

Cameron looked at Chick, then rubbed his hands through his dark curly hair, knocking his sunglasses off in the process. Reaching down and grabbing them, he nestled them back into his nest of hair.

"What the hell ya thinkin'?" Chick asked, taking a long drag off his cigarette.

"I'm working on the setup for the video. I have a clear picture of this. It has to be just right, you see. There's something here. I feel it. It's thick. It's absolutely brilliant. It hit me in pieces. I see it. I have to jot this down," Cameron said, searching through his pockets for a scrap of paper. "You see, this isn't just something we can take lightly. It's powerful. I see just how this needs to play out. I want to begin straightaway before I lose this."

"Cam's got this vision thing . . . ," Chick revealed, swinging his head over to look at Meg, once more wanting to make sure she was all right.

Cameron walked slowly over to Bob, then to Stu, stopping at Kofi for a moment before making his way to Chick.

"Watcha lookin' at me for?" Chick said, trying to snap Cameron out of his fog.

"Don't mess with the vision," Bob said with a laugh.

"Yeah, he's cookin' up something in that little beanie of his," Stu added.

Walking over to Jadon, Cameron stopped cold. He stared, his eyes not moving from Jadon's face. Nodding his head, deep in serious concentration, Cameron slowly looked over his right shoulder at Meg, then back at Jadon who now stared back at him. Cameron kept his eyes on Jadon while he moved over toward Meg, his arms crossed in front of him, his right hand tapping at his mouth.

Meg tried to relax and allow Cameron his moment, just as everyone else so easily did. Instead, she felt as though he were drilling a hole through her soul. Deciding to look directly back at him, Meg stared motionlessly into his large brown eyes. Taking a deep breath, she raised her right eyebrow.

"You two," Cameron said, not changing his stance except pointing at Jadon and Meg.

Jadon dropped his head. This was not what he had bargained for. He just wanted to release what was burning inside of him. He wanted also, in the process, to somehow share it with Meg. Chick crossed his arms over his chest and began to stroke his beard. The rest of the band remained quiet. It was obvious to them too that something was in the air between Meg and Jadon. Chick had said he and Jadon wrote the song, but the song really wasn't Chick's style. And the way Jadon sang and played it, the way he stared at Meg, told all there was to tell. At first they thought Jadon resented her, but it wasn't long before they figured out he was falling for her. Not that they were going to say anything, least of all to Chick. Chick was adamant about that sort of thing within the band. Chick took music and the band seriously, which was one reason why they were such a solid band.

"You write this?" Cameron asked, staring at Jadon.

Jadon kept his head down and looked at his shoes. "Uh, Chick. Chick and me."

Cameron stood staring at Jadon and then over to Chick, who just smiled and nodded.

"Okay, well, whatever, but that's not how it's playing out in my head," Cameron said, turning around. "I have to run, but I want to get this rolling as soon as possible. I have some ideas. I think it's a must. I don't know how some of you will receive it. No bother. It's how it needs to be."

Cameron shot a quick hand in the air, pivoted, and walked out.

Chick turned to look at Meg. "Don't let him creep you out. He's a little on the fruity side. But a good fruity. He's excellent at what he does. He sizes things up spot on and fast," he said, looking at Jadon, who returned the look with a long, flat stare. "I had a gut feeling about this. So I recorded that last session, it was perfect. I don't want to change it. I like it intense. It's got a garage feel to it. We could mix it a bit and tighten it up, but I like it just the way it is. Sometimes people get in there and mess with the sound so much it doesn't sound like real people anymore, sounds like machines playin'," Chick said, already heading over to the sound room.

Meg didn't have a clue that anything was being recorded. Not that it mattered to her either way. Noticing everyone except Jadon was following Chick into the other room, she decided to follow. Putting her violin down, she looked up at Jadon. He looked upset. His eyes were closed, and he was deep in thought. She felt awkward leaving him there, but felt even more awkward staying.

Jadon thought about the animal often created when a song is released into the wild. Everyone gets their hands all over it. He didn't like how long Cameron stared at him. He knew why. He didn't like that it was obvious to Cam, because if it was obvious to Cam, it was obvious to others. Sitting with his eyes closed he thought about Meg's words. *"The most beautiful thing I've ever heard."*

Chick rolled into his driveway late that night, with the unsettling events of the day hanging over his head like a thunder cloud shooting out the occasional, startling bolt of lightning.

As soon as Erin watched Chick kick off his shoes, she knew he was heavy from something. Chick began to pace the living room floor with his hands shoved into his pockets. Back and forth, and with every few turns he would scratch his beard and wipe down his mustache with his fingers.

"Babe? What gives?" she asked gently.

Looking at Erin with exhausted eyes, Chick began to mumble the details, explaining how he had walked in on Jadon the other night and how bizarre Jadon had seemed. He knew the song told the story of what was going on with Jadon. That, in and of itself, was troubling enough; but as the day progressed, and he started to watch Jadon closely, he began to suspect that Meg was at the root of Jadon's turmoil.

"I don't know why," Chick admitted. "I mean the stuff Jadon's feeling is intense." He turned to look Erin in the eye. "But I never see him talk to her. I mean, I could be wrong . . . Damn, I don't think so."

Chick began to pace again while describing the song to Erin, sharing with her how powerful it was. Finally, throwing himself down on the sofa next to Erin, he slapped his hands over his face.

"This is ain't good, sweetness," Chick mumbled through his hands, "If *this* is the shit that's rolling around inside of Jay, it ain't good."

"Well, we don't know for *sure*."

"Ohhh, believe you me, darlin' I think the dude is nuts for her. *Nuts*," Chick continued, talking through his hands while they remained glued to his face like a mask.

"Okay, let's think about this. Let's say you're right. Maybe it'll be okay. We don't know ..."

"Oh yeah, we know," Chick interrupted. "We know. What we know first, is that this is the type of shit that drags a band down into the mud. I've worked too damn long and hard to build this band into what it is. I don't want to watch it combust," he said adamantly, finally taking his hands off his face and throwing his arms out into the air.

"Well, we don't know that things would combust exactly ..."

"When I was harping on the guys about hookin' up and relationships, I never, never once thought this would happen to Jadon. I was thinkin' ... ya know, Bob or Stu. I don't know. The chemistry of the band goes right to shit," Chick said, springing up off the sofa. "Funny thing is I've never seen Jadon hardly show any interest in women. He never wants to be bothered. I mean, he likes them. *God knows* they like him. I asked him one time about it. He said he doesn't want to deal with that crap. He said they're all pretty much the same anyway. I mean, that doesn't sound too cool, I know. But, I understood what he was gettin' at so I never thought much of it."

"I know. That's why I'm thinking ... this could be ..." Erin tried to explain.

"Yeah, I know! This is big shit, isn't it? Fuckity, fuck. Damn!" Chick yelled, putting his hands on his hips, pacing the room.

"Okay. Let's slow this down. How's his playing? You said he *just* wrote this amazing song. Well, he sounds focused to me. Maybe this isn't *bad* chemistry. Maybe it's the type of chemistry that's life-changing. Jadon could use a life change, you know?" Erin walked over to Chick, and wrapped her arms around him from behind.

"Well, man, I can't argue with that. I mean this song. Holy shit, babe, it's fuckin' amazing. I don't think I want to even *know* what's going through his mind, because it's . . . messed up. Tortured."

"Do you think Meg knows? Because, crazy as it sounds, she told me she thinks Jadon can't stand her." Erin chuckled at the thought.

"No, I don't think she knows how Jadon feels. I don't think he wants to touch her with a ten-foot pole. Well, I mean . . . *wants* to, but . . ."

"He fears the wrath of the Almighty, Chick?"

"No, I mean I'm sure he doesn't want to upset me. He's always been straight with me. No, there's something else. Maybe he's afraid of her. Ya know how he feels. What she might feel. Christ. I don't know. I'm not Dr. Phil," Chick said, rubbing his beard.

"Does Meg play in Jadon's new song?"

"Oh, yeah. Her part is, well, it puts chills down your spine. He had it all scribbled out. Looked like cave drawings, but she was able to figure it out. Don't know how. He was emphatic that I be the one that discussed it with her. Shit, he doesn't even want anyone to know he wrote the song."

"All right. Well, did she like it?"

Chick slapped his hands over his face again, letting his body fall lifelessly onto the sofa behind him. "She . . . yeah, she sort of fell apart. Hell, I didn't know what to make of it. I mean, she got all choked up. She kept it together. Sort of. But, it hit her like a train. *Boom.*"

"This is pretty amazing stuff."

"Not good. Not good *at all.*"

"Well, I know it seems that way. At least right now. But . . . you have to admit, it's sort of romantic, isn't it?"

Chick stared at her blankly.

"Well, I'm going to call her tomorrow," Erin said. "You're busy tomorrow with interviews. You'll be with Jay. You might be able to learn something."

"Nope, he's sealed shut. Whatever it is, it's in the vault. I can tell. Anyway, I don't know if I want to know."

"Okay, well, let me learn more about Meg. Hopefully, she's free, and we can spend the afternoon together. It's worth a try. Maybe she's as messed up as Jadon is. Got her number?"

Chapter 7

Who the hell could that be, Meg wondered, not recognizing the number scrolling across the screen of her cell phone.

"Hello?"

"Hey, Meg, it's Erin. Hope you don't mind. Chick gave me your number."

"Oh, no, I don't mind. What's up?"

"Well, the guys will be busy today, as you know. So I was wondering if you would like to join me for lunch. Just hang out. Casual."

Uh . . . Sure. Yeah. I was just writing, but I can always get back to it later," Meg said, closing her laptop.

"Great. I'll be there in about a half an hour. Give me your address . . .wait, I have to find a pen . . ready," Erin said, after searching through her desk.

"3320 Mandalay Bay Drive," Meg said slowly, giving Erin time to write it down.

"Sounds good. See you then." Erin closed the phone, disconnecting the call. "Hey, babe, what's Jadon's address?" she asked, thinking it sounded oddly familiar to Meg's.

"I don't know. He's over on Mandalay Bay. It's in the three thousands. I never remember those things," Chick said.

Pulling her white Jeep into Meg's driveway, Erin stared at Jadon's house.

"What the . . . ?" Erin said, walking up to Meg's front door. "This just keeps getting more and more interesting."

Before Erin had a chance to knock, Meg pulled the door open and greeted her with a smile.

"Ready?" Erin smiled.

"Yeah. Hey, would you mind if Bob joined us?" Meg asked, forgetting that as of yet no one knew who Bob was.

"Oh, I guess not," Erin answered, surprised by the unexpected third person.

"Great. He gets so lonely when I'm gone. He's too used to having me all to himself when I write."

Jumping off the sofa, Bob gladly trotted over and sat next to Erin, allowing her full opportunity to soak in his beauty or scratch his head, whichever she preferred.

"Oh, geez, I thought you meant, ha . . . of course, no problem. Bob? You ready?" Erin said as she opened the jeep door and allowed Meg to lift his hefty body into the back seat.

Within minutes Erin, Meg and Bob arrived at the small café Erin had carefully chosen, situated in the heart of Bay City.

"Azure. Sounds nice," Meg smiled, looking at the blue sign hanging precariously off the front of the brown brick building.

"It is. Chick doesn't care for it, but I like it. He usually gets mobbed though, so going out for a bite with him isn't relaxing anyway."

Meg soaked in the surroundings as they walked to an outdoor table positioned neatly under a large blue umbrella.

After careful thought, Meg finally ordered a salad of mixed greens with grilled free range turkey resting on top. Erin opted for the same.

"Want a drink?" Erin asked slyly, secretly hoping it would help loosen Meg's tongue.

"Sure. I'm game. You choose."

"Ooh. Okay. How about two Santa Margherita Pinot Grigios?" Erin said, pointing at the wine menu so the waiter could see which one she wanted.

Relaxing in her chair, Meg looked at the storefronts lining the main street running through Bay City. People were coming and going from store to store, bags in hand. Young kids, ladies with large hats and sunglasses — just as she would have described it, if she had to write about it in a novel.

"Wow, that was fast," Meg said, startled by how quickly their drinks had arrived.

"Oh, yeah, people around here aren't use to waiting when it comes to service. We wait forever on the freeway . . . but not at our cafés." Erin raised her glass to make a toast: "To hopefully many more outings."

"Hear, hear," Meg agreed, taking a long sip of wine.

Erin didn't know how she wanted to begin. She didn't want to scare Meg. Instead she wanted her to open up.

"Okay, what brings you to Southern California? Other than the sunshine and the chance to play with one of the best rock bands in the world?" Erin said devilishly.

Sitting up straighter, Meg looked out at the street, and thought about how she should answer. Her life had been so complicated, or at least it had some very complicated parts in it. She didn't want Erin to get put off by any of it.

"I wish I could say it was that reason that brought us here. Actually, I had a fan break into my home and try to kill me," Meg said flatly, taking another sip of her wine. Deciding there was no need to dance around the truth of the matter; Meg chose to throw the fact on the table with one big thump, allowing Erin to look at its ugliness instantly.

"No shit. Excuse my language. That's horrible," Erin said, startled by Meg's nonchalant expression, not to mention the upsetting reason for her move. "Well, you're okay. I mean, you look okay. Are you okay?"

"Oh, yeah. I'm great," Meg said, waving her hand in the air to dismiss the concern.

"Where was this?"

"Martha's Vineyard. I had an old home that sat back in the woods off the shore."

Meg went on to tell Erin the gruesome details, taking intermittent sips of wine as she went along. She explained how Devon feared for her safety, and how she couldn't write anymore, couldn't sleep anymore, couldn't stop looking over her shoulder. Meg told Erin how she had just started her latest novel and how the event had stopped her cold. She also told Erin how she and Bob had driven across the country, stopping off at kooky places along the way in an attempt to shake off the feeling of powerlessness.

"I guess I've always lived in this self-imposed bubble. It was safe. The only threat was me. Until that night. When someone, in one pointed move, popped my bubble," Meg winced from the memory of it.

Erin stared at Meg while Meg stared across the street. "How did this young man find you? I mean, how'd he know it was *you* who was the author? You don't use your real name."

"Good question," Meg said tilting her head, contemplating the absurdity of it. "He was clever. He tracked me down, using my publisher. Something Devon has never been able to come to terms with. This young man was able to hack into the company email at the publishing house. It took quite some time, but he managed to piece things together."

"That's really scary, Meg. Christ. Okay, so here you are, this successful writer . . . Tell me, where do you get your inspiration for these novels? What were their names again?" Erin asked with a Cheshire grin slowly spreading across her face.

"You're not an undercover agent during your off hours are you?" Meg joked, taking a deep breath of contemplation before answering. "I guess I just have all this stuff sitting inside of me."

"Well, for all I know you write about personal finance, so I'm not sure how to take that."

"You got me there," Meg laughed, raising her glass.

"Well, it's obvious you're gorgeous. Tell me about the men in your life."

Meg choked slightly on her wine. "I write about the stuff I want: I don't *have* the stuff I want! No, seriously, men. Ah . . . they, just . . . I've just never wanted to allow anyone in."

"In?"

"Into my head I guess. My thoughts. I have a really complex mind. I have a *lot* of shit rolling around in there, Erin. I can't just share this stuff with anyone!"

"I don't believe that."

"Well, okay. I've had a few relationships. But, no one has ever really understood me. And I guess I don't want to waste my time trying. I'm not an easy person, I suppose. I don't think I could be caged, not without dying in the process anyway." With that, Meg let out a sigh of sadness.

"I have a feeling the right guy is out there."

Meg stared at Erin wondering what Erin knew, if anything. There was no way Meg wanted to tell Erin about her nightly interludes with her neighbor. It was too bizarre and too precious all at the same time. Once spoken, it can never be unspoken. It's out. Once out, it can be talked about. Critiqued. Judged. Diminished and ruined. She wanted to protect her moments with her neighbor. They were like air to her.

"So there's no one?" Erin asked again.

"Nope."

"For such a passionate woman, I find it hard to believe you just exist without *any*, you know, sex," Erin said in a whisper, lowering her head over the table to get closer to Meg.

"Well, ha, *that*. I have my rich fantasy life," Meg said, purposely stuffing a large spinach leaf into her mouth. Trying to chew without choking, Meg was happy her mouth was too preoccupied to offer any further information.

"Don't worry; I'll wait until you're done chewing," Erin said, also taking a large bite of her salad.

"Okay, as for me personally, aside from the characters I write about. Well, I mean there is Dev . . . we did have this one night . . . but . . . it wasn't anymore than that."

"Dev is your . . .?"

"He's my publisher. He's also my closest and oldest friend."

"Is he handsome?" Erin asked, her face brightening with the prospects.

"Oh, yeah. He's . . . he's quite handsome, I suppose."

Erin tried to unearth what Devon meant to Meg. From what she could gather, he was dear to her but couldn't seize the passion burning within Meg's heart. Erin thought their night together sounded straight out of a romantic novel, which, in a way, it was. Erin paid careful attention while Meg described how their night together happened, and why it happened. How Meg had been struggling with the plausibility of one of the lovemaking scenes in her novel. Erin was intrigued by that. How plausibility could become an issue during lovemaking fascinated her. Meg fascinated her. The way Meg talked, making her words blend smoothly one into the other, and the way she twirled her hand spontaneously around when she was trying to describe certain things.

"So, let me get this straight. You had this mind-blowing night together. He's handsome, wealthy, intelligent, gentle *and* he adores you," Erin said, looking off as if engrossed in deep contemplation. "No. Doesn't sound good to me either."

"That's good wine," Meg licked her lips, retrieving the last drop, "I didn't say he didn't sound good. He *is* good. He's, well, you'll have to meet him. He's . . . wonderful. He is," she said, feeling the pain of him *not* being the one.

Meg didn't know why he didn't drive her crazy inside. But he didn't. Not like her neighbor. Not like Jadon either, although much of that was most likely due to his hatred for her, and her overwhelming desire to hate him in return.

"No one knows what will ignite the fire within them. Chemistry is a crazy thing," Erin said, realizing this was the perfect opportunity to segue into discussing Jadon. "Chick told me about the new song you guys are working on."

Meg looked up at Erin, startled by the abrupt change of subjects. Although it wasn't a change in subjects at all as far as she was concerned. Jadon had a way of stirring every fiber in her body. And she hated it. She hated how she melted when she was around him. She didn't even have to be around him, just thinking about him made her melt, which made writing about him all the more enjoyable. She could sit behind her safe writing desk, in her safe chair, melting in a private, controllable manner.

"Oh, yeah, it's something," Meg said smoothly, realizing she needed a cigarette even though she didn't smoke.

"Well, what did you think of it?" Erin asked hesitantly.

Much to Erin's surprise, Meg leaned in across the table and said, "I've never heard anything like it before. It's . . . it's amazing, but what it does to me . . . I can barely keep it together when I listen to it."

"I guess Jadon helped write it," Erin tried to find an excuse to bring his name into the mix.

Meg looked up at Erin and nodded. She wasn't sure what to say. Jadon was an enigma to her.

"Maybe, I guess. That's what I was told too."

Erin finally decided to cut to the chase before she burst. "Meg, tell me: what do you think of him?"

"Jadon?" Meg asked, trying to buy herself some time.

"Yes, Jadon." Erin knew full well Meg knew who she was talking about. All the clues that Meg was accidentally revealing showed that she was drawn to him.

"Well, beside the fact that he hates me and stares at me so hard I want to run for the hills . . . well, I mean . . . I'm not going to lie Erin, he's . . . he's damn *nice* to look at. If you like that type," Meg offered, hoping to appease her new friend, but she immediately realized it wasn't even beginning to chip at the surface of Erin's curiosity.

"What type is that?" Erin asked, knowing Meg's answer would give her a clear idea of what Meg thought about him.

Meg looked off across the street. Wrinkling her brow she turned to Erin with exasperation, "Oh . . . you know. That whole, dripping in good looks, lusty, sexy, you just want to ravage him because he's so . . ." Meg stopped herself. She could almost hear the beans spilling across the table as she spoke about Jadon.

"I didn't mean to push a button, Meg. I was just wondering what your take on him was," Erin said, sliding the signed check back toward the side of the table.

Meg felt her face grow hot with embarrassment. Erin hadn't asked anything about Jadon's looks, she merely asked what she thought of him, plain and simple.

Meg rolled her eyes. "I'm sorry, I'm so embarrassed. I don't know what came over me. He just, he gets under my skin. I'm a mess, so if you didn't know already. Hello, my name is Meg Kathryn Scott, and I'm a mess," she laughed, pushing her chair out, motioning to Bob who was enjoying his nap under the table.

Pulling up to Meg's house, Erin stopped the Jeep. "Thank you for joining me today. I really, really enjoyed it."

"Thanks for asking me. I enjoyed it myself. It might not have seemed that way, but I did," Meg said, laughing at her own complexity.

"Hey, Chick said Cam was planning on shooting the new video for that song he heard you guys working on the other day. If you want me to hang out with you, I will."

Meg stood in silence for a moment, "I hadn't realized they would begin working on it so quickly."

"Things in this business can get crazy fast. And Cam can be a handful. I just thought you might feel more at ease with a friend there. Not that the guys aren't your friends; they are. Trust me. All I hear are kind words. I just thought . . ."

Erin didn't want to tell Meg that Cameron had talked to Chick that morning and his ideas for the video were pretty radical. Chick demanded that all members of the band be featured in every video. He didn't like camera hogs. Cam agreed, but said the main theme of the video involved Jadon and Meg. And after hearing what Meg had to say about him, she thought Meg might like a friend on set with her.

"They're all great. They are. Okay. I wonder when it will begin," Meg asked, astonished by the speed of things.

"I don't want to startle you but Cameron wants to hit it while he's still in town. He mentioned starting on it tomorrow."

"Tomorrow?"

"Chick said to come to the studio early. He wants to run through the song a few times before Cam gets there. These things often get shot at obscure times, in weird places. Cam is insane about getting certain angles at just the right time of day. It'll be an experience!"

"Hey. I'm game. Life has been a bit whacky lately, anyway. I'm not an actress, but I can do whatever, I guess." Meg wondered how bad it could possibly be.

"Good, see you then," Erin popped her Jeep in reverse, and gave Meg and Bob a wave as she backed out of the driveway.

Turning onto the road, Erin stared at Jadon's house, wondering if he was there. She couldn't help but think that Jadon *had* to know Meg lived right next door to him. But it was apparent Meg didn't have a clue.

Chapter 8

Meg woke with a heavy feeling lodged in the pit of her stomach.

"Christ," she said, looking over at Bob, who was the picture of peacefulness lying next to her. "What do you think making a music video is like? You don't have a clue. Me neither"

Even though she didn't have the faintest idea what to expect, Meg had been thinking about it ever since Erin mentioned they would begin shooting the next day. The song itself was rough for Meg to get through. She loved it, though. She was captivated by it, almost as much as she was captivated by her moments with her neighbor.

Shuffling into the kitchen, she pushed the button on her coffee machine, happy that she had the forethought the night before to get it ready for the next morning. When it came to mornings, Meg needed all the help she could get.

As she walked onto the balcony, she felt the early morning ocean air sweep over her body. Savoring the memories of last night, she wondered what her neighbor looked like. It took all Meg had not to rush over to his house, burst through his door, throw him down to the ground, and make wild love to him. She wanted to, but in Meg's mind something so perfect risked the chance of being destroyed if changed in any way.

Wouldn't it be a kick if he looked even vaguely similar to Jadon? Meg thought. Shaking her head, she didn't want to imagine it. It meant putting her neighbor in a box, a sexy box, but a box just the same.

Taking her first sip of coffee standing on the balcony, Meg listened to the new song play in her head. She couldn't help but wonder how others would perceive it. It didn't matter: it was breathtaking to her. Hard to imagine, but it was oddly romantic as well.

"That's it. That's why it rips at my heart. That's the type of passion I've always wanted. Suppose that's why it hurts so much to hear it."

A short hour later, Meg flew out of her driveway, already bordering on being late. Putting down the top on her roadster, she let her hair air dry while breaking various traffic laws getting to the studio on time.

"Doesn't look too scary yet," Meg said, getting out of her car and scanning the few cars parked outside the studio.

Erin opened the door to the studio and gave her a quick smile. Relieved to see Erin's smiling face, Meg smiled right back.

"Hey, you," Erin said playfully.

"Hey," Meg said, walking in.

"There she is! Good. I want to run through this a couple of times before Cam has us running all over town," Chick said, already heading to the rehearsal room.

Jadon sat at his drum kit, deep in thought. Having been up most of the night playing things out in his mind, he was finally able to come to terms with how things were unfolding. Deciding that it was going to play out however it was going to play out, all he needed was his time alone with Meg on their balconies. If he had that, he would be all right. Those moments hurled him through countless emotions, but also balanced him. Although they were not physically together, he was making love to her in those moments, and it felt like heaven.

Bob and Stu were already sitting with their guitars, both feeling uneasy, not sure what the day would bring. Each one loved Jadon like a brother and hated seeing him in pain. But they didn't want to say anything. Nothing needed to be said; they would just give him his space. The air felt combustible as they watched Chick and Kofi make their way into the room, followed by Erin and Meg.

Watching Meg laugh with Erin, Bob noticed Meg's large welcoming smile. Her vibrant red hair hung wildly around her face, giving her an almost primal appearance. Glancing over toward Jadon, Bob took note that Jadon was already fixated on Meg, watching her every move as she made her way over to her stool and began unpacking her violin.

Jadon's eyes fell upon Meg as soon as she walked into the rehearsal room behind Chick. He couldn't help but notice how disheveled her hair looked. She had the look of just rolling out of bed, and he couldn't help but wonder if that was how she would look first thing in the morning, a thought that sent an electric current down his spine.

"*Mornin'*, everyone," Chick said with a snap of his gum.

Chick was already sitting comfortably in his chair, his guitar resting comfortably on his lap. He made the whole scene of making music appear effortless. "Ya ready to kick ass first thing in the mornin'?"

Chick watched Meg carefully pull her violin out of its case, and thought about the gossip Erin shared with him yesterday when she got back from her afternoon with Meg. He had to agree with Erin; Meg had no clue about Jadon's feelings. *Feelings,* he mused; *hell of a lot more than that.*

Chick chewed his gum rambunctiously, "Ready, Freddie?" he said looking at Meg.

"Oh, yeah, good to go," Meg answered, surprised by how fast they all had gotten ready.

"Jay . . . ," Chick said, signaling that everyone was in place, while winking at Erin, who was sitting a few chairs out.

Taking the opportunity to watch Jadon, Meg noticed how he collected himself before beginning. His eyes were closed, but always his left knee was hopping to a silent beat that only he heard. Then he began with authority, turning his head to sing.

Meg watched his body as it moved with every beat. It moved to beats she didn't even hear. His body was well toned, but delicate. *He must have been a yogi in a past life,* she thought while looking at him intently. His hair was lighter and fluffier than usual, but by the end of a couple songs it would be wet with sweat. *I like that, too,* she commented silently to herself.

Sliding off her stool, Meg arched her back. Feeling the intensity of Jadon's eyes glued to her, she reached up, and pulled at her first note, hanging on to it as if her life depended on it before launching into the next series of notes.

Right on cue Jadon joined her, his beats propelling her forward, carrying her while she tossed around the complex arrangement that was written for her. Moving to the seductive melody, Meg could think of nothing except the music she was making with Jadon. The way he was able to incorporate the drums into her violin playing was startling. The two don't normally mesh so beautifully. But they did, and they did in a spectacular way. The erotic, forceful blend the two made together made her head spin. She wanted it to last longer, but hitting her last note, she faded to silence before the guys wrapped the song up in a climactic ending.

Walking over to Chick, Erin stared blankly at him. In turn, Chick stared blankly back, not sure what was going through his wife's mind.

"Just a moment, everyone. Come with me," she said flatly, turning to walk into the lounge. Chick followed silently.

"What the hell was that?" Erin asked, once they were alone.

"Well, I know, that's what I was talking about. I told you it was serious shit," Chick said, giving Erin an incredulous look.

"Wow, you weren't kidding!" she said, slapping Chick's arm before peeking back into the rehearsal room. "No wonder Cam was on it. Who the hell wouldn't be? I feel like I just watched those two make love."

"This isn't good Erin. You think it's all romantic and exciting, but this smells of disaster." Chick leaned back, casting a quick glance into the rehearsal room.

"Babe, Jay is madly, *no*, wildly in love with her." Erin looked at her husband for compassion.

"She doesn't even have a fuckin' clue. I can't even *imagine* what must be rolling around in her mind right now. Maybe she thinks it's about someone else . . ."

"She probably does."

"Good, let's keep it that way."

"Wow. I bet he's a red hot lover," she said, trying to grab another glimpse of Jadon.

"Whoa! I so don't want to hear *that!*" Chick said, covering his ears.

"You're *my* red hot lover, but you have to admit . . ." Erin left the thought unfinished.

"I don't have to admit anything," Chick said. "How the hell would I know about that anyway? The dude sounds tortured to me." He nudged Erin back into the rehearsal room.

The band made it through another round of the song, now titled *Longing*, before Cameron and his assistants walked into the rehearsal room.

"Ready?" Cameron said quickly to everyone. "I gotta strike while the iron is hot on this one. I just have these images. I can't get them out of my mind. I have the first few locations getting set up. I need a lot of night scenes though. This song screams darkness."

"Well, ya care to share?" Chick said, getting annoyed with the lack of solid information.

"I would rather throw a lot of this at you in the moment," Cameron said to Chick. "It breeds a more genuine, spontaneous portrayal on screen that way."

"I need some details, dude," Chick said shaking his head, showing Cameron it wasn't going to fly shooting it entirely off the hip.

"I plan to compile a large quantity of clips, short clips of video images. I will do right by it, trust me," Cameron looked around the room to find Jadon and Meg hiding in their respective corners.

Looking up at the ceiling Cameron collected his thoughts. "To start I need a few clips shot in the day. I already have the permits to use the cliffs overlooking the bay. We need to run out there because the damn city wants to give me only four hours. Fuckers. So let's fly. I have make-up, hair and wardrobe waiting," he said turning.

"Ya know, Cam. We're going to appease you. We'll indulge your eccentricities 'cause we just don't have anything better to do," Chick joked, his voice still indicating his reluctance. "I mean, you wouldn't want to run your ideas by the *band*."

Cameron turned quickly and stepped over to Chick. "I need you to bloody trust me. You have something really special here. I know what I can do with it. And it will set the tone for the entire single. I don't, however, think some of the band members will be eager. So, let's just fuckin' act like we're wingin' it, yes?

Chick stared at Cameron and quickly caught on to what Cameron was thinking. He hardly knew how to brace himself for the day ahead. He didn't want his band to implode; as it was, it felt like things were already teetering.

"If *anything* starts to unravel the band, we're outta there."

"Agreed," Cameron replied, happy to get on with the production.

Meg followed the parade of cars out to the cliffs overlooking Mandalay Bay. The cliffs' hard-edged rock formations in brilliant shades of gray made it a magnificent site. The stiff breeze off the ocean nearly blew over everyone as they stepped out of their cars. Chick turned to wave at Meg as she pulled in, his long, black hair shrouding his face as he walked over to her roadster.

"How ya doin' with all this?" he asked.

"I'm good. Why do you ask?" Meg wondered if her turmoil was becoming obvious to everyone.

"Well, hell, first, this isn't your profession of choice. Obviously, if you had wanted to be a musician you could've been, you've proven that. And now within a few days, you're finding yourself standing on a windy ridge getting ready to shoot a music video. Sounds a bit overwhelming to me, don't ya think?"

"I'm good. It might not look like it, and I apologize for that. I don't know what came over me the other day." Meg waved her hand in the general direction of the studio. "I can't really explain it. There's just something about this song that digs into my heart. It's beautiful beyond comprehension, and I'm honored to be a part of it in any way I can."

"All right, sister, sounds good." Chick hooked his arm into Meg's arm as he walked her over to Cameron's assistant, a petite, young Asian woman. "Hey, Charlotte, this is Meg. Meg, Charlotte."

"Hello, Meg," Charlotte said, giving Meg the once over. "We better get started. Cam is over the top on this one. He knows just what he wants, and you're a *big* part of it."

Meg stood silently, startled by the idea of being a big part of anything. Charlotte motioned for Meg to walk into the make-shift white tent, and pointed to the chair next to the table.

"Let's get the hair first, then we move on to makeup, and after that wardrobe," Charlotte said swiftly, a hint of urgency streaming through her voice, revealing the short amount of time she had to work with.

Meg sat patiently while her hair was flat ironed into shiny red sheets that cascaded down her back like deep, scarlet water.

Charlotte stood and stared at Meg's face before pulling out the assorted colors she intended on using. Never bothering to ask Meg what she thought, or if she liked any of it. Meg was shuffled from one chair to the next, with no real conversation exchanged between the two of them. Meg could tell Charlotte was an artist deep in concentration, and tried to appreciate being a blank canvas for her to work upon.

"Okay. Wardrobe," Charlotte said, walking over to the racks set up in the corner of the tent. "Cameron told me your size, but I tend to grab things a few sizes larger and a few sizes smaller. What does he know? I heard the song, so I know what he wants," she muttered more to herself than to Meg. "Okay, this is it. This is it. Go behind the curtain and undress. It's safe, don't worry." Charlotte gave Meg one of only a few smiles offered that afternoon.

Struggling with the outfit, Meg quickly realized it wasn't just a simple dress, it was actually a gown. A long, wispy, black gown, with fabric that clung tightly to her body around her bust and midsection, then swept out into light, long, black layers that pooled onto the ground around her feet.

"I'm a witch," Meg thought. "They think I'm a witch." Moving around in front of the mirror, Meg noticed two vertical slits running the length of the gown beginning high on her thighs, revealing her legs as she walked.

"Thank God," Charlotte sighed, looking at Meg's toes.

Meg looked at Charlotte blankly, wondering what the concern was for, *a sixth toe?*

"I'm glad you don't have polish on. Cam was adamant that you be natural in this shot," Charlotte said, ushering Meg out from behind the curtain. "Let's go."

"Perfect," Cameron said, staring at Meg, "Okay, *I want the song playing,*" he yelled to his sound crew. "It's imperative the energy of the song is felt at all times! Okay, sweetheart, this is one of your easier takes," he said, quickly adding sugar to his voice. "First, we want you to stand near the edge of the cliff and play your violin. Easy cheesy, yes?"

Meg wasn't sure what she thought of Cameron. She could easily tell he wasn't willing to share what he was thinking beyond the now. Once Charlotte handed Meg her violin, Cameron walked her out to the edge of the cliff.

"Play. We will be taping. There is no *wrong.* Do what you feel. We'll edit out almost everything. I want you to *try* to relax, and *feel* the song," Cameron said, turning on his heels and heading back to the group, which was standing near the tents.

Watching Cameron walk away, Meg noticed the entire band standing next to him, including Jadon, who was dressed in a black, button-down shirt that wasn't tucked into his worn faded, blue jeans; he was shoeless. Taking a hard swallow, Meg turned to look over the ocean and couldn't believe the situation she was in.

"Hell with it. I'm going to live this and do this, and just let it happen. I'm tired of living in a box, writing magnificent stories about other people. I want to live something magnificent. As long as I don't make a complete ass out of myself in the process," Meg said forcefully under her breath.

Turning one last time, she motioned to Cameron, who quickly walked out to join her on the blustery cliff.

"Does it matter which way I face?" Meg asked, turning her body to the right, then to the left.

"Darling, we have every inch of you on film, we have many cameras on you; do what feels right." Cameron winked at Meg before making a hasty getaway.

Before she had time to think another thought, Meg heard the music begin. The sound emanated from every angle and every source. Even the rock beneath her feet resonated with Jadon's drumbeat. Staring out at the ocean, Meg stood patiently. With her violin in one hand and her bow in the other, both held low on each side, she allowed the wind to angrily blow against her body, causing her hair to form a thick blaze of red that danced behind her. As did the delicate, wispy layers of fabric around her legs that now flickered in the wind. Slowly she brought her violin up and nestled it on her left shoulder. Her body swaying to the rhythm of the song, her soul was already caught in its beautiful web.

Tilting her head in welcomed resignation, Meg rested her chin on the violin, and waited for her moment to begin. Wishing Jadon were playing along with her, she pictured him instead. Within her mind she watched as he hit the drums with wild abandon, looking at her intensely. Lifting her bow she struck her first chord.

Meg forgot about the camera crew, and about Cameron. Instead she focused only on the images held within her mind, the nights dancing on her balcony with her neighbor, Jadon's face, his liquid blue eyes. She felt his drums beat inside her chest as she swayed delicately through the complicated mixture of notes. Throwing her head back, she dove soulfully into her final chord. Saddened as always by its quick end, she closed her eyes, and stood motionless.

Jadon stared at Meg, overwhelmed by her beauty. He couldn't think of anything except her. Transfixed, he wanted to run to her. He wanted to hold her. None of this was possible, of course, making it almost unbearable for him to watch her.

Erin nudged Chick's arm and nodded her head in Jadon's direction. Chick stood with his arms folded across his chest; slowly he turned his head to look at Jadon, then back at Erin, only to find the look of excitement on her face. Ignoring Chick's look of disapproval, Erin turned and watched Jadon stare longingly at Meg. He was mesmerized. Everyone watched Meg, as she was the one being filmed at the moment. But there was something unmistakably different about the way Jadon looked at her.

Walking over to Jadon, Erin was eager to feel out the situation. "What do you think of that?"

"It's . . .it's just . . .just what it is," Jadon said, turning and walking away.

Not expecting the look of pain she saw in Jadon's eyes before he walked away, Erin felt guilty for acting on her schoolgirl desire to needle him.

"Hey, good job," Erin smiled, walking over to Meg.

"Oh, yeah? Sure feels odd, though," Meg tried to shake off her awkwardness.

"Are you ready to get changed again, Meg?" Charlotte asked.

Walking back behind the curtain, Meg carefully took off the beautiful, black wispy gown, and handed it to Charlotte.

"Here you go," Charlotte said, handing Meg a stack of clothes.

This is more like it, Meg thought to herself, eyeing the faded blue jeans and black, button-down blouse.

"Leave your black lace bra on, Meg," Charlotte yelled over the curtain.

"No problem," Meg said, wondering what the other option would have been.

Stepping out from behind the curtain, Charlotte quickly unbuttoned Meg's blouse a couple buttons.

"I need you in the hair chair for a second," she said, hustling Meg over to the chair positioned next to the table. Rapidly Charlotte threw large, rounded waves back into Meg's hair, a style closer to how she usually wore it. Then as if in a race, she quickly pulled out various containers of make-up, and began dusting Meg's face.

"Close your eyes," Charlotte ordered, applying various shades of lavender eye shadow to Meg's eyelids. Reaching behind her, she grabbed the forest green eyeliner, and applied a thick dark line around Meg's eyes.

"Whoa . . . ," Meg said, catching a glimpse of herself in the mirror.

"I know, it's dark, but it just seems that way now. It changes appearance on film, trust me." Charlotte finished by coating Meg's lips with a neutral shade of creamy lipstick. "I'd use lip gloss, but that wind is going to be hell to deal with. You're good to go."

Meeting them at the edge of the tent, Cameron grabbed Meg's arm and brought her back out to the cliff's edge.

"Where's her fuckin' violin?" Cameron shouted behind his back. "Okay, Meg. This time you're not alone — better, yes?" He said, already walking back behind the camera.

Meg looked around, and noticed Jadon perched neatly behind his drum kit. *When did they get that set up?* she wondered.

"No, no, no! Meg, darling . . . I need you facing this way," Cameron shouted.

"Oh, I thought you said it didn't matter which way I faced. You had a bunch of cameras or something like that . . . ," Meg said, startled that she was the cause of such an outburst.

"Now you're with the band, yes?" Cameron said staring at her. "I need you to be very much like you are in the studio. *So,* you stand like this. I like how you're out in front and the band can see *you,* yes?" he said as he walked away.

Meg immediately felt awkward, "Okay, whatever you say."

Sitting quietly, Jadon watched Cameron move Meg around, pointing her directly in front of him. He didn't care for what Cameron was doing, which was creating a direct connection between the violin and the drums and trying to pair the two. Granted, Jadon knew that this made sense as that's exactly what the song was about, but even so it unnerved him.

Jadon also couldn't help but notice how stunning Meg looked, her large eyes glancing around at everyone. They were spectacular. Her hair bounced in the wind, often getting stuck to her lips. Swallowing hard, Jadon looked around to make sure he wasn't missing anyone's cue to begin.

Cameron watched from behind his large camera. Having all of the camera feeds displayed onto a video screen positioned next to him, he loved what he was catching. He liked the random glances the band made at the ocean and the panorama of Southern California coastline. What most interested him, however, was the look of desire he was catching between Meg and Jadon. He knew it was there. He could feel it.

Cameron signaled for the music to begin. Meg watched as Jadon began playing in the same exact way as before. Easily she found herself captivated by him. *A guy shouldn't be so beautiful to look at*, she thought; *just isn't right*. Her eyes blinked slowly, fixated on Jadon's movements. Biting her lower lip Meg looked at the ocean for a second to clear her mind.

Slowly she turned her head to look at Jadon once more, this time locking eyes with him. Quickly turning to look out over the ocean, Meg tried to keep focused.

Not wanting to turn back around, Meg remained faced away from Jadon as she lifted her violin, and reached for her first note, the most important one. It was the note that allowed her in, giving her a place within the song. It screamed and begged for attention. Holding her finger hard against the neck of the violin, her shoulders pulled back, Meg allowed the full volume of the note to rocket into the air.

Not able to help herself, she quickly turned, facing Jadon exactly as he hit his drums with a commanding thud that tied the two of them together. For the rest of the song Meg swayed gently. Keeping her eyes closed she hit her last note, holding it as long as she could, she turned to look out over the ocean. Suddenly the song ended.

"Meg?" Erin said, walking up behind her. "You're doing great. This stuff is tricky, but you're doing a wonderful job. They're ready to tear down and go to the next location. I told you this stuff is a little nutty. It goes fast sometimes. When Cam is on the scent of something, he just wants to keep going. Knowing him, he'll want to pull an all-nighter."

Meg stopped. "Bob. What about Bob?" She had never even thought that they might work through the night. "His dog walker is done for the day."

"Don't worry, I'll buzz over and let him out," Erin said with bright eyes, pleased with herself for thinking of such an easy fix.

"You wouldn't mind?"

"No, oh no. Bob is quite the charmer. Hell, we can practically see your house from here you're so close. I'll hurry though, so I'm back at the next location, in case you need me."

"Take my car. The house key is on the ring, or easier yet, just use the garage door opener. Thank you, Erin."

Erin walked over to Chick, and told him she was heading to Meg's house to let her dog out. Then shooting a glance toward Jadon, "Of course you could do it, if you're running home?" Erin whispered with a devilish grin before walking away.

"Huh?" Jadon said, startled.

Erin winked at him. "Your secret's safe with me."

Arriving at the next location, a private beachfront lot surrounded by old trees with looming, low hanging branches, arched in a way that gave full privacy, Meg looked around, trying to take in the site. She instantly noticed that the only equipment on site was Jadon's drum kit, placed a few feet from the water's edge.

"Ready, Meg?" Charlotte asked, grabbing Meg's arm again.

"I guess."

"In we go." Charlotte pointed to a much smaller tent than the previous one they had used.

Walking inside Meg waited for Charlotte to tell her what to do.

"This one's going to get chilly, especially now that the sun is going down, so I'm going to be right out there, waiting for you with towels. When you need me, signal, I'll wrap you up. If we're lucky, we can get this in one or two takes."

While Meg's head spun from the unknown, Charlotte motioned for her to go behind the small curtain. Knowing the drill, Meg began to strip down, right on cue. Charlotte handed her a scrap of fabric. *What the hell is this*, Meg wondered, pulling it apart.

"Do you need me to tie that around your neck and at your hips?" Charlotte offered, the assistance helping Meg to realize what she was looking at.

"No. Well, I don't know." Walking out from behind the curtain, the small black string bikini rested perfectly on Meg's petite frame. "This one might make me a bit embarrassed," she said with a chuckle of disbelief, looking down at her mostly bare body.

"I know. It's small," Charlotte said with an apologetic look on her face. "If it's any comfort, it looks very, very good on you," she smiled, making sure the ties were snug and tight.

"Hair?" Meg said, not missing a beat.

Charlotte looked remorseful, "No. Cameron's planning on simulating rain."

"Rain?" Meg repeated, not sure what it literally meant in this situation.

"You'll be soaked. Sorry, Meg," Charlotte said sadly, leading her toward the beach.

"Finally! Okay. This is what I want from you Meg," Cameron said, turning to point at Jadon sitting behind the drums. "I need you to simply walk out of the water, onto the beach, toward Jadon. That's it."

"Okay, go out in the water . . ." Meg began to repeat slowly, pointing out toward the ocean.

"Dunk your head in, get wet so that your hair is *away* from your face. It'll be raining, so don't let that bother you. It adds drama to the scene. *Slowly* walk toward Jadon. He'll be playing his drums. Done," Cameron said, snapping his fingers.

Meg thought it didn't sound too difficult. Considering she was wearing an almost nonexistent bikini, about to slither out of the ocean in front of Jadon of all people, not to mention the rest of the band, and a small legion of strangers.

Nodding her head, Meg slowly made her way out into the ocean, her mind racing with each cautious step. *How embarrassing*, Meg thought. *If I do this right, though, I can be in and out. I can do this.* Meg heard the music thunder through the air, and winced as the cool water shot past her stomach. Gliding her hands across the top of the water, she turned once more to look back at the crew. Soon she heard the small splattering sounds of large raindrops hitting the top of the water. In one quick jump Meg dove in like a fish. Doubling back, she stayed under the water for a second to collect herself.

Jadon watched as Meg slowly emerged from the water. Pounding forcefully on the bass drum, he tried to rein in his mind. His sticks firing rapidly, striking the snare when he meant to hit the mid tom-tom, captivated instead by Meg's body as she slowly moved toward him. Slamming harder on the drums, he tried to concentrate on the words he was supposed to be singing.

Meg felt the rain hit against her face. Her long hair pressed slick against her head and down her back, her body responding to the mix of temperatures. Focusing on Jadon, Meg made sure her steps were slow and purposeful. She felt her chest begin to rise and fall heavily. Keeping her eyes set on him, she watched him move radically to the song. His eyes glued to hers, Meg stepped out of the water, and moved closer toward him.

"Fuck!" Jadon shouted, hanging his head in disbelief. "I dropped my fuckin' stick."

Immediately Jadon began searching desperately to find the drumstick that slipped from his hand. Meg stood a foot away from his drum set, the closest she had been to him since they first met. Looking down she saw the drum stick resting on the sand. Reaching down she slowly handed it to him. Startled and humiliated, Jadon snatched the stick from Meg's hand.

"Thank you," he mumbled, quickly looking down at his drums in a deliberate attempt at false preoccupation.

A sinking feeling filled Meg's stomach before it moved throughout her body. Hurt, she turned and walked back out into the ocean for a second take. Meg felt the sting of small disappointed tears spring onto the surface of her eyes. *I'm a real piece of work*, Meg thought, rolling her eyes at herself. She was amazed at how easily she'd allowed herself to be drawn to Jadon despite everything her mind was telling her. Meg wanted to hide under the water for as long as possible. She wanted to disappear.

Jadon felt his body begin to sweat. Nerves completely took over his mind when Meg began to walk closer to him, and he lost his focus. He never dropped his sticks. He hated fumbling, again. The sting of embarrassment draped over his body. He didn't want to look at Meg. He didn't want her to see his desire for her. He felt like a puppet for Cameron, and an idiot in front of Meg. Now Jadon wanted only to get the scene over with so he could get out of there, and go someplace where his every move was no longer trapped under a spotlight.

Turning under the water, Meg opened her eyes, seeing the glow surrounding Jadon's drum kit she steadily began to swim in his direction. She hated herself for permitting her mind to get distracted by him. As she slowly emerged from the water, her face softly showed her pain. Keeping her eyes set on Jadon, she felt the rain wash her tears away. Blinking slowly, she kept walking toward him.

Angry with himself, Jadon took the anger out on his drums. Pounding harder than normal, he tried not to look at Meg. He didn't care what Cam told him to do. He just wanted to get through the scene. Despite his intentions, his eyes kept being pulled magnetically in Meg's direction as he watched her body glide slowly toward him, her hands hanging down on her sides.

Meg watched as Jadon tried to keep his focus pointed away from her. *Just as well*, she thought to herself. Keeping her footsteps steady and even, she walked out of the water and toward him, slowly making her way up the beach she stood in front of him. Unable to look at him, she closed her eyes and turned away.

"*Cut!*" Cameron shouted.

"Hey, Meg," Erin said, rushing over to her with a large towel in her hands ready to wrap her up. "You okay?"

"I'm great," Meg said, trying to clear her eyes. "How's my favorite guy?"

"Great. He's a sweetheart."

Erin looked around and saw the setup for the scene. Looking over at Jadon who was trying to dry himself off with a towel, Erin couldn't help but feel the uneasiness hanging in the air.

"You sure everything went okay while I was gone?"

Walking behind the curtain to change, Meg looked at Erin for a moment, then nodded her head. "Everything's good."

"No! No! Meg!" Charlotte yelled, running in the tent. "Cam isn't done with the rain scene!"

"Really?" Meg said in disbelief. "I thought he said it would be done in a snap."

"Well, that part. It went well, though, and it only took two takes. You two are naturals. Right now Cam's working with the guys, getting images of them. If it's any consolation, they're getting soaked now, too."

With an arm held firmly around Meg's shivering shoulders, Erin held Meg's towel in place. The two of them watched as Cameron walked the band into the water, positioning each of them in various places, at different depths, before the rain pounded on them. Looking at Erin quickly, Meg then turned to watch the filming. Trying to shake off her anger with herself, she concentrated instead on the guys who looked tired and haggard swinging their guitars just inches above the water.

Taking the opportunity to throw himself down on the beach, Jadon pulled his legs tight in front of him, lit a cigarette and deeply inhaled. His mind raced: he was tired and angry at himself. Jadon looked at the stars, which were just beginning to appear in the night sky. *Meg must think I'm a complete moron,* he sighed, glancing over at her. *She looks cold. She looks sexy as hell. But she looks so sad.*

"Okay," Cameron said, signaling his assistants to get towels for Chick, Stu and Bob. Turning around, rubbing his head, Cam wasn't sure how to best describe the scene without frightening off his main characters. "This will sound a little wild," he said.

Everyone moaned, not wanting to hear what was next.

"But it won't be *that* uncomfortable, especially if we're quick about it. Okay. I want Jadon on the chair. Easy?" Cameron pointed to the chair and back at Jadon. "Now . . ." Looking around, Cameron tried to find Meg. "I want you, darling, to . . . um . . . well, quite frankly, straddle Jadon. And when we have you just right, we'll pour the rain down on you both. It's a *dramatic* scene. All is good, yes?" he concluded. Really not wanting any replies, he quickly walked over to his main camera.

"You have to be kidding," Meg whispered to Erin in disbelief. "Erin, Jadon hates me. He can't even look at me. This isn't going to look right. This guy Cameron's living in a fantasy world."

After hearing Cameron's idea, Jadon slowly walked away. Chick held his arms tightly across his chest, a stance he kept taking throughout the entire day. Knowing the vision Cameron was working on, Chick had to agree it caught the essence of the song.

"Holy hell, what a scene," Chick sighed.

Jadon didn't look pleased about it. Chick glanced at Meg and noticed she looked as though she had been ordered to walk the plank.

"Okay, okay," Chick said, trying to rally the two of them together.

"Hey. I'll do it," Bob offered slyly.

"Me too," Stu added.

Chick stood rubbing his mustache and beard in one fluid repetitive motion. "Jay, come here. Meg. If you both just do this, it'll be done in minutes. Half hour tops. I see where Cameron is trying to go with this, and I have to say I agree." Chick paused to run his fingers through his hair. "It's obvious that neither of you want to do this. And that's cool. Just give it your best shot. I know you both . . . have it in you," he said with a quick look at Erin.

Meg stiffened her back and gave Erin her towel. "Let's just do this," she said forcefully, walking over to the chair and motioning for Jadon to sit down.

Staring at Meg, Jadon couldn't believe she was going to go through with the scene.

"Time to step up to the plate, big guy," Chick nudged Jadon toward the chair.

Reluctantly, Jadon walked over and sat down throwing his arms across his chest, causing Cameron to rush over, not wanting anyone to back out at the last minute.

"Okay, well obviously that won't work," Cameron pulled Jadon's arms apart, "Meg, climb up here."

Looking around for a moment, Cameron motioned for Meg to wait. Pointing to Charlotte, who immediately ran to his side, he whispered something in her ear. Charlotte smiled and nodded before running off to one of the equipment vans.

"Nothing!" she yelled back.

"Fucking bastards got into my stash. In my trunk then!" Cameron yelled.

Charlotte quickly popped open the trunk of Cameron's rental car, grabbed a bottle of tequila, and ran back to Cameron.

"Oh, you're a sly motherfucker, Cam," Chick shook his head.

"Hey, liquid courage. Never ever, underestimate its power," he shot back. "Okay, ladies first," Cameron handed Meg the elaborate bottle of tequila. "Drink it, darling. It won't work unless you drink it."

Pulling out the thick cork, Meg took a sip, discovering it was far smoother and easier to drink than she first anticipated.

Cameron handed the bottle to Jadon, who glared at him. "Don't be a chicken, Jay, most men would beg to be you right now."

Taking a swig of the tequila, Jadon handed it back to Meg, who didn't realize they were planning on having more than one drink. Looking at Jadon, Meg again felt the pain he sent shooting through her earlier, and decided to take an especially long drink.

"See if you can top that, tiger," Cameron said sadistically, handing the bottle to Jadon, who met his challenge with a long lingering swallow.

"That's quite enough, Cam, Christ! We got more filming to do tonight!" Chick piped in.

"They're good, they're good. Give it a second," Cameron said, hastily turning around, heading back to the group. "I want that song *on!*" he shouted angrily. Within seconds the song thundered through the night air.

Feeling her body warm from the tequila, Meg noticed her skin soften under its slightly numbing, relaxing effect. And just as Cam had promised, a new found courage rose up inside her.

"Are you okay?" Erin whispered.

"Yup. Never been fuckin' better," Meg blurted unabashedly. Even though the numbness did nothing to lessen the pain of Jadon's loathing that rested firmly on her chest.

"Jay?" Chick asked, wondering if Jadon was coming unhinged.

"Good. I've never been fuckin' better," he said in amusement.

Jadon's humor wasn't lost on Meg; she felt it sting through her body. She was angry. She was angry at him for his dislike of her. She was angry at him for being so wildly attractive. She was angry at him for helping write such a passionate song. She was angry all around. And she missed her evening with her neighbor. She was thoroughly pissed, and the tequila helped her realize it.

Feeling the music pound through her chest, Meg turned to face Jadon. Slowly she placed her hands on his shoulders, causing her breasts to move within inches from his face, and his long strands of blonde hair to brush against her chest. Closing his eyes, Jadon tilted his head back while Meg's body moved in front of him.

Sliding her right shin onto Jadon's left thigh, Meg repeated the same on the other side. Bringing her body completely on top of his, her face arched over his, her long graceful legs straddling his warm body between hers. Instinctually Jadon's hands made their way slowly onto Meg's thighs, and cautiously on to her back.

As the rain began to pour heavily down on the two of them, Meg saw Cameron out of the corner of her eye motioning for her to move her body. *This is unreal,* Meg laughed to herself, not fully believing the moment her life was engrossed in. Pulling her head back she allowed the rain to fall across her face.

Sighing in pleasurable discomfort, Jadon stared at Meg's long neck, his hands moved slowly up and down her back, while the outside world faded into nonexistence. Feeling the rain fall onto his face, Jadon licked the drops of water off his lips. As the heat from Meg's body penetrated into his skin, Jadon held her tighter.

Slowly running her hands over her wet hair, Meg turned her gaze directly down at Jadon. Their eyes locked onto one another, and Jadon's breathing settled into a noticeable, heavy rhythm. Pulling Meg closer, he began to open his mouth, unable to resist the desire to touch her lips with his.

"*Cut!* Wonderful! Wonderful! I knew you two crazy kids could pull it off," Cam shouted, lighting a cigarette while trying to walk off the intensity of the moment.

Jadon didn't let go of Meg. Instead he held her tight, and stared into her eyes.

"Crap, cat's gonna come flyin' out of the fuckin' bag now," Chick moaned, kicking the sand with his foot.

Bob and Stu kept their eyes on Jadon and Meg, not knowing what was going to happen next.

Meg found herself getting lost in Jadon's eyes. He wasn't releasing her from his hold. Instead his hands moved up her back and into her hair, pushing her closer toward him. Wanting to pull her into him, short of a hurricane pulling them apart, Jadon wasn't planning on letting her go.

Meg opened her mouth gently as Jadon brought his mouth closer to hers. Meg panicked. She didn't know what was going on.

Nothing was making sense. She didn't want him doing something because he thought he had to, because Cam wanted a good shot. She didn't want him, not like this. She didn't want to open herself up, so he could turn away from her again.

"I . . . I'm sorry you have to do this with me," Meg whispered, her mouth brushing against his as she pushed herself away.

Chapter 9

"I need a cigarette," Meg said with agitation, hitting the ignition of her roadster.

"Do you smoke?" Erin asked, jumping in beside Meg.

"No. But, I really think this is a good time to start. Hey, thanks for being here. I'm . . . not the best at this *girlfriend* thing. I'm used to talking to Bob," Meg said, looking down and tapping the wooden shifter knob with her finger. "But I just want you to know it means a great deal to me. So thank you."

"Not a problem. I'm here because I want to be. *And* if you *ever* decide you want to talk about what's rocketing around inside your mind, I'm all ears. But until then . . . ," Erin said, putting on her seatbelt. "Or if that day never comes, I'm still gonna be here."

"Jesus Christ, that was really nice," Meg said shoving her car in reverse. "Did anyone ever think of bottling you and marketing your sweetness to the masses?"

Taking the moment between locations, Meg let the warm nighttime air smack her back to her senses. Darting in and out of traffic, Meg's car sailed down the freeway in a gray blur while Erin sat peacefully with her hand dangling out the window. *She seems so complete, so balanced and happy*, Meg mused, looking at Erin from the corner of her eye.

Shooting off the freeway and onto a side street, Meg careened her car into a convenience store parking lot.

"Need anything?" she asked Erin.

"Ah, no. But, I think you need clothes," Erin said, pointing at the towel still wrapped around Meg.

Looking down at herself Meg rolled her eyes, "Damn it, I was in such a hurry to leave."

"What do you need? I'll get it."

"You'll hate me. But I really could use a cigarette."

"No problem," Erin said, knowing Meg needed whatever Meg needed at the moment. "Any brand?"

Meg shook her head. She didn't care. She just wanted to project her frustrated energy into something, an object beyond herself. There were many healthful alternatives, none of which interested her at the moment.

Tossing the pack of Marlboro Lights onto Meg's lap, Erin hopped back into the car.

"Excuse me," Meg said opening the glove compartment door, before searching blindly for the lighter she had tucked away for emergencies. Such as the one she was currently experiencing. Erin watched as Meg slowly lit the cigarette, and took a deep inhale without showing the slightest signs of discomfort.

"Okay, I know what you're thinking. No, I don't smoke," Meg said. "But while I was writing my last novel, my lead . . . she smoked. I was so immersed in her." Meg took another drag, shaking her head. "I picked up some of her habits. Strange, I know."

"I don't think that sounds strange. Actually, I think it sounds fascinating. I think you're fascinating. Meg. You don't even realize how much," Erin said, looking at the street in front of them. "I love my life. Don't think I don't. Because I do. But, sometimes I don't feel creative, raw. I don't feel edgy. At times I want to be edgy. Like you."

"Me? You've got to be kidding. You know, I think we could use a drink," Meg said, shooting a quick look at the convenience store behind them.

Erin's eyes twinkled at the thought, "I think we do. Be right back."

If she only knew. I'm fucking falling apart, literally right before everyone's eyes, Meg thought, taking the moment alone to stare at her cigarette and the lipstick her lips left on its filter tip.

"I'm back," Erin verbalized the obvious as she jumped back in the car. "I didn't know what to get, so I got beer. Hope that's okay. This place isn't exactly stocked with top shelf choices," she said happily, digging two long neck bottles of cold Coors out of the bag and handing one to Meg.

"I know we aren't supposed to be gone long . . ."

Erin waved a dismissive hand in the air. "Cam will live. Anyway, I think we need a moment. Meg, what happened back there? Between you and Jadon?"

Meg took the last hit of her cigarette, and stared at her beer bottle, wondering what to say.

"I don't know. Sounds stupid, I know. But that's the truth."

"Tell me about this lady in your novel, the one that smoked," Erin asked, deciding to leave it alone.

"Well, she was in a rock band," Meg said raising an eyebrow, lifting her beer in the air before taking a drink. "And she had this energy about her. She was great. I miss her. I loved living in her life for a moment. It was complicated, but I loved it."

"Hello. Sounds a bit like reality, doesn't it?"

"Well!" Meg shot out a raspy laugh. "I'm not the lead singer. I'm just trying to fit in. I feel like I'm barely hanging on."

"You're doing great, and it sounds similar to me."

"I will admit to similarities, but . . . Bertie had such a commanding personality that she was able to orchestrate an incredible life for herself. I feel like mine is spinning out of control."

Erin turned to look Meg in the eye. "How's that? You seem so put together. So on top of yourself and everything. Anyone who plays the violin like you, Meg, knows what they want."

"Knowing what you want is entirely different from getting it. Believe me."

"What do you want?"

Meg turned back in her seat to watch the traffic. "I'm not an easy person, Erin. I'm not all sweet and sunshine like you. I . . . I have so many thoughts. And honestly, I don't know if I want to risk opening myself up. Anyway, people want to put people in cages. They want to label them, and make them acceptable and easy. And I don't blame them. I'm just not one of them," she said, grabbing another cigarette, feeling awkward from her sudden burst of openness.

Meg lit it with one fluid motion. Pulling on the cigarette, she thought about Jadon, then about her neighbor. She missed him. She wondered if he missed her.

"Well, if you don't want anyone to put you in a box, maybe you shouldn't put others in a box. Maybe there's someone out there with the same amount of passion and wild spirit. You just haven't found him yet. Maybe it's fate, your moving here. Maybe he is here," Erin grinned, thinking of Jadon.

Meg sighed and thought about her neighbor, and the way he made her feel. During the moments they were together, it was perfect.

"If I could just find someone like my neigh . . . ," Meg whispered to herself, realizing too late that Erin was glued to her words.

Erin spun around in her seat, "Who? Your neighbor? Did you say neighbor? I didn't realize you *knew* your neighbor."

"Well, uh, oh, God," Meg began to stutter, "I . . . I don't *know* my neighbor. You see, I just hear him play the piano. It's . . . I don't know who the hell he is, Erin. I don't even know if it's even a *he*. Christ," she said clearing her throat. Leaning forward she brought her car to a roaring start.

"Oh, I thought . . ."

Meg nodded her head. Erin heard her right; she just accidentally said too much. Pulling the car out of the lot, Meg made their way back onto the freeway.

After finally finding the remote location, buried in a near desolate part of town, Meg wheeled her roadster next to the curb behind Chick's BMW.

"Meg!" Charlotte shouted, running on the sidewalk. "We have to get you dressed, girl."

Grabbing Meg's arm, Charlotte swiftly led her up a stairway that opened to an upstairs apartment. Looking around, Meg noticed everyone who was suppose to be there, was there. She was late. But she needed those few minutes she stole to clear her head. Moments ago there was a paper thin line separating her from taking Jadon's face in her hands, and finally unleashing her frustrations on him in front of everyone. Short of dying, there was no way to turn off her attraction to him. At the same time, she couldn't stand him. Truthfully, she couldn't stand how much he couldn't stand her.

Charlotte waited until Erin entered the small room before closing the door, "All right, Meg, you know the drill. Go ahead and sit down in the chair," she said, pointing toward the chair positioned next to a small vanity surrounded by bright lights. Charlotte tussled with Meg's hair, finally grabbing the hair dryer in an attempt to bring it back to life after the turbulent ocean water had its way with it. Meg cut a quick look toward Erin as Charlotte made it appear as though she just rolled out of bed after a wild night of sex. Working feverishly, Charlotte next created a dewy glow to emerge across Meg's face. Like an artist, Charlotte worked to bring out Meg's seductive eyes, giving them a sensual softness, finishing by frosting Meg's lips with gloss, instantly causing her lips to look wet.

"Wardrobe?" Meg said, feeling confident the outfit she would be given would be a real shocker.

"Nope. I just need you to strip down. I put a lace thong in there for you. Other than that, I have a black blanket I need to wrap around you," Charlotte answered without blinking.

"Hang on to your hat, Meg!" Erin teased.

Reaching an arm out from behind the curtain, Meg hoped it would signal Charlotte to hand her the blanket. Quickly Charlotte pulled the blanket around Meg covering her front side.

"Charlotte, my entire backside is sort of . . . hangin' out?"

"Don't worry, Cam will shoot at just the right angle. Trust me," Charlotte said, ushering Meg out into the main room where everyone was gathered.

"Great. Glad you ladies could finally join us," Cam said with an air of frustration.

"I'm glad we could, too," Meg shot back, not wanting to be pushed around.

"This scene ought to be a riot," Bob said, once Meg walked into the room.

"Jadon!" Cameron yelled. "Over here. Over here," he said, pointing to the small dark room off the main room they were all gathered in. "Meg, you too. I only have one more scene besides this one we need to get through tonight. Tomorrow we'll finish the rest," Cam said, waving his hand in the air before running his fingers back into his hair. "Meg, I need you to stand here. Erin, you'll have to let go of the blanket, sweetheart."

Meg looked around the room absorbing every detail. There was one window, located off to the side. Through the window Meg could see the lights from the street below shining brightly. Glancing around, she noticed the only pieces of furniture in the small room were a tall, dark dresser with an intricately carved crystal glass half full of water sitting on it and a white mattress lying on the floor. The room was dark, stark and bleak. Suddenly cold, she pulled the black blanket closer to her chest, relieved no one was standing behind her.

"Jadon!" Cameron screamed, looking around, trying to locate him through the small group of people.

Chick felt pensive, his arms were folded tightly across his chest. He turned to look, finding Jadon standing directly behind him. "Dude. Looks like you're up."

Jadon walked over to Cameron. At once Charlotte dusted his face with powder, before whipping his hair into a nest.

"Unbutton his shirt," Cameron snorted, rubbing his hand over his chin, eyeing Jadon intently.

Jadon stood passively as Charlotte prepared him for the scene. Cameron then pulled Jadon behind Meg, positioning him an inch away from her mostly exposed rear. Placing Jadon's hands on Meg's bare waist, Cameron pushed Jadon's head into Meg's disheveled hair. Pulling his head back abruptly, Jadon directed an angry glare at Cameron.

"I didn't mean to push. I just want you to have your head buried in her hair."

Trying to swallow, Jadon slowly looked down at Meg's bare back, his eyes stopping at her delicate lace thong. "I can't do this," he said, backing away.

Putting his hands over his face, Chick began to rub his forehead. Meg bit her lip in mortification. Walking over to Meg, Erin wanted to ease her anxiety, even though she had no idea where to start.

"He sure knows how to crush a girl's ego," Meg whispered.

"That isn't it, Meg. That isn't it at all," Erin offered kindly, knowing it was actually just the opposite.

"What do you mean you can't do it?" Cameron shouted. "We've *all* put in a solid day of grueling work, and you're telling me you can't stand with Meg for a few minutes so I can grab some tape?"

Jadon took a deep sigh and walked back behind Meg. He didn't want the attention his outburst was creating. He also didn't want to further upset Meg. He knew she was still upset from the earlier scene they had together. Everything he was being told to do, he wanted to do with every molecule in his body. But controlling himself was getting increasingly more difficult. Stepping closer toward Meg, Jadon placed his hands on her waist. Letting his eyes fall onto the graceful shape of her back he rested his head on hers.

"Bring your head back, Meg!" Cameron bellowed, stopping Meg from getting swept away by the feel of Jadon's breath falling hard on her neck.

As Meg slowly pulled her head back, her nest of hair completely covered Jadon's face. Moving his head slightly, Jadon took a deep breath, smelling Meg's perfume. Savoring the scent, his hands tightened on her waist.

"Move her hair to the side, Jadon!" Cameron yelled.

"What?" Jadon shot back, startled and frustrated.

"*Move* her hair *off* to the *side*. I want to see her neck."

Slowly sliding Meg's long, red hair to the side, Jadon revealed her slender neck and shoulder.

"Keep your eyes closed, Meg!" Cam's voice boomed.

Jadon looked at Cameron, then at Chick, who had his hands covering his face, except for a slight gap where his fingers were spread to see what was going to happen next. Looking back at Meg — her head was tilted to one side and her eyes closed — Jadon reached up to touch her neck.

"*No!*" Cameron yelled. "No, *don't* touch!"

"What? I don't know what the hell you want!" Jadon shouted.

"I know, I know," Cameron said, trying to lighten his voice, sticking his head around from behind his camera. "This is looking perfect. Just . . . um, smell her neck, you know, run your nose up and down her neck. I want that on tape."

"*Music!* Where the fuck is the *song*? Are we turning into complete imbeciles? I said I wanted the song *on*, at all times!" Cameron yelled, noticing the room was stone silent.

"Why the hell do we need that on?" Jadon said bitterly.

Despite Jadon's protest, the room instantly pounded from the sound of his drums, and his voice.

"*Go!*" Cameron shouted, stepping back behind his large camera.

Stepping closer to Meg, Jadon looked around the room again, trying to center his mind.

"Don't look at us! Look at her!" Cameron yelled angrily.

"I know, Cam, I know!" Jadon snapped, his heart racing.

Feeling Jadon's hot breath against her skin, Meg opened her eyes. Turning her head slightly, she saw his mouth move closer to her neck. As his lips and hair brushed against her skin, she closed her eyes and dropped her head back to the side.

Bringing himself closer, Jadon felt her bare back against his chest. Softly opening his eyes, he looked at Meg's face and tried to memorize her delicate features. Pulling Meg tightly into his body, he ran his lower lip up her neck toward her ear.

"Now move *in front* of her!" Cameron shouted, keeping his head glued to his camera screen.

Jumping back, Jadon threw his hands onto his forehead. "What? You want this! You want that!" He said spinning around, facing away from Meg. "Do you even know *what* the fuck you want?"

"Just a little more, Jay?" Cameron said, stepping out from behind his camera. "Just a little more, this time I want you in front of her that's all."

Chick ran his fingers through his long black hair before returning his hands to their resting place at the back of his head. All the while he was watching what he feared would happen, happen. Jadon was beginning to implode.

"In front? You don't *fuckin'* understand," Jadon shouted, grabbing the crystal glass from the dresser and whipping it across the room, where it shattered against the wall, sending a wave of small crystal shards spiraling through the air.

Meg winced. Something hit her cheek right below her right eye. Her heart pounding profusely; she didn't know what was going on anymore. Her mind and body couldn't take the emotional roller coaster ride she was on.

Cameron ducked behind his camera, excited with the drama he was watching unfold.

Meg felt something warm slowly stream down her cheek, but she didn't move. She stood straight, holding the blanket close to her chest staring at Jadon, watching him stand with his hands over his face. His long blonde hair was draped over his fingers.

Jadon's ears thundered from the sound of his own drums that filled the room with a thick mass of volume. His thoughts were fragmented and scattered. He couldn't continue being played with. Cameron's incessant stopping and starting. Moving, wanting more, pushing him to go beyond the point of return. He wanted it all to stop.

Opening his eyes, Jadon looked at Meg, standing quietly, her chest moving heavily with each weighted breath. He tried to look into her soulful eyes but quickly noticed a thin red line running down below her right eye.

"Oh, my God. Oh, my God," Jadon whispered, rushing over to Meg.

Standing in front of her, he watched the blood slowly move down her face, forming a drip that was about to fall. Jadon's eyes searched Meg's face, then her tear-filled eyes. Slowly moving his hand toward Meg's face, Jadon put his finger next to the drop of blood. Stopping himself, he cautiously pulled his finger away. Touching Meg's left cheek, he moved his mouth closer to her face and began kissing the blood that was about to drop. Pressing his chest against hers as he pressed his lips harder against her cheek he delicately eased his mouth cautiously up Meg's face. Meg winced from the pleasure as Jadon crept his way slowly toward her eyelashes, erasing her tears and blood within his lips. Stopping where she had been cut, he paused for a moment to gently kiss her soft skin.

Pulling himself abruptly away, Jadon ran his hands through his hair. "Oh God, what am I doing? I'm sorry. I'm so sorry," he whispered quietly to Meg, startled by what he had just done.

Turning quickly he walked out of the room and down the stairs leading to the street outside. Meg stood motionless.

"I'm going to go find Jay," Chick told Erin. "I have a feeling he isn't doin' so good right about now."

"I'll take care of Meg."

Stepping out of the building, Chick looked down the street and saw Jadon sitting on the sidewalk, his back against an abandoned storefront a few buildings down. Walking over, his hands in his pockets, Chick didn't have a clue what to say.

"Don't fuck with me, Chick. Not now," Jadon said looking up at him.

"I'm not sayin' a thing, dude." Chick sat down next to Jadon. "I'm just here to listen. Maybe help, if I'm lucky," he said, wondering if help was even possible at this point.

"You don't realize, I can't keep doin' this shit with Meg," Jadon said angrily, throwing one hand in the air, puffing quickly on his cigarette with the other.

"Okay. Well, you don't have to. I don't want *anything*, ya know." Chick struggled for words to describe what he was thinking.

"No one's *anything*," Jadon said. "I mean, don't think anything is going on. It's not. Nothing. You have to know that. Nothing."

"Okay," Chick said nodding his head, knowing differently.

"I know you want to know what *that* was . . ." Jadon shot his thumb in the air, pointing up toward the apartment.

"No, I don't need to know anything," Chick said soothingly.

"I don't know what that was," Jadon said. "I just, I don't know . . . let's leave it there. Cuz, I don't fuckin' know what *that* was," Jadon repeated, still feeling unsettled by his own desires for Meg.

"That's okay," Chick replied as he continued nodding his head. "We don't need to figure anything out. I just want to know that you're okay."

116

Jadon looked at Chick, wanting to admit he didn't know anymore.

Chapter 10

Please place your item in the bag, repeated the computer generated voice in the self-checkout lane of the D&P Save-More. *Please place your item in the bag.*

"I'm placing it in the goddamn bag you stupid ass machine, you just don't seem to want to notice," Jadon whispered with exhaustion.

Please wait for customer assistance.

"You've got to be kidding."

Looking around the checkout area, Jadon saw only one cashier, and she was occupied on the telephone. He tossed the troublesome box of crackers off to the side, forcefully pushed the checkout button, and grabbed his things. Walking into the parking lot, he stared at the few cars traveling down Melbourne Street that morning. Not surprised that his car was the only one in the lot at 5 a.m., Jadon pressed a button on his key fob, unlocking the car's doors.

As he drove home, the images from the night still raced through his mind. And in every image was Meg. The picture of her long slender back draped with a blanket was carved into his mind like a perfect sculpture.

Walking into his house, Jadon threw his keys on the counter, then threw himself onto the sofa. Sitting quietly, he tried to find some level of balance while his mind rocketed erratically from thought to thought. The most piercing of thoughts was what Meg was thinking of him, and how uncontrollable his level of desire for her was.

"She probably thinks I'm some kind of freak. God, I hope not," he said painfully.

"*Bob! No!*" Meg yelled, too exhausted to move.

At the sound of Meg's voice Jadon shot off his sofa, and quickly went onto the balcony. Standing like a statue, he looked beyond the railing at Meg sitting on the edge of the water, staring out at the early morning ocean.

"Bob. Jesus Christ. Get *over here*. Regardless of what you might think, those runners don't want you to run with them," Meg said, beckoning Bob to stay near her. Naturally he wanted to scamper off with the ever changing parade of joggers taking their morning run on the beach.

"Bob? *No* fuckin' way," Jadon thought in pleasant disbelief. "All this time . . . and Bob was her dog. He's her dog."

"Come here, baby. I need you more than ever," Meg ordered, grabbing Bob's auburn colored head in her hands. "I need your advice, Big Guy."

Slowly lowering himself prone onto the floor of his balcony, Jadon still couldn't hear what Meg was saying, except when she had to shout to keep Bob away from the joggers.

"Well, I think I'm losing it." Meg looked Bob directly in the eye. "What do you mean I was always losing it?" she joked. "Seriously, there's this guy — two guys really . . . "

Jadon's eyes held steady onto Meg, watching her red hair float around behind her head as it was moved carelessly by the wind, her arms wrapped around her dog.

"I can't believe that's Bob," Jadon said.

"Bob! Stay here. Christ, what has gotten into you lately? I know, let's back it up a bit," Meg said, jumping up abruptly.

Grabbing Bob's collar, she turned to face the beach house behind her, rocketing a quick glance up onto the balcony in hope of catching sight of her elusive neighbor.

Startled when Meg sprung up like a jack in the box, Jadon quickly dropped and pressed his face against the balcony floor, terrified she would see him.

"Holy Christ," Jadon whispered, his chest firmly planted on the floor.

Looking at the balcony for a moment, Meg didn't see anyone. *I suppose that isn't a bad thing. If I don't see him, then I can't get disappointed,* she reasoned, all the while wishing she could see him.

"This will do. From here we can *watch* the joggers. Notice the word *watch*, Bob?" Meg sighed, settling down onto the sand, a few yards back from the water.

Slowly pulling his body up, Jadon peered down between the balusters of his balcony. He saw Meg sitting a stone's throw away. He crawled closer to the edge, trying to settle into a comfortable position where he could hear what she was saying.

"Are you finally ready to listen?" Meg asked, looking out at the ocean. Sitting next to her, Bob also stared out at the ocean.

Resting his head against a baluster, Jadon savored the moment, a moment that allowed him to be fully captivated by Meg's gentle ease with her dog, her playfulness, her smile, the way she sunk herself repeatedly into Bob's furry coat.

Meg sighed. She wasn't sure what she wanted to get off her chest. "On the plus side," she earnestly told Bob, "my writing is phenomenal. And it's more fun that it's been in years. You have to admit, he really, *really* is fun to write about, right? Am I wrong? Try to tell me I'm wrong. I didn't think so." Meg turned her gaze back toward the ocean. "He's . . . well words don't really do it justice. Sometimes though, I wish I were Elle."

Jadon lay motionless, soaking in Meg's words and trying to make sense of them. What was most important, he thought, was that she was happy.

"I couldn't have found a more perfect person for this novel. I mean, I was stumped. You know I was stumped. Remember? Now, I feel like I'm alive. He makes me feel . . . beside myself. Of course, the real version can't stand me. That's a slight problem. He doesn't want to be near me." Meg touched the cut on her face, wondering what had been going through Jadon's mind when he touched her the way he did last night. "I need to Google . . ."

Oh, you're the best friend that I ever had.

I've been with you such a long time.

Jadon jumped to his feet, fumbling for his cell phone that loudly played the new ringtone Chick had downloaded onto it. Flipping his phone open, Jadon silenced it instantly, while launching his body into his living room.

Meg quickly twisted around and tried to see who was on the balcony. Getting up slowly, she slapped her thigh, motioning to Bob that their therapy session was over. Walking slowly backward toward the beach, she eyed her neighbor's house.

"What?" Jadon barked into his cell phone.

"It's Cam. He isn't done torturing us yet," Chick said dryly.

"Screw him."

"Can't do that. Don't want to do that," Chick sighed, equally fed up with Cameron. "He wants us to meet at the corner of Melbourne and Delaney, ya know . . . down by the beach."

"Damn, what's with this guy? Go here, go there . . ."

"You know, he just wants to do a good shoot. Once that's done, then we can get this ball rolling and hand the song over to Neil. Once produced, it's out, breathing on its own."

"Normally we produce the record first. This shit's all twisted around," Jadon said, uncomfortable with how upside down things had become.

"I know. That was chance. He caught you raw man. He liked it. He wanted to nail it down while he was in the States. Let's just roll with it."

"Yeah. I'll be there. Who else is coming?"

"Well . . . ," Chick snapped his gum at the obvious answer, "I suppose the band, Jay. Ya know, the people who are in the song."

"Yeah. Yeah." Jadon stepped slowly back onto his balcony, cautiously trying to see Meg. "She's gone."

"Ya cool?"

"Yup," Jadon said flipping his phone closed.

Bob and Stu sat on the curb at the corner of Melbourne and Delaney streets, watching the early morning joggers trot breathlessly past the early morning yogis, who stood motionless along the ocean.

"You do yoga?" Bob asked, staring at everyone on the beach.

"Why the hell would I want to do that?" Stu replied, pushing his sunglasses up on his forehead and eyeing the slender bodies scattered across the sand.

"Look at that guy . . ." Stu shot his arm out, pointing at the man who was steadily bringing his body into a head stand.

Watching Chick, Bob shook his head, "You're gonna' wear down the pavement."

Breaking his stride only briefly to face Bob, Chick then continued to pace again, stopping occasionally to kick the stones scattered randomly on the side of street. Looking up, Chick spotted Jadon's black Porsche dart into a nearby parking space.

"Boardshorts? You're gonna wear an old t-shirt and boardshorts for the video?" Chick laughed.

"Hey, I'm here. That should make the bastard happy. Speaking of bastards, where the hell is he?" Jadon asked, looking around for Cam and his camera crew.

"Beats the hell out of me. He's screwier than screwy on this one. Maybe he's gonna come flyin' in on a low helicopter or somethin' nuckin' futs like that," Chick said, darting his hand out like a low flying plane.

Jadon shoved his hands in his pockets and nodded while looking around for Meg.

"She's not here, dude," Chick said with a loud snap of his gum, before sitting down on the curb next to Bob. Jadon followed, leaning his arms back on the sidewalk next to Chick.

The rumble of Meg's roadster echoed between the cars as she slowly made her way closer to the corner of Melbourne and Delaney. *There they are. There they ALL are*, she repeated, noticing Jadon relaxing next to Chick.

Meg downshifted abruptly, causing Bob's body to skid forward on the seat.

"Sorry, babe," she said looking over at Bob.

Meg hoped bringing Bob would be all right with everyone. He was lonely and she didn't want to be away from him. He kept her grounded. And every time, without exception, she had to be near Jadon, her mind left her body. Perhaps with Bob near, he would safely keep her tethered to something steady.

The guys watched as the two redheads slowly approached them. The low grumble of Meg's car came to an abrupt end when she cut the engine and stepped out of the car. Their eyes followed her as she walked over to the passenger door and opened it, allowing Bob to casually hop out onto the sidewalk, his tail wagging at the possibilities a new place offered.

Jadon's eyes, hidden behind his sunglasses, had the unrestricted opportunity to watch Meg and Bob as they gracefully made their way toward the band. Tilting his head to one side, lost in concentration, he looked over Meg's body, noticing her blue jeans, which appeared more faded and ripped than normal, her long red hair that bounced around her face and onto her shoulders as she walked, and her thin, snug t-shirt that displayed a crudely drawn hand, with an extended middle finger, unapologetically telling everyone what she thought.

"Love the sentiment," Chick smiled, pointing at Meg's t-shirt. "You gonna introduce us?"

"Gladly" Meg said proudly, kneeling next to Bob. "Bobby, these are the jokers I was telling you about."

"Aren't you handsome? Good name too," Bob said in a low baby voice, kneeling next to Bob.

"So, *this* is your main man?" Stu shook his head, stroking Bob's long silky ears.

"This is him," Meg said. "You don't mind my bringing him, do you?"

In unison, Chick, Bob and Stu shook their heads *no*. Bob was welcomed. Reaching over to pull Bob closer, Chick began to rub his neck.

"I think we have a new mascot. Equinox Bob. Yeah. I like that," Chick said, enjoying the moment with an untroubled soul.

Letting out a soft bark, Bob swaggered over to Jadon. Leaning forward Jadon stared at Bob, slowly running his hands over Bob's head and down his body.

"I'm really fuckin glad to meet you Bob," Jadon looked Bob in the eye. "You're a pretty important fella' aren't ya? Important to me, that's for sure."

Pleased to finally meet his new neighbor, Bob sat next to Jadon, pushing his body close into his. Meg watched as Jadon showed a side of himself she hadn't seen before. He was gentle and delicate. His words fell softly into the air as he spoke them, and emanated warmth. Meg also couldn't help but notice that his smile propelled his handsome good looks well into the stratosphere.

Looking up at Meg, Jadon continued to run his hands over Bob's head and down his neck. Spotting the cut on her face, Jadon felt the sudden sting of embarrassment, and dropped his head, looking back at Bob.

"Where the hell is Cam?" Stu growled, standing up to look at the street sign in case there was something they missed about the location.

"Dude, we *all* couldn't possibly have ended up at the wrong spot. I'm not going to give him much longer. This is ridiculous," Chick said, grabbing his cell from his front pocket. "Where the fuck are you?" He asked once Cameron picked up on the other end. "Well, yeah, we're all here. We're tired, Cam. You had us up all night running down the street at 3 a.m. We're ready to crash." Chick paused listening to Cameron. "Fine, but we're not waiting any longer than that."

"What gives?" Bob asked, standing up to stretch his back.

"Says he's caught in traffic." Chick looked around. "Something doesn't seem right."

For the next half hour the five anxiously paced the sidewalk, kicked stones, ran their fingers through their hair, folded their arms, threw themselves down on the sidewalk in disgust, and waited.

"Fuck it. Let's go," Chick ordered.

Jadon tossed his keys onto the kitchen counter and wondered what just happened at the beach. Cameron, at the very least, was focused and professional. Making them sit for an hour wasn't the norm, even for someone as unorthodox as Cam.

Jadon stared at his piano, then out the window at Meg's house. *I know she's home,* Jadon thought to himself. Driving home he pulled around a corner, safely out of sight, and waited until Meg pulled in her driveway before he proceeded. He wasn't ready for her to know yet. To know *he* was the one that nightly asked her to play music with him. Sitting down at his piano, he tapped softly on the keys, hoping she would come to him, delicately creating a rhythm that bounced effortlessly between the keys and into the air. *It's early,* he told himself. *She might not be comfortable with the idea.*

"Where are you?" Jadon whispered, waiting longer than usual for Meg's response. "Where are you? Damn. It's not good to be so lost in someone. Come on Meg . . . "

The warm, rich sound of Meg's violin suddenly soared across Jadon's balcony, instantly filling the air with her presence. Closing his eyes in relief, Jadon smiled. Taking a deep breath, he took a moment to find his place within her rhythm.

"Give me a sec . . . give me a sec, Meg," Jadon whispered, settling into her notes. "There's my girl, okay . . . we're still okay."

Meg swirled with excitement on her balcony, caught off guard by the sound of the piano so early in the day. "Oh, I've been needing you."

As the music poured from the two homes, dusting the beach with its deeply sensual mixture of notes, Jadon felt both of them becoming complete within one another again.

Chapter 11

Meg and Bobby made their way into the studio. Ready for a late morning nap, Bob plopped onto the sofa, making himself comfortable next to Stu, who was busy looking at the latest *Drummer World* magazine.

"Hey, Meggie Peggie," Stu said, throwing the magazine onto the table in front of him and then grabbing a cigarette. "Pretty boy's on the cover."

Sitting down next to Stu, Meg tried not to appear eager, making sure to first scoot the magazine around on the table before officially picking it up. Looking at the front cover, she allowed her eyes a few seconds to absorb every nuance of Jadon's image.

"Page 43," Stu said discreetly, leaning closer to Meg for her to hear.

Meg nodded. Thumbing through the pages, she stopped periodically to throw off any suspicion as to the level of her curiosity. As it was, she Googled Jadon after she finished writing last night. She was amazed by the hits she was able to retrieve by simply typing Jadon Hastings into the search bar: 551,000, more or less. She made a mental note of it. She now knew he grew up in Northern California and was one year younger than she was. He was an Aquarius, not that it mattered. Meg didn't believe in horoscopes. But from what her digging was able to unearth, Aquarius and Libras make passionate lovers, a fact she also noted.

She downloaded numerous four-minute segments of his appearances from YouTube. She saw how light-hearted he was during his interviews, and realized what a playful personality he had. Meg also couldn't help but notice all the female admirers he had, although her search didn't bring up anything regarding a wife, past wife, or present girlfriend. Not that any of that mattered. Because it didn't.

Briskly reading the article, Meg quickly realized it was taken just prior to her audition with the band. Jadon sounded excited about the new acoustic songs they were about to record. He sounded equally excited about Kofi's joining the band for the recording and tour. *What tour*, Meg interrupted her thoughts to ask herself. When questioned about the new violinist, Jadon didn't seem to offer up much information, except to say, "*Hope they can keep up.*"

"Hope they can keep up?" Meg grumbled, throwing the magazine down on the table.

"Rubbish. All that stuff. Just bullshit. You're a writer, you know," Stu said, nudging Meg with his elbow.

Chick stuck his head around the corner. "We're recording today. Consider yourself warned." He then retreated toward the sound room.

"Can't say I will be doing anything different than I do every other day," Stu yelled.

"*Good!*" Chick shouted.

Bob and Kofi strolled through the door, engrossed in a debate over the best arrangement on a Who album that Meg had never heard of. Happy with their conversation, they didn't seem to care when Chick bellowed that they would be recording.

Bobby barked moments before the door opened, and Jadon breezed in, his energy level high, filling the room with electricity. *Or is that just me?* Meg wondered. Jumping off the sofa, Bob claimed his place at Jadon's feet, causing Jadon to instantly kneel down.

"How's Bob?" Jadon asked, drawing his thumbs between Bob's eyes and down his head.

Looking over at Meg, Jadon smiled. It was smile that shot through Meg like a rocket.

"In a sec Chick will want to start recording," Kofi said.

"Cool," Jadon said, a quiet contentedness resting comfortably on his shoulders.

Even though his heart was about to leap from his body, he felt good. He knew what he was going to do. Hell or high water, he was going to move forward in Meg's direction. The only concern that really mattered was how Meg would feel about it.

"Hey, Jadon," Erin said, scooting past Jadon who was still camped at the front door petting Bob. "Hey, Bobby. Chick?"

Hearing his name, Chick stuck his head around the corner.

"Hey, babe . . ." Chick said, wondering what brought her down to the studio.

Erin waved the small box in her hand. Walking over to her, Chick read the label and wondered how its contents would affect the first day of recording the new album.

"Goodie. Goodie. Guys, this is the video of Jay's . . . and my new song. Our song, the band's song. Christ, Cam must have been up all night slapping this together. Cam's note says — he paused as he held it up to the light — "it's the first rough cut, but it should give us an idea of how it'll look once he's done with it." Chick stopped, not ready to unwrap the package.

Erin grabbed it and quickly ripped open the box. Pulling out the DVD, she fed it into a player on the shelf near the flat screen TV.

Staring hesitantly at the TV, Chick wasn't sure what would happen. *Could go fine, could be disastrous. Things are so combustible lately,* Chick said to himself. He glanced back at Jadon, who wore a big smile while engrossed in rubbing Bob's stomach. It was not an expression Chick had expected to see after the other night.

"Hey, nice teeth . . ." Chick joked, shooting Jadon an equally large smile.

Kofi adjusted the window shades, creating a semi-darkness that made the images on the TV screen brighter.

The Berkshire logo and the phrase in cooperation with A&E Records appeared on the screen before fading to black. Then the first dark image appeared, a single leafless tree on a barren hilltop. The camera panned, keeping steady with Jadon's rhythm on the drums before settling on a heavily wooded river, with water as still as glass. Just as Jadon's voice rockets with his first word, a flock of geese spring from the water and fly over the leafless tree. As Jadon's beats increase, and his words intensify, the black and white images cut rapidly but fluidly, one to the other. The guys in the ocean. The geese. The six of them, including Bobby, at the corner of Melbourne and Delaney. As if orchestrated by an invisible conductor — the wind blowing their hair as they stand, they sit, they wait. Suddenly the images cut to Meg, then back to Jadon. His eyes rest softly on her. The guys strum their guitars on the street while Jadon runs after Meg.

Jadon hits hard on the bass drum, the geese fly low over the river, skimming the surface. Meg emerges from the water, rain washing over her body. Jadon's eyes pull in her direction. Tears fall from Meg's eyes as she steps out of the water. Standing in front of Jadon, she looks away. He slams harder on the drums. Her mouth skims on his in a seductive embrace, his fingers slide up her back, the rain streaming down her skin.

As Meg hits her first overpowering chord on the violin, the video cuts to the image of the crystal glass soaring through the room, slowed to match the speed and length of her note. The image swiftly cuts to her on the cliff, her eyes slowly falling on Jadon. He hits the drums forcefully, then looks at Meg. Chick and Bob strum violently on their guitars. The powerful wind from the ocean blows their hair in every direction, giving the impression of things spiraling out of control. Jadon hits the drums in anger. Meg sways with her violin on the cliff, her gown flowing behind her. Then appears the image of Meg's face, a drop of blood running down her cheek. Jadon's mouth slowly kissing her blood. The cliff. The chase. The leafless tree blown mercilessly by a forceful wind. With the final hit on the drums, the geese land back on the water.

Meg felt her heart tighten. Every desire lurking under the surface of her skin was in the video.

No one said a word. Chick kept his hands firmly planted behind his head, as he continued to rock on his heels, snapping his gum, silently thinking. Erin kept one arm across her chest, one hand softly resting on her lips, equally stunned by the beautiful, passionate images.

Jadon felt his body erupt into a volcano. The embarrassment from the other night landed back onto his shoulders. He started to feel a slow anger surge through his body. Anger at Cameron for exploiting his song, for exploiting his feelings. Everything that was tormenting him for weeks was strewn wildly throughout the video. His song, combined with the powerful images made his knees too weak to stand on.

"Ya know . . . they sure know how to manipulate those damn clips," Stu moaned, trying to offer a plausible out for Meg and Jadon.

Not missing a beat, Chick quickly added, "Yeah, that's what Cam is known for. Wow." But Chick was hardly able to believe what he just saw. It was amazing. Jadon's song was unbelievable, and when mixed with the images though, it was unsettling. The raw intensity between Jadon and Meg was nakedly evident throughout the entire video.

"I . . . I have to . . . I'll be back," Meg stammered, making her way quickly to the restroom tucked behind the sound room.

Jadon watched Meg, unsure of what her response to the video really revealed. Walking outside with Bobby, he lit up a cigarette, and leaned against the building.

"She must think I'm a real monster," Jadon said, feeling his throat tighten.

Closing his eyes, the image of his throwing the crystal across the room exploded into his mind. As did the look of pain in Meg's eyes.

"Real cool, Jay. Real great," he told himself. Jadon took another drag from his cigarette and looked at the buildings lining the alley. All the while his mind feverishly replayed the images of Meg's body on his. The drop of blood running down her cheek. The scene of his being overcome with passion, kissing her face.

"Caught that on film. Real nice, Cam," Jadon mumbled, knowing Cam didn't have to work hard to catch anything. It was all there, plain and easy to see. His love for Meg was blatantly obvious, and by the sign of her reaction to the video, it wasn't mutual.

Chapter 12

Pulling up in front of the Paladia Theatre on Delaney Avenue, Meg took the ticket the valet handed her and pulled her violin case from the passenger seat. Tonight was Equinox's premier of their new acoustic album. Although the guys seemed pretty relaxed about it, Meg felt as though she was overdosing on nerves.

Tonight they were also introducing the song *Longing*. Meg understood that, like a good book, it needed to be released, allowing everyone the chance to swim within its words. However, she wasn't sure if she was ready for the entire world to watch the music video.

Meg tried to shake off her uneasiness, thinking instead about Jadon. He seemed different lately. Kinder. He still stared at her. Relentlessly, but it felt different. *No, no*, Meg thought, *not different, very much the same, but without the edge.*

"Hey, girlfriend," Erin said warmly, waiting for Meg to arrive so Erin could show her where they needed to go backstage to set up. "Wow, you look . . . amazing, Meg. Spicy."

"Good spice or bad?" Meg asked, leaning in toward Erin's ear.

"Beautiful spice," Erin answered, latching her arm around Meg's.

Meg hated being nervous. Hated doubting herself. Walking backstage, she felt her nervousness and doubt landing on her skin like a thousand hungry mosquitoes. She was out of her league here, and out of her element. Ask her to write a bestselling novel, done. Play violin in front of a crowded room full of people, who will by night's end be watching a very seductive video featuring her, not so easy.

"Hey, Ant," Erin grinned, as the bodyguard opened the heavy, thick door leading to the backstage. Standing like a boulder, he didn't bother to ask Erin who she was. It was obvious, Meg assumed.

"Where is everyone?" Meg asked, looking around.

"Oh, they're goofy. They like to work their nerves out. Jadon especially. He gets pretty nervous before a live show."

"Interesting." Meg never considered for a moment that any of them would be nervous.

"Hey, pretty ladies," Bob offered easily, strolling in and smoking a cigarette. Wearing a dark gray suit, his bleached blonde hair was spiked erratically on top of his head.

Stu and Kofi ambled their way in from a different back door, both dressed in slick sport coats and dark jeans. Meg smiled at the sight of them as she handed her violin case to Roach, the main roadie in charge of keeping things organized.

Hopping around in the back alley, Chick tried to get his blood pumping.

"Why the hell do you have to do that?" Jadon asked. "God, my heart is pumping hard enough." All the while he was hitting the ball attached to the paddle he gripped tightly in his hand, firing off rapid hits in a blurred succession.

"Paddle ball is for wimps, dude," Chick replied, trying to run up and onto the wall of the building before hopping back down to the ground.

"Yeah, right. You're just pissed because you suck at it," Jadon said pleased with himself, opening the door for Chick to enter.

Walking to his drums, Jadon's eyes instantly locked onto Meg. Her back was facing him, and he was entranced by her silhouette — her bare lissome back showing itself exactly as it did the night they worked on the video. Her long slender legs gracefully gave way to her high-heeled leather boots, with a flash of red peeking from the soles, signaling an air of seduction hovering patiently around her body.

Glancing around the room, Meg saw Kofi play on his piano, Bob pace next to Stu, and Stu sit casually in his chair as if he were enjoying a day at the beach. Meg envied his cool confidence. Pulling herself onto her stool, she crossed her legs in front of her, and casually turned her head in Jadon's direction. Catching her breath when his eyes met hers, Meg came to the firm, albeit repetitive conclusion, that she had never seen a man so unbelievably attractive.

"Tonight. Tonight. Tonight," Jadon said softly, sitting down behind his drums, giving Meg a small warm smile. Without thinking, Meg gave him the same.

Smacking his gum loudly, Chick sat down in his chair, located front and center of the stage, and glanced over at Meg.

"Whoa. Holy smoke, Meg. Spicy." Chick gave her a quick wink, not wanting to look at Jadon, confident his eyes would be cemented onto Meg. *Let's hope he can hold it together,* Chick thought, grabbing his guitar.

Meg felt herself relax as the show progressed. She liked the calm, controllable setting of the theater. She liked that she wasn't directly in front. That spot was reserved for Chick. From the moment the curtain rose, he controlled the audience and the band, including her. His eyes sent millions of cues, making sure everyone fell into place perfectly. His comfortable ease created a feeling of oneness that descended over the audience. They loved him. He loved to perform, and it showed.

She watched as the band smoothly transitioned from song to song, expertly displaying their craft. She liked how good they were. She liked that she was among such incredible musicians. She watched Jadon from the corner of her eye. Her body flushed at the intensity of his movements. And the way his eyes would continually fall back onto her.

Meg sat amused as she listened to Chick introduce the band members, asking them to do impromptu solos. Slowly she realized he was about to do the same with her. Meg's eyes began to shift, not knowing who he was going to introduce next. It was down to her and Jadon, so it was safe to assume her moments were numbered.

"Okay, okay," Chick told the audience. "I gotta tell ya somethin'. We've got a new addition."

Oh God, Meg thought.

"I would like to introduce . . . the new-and-improved . . . Jadon Hastings!" Chick yelled, shooting a devilish grin toward Meg, and an arm back toward Jadon.

Without missing a beat, Jadon broke into a feverish drum solo, his hair flying madly around his head before he settled into a repetitive beat that filled the room with a funky, slow rhythm.

"I was messin' with ya a bit. Just havin' some fun. Seriously though . . ." Chick whipped his head around to look at Jadon. *"That* was a fantastic solo. However, we met this spectacular musician not long ago and . . . ," he said, relaxing into his chair, deliberately taking his time, "and she has had us in a tailspin ever since. We're fuckin' never gonna be the same. Think you're ready for your solo?"

Meg nodded, comforted by Jadon's steady drum beat, thoughtfully keeping her company.

"All right, Meg Scott . . . I would like you to meet everybody. Everybody . . . this is Meg Scott." Chick let his hand flow out in front of him toward the audience, then back toward Meg.

Sliding off her stool to stand upright, Meg raised her right arm and swept her bow across the strings of her violin. Not sure how to begin, she just started. In the process, she sent a blend of notes that swept their way through the theater, fluttering mystically between the beats Jadon continually offered. Not wanting to disappoint, she turned to look at Jadon, and picked up her tempo. Smiling, Jadon stepped up his beat, matching her playing, and watched as Meg demonstrated her authority over her violin — an authority that demanded the notes burn the air that filled the room. Together with Jadon, Meg ended her performance in a blaze of complex notes that gave her violin ownership of the auditorium, and everyone in it.

"*Whoa!* That just amazes me every Goddamn time!" Chick yelled, visibly thrilled by Meg and Jadon's performance.

Meg bowed gracefully, turning to give Jadon his due. Listening to the audience explode with approval, Meg gave him her smile again.

"All right, well, gee, how do we beat that?" Chick rubbed his beard, sitting back and crossing his legs in one slow, fluid move. "I got an idea. Well, we have another new song; it's gonna be released this week . . . we think it's pretty cool. It's a bit on the heavy side," he cautioned the audience by lowering his voice, causing the crowd to fly into a frenzy of anticipation. "But I think you're gonna like it."

Bracing herself, Meg slid back onto her stool, and turned to see the large screen that flickered high behind the band with the Equinox logo emblazoned on it. Watching the video for a moment, Meg lowered her eyes slowly onto Jadon, and watched his hair dance in front of his face as he sang. Slowly she moved her eyes back onto the large screen, to see the video image of Jadon's eyes watching her while she moved slowly out of the ocean.

Sliding off her stool, Meg readied herself for her moment. Needing to focus she closed her eyes. Raising her bow, she grabbed her first note, sending it through the theater like a launched missile. She turned her eyes toward Jadon, who was waiting for her, waiting for his moment to fall into place with her. Joining Meg at exactly the same moment she dropped into her third note, he and she began their melodic dance.

Meg felt Jadon's drum beats seductively force her into every series of chords, every blended mixture of notes. The violin screamed through the silent crowd, the drums running next to her, intertwined instinctively. Meg's eyes glanced across the screen, to see the larger than life image of Jadon kissing her face, her drop of blood resting on his lips.

Meg closed her eyes and focused her energy onto her last melodic phrase. Once done she dropped her bow, and quickly sat back on her stool, listening to the band thunder through two more riffs, then a crashing end. The crowd exploded, jumping to its feet and creating a deafening rumble that filled the large hall.

"Thank you. Thank you. I want to thank you. All of you. We've enjoyed sharing the evening with you. You guys were great," Chick said with a final wave, as the curtain fell quickly from the ceiling.

Meg took a deep sigh. It was over.

Walking over to Meg, Chick shook his head smiling. "You just keep on surprising the hell out of me."

"You're awesome, Meg. Christ," Bob shot out quickly. Stu and Kofi were already making their way behind him.

"Oh, yeah, this is going be a fun, fun tour. Can't wait," Stu agreed, lighting up a cigarette.

"Well, hey," Chick said. "We're gonna wrap it up. We have a photo shoot tomorrow, so be ready around noon. We're about to head out for a drink, if you want to join us," he said to Meg. "Erin will be there."

"I'd love to. Where?" Meg asked.

"What the hell is the name of that place? Square . . . what the hell is it?" Chick looked at Bob and Stu, waving his finger for input.

"The Round Dog?" Bob asked tentatively.

"That's it. How the hell did I get square outta that? Don't take too long, 'kay? We're outta here," Chick said, walking out the door, followed by Kofi, Bob and Stu.

Meg nodded, carefully putting her violin back into its case. Closing the lid she looked up and noticed Jadon quietly fussing with his drums, raking his fingers through his hair repeatedly in the process.

Meg paused, not sure what to say, or if she should say anything. The moment screamed awkwardness. Beginning to walk toward the door, she stopped.

"I'm sure it's just routine for you but, well, it was really great that you continued to play while I had my solo. Thank you," Meg said, uncomfortable with herself, and her desire to thank him.

Sliding off his stool, Jadon stepped over to Meg. Having waited for it all day, he wasn't going to let the moment pass. Staring into Meg's eyes, Jadon quickly turned, throwing his hand through his hair.

"God. That? I didn't want you to think . . . I don't know . . . that you were alone or somethin'."

"Well. I didn't," Meg nodded, overly aware of the sound of her own voice. "So, thank you. I think the drums are amazing."

Jadon pulled his head back in surprise, "Not what I thought I'd hear from a master violinist."

"Master. Right. I caught that," Meg laughed, feeling a bit more at ease, and finding it impossible not to smile. "Well, I just don't understand the drums. Well, I *understand*, I just don't know how one gets their body to play them."

"Shoot. It's really not that hard. I mean, I could, show you," Jadon offered, looking at Meg out of the corner of his eye.

"I think you might regret that offer." Meg felt her body temperature rise to near lethal levels. "I'm not an easy student."

"I don't think it'll be a problem."

Meg studied the drum kit from across the room. "How about this, you teach me your craft, I teach you mine."

"I like that. I like that a lot."

Bending down to place her violin case on the floor near the door, Meg walked over to the drums, eyeing them like a problem to be solved.

"First, oddly enough, you have to sit on the stool," Jadon said playfully.

"Of course."

Meg situated herself behind his drum kit, still eyeing each piece cautiously.

"All right, take the sticks and hit something."

Meg looked at Jadon, smiling at the simplicity of the first task.

"That pedal, it's for your right foot," Jadon leaned over the tom-tom, pointing toward the large bass drum and the pedal attached to it.

"Step on that?" Meg asked, aware that her dress was creeping higher on her thighs as she moved. Stomping on the pedal, she produced a low, resounding boom. "I like that, it sounds loud, but soft."

Jadon smiled. "That's right. Okay, how about hitting the snare, right here . . ."

Meg plunked it with the stick, unimpressed with the sound she made.

"I guess that one takes some skill."

"Well, it's all in how you're hitting it."

"Oh," Meg said, hitting it again with the same results. "Can we skip that guy?"

Jadon tilted his head back, a smile on his face. "No, you don't get to skip stuff. It's easy. It's . . . just, you're off on how you're hitting it."

Walking behind Meg, Jadon positioned the stick into the correct striking position.

"Oh, I see you sort of hit it while you're drawing your hand back. Okay."

Meg plunked the snare again, still not able to get a nice sound to emanate from it.

"Do I switch hands? Your hands are going all over the place. Am I using the wrong hand?"

"Let me . . . well . . . um . . . if," Jadon stammered. "If I can help direct your hands, you'll get this. I need to sit behind you," he said, searching for something to sit on.

Finding a small square table, he quickly brought it to the drums and swapped it with his drum stool.

"Okay, you can sit back down," Jadon said.

"Will this thing hold both of us?"

Meg eyed the legs of the small table. Feeling Jadon's body inch closer behind hers, she dropped her question.

"Okay, let's do this," Jadon said, pulling Meg's hands gently, gliding the stick across the head of the snare drum.

"See, that sounds like something," she said.

"That's okay," Jadon said softly, his breath falling onto Meg's cheek as she turned to look at him, giving him a smile of appreciation. "Let's get the right hand doing something. Now get your foot going; don't forget about that guy . . . down there."

"Oh, that's right," Meg said, surprised she had so easily and mindlessly forgotten to move her foot.

Feeling too comfortable in his arms, Meg was swept away with the natural ease Jadon had when playing the drums. It was as if he had been brought to earth for the purpose of making those exact sounds.

"Let me help with the foot. Maybe it's the high heel you have on. That's probably throwing you off," he offered, gently pulling his body tighter against hers.

"I bet that's it. Gotta be. It's that blasted heel," Meg said, hoping he wasn't as aware as she was, that her body was quickly turning into a shameless puddle of lust. "Promise you won't quiz me. I'm not exactly catching on too quick."

"Never."

Jadon wasn't sure if what he was doing sounded like anything. He just wanted to feel her in his arms. She fit perfectly. Brushing his cheek against hers, he smelled her perfume. Jadon said nothing, except his desire that was told easily by his breath that fell gently on Meg's face. Cradling her in his arms, he held her hands, moving them rhythmically back and forth, wanting to make time stand still.

Meg felt her body soften. Whether it was right or wrong, if given the chance she knew she would risk everything and finally give in. Out of pure panic, Meg smiled, and felt his face form a sensual smile in response to hers. *Oh God, I want this man*, Meg thought, tilting her head to the side, giving her the chance to record the image of him exactly as he was within her mind.

Feeling Meg's head pull away, Jadon opened his eyes slightly. Eager to touch her skin, he ran his nose next to Meg's ear, and pressed his warm lips against her neck.

"Jay?" Chick said in a rigid tone, causing both Jadon and Meg to jump clumsily to their feet.

Dropping the drum sticks on the floor, Meg busied herself trying to find them, while Jadon stood speechless, running his hands through his hair, staring back at Chick.

"Let's get going," Chick said flatly, turning and walking back out the door.

Because Chick left the door open for Roach and his crew, the room instantly flooded with people ready to tear everything down, something the crew held off on when they walked in on Jadon and Meg earlier.

Chick sat in his car outside the Paladia and thought to himself. *It was one thing to let things gurgle under the surface, it was another to let the monster bring its ugly head above the water, and start walking ominously onto the beach.*

Seeing Jadon walk outside, Chick stepped from his car. Chick's stare was impossible to ignore. Jadon stared back and walked directly in his direction.

"What's this?" Chick asked.

"What do you think it is?" Jadon snapped.

"This isn't good. This isn't going to work."

"It's good. And it is going to work."

"I know you think that. It was a powerful show tonight. Ya know. I know. I was there. Fuck. You just need to pull back, dude. This can't happen." Chick shook his head with certainty.

"What? Are you fuckin' serious?" Jadon yelled.

"Yeah . . . oh, yeah. I'm beyond fuckin' serious."

"You think this was some after-show power trip? You have to be kidding me."

"I don't know *what* it is. Meg is in the band, and we have a tour. That's months on the road, man. And God only knows what else from there. This will ruin the band."

"Where do you fuckin' think that song came from? You *love* the song. Sounds like *what this is* is working out pretty fuckin' good for you!"

"You need to end it. Just end it now," Chick demanded, knowing it wasn't even a remote possibility.

"*No*. No, I can't." Jadon shook his head slowly. "I can't fuckin' stop anything. I can't act like I don't love her. Christ, I would rather *die* than turn back now. She's all I think about. I can't imagine my life without her in it. Fuck the band, I don't care anymore. Get rid of me, then. Get rid of me. You're asking me to stop breathing. Make your choice. Because I'll go. You decide. I *won't* end it, so don't even think about asking me. I've just gotten this far."

Meg poured herself a glass of wine after walking Bob. Her mind was flying full speed. From the look on Chick's face, she didn't want to join the band at the bar. It didn't feel right. She felt she had crossed an invisible line she didn't know was even there.

Sitting down at her desk, Meg opened her laptop and brought her novel onto the screen. Staring at the lines appearing before her, her mind wouldn't stop thinking of Jadon. The feel of his breath on her neck felt so right. It felt more right than anything she had ever experienced.

Meg pounded mindlessly on the laptop, trying to harness her thoughts back onto the life of Elle, but every time she saw Jadon's name on the screen, she saw him holding her and felt his warm body up against hers. *Maybe I should make them break up*, Meg thought, wondering if it would help her to focus. She didn't want to stop writing about him, though; instead she wanted to keep reliving every experience she had with him. Slowly Meg started to craft the next chapter in her novel:

Elle and Jadon arrived at the Grand Hotel Wien in Vienna just before dawn subtly made its appearance. The snow fell heavily through the air like small, delicate scraps of white paper, cascading down from heaven before draping heavily everywhere, giving the appearance of thick white downy blankets covering the shrubs, trees and ground.

Impulsively, Elle confronted Jadon as they stepped out of their car, accusing him of embezzling millions from her art gallery.

Jadon turned slowly, stunned by her words. He's not embezzling anything; the bitter accusation shoots through him like a bullet to the chest.

"How could you think . . . ," he muttered in disbelief, his face wrought with pain.

"I have proof. Simon dropped off the bank records. It's all there . . . ," Elle yelled in desperation, her eyes filling with tears, her voice filling with anger. "Damn you. Damn you, Jadon. I trusted you."

"Simon set me up. You know I wouldn't do anything to hurt you. I wouldn't use you. I love you. I've always loved you," Jadon pleaded, his words echoing through the frigid Vienna morning.

"I don't know. I don't know who to believe, anymore," Elle panted, rushing to the stairs leading to the side entrance of the hotel.

Running after her, Jadon grabbed her arm, attempting to keep her from leaving. Slipping on the icy step, Elle fell, hitting her head on the jagged steps. Rushing to her side, Jadon turned her face toward his, horrified by the blood dripping down Elle's cheek. Kneeling down Jadon began . . .

"Too drippy. Too . . . too something. Not right," Meg grumbled, hitting the backspace key repeatedly, watching the fresh words disappear. She couldn't stop thinking about the moments when Jadon had touched her. She kept throwing the moments into her novel, trying to relive them. She didn't care if it read well. She didn't care if readers would enjoy it. She just wanted to capture it.

Putting those moments on paper made them permanent. In the process, Meg described his touch with words that rippled from the page. Once written, she owned the moment, hers forever.

After hours of work, Meg finally hit send, shooting her latest version to Devon. It was another fifty pages, bringing him up to speed. It was already 2 a.m., and she was tired. She worked and reworked the scenes in her head until she was finally pleased with the outcome. She never wanted to rush her characters, even if only for her own personal gratification. Instead, Meg eased them from scene to scene, making sure everything stayed true to the theme she was carefully developing. It took longer than she wanted, but finally she was able to make the scene work where Jadon gently kissed Elle's tears, which were mixed with blood from her cheek.

Closing her laptop, Meg thought about her neighbor with a pang of guilt. The lights were still off next door. They were off when she arrived home. She didn't walk through the door until after ten o'clock, but she made sure to watch for his lights to come on. They never did. Reaching over, she pulled the metal string of beads that hung from the lamp on her desk, instantly allowing the darkness its chance to fill the spaces of her home.

Jadon pulled into his driveway, making sure to look for signs of life from within Meg's house. There weren't any. Making his way through his living room, he checked again for the faintest glow radiating from her laptop, hoping she was up late writing. Nothing.

"Damn" Jadon said, lying down on the sofa. *Should've just driven home*, he realized quietly.

It wasn't until he walked back from the cliff overlooking Mandalay Bay that he noticed he missed Erin's call letting him know Meg never showed up at The Round Dog. But he needed time to sit and think. He never felt more right about anything in his life. The threat of risking everything to get it didn't terrify him anymore. He wasn't going to let her go. If she would have him, he was hers.

Chapter 13

Devon sat motionless before his computer, hesitating a moment before reading Meg's latest installment. Her emails were getting increasingly short, Devon noticed. Their conversations over the phone were hurried. With every day that passed, he felt Meg drift further away. She was happy. This he knew. It was obvious in her voice. Devon could easily see that Meg enjoyed the band, but the heaviness in the pit of his stomach made him wonder if arranging the audition might have been the worst idea he had ever had. He struggled constantly to contain his emotions. He was succeeding in giving her what she needed, while failing to be the man she wanted.

Nodding in silent resignation Devon reached onto his desk and pulled the loose white pages of Meg's book onto his lap. He settled back into his chair. Letting his eyes flow across the words she carefully painted onto each page, he quickly resumed the fast-paced journey Meg was swiftly leading him on. After his mind absorbed Meg's last sentence, Devon paused for a moment.

"Fuck," he hissed slowly, throwing the newly printed pages of Meg's novel across his desk. After running his hands over his face and through his hair, Devon sat with his hands pressed together, his fingers resting firmly on his nose.

"Fuck," he whispered again, closing his eyes.

The words in Meg's novel poured through his body like acid. The pages were wet with sensuality. Meg was known for passion. This he knew. But it was the energy hiding beneath the words that enraged him. The imagery was striking. Startling, in fact. Her writing was different than usual, immediately alerting him to the unsettling possibility that one, if not both, of Meg's characters might not be fictional at all. Her descriptions were sumptuous and rich to the point he could taste the images as he read them. The feelings exchanged between Elle and Jadon were overwhelming.

"Meg, Meg, Meg . . . what are you up to?" Devon whispered.

The detailed images of Jadon kissing Elle spun in a million different directions inside Devon's head. Elle's uncontrollable desire for Jadon burned in his mind.

"Jadon, Jadon . . . Who the hell are you?" Devon said, waking his computer from its sound slumber.

Meg allowed the lull of sleep to rock her gently between wakefulness and unconscious thought. Pulling the pillow tight under her head, she gazed out the large French doors that revealed the early morning brilliance of the ocean; its ebb and flow were reassuringly constant despite all of life's turbulence.

The words she wrote in her novel last night floated across her mind. Meg sighed, pleased with how her last two chapters had finally eased themselves out of her. Her choice of words was crucial, as it always is for a writer, but this time it was different. For the first time in her life she was writing about something she personally felt, had felt, and was hoping to feel again. Once she gave herself permission to let it flow, the words poured forth. Like watercolors exploding onto a damp canvas with every brushstroke, her words were fluid and alive.

Consumed with the need to find the perfect words, Meg savored each one as she thoughtfully chose it. She carefully rolled each around in her mind, making sure it captured the essence of Jadon with its subtle and sometimes not so subtle references.

He's decadent. Sweet, but not too sweet. Rich with flavor, overpoweringly so. Like a fine dessert, Meg smiled, nodding her head in agreement with herself. Wanting a metaphor easily accessible to all her readers, she chose to describe Jadon using the simple act of tasting something divine. The way it startles the system as it settles itself on the taste buds. The uncontrollable, undeniable need one has to devour every last morsel of it. The painful feeling of restraint that always looms in the background. The memory of the taste as it lingers throughout the day. The pleasurable experience of hoping to taste and experience it again.

Pulling herself onto the side of the bed, Meg pondered the literary aspects of her latest novel. The words of Elizabeth Bowen kept repeating themselves in her head: *"Any fiction . . . is bound to be transposed autobiography."*

"Ugh," Meg mumbled, standing to look out the French doors of her bedroom. "That is precisely my problem."

The primal nuances and desires for Jadon, set down on paper, were all her own. Pure autobiography. Not that anyone would know, she supposed. *But was it too much?* She couldn't help but wonder. *No, it wasn't.*

Bob and Stu were already perched on top of the rock formation that capped the cliff overlooking the bay. Waving their hands, they motioned for Meg to join them. Bob tapped the raw rock next to him with his hand, letting Meg know to take a seat.

"This is breathtaking," Meg said, casting her eyes across the open vista.

Soaking in the stunning view, Bob and Stu nodded their heads in agreement.

"How ya holdin' up, Meggie?" Bob asked.

Glancing purposefully back at the ocean, Meg sighed and shook her head. "It's been interesting. It's been embarrassing . . . ," she added with an air of remorse, picturing how she appeared in the video and what Chick walked in on the other night.

Shrugging his shoulders, Stu scrunched his nose, "Nothin' to be embarrassed about. What do you have to be embarrassed about?"

"Don't worry about it," Bob interjected, suddenly standing up to arch his back. "This business, it can rip you wide open. Just say fuck it. Ya know. Who cares what people think. *God*, you looked great in the video Meg..."

"It's more than that. It's the . . ."

Meg's sentence was cut short by the sudden arrival of Chick, who jogged up the stone steps, his face showing the residue of a hard night.

"'Bout fuckin' time you showed," Stu said. "Now all that's left is pretty boy."

"He loves it when you call him that," Chick said, sinking into his favorite position with his arms folded across his chest, before turning to give a hard inspection of the ocean.

"That's precisely why I do it. He ain't *that* pretty," Stu joked, winking at Meg, who felt the prick of awkwardness when she realized the comment was directed toward her.

"There he is," Chick said, not changing his stance.

Jadon parked on the dirt road leading to the cliff, the same place where he spent much of last night, and walked to the edge over looking the water. He felt heavy, not knowing how the day would play out. Turning around to take in his surroundings, he noticed everyone gathered high near the rock formation, which stood like a lighthouse peering regally over the cliff. Slowly he made his way up the hill toward them, considering with every step the uncertainty of the day — and of the situation.

"Hey, Sid," Chick shouted, nodding his head toward the photographer whose large camera bag appeared small against his even larger frame.

"Hey, Chick. Bob. Stu," Sidney said, pausing for a moment to smile warmly at Meg. "And this must be, Meg."

Towering over everyone, Sidney surveyed the surroundings. His warm chocolate skin was set off by his white shirt; his sunglasses were perched precariously on top of his shaved head.

"This is going to be great. I like it. I *always* like this location. Hey, Jay," Sidney quickly added, noticing Jadon sitting down behind the others.

"That's Sidney Paul," Chick said, sitting next to Meg.

Meg nodded her head to show she was listening, all the while her mind jumped heavily from thought to thought. Remembering the far off rapturous place she was in when Chick walked in on her and Jadon, she cringed in silent embarrassment. She stared down at the small gray aliens peppering the fabric of her sneakers and shuffled her feet on the ground before gazing back at the ocean. Its overwhelming presence was never ignored for more than a moment by anyone who had the fortune to be near it. Thinking again about her writing, Meg couldn't help but wonder what Devon would have to say after reading her latest chapters. They were wildly erotic. Meg wondered if the scenes themselves were erotic or the way they made her feel was erotic. Either way, regardless of how many times she read them, her body erupted into a heated sweat each time. *Would it be too much?* she wondered again and again.

"No," Meg said softly. Those moments, regardless of the unorthodox way they came about, had changed her. They changed how she viewed the world, and what she wanted from it. Taking a deep sigh, Meg tried to clear her head of her thoughts before they became visible to others.

Glancing at Meg, Chick wondered whom she was talking to, all the while his mind weighed heavily with what he needed to tell her.

"Where's Equinox Bob?" Chick asked kindly, feeling Meg's tension he pushed back the words standing first in line to be said.

Relieved by the question, Meg answered easily, "I wasn't sure what the day would bring."

Looking at Meg for a moment, Chick scratched at the scrappy hair resting under his chin. "He's always welcome. He's our mascot, for Pete's sake. From now on, bring him."

Nodding her head deeply, Meg felt slightly better. His answer gave some indication as to her future with the band. *Please let that be it. Let last night never come up. Let last night never come up*, the words tumbled repeatedly inside of Meg's head.

"Meg," Chick began, slowly bringing his hands together in front of his face. "I don't know what's going on between you and Jay. But whatever it is, it has to stop, for the sake of the band." He let the words trickle slowly from his mouth, not feeling completely satisfied with any of them. "I don't want to lose you. I don't want to lose Jadon. Without question, though Meg, there can't be anything . . . ," Chick began to flutter his hand in front of him, "between band members. I've been watching as this *thing* has been spiraling radically out of control, and it just can't happen. These things tend to ruin bands. Absolutely ruin them."

Chick's words sliced through Meg like a sword painstakingly sharpened against a grinding stone for days. Not sure how to react,

Meg sat silent, immobilized by humiliation and the immense obviousness of everything.

Liking what he saw, Sidney stared at the rock outcropping the band was scattered across. Instead of moving them around like mannequins, he decided to start snapping pictures continually as he weaved his way around each of them while they resettled themselves on the expansive cliff. Looking through his lens, he liked the way life rested on each of their faces. Some smiled, some looked tired. Others so weighed down with thoughts, their faces were easily read like handwriting on paper.

Moving his gear from in front of the group, Sidney found a level clearing behind them instead. He crawled on his knees until he found a spot that allowed him to capture them from a different perspective. By coming up from behind, the images appeared stolen.

He knew he had his shot when he heard the shutter click, and their image flashed before his lens. The photo spoke volumes with its subtle tones. Each one sitting next to the other, Chick on the right end, his elbows resting easily on his legs, looking up at Bob, who was now sitting directly to Chick's left. The puzzled look on Chick's face as he watched Bob stretch his arms out into the sun, absorbing its sunshine onto his already well tanned and tattooed body. Meg sitting next to Bob, her faded jeans and loose t-shirt trying unsuccessfully to hide her beauty under a carefree, worn facade. Meg's turned head was looking to her left and directly at Jadon; her long hair blowing like wisps of fire burning Bob's back while he reached for the sun. Stu settled casually next to Meg, resting his left elbow on his left knee, staring peacefully out at the ocean, the cigarette between his fingers sending a swirl of gray smoke twirling upward into the sky. Finally Sidney saw the part of the picture that gave the black and white photograph its color.

Jadon was sitting on the far left, leaning back on the ground, resting his weight on his elbows buried within the scrappy wildflowers that dusted the hillside. His head was turned facing Meg, his face softly frozen. His stare unmoving. His blonde hair made white by the sunshine as it floated past his face toward Meg.

"We're good," Sidney said, pulling himself off the ground, gathering his things, and placing them neatly back into his bag.

"That was one of the easiest photo shoots I've ever had to go through," Chick said, startled that it was already over.

As they began to scatter, Meg walked slowly down the hillside. Veering off the path deep in thought, she came to a halt at the cliff's edge. Extending her toes beyond the ground that protected her from falling, she stood motionless. Spreading her arms wide Meg, pushed her body against the wind, trusting in its ability to hold her steady, reminding her that there was something bigger than herself in control.

"Why does the thought of not allowing myself to feel what I feel, feel like death?" Meg whispered, keeping her eyes closed trying to make sense of it. "Because, whether he knows it or not, whether he should or shouldn't, moreover, whether it's right or wrong, Jadon has become the beat of my heart. It can't kill you, Meg, to let go of something you didn't quite have."

Sitting alone on the warm rock outcrop, Jadon watched as Meg looked out at the ocean, admiring the spiritual connection she had with the universe. It was, he was sure, the same force that allows the earth to keep spinning and the stars to remain safely seated in the sky.

Even though he tried to ignore them, Chick's words landed on Jadon's mind, singing their miserable song repeatedly. He shouldn't have agreed with Chick's conditions. But as Chick pointed out, the welfare of the band was at risk. That was the last thing Jadon wanted to hear. But once he heard it, he couldn't ignore it.

"Just for a couple months, Meg," Jadon whispered, watching her hair carelessly succumb to the strong ocean wind.

Chick had told Jadon to hold off until after the tour. And against the natural desire of every atom in his body, Jadon agreed. He didn't want to hurt anyone. Although, he wasn't sure how it would. What harm would come of his love for Meg? Everything about it was perfect. He never felt more connected with his music than when she was near.

Pulling his arms around his legs, Jadon continued to watch as Meg eased herself away from the edge, never feeling concerned she would fall. If she had, he would have fallen with her.

Chapter 14

"Isn't it kinda cold to be out here this early?" Meg asked, trying to ignore the frigid early morning ocean air.

"Flora says it's good for us," Erin answered, taking the last sip of her mocha.

"Christ," Meg complained, pulling her foot up behind her, trying to ignore how anxious she felt about attending Flora's yoga class.

"She doesn't like closed in spaces," Erin continued. "She feels the open air helps the prana to flow . . ."

Puzzled, Meg cocked her head. "What the hell is prana?"

Erin stared for a moment before answering. "Well, it's like energy, or something like that. Flora told me, I just get it a little confused with chi," she mumbled before throwing her body into a deep forward bend. "Or maybe they're the same thing. God, I don't know; but it's important, I know that."

Meg nodded her head, trusting that it probably was important. Flora seemed the type that had a good understanding of what was important. Having just met her the day before, Meg quickly noticed Flora was the type of person whose eyes easily pulled aside the curtains of one's soul.

"I like Flora. She probably knows what she's talking about," Meg added, trying to swing effortlessly into a forward bend like the one she had watched Erin do so easily. "Oh, God, that sort of hurts."

"Make sure you take it easy. Flora will be all over you if you push yourself too far, too fast."

"Gotcha," Meg said, swinging her head upside down so she could look Erin in the eye.

When asked to come to one of Flora's classes, Meg couldn't help but feel as though it wasn't so much a question but rather guided advice. Much like when a doctor eyes your body and advises you to lay off fats and sugars.

"I'm not so sure we gave our bodies the right kind of fuel for this mission," Meg said, regretting the chocolate glazed donut she inhaled shortly after they zoomed out of Winchell's parking lot.

Stretching her arms up into the sky, Erin had to agree. "Yeah, next time we'll go someplace else. Those damn donuts, though, they really know how to scream my name."

"I know. Bastards. Winchell's, Krispy Kreme...Dunkin. Ruthless bastards. All of them."

"Namaste," Flora said calmly, standing in front of the small crowd that had gathered on the beach.

"What? What did she say?" Meg whispered, not sure if it was something she needed to know.

"Namaste. It means . . . crap, I'll tell you later," Erin tried to whisper.

Concentrating on Flora's movements, Meg tried to bring her body into some sort of resemblance of Flora's as they moved through the various poses. Some of them felt wonderful, others felt like a form of torture. Her shoulders were always her worst enemy, for they held within them all of her writer's tension. Tension that, as of late, had increased tenfold compared to her past novels. Trying to remove Jadon's narcotic effects from her system, and write about him at the same time, was proving to be excruciatingly painful. All the pleasure Meg was basking in while she bounced the words around on her laptop, describing her borderline unholy lust for the man, had now turned to immense sadness. It showed in her writing, Meg knew as she reread her phrases, often crying while pulling her characters apart, much like she felt pulled away from Jadon. It was impossible to keep the lovers in her novel together while she was forced to do otherwise. Finally giving in, Meg caused the two of them to be parted under nefarious circumstances. Giving both characters a mountain of pain to carry around in the process, just so she didn't feel quite so alone with her own heavy burden.

After the class had silently ended, Flora flowed casually over to where Erin and Meg were still curled on their mats.

"I'm so happy you both were able to make it," Flora said with a smile that proved her words to be honest and sincere.

Meg flipped her head up from her mat to see Flora hovering over her like a statue of Christ, the sight of which caused Erin and Meg both to hop to their feet abruptly.

"It was *awesome*, as always," Erin beamed.

"Wonderful. You ladies have a wonderful day. Namaste," Flora said, bringing her palms before her face and then gracefully walking toward the other members of the class, who were anxiously clamoring for her attention.

"What was that again? Nam . . . what?" Meg said wrinkling her face.

"Namaste. Okay. *That* means, 'The divine in me recognizes the divine in you.'"

Considering the statement for a moment, Meg wondered what its true implications were. *So many people don't seem divine at all,* she thought.

"She kind of creeps me out a little. Something in her eyes, when she looks at me. Do you feel that?" Meg hoped Erin felt the same.

"No. No, I really don't. She is psychic though," Erin said in a low whisper.

"No shit," Meg blurted, stunned by the consequences of being around someone who had the potential to tap into her mind, the only sacred place she had left. "No wonder she looks at me so funny."

"Hey, I have a great idea. Flora asked if I would like to go to a workshop with her, and I said yes. I want you to come too. Say yes. Soon we'll be on tour, maybe a workshop is just the thing we need to put us in the right frame of mind before we go."

"Well, yeah, I'll go," Meg answered, trying to find every possible thing to occupy her time with. "But, well, what kind of workshop is it? I mean, how to do your taxes; tax time is inching up on us. Pottery . . . I've always wanted to throw clay ever since I saw the movie *Ghost*."

"Oh, no. This is mind-blowing stuff. It's about letting go, and allowing the Universe to bring what you want into your life."

"Why not?" said Meg. "My mind has already been stretched beyond the limits of healthy expansion. Sounds good. Anything to keep me busy."

Erin glanced at Meg. She knew Meg was trying to keep busy in an attempt to purge Jadon out of her system. Chick told her everything shortly after it happened. It was already painfully obvious how strongly they were drawn to one another. But then Chick walked in on them after the show at the Paladia. He told Erin what he had seen, saying how the sight of it cut him in two. One side of him felt overwhelmed for his dear friend, wanting beyond belief for him to experience the feelings that were finally finding the courage to step out from behind the door of his heart. The other half, though, weighed the tragic possibility of what such a relationship, any relationship among band members, would ultimately do to the band.

Chick also feared the combustibleness of what was felt between Meg and Jadon. *It was intense,* Erin thought to herself. But it was also beautiful to witness, except now it ripped her heart watching both Jadon and Meg silently try to handle the forced separation: the glances they would quietly pass to one another over the past two weeks, the sighs of discomfort when they rehearsed together, the smiles that immediately formed on their faces when they saw each other, only to quickly fade as they tried to keep themselves from feeling what they were feeling.

"When is this workshop?" Meg asked.

"Tonight!" Erin answered quickly. "Hey, let's get together at the house. We'll have a barbeque, get everyone together. Yeah. Chick loves barbeques, and it's always good for the band to have time to chill together. How about three o'clock?"

"Sure," Meg offered, suddenly feeling the pressure of having to try to relax around Jadon again.

Pulling up to Chick's place, Jadon parked his Porsche alongside Erin's white Jeep, tucking it between her car and the large wall of shrubs lining the driveway, hoping to keep it out of plain sight.

"Dude!" Chick shouted, sticking his head out from behind the garage, waving a pair of tongs in his hand.

Jadon smiled and nodded as he walked slowly in Chick's direction.

"Beer?" Chick asked, putting one in Jadon's hand.

"Yeah. Thanks," Jadon answered, taking a long drink as Meg breezed past him. Watching her walk by, Jadon gave Meg a long purposeful stare, then turned his eyes to Chick. "Two months . . . three weeks and four days. That's it. Not one day longer."

He's fucking counting the days. Chick said to himself, finishing his beer, before turning to join everyone. It was obvious Jadon was dead set on pursuing Meg. Although Chick was the one who had left the door open for that after the tour, he was beginning to regret his words. Chick was already bombarded with offers for the band to extend their tour, and to continue with a second album. He couldn't help but wonder how all of this was going to play out. Erin wouldn't stop badgering him, either, pushing him hard to lighten up on Jadon. She felt certain that, if pushed beyond the original agreement, he would leave the band to pursue Meg. It was a point Chick couldn't argue with. Erin also pointed out how the energy during rehearsal was strained and heavy, which was what Chick wanted to avoid in the first place.

"Meggie Peggie!" Stu and Bob shouted as Meg walked up to the table. "Give this lady a drink, Chick!"

Chick waved his tongs to signal he heard the request, and was on his way.

"Name your poison, sister," Chick said warmly.

"Lay it on me," Meg shot out, needing something to slow down her racing heart. Still not able to think and easily contain herself around Jadon at the same time.

"Hey, Kofi, Flora," Chick shouted, spotting the two making their way up the long walk that bordered the garage, leading to the spacious, tastefully landscaped backyard overlooking the ocean. "We threw some veggie burgers on for you, Flo!"

"Thank you, Chick," Flora said, walking behind his chair, hugging his head into her side.

Meg noticed the maternal gesture, and how it seemed so natural. Flora was the embodiment of a walking, talking, breathing incarnation of Mother Earth. Her long natural curls flowed midway down her back, their blackness disrupted only by the long streaks of silver that accentuated the spiraling curls. Her face was left natural, beautiful in its own intrinsic way. Her body buried under long draping pieces of fabric, all of which heightened her Mother Earthiness quality.

Flora casually took the seat next to Jadon, which Meg noticed made Jadon sit up straighter in his chair. *I wonder if she is reading his mind*, Meg caught herself wondering. *I wonder if she is reading my mind, which is wondering if she is reading his mind.*

How are you, Jay?" Flora asked, taking her hand and placing it over his.

"Good," he stammered, thanking God he had his sunglasses on, which he hoped was preventing Flora from seeing into his mind.

"Hmm . . . ," Flora offered.

Meg wondered what that meant.

Jadon wasn't pleased with Flora's response, and tried breaking her concentration by shifting her focus. "How are you, Flora?"

"Good, sweetie, and don't worry. I won't tell anyone what I saw," she said easily, patting his hand gently before taking her glass of wine off the table.

"What the hell does that mean?" Chick shouted with a smile. "You know that stuff freaks the shit out of me."

"I know. Maybe that's why I do it."

"*Right*. You're doin' your thing. I can tell. You always do that thing. I love it and hate it all at the same time," Chick laughed.

"Okay. I will admit, the energy is thick this afternoon," Flora glanced casually around the yard, causing everyone to fidget slightly.

"I bet you're busy during the Halloween season," Chick teased.

"You know I don't practice in that way."

"You should do some readings tonight!" Erin said excitedly.

"*Oh, God!*" Meg blurted, not having considered the possibility of such a thing.

"Let's just leave that for another day," Jadon said, hoping Flora liked his suggestion.

'Don't worry, I already know what's going on in your mind. I didn't even have to look. It showed itself to me," Flora said, turning to look at Jadon directly, a gesture that gave her words a prophetic feel.

Returning home from the workshop hours later, Meg drove into her garage, noticing in the process that her neighbor's lights were still off.

Snapping Bob's leash onto his collar, Meg smiled thinking about the rendezvous she had with her neighbor the night before. He had been more forceful than during previous times. Meg enjoyed it. She enjoyed feeling him command both of them through their sensual moment together. It drove her mad not knowing who he was. Between her feelings for Jadon and her feelings for this man, she felt as though her body was literally being ripped in two. Meg cringed, recalling walking up the steps that led to his door last night. But she couldn't handle it any longer. She needed to act on her feelings. Her hand had already been slapped concerning Jadon. All of it mixed together was pushing her off the edge.

Returning from the walk, Bob jumped up on the sofa. He watched Meg charge from the bedroom, shoving her iPod into the speaker dock positioned next to the TV.

"Wanna dance?" Meg turned, giving Bob a devilish grin before taking another long sip of the pinot noir Erin had given her after they returned from the workshop.

Flipping off the lights and turning up the volume, Meg spun her body around the living room. Despite the cool nighttime temperatures, she threw open the French doors leading to her balcony and began dancing to the music that roared through her home.

Jumping onto the sofa next to Bob, Meg burst into a series of complicated air guitar riffs. With her head swinging wildly she jumped off the sofa, and continued to thunder her body around the living room. Her heart racing from the aerobic activity, Meg began to hammer imaginary drums, positioned high in the air.

It wasn't until Jadon opened the door to his house that he heard the music reverberating from Meg's home. Looking out his kitchen window he noticed her lights were off, a fact he already knew when he drove up and assumed she wasn't home from the workshop yet.

"Is that Motorhead?" Jadon questioned, listening to the noises booming from Meg's balcony. Turning slowly to toss his keys on the kitchen counter, he walked out onto his balcony. "Zeppelin. So far so good," he smiled, letting his eyes linger on the inky black ocean, admiring the crowns of white cradling themselves on top of each forceful wave that rolled in.

"ABBA.. Nice touch," Jadon laughed once the next song began, enjoying the contrasting mix that seemed to fit Meg so well. "Gotta have some ABBA..."

Lowering himself onto the floor of his balcony, Jadon rested his back against the railing. Breathing deep, he listened to the music, and wondered what Meg was doing.

"Hope she's okay," Jadon said, realizing he had never heard such loud music from her place before. *What if something's wrong? What if someone broke in?* He wondered. Once the questions were allowed to form in his mind, Jadon felt his body tighten with worry.

"Equinox . . ." Jadon smiled cautiously, pleased that Meg was listening to his music, but still hoping for a clue revealing if she was all right.

Crash. Boom. Smash.

Hearing the loud, unexpected noises from Meg's house, Jadon was instantly out the door. Within seconds arriving at Meg's front door.

Chapter 15

"Lately I've been living in my head, the rest of me is dead. I'm dying for truth," Meg sang forcefully. "Okay. Okay. For Pete's sake Bob, stop barking. Where the hell is that remote? *Got it!* Who the hell is ringing the doorbell?" she grumbled. Fumbling her way through the darkness, Meg eyed the clock on her coffee maker. "It's almost eleven at night, for Pete's sake."

Zigzagging through the living room toward the door, Meg shot a quick glance in the direction of her neighbor's house. It was just as dark as it had been earlier. Standing on her toes, she looked through the peephole and tried to see who was standing on the other side of her front door. Not able to see anyone, she flipped on the outside light, flooding her front porch in a warm yellow glow.

"Oh, my God," Meg said stunned.

Knowing she would have to open the door eventually, Meg swung it open quickly, trying to hide her shock.

"Hello, darling," Devon said smoothly, standing casually at Meg's door.

"Devon," Meg said, trying not to sound alarmed by his unexpected presence. "I had no idea."

"I know. That's precisely how surprises are intended," Devon offered effortlessly. "I don't know exactly how you Americans do it, but I believe . . . when one flies in from London, they're normally invited into one's home shortly after arriving at their front door."

"Oh. Oh, yes. Of course. God, I'm sorry. My mind was elsewhere."

Holding the door open wide, Meg stepped aside, throwing her arm out toward the living room in a gesture of invitation.

Gracefully stepping into Meg's home, Devon noticed her living room was in a state of complete chaos.

"What have you been doing?"

"Dancing. I've been . . ." Meg said, slowly shutting the door, "dancing."

"Looks like you've been raising bloody hell in here," he continued, noticing the desk lamp broken on the floor.

Easing himself out of the thorny bushes that lined the side of Meg's front porch, Jadon quickly crept across Meg's front lawn, and back to the safety of his own home

"Who the fuck was that?" Jadon asked himself, not having considered another man already in Meg's life. "Don't know who you are pal, but you're not going to mess up my plans," he said in disgust, not liking Devon as soon as he heard his British accent.

Jadon painfully wiped his face, arms and legs. The latter two mirrored the appearance of his battered face, the result of landing awkwardly in the bushes after throwing himself face first over the railing that bordered Meg's front porch. Startled by the sudden sound of a car door slamming shut in her driveway, Jadon panicked, and tried to disappear the only way he could. Lying in between the thorny bushes, it felt like an eternity before Meg finally opened the door welcoming Devon inside.

Standing in front of his kitchen sink, Jadon systematically began pressing the small wads of toilet tissue onto his cuts while looking into Meg's house, through what appeared to be her kitchen window.

Devon walked steadily through Meg's house, his hands buried casually into the deep pockets of his perfectly pressed gray trousers.

"I was a bit surprised by how frigid the air felt." Devon said, closing the French doors leading to Meg's balcony. Walking over to pet Bob, Devon couldn't help but notice Meg was acting very different than her normal, relaxed self. "Hope my little surprise hasn't caught you at a bad time."

"Nooo . . . ," Meg said in a raspy voice, looking up at Devon, giving him a warm smile. Just as quickly she looked back down at the magazines scattered across the floor. Gathering them together she stacked them back into a neat pile on the coffee table.

Devon opened the door to Meg's refrigerator, half out of curiosity, half out of the desire for something to drink. Settling on a bottle of vitamin water, he slowly closed the door and walked to the kitchen window to stare at the dark surroundings.

"Jesus!" Jadon dropped down to his knees, "What is it about this guy?" he said to himself, easing his body back up to the window, figuring out that Devon couldn't see him, but because his lights were off he could see Devon.

Enjoying the freedom that being hidden in darkness provides, Jadon stood calmly looking out his window watching Devon.

"He's tall," Jadon noted. He wasn't happy with the observation, feeling slightly disappointed with his own height in the process. Watching Devon, Jadon felt every insecurity he had bubble up inside.

"So!" Devon began crisply, unable to resist his need to learn more about the fuel Meg's mind had been running on to create her latest chapters. "I've been reading your book.

"Good, good. I like it." Meg sat down on the sofa next to Bob. "So, you came *all* the way over here, to discuss the book? Hmm . . ."

"I do have a couple of engagements while I'm this close to Los Angeles, but yes, yes, I mainly came here to . . . to talk with you. Find out how you are." Devon lowered himself onto the chair facing Meg.

"I'm great. Couldn't be better."

"I don't believe that for an instant."

"Ha, well. It's true. I'm great. I think the book reveals that, don't you?" Meg said, hoping Devon would drop the subject.

"Yes," Devon said slowly. "It does seem to reveal something . . ."

Meg smiled. *Damn he's good,* she mused. *He's light years away from being able to read souls like Flora, but he's good.*

"It's just a book," Meg said staring at her fingernails.

Watching Meg, Devon could tell instantly more was going on than she was willing to share. Not wanting to push the subject, choosing instead to leave things open so he could pursue it later, he walked over to Bob.

"Well, looks like your mum is getting pretty tired. Must be all that dancing." Devon gave Meg a sexy wink to match the sexy grin adorning his face. "I don't mean to keep you dear. Really, I just wanted to drop by. Let you know I was here for a couple of days before heading to New York."

"Oh," Meg said, surprised by his sudden desire to leave so soon. "Thank you. But, you don't have to leave so soon."

"Yes I do. You're tired. And quite honestly, I am too. I'm staying at the Hathaway Grand in Beverly Hills, but as always I have my cell in case you need me. I would like to meet your new friends tomorrow if that is possible," Devon said, finally bringing up the reason he flew all the way across the Atlantic Ocean.

He desperately wanted to meet the musicians Meg was now spending her days with. That's not entirely the truth. He wanted to meet Jadon. He didn't want to read about him, he didn't want to see his picture or the godforsaken video of him and Meg one more time. He wanted to stand face to face with him.

"Oh, of course," Meg said, bringing herself up off the sofa, wondering what was rolling around in Devon's head.

Jadon watched as Devon walked closer to Meg and leaned down. Much to his frustration, he couldn't make out any more than that, but felt relief when he noticed Meg walking back into her living room alone. Just to make sure, Jadon looked out onto the street. Watching Devon back out of Meg's driveway, he quickly made his way to the piano, hoping that after all the commotion she would still want to make music with him. Lowering his fingers onto the piano keys, Jadon called out for Meg to join him. Hearing her balcony doors open, Jadon smiled, knowing that at least for now, in this way, she was still his.

Chapter 16

"Who cares if I pee in the shower?" Stu grumbled at Bob while flipping through the channels on the TV they both were staring at that hung on the wall of the studio.

"I do. It's gross," Bob snapped, disgusted by some of Stu's more questionable habits.

"Says who? Who says it's gross?"

"I do. It's disgusting. Just piss before you get in the shower."

"Why would I do that? The water all goes to the same place!" Stu swirled his finger down an invisible drain.

"That's not the point."

"That's precisely the point. Think of all the water I'm saving!" Stu snuffed out his cigarette in the ashtray sitting on the table in front of them.

"What?"

"The water, by not flushing . . . what is that? How many gallons? Consider it my small way of going green. You're just miffed 'cause you hadn't thought of it."

"I doubt peeing in the shower makes you a conservationist."

"Kofi would agree with me. He and Flora are all about the environment. Wait till he gets here. He'll tell ya you were an idiot for not thinkin' of it yourself," Stu said, turning to see who was about to walk in the door.

"Hey," Meg said, opening the door for Bobby to come charging through.

"Bobby!" Stu shouted, slapping his lap, giving Bob the all clear to join them.

Jumping onto the sofa the best he could, Bob sprawled his body over both Bob and Stu.

"Who's your daddy, yeah, who's your daddy?" Bob cooed, rubbing noses with Bobby.

"Guys, this is Devon," Meg blurted, breaking up the heartfelt reunion between Bob and Bob and Stu.

"Hey," Stu offered, taken back by the tall picturesque man standing beside Meg.

"Devon, this is Stu . . . ," Meg said, pointing a casual hand toward Stu who was still buried under Bob's wagging tail. "And this is Bob . . . ," she added, pointing to Bob, who merely nodded his head, not impressed by the sight of Devon.

Unable to ignore Devon's overpowering vibe, Stu slid himself out from under Bob, and offered a hand to Devon, in hopes of making Meg feel more at ease. "How ya doing?"

"Very well, thank you," Devon said, revealing his prominent accent.

No longer inclined to stir up conversation, Stu turned around. Settling himself back onto the sofa, he picked up where he had left off with Bob's rub down. Rounding the corner in a flurry, Chick stopped suddenly when he noticed a new face standing in the studio.

"You must be Devon," Chick smiled, offering a firm handshake. He was well prepared for his arrival due to Meg's phone call earlier that morning. No, he assured Meg, he didn't mind a visitor, even though he couldn't help but sense Meg's hidden reluctance when she asked.

"Kofi's running late. You guys ready?" Chick looked at the sofa covered in lazy bodies.

"Yup!" Stu said, prying his body out from under Bob again. "Just a sec . . . Bob was needing a massage."

Bob snaked his way off the sofa as well, setting Bobby's furry head back down so he could nap, then changed the channel over to Animal Planet.

Devon watched and followed as everyone ambled into the rehearsal room. Walking over to her stool, Meg made a point not to look in Jadon's direction. In no way did she want Devon to sense any form of attraction coming from her toward Jadon. Because her attraction was almost impossible to hide, Meg wanted Devon out of town as soon as possible. Devon wasn't doing anything wrong by being there, Meg reasoned, she just didn't want questions. She didn't want the wretched awkwardness of someone who likes someone discovering that the person they like likes someone else.

Jadon sat still, trying to be patient, while waiting for everyone to finally begin rehearsing. He was tired of rehearsing. Chick was adamant the band be completely in synch before hitting the road. But they were in synch, and Jadon just wanted to get the next couple months over with. Rolling his head around to loosen his neck, he also thought about Devon. Chick had called letting him know in advance that he would be there at the beginning of practice. An act of kindness, perhaps; he wasn't sure. Either way, Jadon watched as Chick strolled in to the room, followed by Meg and Devon. Looking away briefly in disgust, Jadon quickly returned his sights to Devon, giving him the once over, not pleased with what he saw. Just as he had remembered, Devon was well over six feet tall. A fact that made Jadon's height of five-foot-nine seem even shorter somehow. Jadon couldn't help but notice that, for all intents and purposes, Devon was the complete opposite of himself when it came to appearances. And, he was quite sure, in terms of personality as well.

"Looks like a real jerk," Jadon sputtered under his breath, watching Devon softly touch Meg's waist before sitting down.

Jadon couldn't stand the fluid way in which Devon carried himself. Instantly concluding that Devon acted like he popped out of a movie, one in which he was the debonair romantic leading man. Striking the drums exceptionally loud, Jadon pounded out a wickedly fast drum roll, prompting Chick to turn, and look in his direction.

"Devon. The loud one back there . . . that's our very own Jadon," Chick threw a casual hand back toward Jadon, not realizing the weight his simple introduction carried with it. Watching Devon cock his head in examination of Jadon, Chick couldn't help but notice the sneer emerging across Devon's face.

Chapter 17

Erin sat quietly next to Meg, watching the circus of people scattered across the beach. And the bright sun, finally awake, settled in its resting place above everyone.

"Jesus Christ, I'm glad Flora up'd her class to eleven o'clock. At least the sun has had a chance to introduce itself before we start disfiguring our bodies into all those weird poses," Meg griped, ripping open the wrapper of her Luna bar. The two of them were sitting comfortably in Erin's Jeep in the beach parking lot.

"Meg," Erin said, the full inflection of her voice showing she'd been thinking hard about what she was about to say. It was a sign that made Meg's head dart abruptly, no longer consumed with trying to dislodge her breakfast from its shiny wrapper.

"Uh oh."

"No. Nothing bad. Just the opposite really. I . . . I just want to talk. I mean, really talk. There's a lot going on, and you're trying to keep it all inside. I don't want that. *Not,* unless *you* want that, which, then I guess, I want that too. But I really don't want that."

Knowing Erin's motives were genuine, Meg nodded and braced herself slightly for what was about to come.

"Meg, Well . . . I don't know where to start. Except that, I don't want you to always be this mysterious person. I want to know you. Sarcasm aside. Not that I don't enjoy your sarcasm, I do. But I can tell it often hides something much deeper. Let's start with something easy. Tell me about your mom." Satisfied with her delivery, Erin grabbed her mocha.

"Well . . . Okay, she used to . . ." — Meg looked deliberately at the ocean that raucously rolled in front of her eyes — "wear one little squirt of men's cologne in addition to her own perfume. One morning when I was about seven or so, I sat and watched as she got ready for her day. And, as I sat there . . ." Meg paused, feeling the pain of the memory in her eyes. "I watched as she sprayed her perfume on. It was such a beautiful bottle. I remember it. It looked like it was straight out of a fairy tale. Then, she put it away and grabbed a small square bottle that was filled with a real dark liquid, and gave it one light spray onto her chest. I asked her why she did that. Because I thought the stuff in the pretty bottle was the only one she could possibly need." Meg began to shake her head. "No, no, Mom said, turning to look at me. Sort of like she was about to hand me a secret, revealing a magical truth. She said a woman's beauty, her essence is always brought forth tenfold by a deeper, magical scent. She said that all things need a certain passion that allows their beauty to expand with depth. And in that depth is where life is hidden."

Erin felt her eyes well up. Not knowing why, really. Just knowing that the words she heard were so beautiful they hurt.

"That was beautiful. You two must be very close. She sounds so like you."

"She's gone. She and my father were killed shortly after I turned ten," Meg said, folding her Luna bar wrapper into a small accordion fan.

"Oh, God, Meg. Christ. I'm sorry."

"What for? Gee, what's done is done. The universe is a cruel place sometimes," Meg said, trying to make light of what was the most venomous demon living within her soul.

"Sometimes the universe tries to make amends."

"Yeah. Well. It hasn't gotten around to calling my number yet . . ."

"Can you tell me more about her? If you can't, that's okay. I understand. The last thing I want to do is cause you pain. It's just that she sounds like someone I would have loved to know."

"Me, too," Meg said, her eyes becoming too blurry to see the ocean. "Well...she was an artist."

"Ah . . . the pieces of the puzzle begin to fall into place."

Meg cocked her head, not seeing the connection Erin felt so confident about.

"Let me think . . . ," Meg began, buying herself an extra moment to sort through the limited but weighty memories she had of her mother. "She was elegant. Yeah. Very elegant. I remember thinking she didn't fit in her own life. She sort of looked like she was just gliding through a movie set. A movie she wasn't perfectly cast for," Meg said, turning her head to notice the car pulling into the parking spot next to Erin's. "She wasn't happy, I don't think. I mean, she seemed happy, but not fulfilled. I guess that might be what I want to say."

Meg struggled, remembering how her mother smiled easily, but behind her smile were a million unhappy faces. Turning her head back toward the ocean, Meg brought to life memories she normally tried not to allow into her mind.

"I remember this one time, I was nine and we were stuck in the car for hours. We lived quite a ways away from any large city, so when it came time to get all my school clothes, it usually involved a full day out. A full day of shopping. And, out of the blue — you know, how kids sometimes do — I just turned to her and I said, 'Mom, how come, you seem sad so much.' I just launched this loaded torpedo out. And you know. She didn't even seem fazed," Meg chuckled.

Closing her eyes, Meg remembered the scene vividly. She could still see her mom casually wheeling their 1976 Continental Mark IV through the curvy roads that eventually led to Buffalo. Her mother's long chestnut colored hair was in a French twist that rested snuggly against her head. Large black sunglasses covered half of her face, leaving only her delicately shaped nose peeking out, and her vibrant, red lips that usually only held two shapes, a radiant smile that could light an entire room, or complete non-expression, like a porcelain doll, neither smiling nor frowning but instead suspended somewhere in between.

"Why wasn't she happy, Meg?" Erin asked.

"Well, I don't know. Not fully anyway. When I was young, I just watched. I just watched my parents. I watched my mom paint. I loved to watch her paint. It was like watching a bird dance gracefully above the trees. She used to mystify me," Meg stopped to push back her tears. "After I asked that question, Mom just sat there, staring at the road. Finally she took her long delicate finger, and ran it slowly down her neck. I could tell she wanted to make sure she got her words just right."

Erin casually shifted her eyes in Meg's direction, wanting to see how she was handling the memory. She saw that Meg's eyes were wet with tears but except for that she seemed almost calm.

"She said finally that people are like birds in a way. They're so busy flying around that sometimes, without even noticing, they swoop quite unintentionally into a cage. They fly there because the cage looks lovely — in fact at the time, the cage looks like the loveliest place on earth. But once inside, once they're settled and so convinced they like this new place, they take a deep breath and try to spread their wings, wanting to enjoy this new cage and their own wingspan at the same time. And it's then they find out that their wings don't fit. They're too big. So they pull them down onto their side. They tuck them in, saddened by the discovery. And with that, my mom looked at me and grinned. I remember it so well. Like it happened this morning. At the time, I didn't know what she was saying. I just thought it was beautiful. I liked the way she used her words. She painted pictures not just with her hands but with her words as well. And I thought she was radiant."

Erin felt a soft tear roll down her cheek, unable to control how deeply Meg's words had touched her.

"I remembered her words. Always. They were the soundtrack that played in my mind as I watched my mom gracefully and faithfully complete her days. I would watch as my dad struggled with my mom's uniqueness," Meg continued, drifting her memories onto her father, feeling her love for him well up inside of her stomach. "He was great. God. He was great. He was her opposite in so many ways. Making it even more ironic that the thing he struggled with the most, her uniqueness, was the very thing that had drawn him to her."

Meg remembered how her father always worked to keep up with her mother. Not that her mother was doing anything. She wasn't. But for every move her mother made, her father would try to counter it. His insecurities overcame him often, causing the real him to fade into the distance just to be replaced with a weaker, less attractive, less fun, less everything version. Allowing her mind to plunge deeper into the back recesses of her mind, Meg described to Erin a moment in time she felt changed her mother forever. Struggling with the words, struggling with the emotions that still hung thick to the memories, Meg described a painting her mother had completed.

"God, it was beautiful. It was the most beautiful painting I had ever seen. No, erase that, it was the most beautiful *thing* I had ever seen, and still is to this day," Meg said, unable to stop the tears flowing freely from her eyes. "The colors my mother used were unbelievable. I mean, you would think, colors are colors. Once you've seen them all, how surprised can you be? But I was. I remember walking in on her when she had just finished it. Her smile was radiant. I can still see her stepping back from her easel, as if the further away she stepped the more alive her painting would become. Her smile was . . . it was divine," Meg added, not wanting to break the rhythm of the memory. "She put her arm around me as we both stood there, staring at it. My mother's paintings always allowed for a great deal of interpretation. She used to say life was better when the door was left freely open." Meg paused, not sure if she could continue. "We, uh . . .we just stared at it. It was an oversized painting. My mother always painted on large canvases. It was this image of a man, not in so much detail as to be able to decipher his shape really, but you could easily make out his gracefulness. The man wasn't doing anything in particular in the painting, but something about the way his body was positioned, he . . . he seemed fluid, kind of reaching for something. Wanting something. The painting had a heavy feeling about it. I asked my Mom what she was going to name the painting. And she said, nothing. She wasn't going to name it anything, because it embodied too many things. Naming it would clip its wings."

"Do you have the painting? Can I see it?" Erin hoped she could stand, and look at what Meg's mother had created.

"Ha . . . well . . . ," Meg said, bitterness creeping into her voice. "You see, that . . . no. No, I don't. I remember how my father loved the painting, at first. Who wouldn't, it was magnificent. But in the days that followed, his feelings changed. Slowly he would drop little comments, things about men. He kept questioning her, and questioning her. Well, I could tell his questions, which without him saying so, were linked to this painting. It just . . . I don't know. It killed her inside. It killed her desire to express herself, because . . ."

Meg sat up straighter in her seat, not wanting to break down fully. Putting her hand straight in front of her, she tried to steer the painful memory to a close. "I was walking next to my Mom's studio a couple weeks after she finished the painting. And I saw her out of the corner of my eye as I made my way by the window that was next to the door. The door wasn't opened, something I noticed right away, because she never used to close the door. I stopped, and . . . I watched as she took a narrow, flat paint brush, and slowly moved its black paint across her painting. Line for line. Row for row. I just stood there. I watched. I watched until the entire painting was turned black."

Chapter 18

"Well, I don't like him. I think he's a dick," Stu said, not ashamed of his opinion of Devon.

"Something about him . . . yeah, there's just something," Bob agreed.

Sitting comfortably on the sofa at the studio, his foot resting against the coffee table in front of him, Jadon listened to the comments about Devon. He was enjoying the unanimous disdain he was hearing from the band. He sat relaxed, running his fingers through Bob's wavy, auburn fur.

Having grabbed Bobby out of Meg's car before it hardly reached a stop that morning, Chick ushered him quickly into the passenger seat of his BMW, wanting to make certain Bob would be at the studio all day. Bob's love was infectious. All who met him, loved him. Some, just wanting a pair of receptive, forgiving ears to talk into. Some, wanting the energy only a dog can provide. Energy that says, no matter how crazy life seems, it'll be okay. But Chick had a motive. Jadon lit up when Bob was around. Chick knew that whenever Bob was near, Jadon would once again resemble an intact, glued together person. Without Bob or Meg, he was empty. It was an emptiness that filled the space around Jadon wherever he went.

Amused with the negative judgments thrown around the room regarding Devon, Jadon kept cooing at Bob, all the while agreeing silently within himself at every sneer and snort of dislike.

"What the hell do you think of the guy?" Stu blurted, looking toward Jadon.

Slowly lifting his head, Jadon looked at Stu, then at the others who were waiting for his response.

Everyone except Chick was eager to hear Jadon's take on Devon. Knowing his feelings for Meg, they couldn't help but think he would have more to share on the subject.

"I'm sure Jadon feels like the rest of us. Ya know. So what, Devon's a creep," Chick interjected, trying to accomplish two things in the process. One, releasing Jadon from the obligation to answer. Two, prevent everyone from discussing the elephant in the room that had become a new member of the band since Jadon's eyes met Meg's.

"Wonder what Meg thinks of him?" Kofi said.

"I Googled the fucker last night," Stu grunted.

"Since when do you Google anything?" Bob asked.

"I'm on all the time. God, I'm on YouTube like a fly at a picnic, buzzing around, hoppin' from one video to the next. They got this one . . ."

"Well, what did you find out?" Bob interrupted.

"Well, it seems our little friend Devon Mitchell Hathaway is one rich motherfucker. Yeah, his family has big . . . *big* money," Stu said.

Jadon rolled his eyes, not happy with the first nugget of information Stu doled out.

"Let's see . . . ," Stu said, pulling a cigarette from the pack tucked in his pocket, taking the moment to mull over his findings from the other night, enjoying the suspense he was able to provide in the process. "His family owns the Hathaway Grand Hotels. They're all over the world."

Chick sighed with displeasure, "Those are *nice* hotels. Hate to tell ya but, uh, we're stayin' in one while in London."

"Well, that's just fuckin' special," Stu groaned before continuing. "He, uh, well, he's one of two sons. His older brother, Daniel or Douglas or David — it's a D name — races yachts. Our little friend Devon runs a publishing house. He's the big banana over there in London at their main office. He manages only a handful of authors, though. Some pretty big names."

"Like who?" Bob asked, eager for more information. "Meg? She's gotta be one of them."

"I didn't see her name."

"She writes under an alias. Erin told me." Chick smacked his gum, enthralled in the conversation.

"He's never been married. I read that. Uh . . . he's a vegetarian. I read that, too. He's only forty years old. Don't ask me what sign he is 'cuz I don't know." Stu swished his hand in the air, indicating to everyone he didn't have any more information to share.

Bob let out a disgusted snort. He was not pleased with Devon, not pleased with anything about him. "He's too fuckin' good lookin'. Hey, I'm not gay. But damn, that guy makes ya feel like a mutant when you stand next to him."

"That solves it. That's our plan. We can't stand next to the wanker," Chick said, pleased with his use of British slang.

"You haven't said one word since we started talkin' about our little friend," Stu said to Jadon, slapping him on the shoulder.

"He's not my fuckin' friend," Jadon said, running his fingers through Bob's fur.

"Well, he's Meg's, so . . . I guess we have to at least *act* nice," Chick recommended.

"Yeah. For Meg. Anything for Meggie Peggie," Bob said.

"Vince says we're clear for takeoff tomorrow," Chick said, not feeling the need to get too amped up over the tour they were about to take.

Except for one show already scheduled in London, planned well before the acoustic dates were mapped out and put into place, the whole tour was pretty low key. Something Chick was looking forward to; he was feeling worn from years of performing fast and hard.

"What the hell time is it, anyway?" Bob glanced over his shoulder at the clock on the microwave. "Oh, crap. I don't want to be late. I told Meg I would grab Bob and meet her at Dr. Banard's." He snuffed out his cigarette in the ash tray just as his cell phone rang. "Christ. Who the hell is calling me now? I've been sitting here all day, and not one call. I'm late, and walking out the door, and the phone rings."

The wheels in Jadon's mind began turning, "Hey, I got him," he said, pointing at Bobby. Grabbing onto his collar, Jadon ushered Bobby toward the door.

"You sure? I got Roach on the line. He wants to go over my equipment list one more time. You know where Dr. Banard's is? It's that vet clinic over on Ocean View."

Even though he didn't have the faintest idea where the clinic was, Jadon quickly nodded his head, anxious to make his getaway with Bob.

"Ya know, Jay. Why don't I . . . ," Chick began, turning to grab his cigarettes off the table behind him.

"You need to talk with Roach, run over the equipment list with him again before we head out," Stu interrupted, hoping to give Jadon the moment he needed to wiggle out the door with Bob.

"What? We've been over that list . . . like twenty times!"

"I heard Roach say something about not being sure which mike Henchel was planning on using. An MD 431 II or the other one you guys toyed around with, so he didn't pack any." Stu fired off rapidly, having just come up with a smooth lie.

"*What?* That's insane. What the . . . ? Henchel's been our sound tech for five years," Chick said, amazed at the horrific oversight.

"I mean, maybe I heard him wrong, but while Bob's got him on the line . . . ," Stu said calmly, trying to smooth things over. His objective wasn't to get Henchel in trouble, it was to allow Jadon a moment around Meg without Chick's domineering eyes glooming over him. Stu couldn't help it. Neither could the rest of them. They all wanted to see Jadon united with Meg. Watching Jadon fall apart because of a broken heart was slowly beginning to kill them all.

Meg paced in circles inside the waiting room of the veterinary clinic. It was after four o'clock, and Bob and Bobby should have already been there. Trying to distract her mind from watching the clock, Meg busied herself with the photos push-pinned to the cork board on the waiting room wall. Scattered across its surface were pictures of happy clients and patients: dog and cats of all sizes, with the occasional snake, rabbit, and bird thrown in for good measure.

All the while, in the pit of her stomach Meg could feel herself get nervous. Although having flown to Europe several times, she'd never done anything even remotely close to a tour before. She didn't have a clue what to expect. However, she did look forward to seeing Jadon daily. That idea she liked — and didn't like at the same time. Seeing him only reminded her that she couldn't have him.

"Arg," Meg sighed, letting out the only word that summed up how she felt.

"Hey," Jadon said, his eyes sparkling from the sunshine that spread across the waiting room floor as he opened the door to the clinic.

"Hey," Meg said, drawing the word out long.

Possessing a smile that wouldn't release its fixed position on his face, Jadon stared at Meg for a moment, "I . . . I thought I would run him over here."

Meg's mind went blank. "Thank you. You didn't . . ."

"I know. I wanted to."

"Ms. Scott," the assistant behind the counter called. "Ms. Scott."

Not wanting to release her gaze from Jadon's gentle face, Meg slowly turned her head in the direction of the noise she was beginning to recognize as a voice calling her name.

"Hmm? Yes. Yes. That's me. That . . . would be . . . me."

"Yes. I know. I need some information," the young man said slowly.

"Oh. Of course." Meg glanced over toward Jadon and Bob as she walked to the counter.

Jadon tapped his leg, motioning for Bob to stick close to him as he walked over to Meg at the counter.

"I don't think we have your address."

"3320 Mandalay Bay."

"Manda?" the young man asked, squinting at the computer screen in front of him.

"M-A-N-D-A-L-A-Y . . . Bay" Meg repeated slower this time.

"Mandalay?"

"Yeah, Bay. Mandalay Bay," Jadon repeated.

"Got it. Got your phone number. Good. We received Bob's records yesterday, so we're good there. Oh. Emergencies. Who should we list in case we can't reach you?"

"Well, um . . ." Meg paused.

"Jadon Hastings. J-A-D-O-N H-A-S-T-I-N-G-S. 310-555-0010. I'm kinda like Bob's dad. Make sure you get that in there, get that in your records," Jadon quickly said, pointing at the computer screen. Flipping his hair off his face, Jadon looked at Meg. "He doesn't already have a dad does he?"

"No . . . ," Meg said, her words still peculiarly slow. "No. We've always been a single parent household."

"You don't mind do you?"

"No. I can't think of anyone I would rather . . ."

"Bob?" Dr. Banard called, looking around the waiting room.

"I guess you better join us then," Meg motioned to Jadon.

"I guess I better," Jadon said, pleased with himself and the way he insinuated himself into the perfect situation. But the situation fit. He loved Meg. And he loved Bob. There was no place, he would rather be.

"Meg," Dr. Banard said, pressing his hands and stethoscope onto Bob's body while glancing back at his chart. "I have some reservations about such a lengthy trip for a dog Bob's age," he said while reading over Bob's chart. "Flying in general is tough on pets. We'll make sure you have enough medication to sedate him. But sedation has its drawbacks. It isn't good for a dog to go in and out of sedation."

"Well, we . . ." Jadon looked at Meg as he waved his finger between the two of them. "We, uh . . . and everyone that we're flying with. Well, Bob is going to be sitting with us. I mean . . . he shouldn't need to be put under. Unless he begins to flip out or something."

"That's right. We aren't flying the standard way. Well I mean, *we are* obviously on a plane," Meg laughed at herself. "It's a chartered plane, just for us and the crew, so Bob can move around freely."

"Yeah, we've used this type of plane before and there'll be plenty of room for him to sleep and walk around," Jadon added.

"I still have to warn you. This will be tough on him. As you're already well aware, Meg, his hips aren't in the best of shape. His medicine helps, but . . . Well, make sure he takes it easy. Any problems, call me. And I'll try to get you hooked up to a vet wherever you are," Dr. Banard said, giving Meg a detailed sheet of instructions, and the medicine Bob needed for the trip.

Stepping out of the clinic, Jadon knelt down to rub Bob's ears. Looking up at Meg, he noticed her eyes were filled with the same concern that filled his.

"He'll be fine. We'll make sure of it. All of us. He's one important dog," Jadon said, hoping to lighten her heavy heart.

"You're right. Think good thoughts. Think good thoughts. Allow only goodness," Meg repeated, trying to practice what she'd learned at the workshop with Erin and Flora.

Jadon stood up to look at Meg. "I was wondering, would you like to . . . maybe . . . ," he began, knowing he was venturing into dangerous territory. In the process, going against everything he promised Chick he would do. "I don't know if you would want . . . Not that I'm even supposed to. I just . . ."

Meg's body jolted from the sound of her cell phone ringing.

"Just ignore it," she said quickly.

"No, go ahead."

"Well, hell. I don't really want to . . . Just a sec, don't move," she said, grabbing her phone.

Jadon watched as Meg shook her head repeatedly at the voice on the other end of her phone. Taking the moment suddenly given to him, he answered the message Chick left on his phone earlier.

"I know. I plan to wrap it up. It's a novel, Dev. One doesn't just decide when to end it, and end it. It ends itself. You know, you've really been pushing on this lately. I have to go. We'll talk about this later," Meg said, ending her call.

"Are you okay?" Jadon asked, disappointed that he wouldn't be able to act on the plan he had earlier of asking Meg for a walk on the beach. Instead he needed to head back to the studio.

"Oh, Dev's just a real piece of work lately," Meg answered, shaking her head. "What, um . . . what did you want to ask me?"

"I . . . I guess . . . ," Jadon slowly started, "for the first time in my life, Meg, I'm going to do this right. I'm not going to fuck it up. I . . . I know, that doesn't make sense right now. I know. I . . . uh . . . just know that I think you're . . . beautiful. Know that. Know that I think you're beautiful," he whispered, walking slowly backward toward his car.

Watching him drive away, Meg stood stunned. Not sure what to make of the moment, knowing only that she wanted to bottle it and keep it forever.

Bob and Meg walked the shoreline, taking the moment to enjoy their last effortless attempt at exercise before they boarded the jet the next day for the European tour. Meg's mind and body hung warmly onto Jadon's words, replaying the moment over and over again in her mind.

"What do you think that meant?" Meg asked, looking down at Bob.

Breaking their stride only occasionally to gather stones, Meg and Bob marched farther down the beach than they'd ever gone before.

"Is it possible to let all these feelings boil under the surface without acting on them?" Meg questioned. "That's the plan, though. I've lived in my head most of my life, so . . . relatively speaking, this should be a piece of cake, right?" she asked, once again looking down at Bob, who this time looked up at her as they made a u-turn on the beach and headed back toward home. "As long as I don't do anything stupid, just keep the lid on, don't let any of the stuff that's bubbling inside get out. Oh, God, Mom, I wish you were here."

Taking a deep breath, Meg let her mind rewind itself, recalling the sadness that settled into their home after her mother turned her final painting to black. Meg couldn't help but feel a cloud had filled their home; like the grayish cloud that fills a tavern crowded with smokers. But, instead of smoke created from time spent with friends, this smoke was created by two souls, discontent with their journey.

Biting her lip, Meg winced, reliving the pain she felt watching her parents grow farther apart: apart from each other, and apart from themselves. Knowing she'd witnessed a slow death well before the tragic accident that had, in one quick instant, ended her parent's lives. Meg couldn't help but wonder, if somehow, in some way, her mother had secretly willed herself to be released from the bondage of an unfulfilled, smothering life. It was a thought that seemed entirely plausible, especially when she remembered how ethereal her mother had seemed. She was like a spirit that started to emerge into a physical shape, only to notice the pain inherent to living on earth. Then the spirit trying desperately to pull itself back, discovers suddenly and sadly that it's too late. There it remains, forever stuck between the two worlds.

It took years for Meg to come terms with her father. Remembering at a young age how her father's insecurities ruined not just him but the one he loved, her mother. Crippled by his fear of losing the life he had with her mother, he turned bitter. Meg shook her head slowly, looking out over the ocean and remembering walking in on her father as he rifled through her mother's belongings, reading her journal, looking through her letters. Instead of loving the butterfly her mother was, he wanted to catch it, push-pinning it to a cork board, keeping it frozen in place where he could always see it. He never once considered that by doing so he would cause this lovely butterfly to lose its beauty because it can no longer fly.

"God," Meg said bitterly, throwing the last gray stone she held in her hand out into the ocean. "I hope they're happy now."

Not caring what people would think, she let herself mourn her parents. Mourn the life that'd been extinguished. Mourn the time with her parents that'd been stolen from her. Not just the time after their death, but the time while they were alive, but were both too troubled to live.

Walking back from her mailbox, wiping her tears with the back of her hands, Meg stopped at the sight of a long, white box sitting at the foot of her front door.

"Hardly anyone knows I live here," Meg said, opening the envelope tucked under the red velvet ribbon tied around the box.

My Dear Musical Neighbor,

It pains me to tell you that I'll be away on business for some time. I didn't want you to think I didn't still long to be with you. Because I do. I do more than you will ever know. I tried to find flowers that reflect your beauty, with all of its depth and complexities. Although, please know I think you're far more beautiful than any flower could ever hope to be.

Also, know my heart will be only a shadow of itself while I'm away, without your music to complete and fulfill it. Once back, I hope we can meet. I would very much like that, if you would like that also. I hope you do.

Love ~ Your Piano Man

"My piano man," Meg said, spinning around to look at her neighbor's house. "This is amazing. Today has been, freaking amazing. I don't know what to think. This letter, it's so . . ." she paused, "beautiful."

Moving in slow motion, Meg picked up the box and drifted into her house. Setting it down on the large island sitting in the middle of her kitchen, she untied the ribbon. As if dismantling a bomb, she carefully eased the top off and placed it quietly on the counter. Pulling back the layers of tissue paper, she gently ran her fingers across the rainbow of roses that sat nestled inside.

Chapter 19

Jadon curled his leg beneath him in the plush leather chair, one of only four located in the front of the plane. He stared at Meg as she sat reclined in her chair. He watched as her fingers moved across the keyboard of her laptop in a blur, stopping only for a moment to stretch her left arm over her head or drop her right arm down to scratch Bob while he slept peacefully on the floor next to her. Noticing she was pointed away from him, Jadon couldn't help but wonder if he'd startled her with his sudden burst of honesty outside of the vet's office yesterday. For whatever reason, almost every moment of intimacy he was able to share with Meg was always startling, overwhelming or extreme.

Biting at the skin lying helplessly at the side of his nail, Jadon wondered what Meg thought of the flowers. He had spent an hour painstakingly selecting them, one at a time. He didn't care that Chick had asked to meet him at the studio immediately. He wanted to make sure Meg knew that her neighbor, the man she shared music with, thought she was wonderful. He also didn't want her worrying while she was away that she couldn't explain her absence — even though no explanation was necessary, as he would be gone, too. Wanting a way to calm his mind, Jadon whispered for Bobby to come over.

Opening one eye at the sound of his name, Bob began thumping his tail on the floor of the plane. Easing his heavy body from the floor, Bob made his way over to Jadon and pushed his head into the bear hug that was waiting for him.

"Hey, Meggie Peggie, whatcha' doin'? Stu asked.

"Killing someone," Meg answered without a hint of remorse.

As Meg felt pushed to finish her book, she tried to find closure for Elle and Jadon. A large part of her didn't want to let go of the life she had given them. Once done, once published, she forfeited her right to mess with their lives anymore. But as soon as Meg opened her eyes that morning, the ending of her novel downloaded itself into her mind. Knowing it was right, she surrendered. Now she sat on the plane headed for London, obediently tapping out the words streaming through her conscious mind.

"Whoa, that doesn't sound friendly," Stu said, peering over Meg's shoulder.

"Life isn't always friendly. Hey, hey, hey, no peeking."

"Fair enough. Just as long as I get to read it once it's done."

Satisfying Stu with a preoccupied nod of the head, she turned her attention back to her laptop and resumed work:

"Damn you, Simon. Damn you," Elle said repeatedly, as her trembling hands riffled through the banking records that arrived at her office that morning. "You lying bastard. Bastard!" She shouted, fumbling through her purse to find her cell phone. "Trish! Where the hell is my cell?" She screamed breathlessly to her assistant.

"It's right here, Ms. Shelton, right next to the cappuccino machine," Trish answered, handing Elle her cell phone.

"Oh, thank you. Thank you. Trish. I'm just . . . I have to talk to Jadon. I have to reach him in time," Elle said, waving Trish out of her office, as she punched repeatedly on her cell phone, bringing up Jadon's number. "Answer. Answer," she whispered.

Elle sat motionless, listening to the ring repeat itself as the call shot through space, within seconds arriving on Jadon's cell phone, which hung precariously onto his hip as he wiggled his way through the crowded streets of Havana.

"Elle?" Jadon answered, surprised to see her number flash across his phone. "Is that you?"

"Yes. It's me." Elle's words pleaded through the choppy connection that interrupted her every other word.

"I can't hear you Elle . . ."

"I . . . I just need to tell you. I know."

"Elle? Are you okay?"

"Come home. Come home," Elle repeated frantically. Suddenly the call was dropped.

"Damn!" she screamed, throwing her cell phone across her office.

Tossing her Valentino tote over her shoulder, Elle stormed out of her office, quickly making her way onto the street in front of her gallery. She signaled to the valet, taking in a deep breath of the cool New York air. Two minutes later she slid herself behind the wheel of her 1965 Ferrari. Elle made her way through the busy Manhattan traffic, then past the parking attendant that nodded while raising the gate that allowed her to enter the subterranean garage beneath her high-rise co-op building.

"I'll just give it a minute. Once he's settled at his hotel, he'll call me. That's it. That sounds good," Elle mumbled, trying to console herself while she scrambled through the various bottles lining her medicine cabinet, wanting only to have Jadon back in her arms, back in her bed, back in her life. She was suffering from the crippling pain of having forced him away, of not trusting him — him, her soul mate. Elle began to yell at herself, angry for all the damage she'd done.

Elle poured a handful of pills into her hand, convinced they would ease the immobilizing tension holding her body prisoner, and help silence the voices that dinned through her mind. Taking a big drink to wash down each pill, Elle slid herself onto her bed. Closing her eyes she pictured Jadon's face in her mind. Smiling gently, she looked into his eyes, seeing within them her heaven. Giving in to the magnetic pull that crept over her consciousness and body, Elle fell rapidly asleep. And in doing so, she gazed peacefully within her mind at the only face she wished to see.

"Elle!" Jadon yelled frantically, rushing through her bedroom door. His body was tired and his face revealed the days of travel he just endured trying to get back to her. "Elle!" he screamed trying to wake her. "Elle! Elle! No . . .No . . . " he cried, rocking her lifeless body in his arms.

"That's about right," Meg said, staring out the window.

It wasn't exactly how she wanted it, but she was on the right path. The end was drawing near, and she had a firm grasp on it. Meg knew the story's conclusion wouldn't bring a smile of satisfaction to her face, but it ended exactly as it needed – tragically.

"Hey, you," Erin said brightly, tossing her body into the chair across from Meg. "You look way too serious. I can't even imagine how hard it must be to write a novel."

Meg glanced over at Bob, finding him content, welded into Jadon's arms. She envied Bob so often lately. Without limits, without judgment, he was allowed unencumbered access to the most beautiful human being she'd ever seen.

"Sometimes it's not so fun," Meg answered, looking back at Erin.

"Why do you do it then?"

Meg thought about the question, realizing she had never considered doing anything else. It was safe.

"Tell me another story about your mother. Please?" Erin asked, wanting to hear something beautiful.

Looking out the window, Meg thought about Erin's request. For the first time in her life she was able to see the beauty in reliving the precious moments she had with her mother.

"I remember one time," Meg began, not breaking from her stare out the window, "she was sitting outside, rocking slowly in the chair swing, enjoying a cigarette. And she motioned for me to sit next to her, so of course I did. Moments with Mom always felt like I was sharing time with Cleopatra. She looked over and smiled at me as we pushed off harder on the porch. Thinking this was the time to dive into the labyrinth that I thought was my mom's mind, I asked why she used some of the weird colors she did in her paintings. She looked down at me as if she was trying to absorb more than my words."

Meg curled her knees up in front her, and continued. "My mother took a long drag on her cigarette, and exhaled slowly, sending a long brilliant swirl of smoke into the air. Then she said, 'There are no weird colors. All colors are beautiful in their own way. Sometimes it's only when we use the colors our eyes don't naturally gravitate to that we stumble upon a masterpiece. I want you to look at colors this way; each color is a shade of love. And life is at its fullest most divine state when all types of love are allowed to dance and play upon the canvas. Some colors are subtle, and help build up the painting. They are vitally needed because they help ground the other colors that rely and depend upon them to bring out their own beauty. Others blend the colors. Those colors have the ability to pull the other colors together. Ah, but then there are those certain colors that, once your eye falls upon them, your breath is quickly and dangerously stolen from your body. Those, those are the best colors. But all are important. Don't ever exclude a certain shade of love from your life; instead, experience it, treasure it for what it is, even if only for a season.'

"It's as if I can remember every word she said that day on the porch. My mind buzzed with her words. Often I would go and write them down, just to make sure I didn't forget them. I loved her words. I guess . . .," Meg paused, feeling the sadness weigh on her heart. "I guess that's why I love words so much. It was within words that I felt the closest to my mom."

"You should write a novel about your mother, Meg. Give her the life you think she would've loved. Fill it with exquisite passion, adventure, art and laughter."

"That is . . . one of the nicest things I have ever heard. You know, life has really swung radically out of control lately. Some of it, to be honest, I don't like. But other parts . . . Can I tell you something?"

"Like you have to ask?"

Eyeing the cabin of the plane suspiciously, Meg tried to decide if everyone was out of earshot before she began.

"Yesterday. Well, Jadon showed up at the vet's office with Bobby. He met me there, and he was . . . he was so . . . well, if you're not a dog lover, you might not fully understand the impact of what he did, but . . . he told the guy at the vet's office that he wanted to be the one to take care of Bob if something ever happened to me."

Erin pulled herself in closer, twirling her hair with her finger as she eased her eyes over in Jadon's direction, excited that he was still moving ahead with his feelings for Meg, even if behind the scenes.

"Okay, well, I know that probably doesn't have the impact on you that it did on me, but I have to tell you, Erin, it was like some man, the man of my dreams, wanting to adopt my son. Well, *man of my dreams* sounds a bit high school and, well, too strong . . . I mean . . . well . . . I'm not sure where that came from. So anyway," Meg sighed, not entirely happy she'd let that last comment slip out. "We're standing outside and he was going to ask me something. I don't know what. I don't have a clue. My phone rang. It was Devon. While I was trying to make Devon go away, I noticed Jadon was also on the phone. Then he had to go. But before he does, he tells me, well . . . that he wants me to know he thinks I'm beautiful. He said it and just stared at me. I didn't know what to do. I know what I want to do," Meg said rubbing nervously at her neck. "But, I can't. Then, well, I need to tell you something. I haven't told you about this because I didn't want you to think I was a nut job. But I've been having this rather unorthodox relationship with my neighbor."

Erin beamed with delight, enthralled by the deeply romantic moments Meg was sharing with her. Equally enthralled because she knew it was Jadon who was secretly serenading Meg.

Chapter 20

Throwing herself onto the oversized bed that commanded the luxurious space surrounding it, Meg quickly slid back off the bed and gently hoisted Bobby up so he too could enjoy the regal comforts of life at the Hathaway Grand London. As she walked around her suite, she noticed all the small details that had been carefully taken care of. Then she opened the small envelope propped against a rose on her bed and read the message written for her:

Darling Meg ~

I hope you find your room to be to your liking. I made sure everything was perfectly in place before your arrival. Please have dinner with me tonight? You may invite your friends as well. I look forward to seeing you.

Yours ~ Dev

Sliding across the shiny black bedspread, Meg looked Bob in the eyes. She felt blessed by his love and his companionship. She wrapped her arms around him and nuzzled her face into his warm welcoming neck, delighted in the fact that she could still smell Jadon. *What a wonderful world, to hold my best friend in my arms and smell the scent of the man I love*, Meg thought to herself.

"Brilliant," Devon said smoothly, his body leaning casually against the doorway separating Meg's bedroom from the rest of the suite. "What a beautiful sight."

"Oh!" Meg sat up abruptly, "I didn't even hear you," she said, trying to force a smile to settle onto her face.

"Darling, I do live across the hall. I'm glad you and your little friends made it safely." Devon said, a hint of bitterness in his voice. "Are they joining us for dinner?"

"Yes," Meg answered quickly, not having asked any of them yet, but hoping they would. "They have their show later tonight so . . ."

"Yes, but it's at the Ashby, and that's right across the way. I think it's good that I get to know the people presently taking over your life."

"No one is taking over anything," Meg shot back briskly, not enjoying his tone. "What time?" she added more gently. "And thank you for getting things ready for us, for Bob. It was really nice of you."

"Of course. I would do anything for you, and for Bob. How is my special young man? He looks tired. Perhaps he should stay with me as you hop from country to country."

"I don't want to be without him. The doctor thought it would be all right," Meg lied. "Anyway, the band adores him. He has won their hearts," she added, wanting to ease the tension that walked into the room with Devon.

"Fine. Well, then. I will meet you at four o'clock at Darby's. I already have a large table over looking Hyde Park reserved. I think your friends will find it very much to their liking," he said, bending down to give Meg a small kiss on the forehead.

Jadon sat patiently at Darby's between Bob and Stu, listening to their idle chatter. His heart was racing as he awaited Meg's appearance. He also couldn't help but feel apprehensive about Devon. According to Erin, Devon had a previous engagement for the evening, so once dinner was over, he would need to move on. It was a thought that brought Jadon great relief as he nervously slid his spoon back and forth on the white tablecloth in front of him. He wanted Meg all to himself, and if there was an opening anywhere in the evening allowing for it, he was going to seize it.

"Hey, there's Meggie," Chick pointed out, noticing Meg standing next to the maitre d' guarding the entryway of the restaurant.

Jadon's head and heart jumped quickly as he tried to catch a glimpse of her. Only when the maitre d' backed away and directed her to their table did she become visible.

Walking slowly toward their table in the small, red cocktail dress she had carefully chosen, Meg gave them her largest, welcoming smile. Looking at everyone sitting around the table, she knew without a doubt that she loved each and every one. Some in different ways than others — in different colors, as her mother would have put it — but each one was without question a different shade of love. Meg's eyes glazed over as the true meaning behind her mother's words, spoken to her as a child, finally manifested themselves in her own life.

"I really like you guys," Meg said, shaking her head lightly while sitting down.

Caught slightly off guard by her own abrupt honesty, Meg looked up and smiled at Jadon, to find his blue eyes held steady onto hers. *I could stare at him forever*, Meg thought.

"Wonderful. Looks like everyone is here," Devon said, suddenly appearing out of nowhere. "Meg . . . You're absolutely stunning. Just stunning."

Owning his words as he spoke them, Devon gladly took the last remaining seat, which was next to Meg.

"Thank you. Thank you, Devon," Meg smiled.

"And don't you look lovely, Devon," Erin interjected, trying to lighten the dampened mood that appeared once Devon arrived.

"Thank you, Erin. You're too kind." Devon raised his wine glass.

"This is a beautiful hotel, Devon. I'm sure you're very proud of it. Where do you live? Here in London?" Erin asked, trying to pass the time, also unable to suppress her curiosity.

Erin couldn't help herself. After all, Devon was debonair, charismatic and poised, but he also had a biting edge, a dangerous combination she couldn't help but notice.

"Oh, I live in the penthouse suite. Actually, I'm across the hall from Meg," Devon said, pointing a finger up in the air and shooting a quick glance at Jadon in the process.

Noticing Devon's repeated glare throughout dinner, Jadon made a point to never let his eyes back down; instead he chose to keep them held steady whenever they were met with Devon's. Whether Meg was aware of it or not, Jadon knew Devon was claiming ownership over her. The mere thought enraged him. Taking a long drink from his beer, Jadon wasn't interested with the dinner that sat artfully displayed in front of him. He just wanted to get out of there, preferably with Meg by his side.

"So, tell us how long have you known Meggie Peggie?" Stu asked, not concealing his mouth full of raw spinach.

"Meggie Peggie. How interesting. Well, we've been working together for ten years. It seems like just yesterday that we were introduced. Her writing was so striking; she was referred to me directly. And thus began our wonderful partnership," Devon said, savoring the history he shared with Meg. "Actually, I was the one who recommended Meg audition with you. Funny how things work out." His words failed to hide the regret in his voice.

"How so?" Chick asked abruptly, not liking the implied meanings tucked within Devon's tone, not to mention his words. "The way I see it," he said, wiping his mouth with his napkin before covering his plate, signaling to everyone dinner was officially over, "I think Meg would have found her way to us, one way or another. Fate. I like fate. It manipulates things, arranges and orchestrates circumstances, brings about things that are meant to be. Meg is family now. It just took some *funny* circumstances to bring her home."

"Well, I guess we need to be going," Meg said rising quickly from her seat. "They have a lot to prepare for. So, they need to have plenty of time. Thank you for arranging dinner. As always it was wonderful."

Devon leaned in and gave Meg a kiss on the forehead, while making certain his eyes landed in Jadon's direction.

"Wonderful. I'm glad you enjoyed it. I must beg off myself. Enjoy your evening, Meg."

Meg watched as Devon turned and walked gracefully out of the restaurant. Turning to Erin she said, "He's usually nicer. He hasn't been himself lately. I don't know what's going on with him. Don't forget, I need to let Bobby out one more time before we head over."

"Okay. See you guys. We'll be right over," Erin said, motioning for the rest of them to head across the street to the Ashby.

"So, you're way up here?" Erin said, giving Meg a grin as the elevator doors opened onto the floor of the penthouse suites.

"Yeah. Devon. He . . . he likes nice things. I guess he thought I would, too. Not that all the rooms aren't remarkable. Hell, I don't know why I'm up here," Meg added, shaking her head and running her card through the lock on the door.

"Uh, I think so that you're right across the hall from his suite," Erin said, swinging her finger back and forth.

"You have quite the imagination."

"Trust me. No imagination is needed. It's obvious. His motives are quite apparent. He has some serious feelings for you, Meg. I think it was felt across the table."

"Really? I don't know. I guess, he does sort of hint to it . . ."

"*Hint?*" Erin said incredulously. "Hint? You have to be frickin' kidding me? No, Meg. There isn't any hinting involved. For someone who creates legions of people within her mind, I'm amazed you can't read his intentions."

"I guess, well, I don't view him in that way, so . . . I mean, I know he's attracted to me. But, I don't feel the same. Not that he isn't attractive. He certainly is. He's just not . . . you know . . . ," Meg sighed.

"Not Jadon," Erin added nicely, knowing that Jadon, whether he knew it or not, held Meg's heart in his hands. And it was painfully obvious to everyone that Meg held his.

Following Erin, Meg walked into the Ashby, wiggling her way through the various doors leading backstage where the band was preparing for their show. It was the final show booked before Chick adopted the acoustic sound, which meant that Meg would be part of the audience instead of part of the band. Looking around, she noticed each of the band members was carrying out his pre-show ritual, noting in particular that all of them, regardless of what they were doing, puffed ardently on a cigarette. Erin made her way over to Chick who was perched on the windowsill, holding his cigarette out the window, his knee bouncing with energy soon to be released in front of thousands of screaming fans. Meg's eyes drifted around the room, looking for Jadon.

"Nuts," Meg mumbled.

"What was that?" Jadon asked, sliding his body alongside hers in the doorway.

Looking at Meg, Jadon gave her a warm, sexy smile that brightened his face with boyish charm.

"Did I say that out loud?"

"How's Bobby?" Jadon asked.

"He's good. He's zonked out on my bed."

"Maybe . . . um, after the show I could . . . ," Jadon whispered, looking over at Chick and Erin who were busy talking by the window, "come by and check on him. I mean . . . I would like to say goodnight. Maybe I could take him out for a walk before bed. Or something."

"I would, *he* would really love that."

"He's pretty important. I really love that guy," Jadon offered quietly, not dropping his gaze from Meg's.

"Well he's one lucky guy," Meg said, once again envying Bob.

Jadon didn't want to let go of the moment, but instead felt his desire for Meg obliterate his awareness to everything around him.

Leaning over he whispered softly into her ear, "You look beautiful tonight."

"What's *he doing?*" Chick said, startled by the sight of Jadon's face cradled next to Meg's ear. "Jesus!"

"Honey, leave him alone," Erin said, pulling on Chick's arm as he moved away from the window.

"Dude! Time to fly," Chick said, smacking his gum loudly in Jadon's ear as he walked briskly past him, followed by Bob, who nudged Jadon playfully away from Meg, and Stu, who gave her a wink as he walked by.

"Oh, I suppose that didn't look good," Meg said to Erin.

"Forget about it. Let's enjoy the show," Erin smiled.

Sitting at a small table situated off to the side of the main auditorium seating, Erin motioned for the bartender.

"What are you in the mood for? Want to shake it up a bit? Martinis?" Erin looked at Meg for the official go ahead.

Nodding her head, Meg didn't care what they drank. Instead she sat enthralled watching Chick march onto the stage with purposeful steps. She noticed how casually Bob and Stu ambled over to their guitars, and how Jadon walked behind his drum set, shifting and fidgeting before finally positioning himself comfortably. Because of the position of the table Erin had chosen, Meg could easily see him. When the lights flashed, she was given the chance to see his facial expressions as he moved his body demonstratively; giving each song its thundering beat.

Pulling the olive off the small plastic sword in her drink, Meg sat engrossed throughout the entire concert, her eyes breaking away from Jadon momentarily to watch as each musician poured himself out onto his instrument, all the while Chick commanding the space, making it clear to everyone that he owned the stage. Turning briefly to smile at Erin, Meg watched as Chick erupted into a scream that rocketed itself across the audience.

After a quick trip to the ladies room, Meg returned to their table to find Erin talking to a thin blond woman. The look on Erin's face showed she wasn't excited with the conversation. Sliding onto her seat, Meg quickly turned away from the twosome, wanting to catch every moment of the show.

"No, no, right after this we're heading out. I don't know where we're going!" Erin yelled, ensuring that her words would be heard over the volume of the music.

"Well. I'll be back," the young woman shouted before storming away.

Meg turned toward Erin, and raised her eyebrow. Erin waved a dismissive hand as if shooing away a pesky gnat, even though she wasn't sure how to handle the dismal situation that presented itself. Erin had told Chick that she and Meg would wait for them at this table, but now that the show had ended she wanted to leave immediately.

"Let's scoot," Erin said, hustling both of them away from the table and past the young woman who'd been at their table earlier.

"I thought we were going to hang out?" Meg questioned.

"I already called Roach and told him to tell the guys we would meet them over at the hotel. It makes more sense this way," Erin said hastily.

"Hold up, Speedy Gonzalez. Christ, a couple martinis and you're still Steady Eddie," Meg said, gliding quickly behind Erin as they made their way across the street to the hotel.

Flopping down on one of the ruby red chairs dotting the trendy after-hours bar next to the lobby of the hotel, Meg glanced around the dimly lit room and watched the people of all different shapes and sizes mingle and cavort.

"I think I need water," Meg declared, still suffering from the hurried trip they made from the Ashby.

"Two waters, two martinis," Erin said, tilting her head back so she could look the waiter in the eye as she ordered. "Very dry, straight up, with olives."

Jadon whizzed around the corner, stopping only for a second to scan the bar, looking for Meg and Erin. Waving her arm in the air, Erin motioned for Jadon to come over. Bob, Stu and Chick were following behind, trying to keep pace with Jadon's breakneck speed.

"Christ, Jay," Chick barked, throwing his pack of Lucky Strikes on the table, before plunking his body down next to Erin's, flustered by the race they just made through the lobby. "Swear we were being chased . . . ," he said, lighting up a cigarette.

Stu tried to catch his breath while asking the waiter for water, looking at Bob to see if he also wanted one. Neither Stu nor Bob, wanted to harp on Jadon for the sprint they just made down the halls and through the lobby. They didn't want to shine the light any brighter on his motives. Instead, they wanted to help him along, aiding him in his quest to steal a forbidden moment with Meg.

"Well . . . what do you think?" Jadon asked looking at Meg, then quickly looking back down at the beer bottle newly placed before him.

"You're amazing. You all are . . . amazing. It was an incredible show. I loved it. I just loved it. Every minute of it. Even when Erin was yelling at that girl. I was still mesmerized."

"What girl?" Chick asked.

"Oh, it was nothing," Erin answered, not wanting to discuss it in front of Meg.

Noticing Chick wasn't appeased by the answer, she leaned in and whispered into his ear.

"Ugh," Chick sighed, after hearing the visitor's name. He then turned his attention to Jadon. "If your chair was any closer to Meg's, you'd be sitting on top of her, Jay," he said, flipping the tip of his cigarette into the ashtray.

"I couldn't hear what she was saying," Jadon answered with mingled innocence and annoyance.

"Odd. I could hear her great and I'm two chairs away," Chick said, realizing Jadon was quickly losing sight of their agreement.

"Well. You just have fuckin' better ears than me," Jadon said.

"That was a great show," Stu said, slamming his quickly emptied beer bottle on the table.

"Great sound in that room," Bob added.

"You think Bobby's ready for his walk?" Jadon blurted out with too much enthusiasm, startling Stu who was lounging leisurely next to him.

Turning to look at Jadon, Meg found the same look in his eyes that was there earlier, the look that made her forget her name.

"Yes. Yes. I think he would love a walk right about now," Meg answered.

Jumping to his feet Jadon slowly pulled Meg's chair out from behind her, "I . . . um, promised to take Bobby for a walk before bed tonight," he announced, not bothering to look at the others, who were captivated by his captivation with Meg.

"Thank you for the night. I was in awe of each of you. You're all so talented. I'm so honored to be here with each of you," Meg said. The sincerity of her words floated across the table, landing in the hearts of everyone. "Goodnight."

"Goodnight, Meggie Peggie" Bob said, holding back the urge to give her a hug.

"Yeah, we think the same of you, Meggie. Don't ever forget that," Stu felt his chest tighten from Meg's sincerity.

"You get plenty of rest and give Bobby a hug for me," Chick sighed, not having the heart to interfere as he watched Jadon glide away from the table and slide his body next to Meg's as they made their way out of the bar.

"Thank you for helping me take care of Bob," Meg said, stepping onto the elevator.

"I . . . I would do anything for him," Jadon paused, "Oh yeah, you're on the top floor," he said, pushing the button marked with "P."

Meg leaned against the side of the elevator. Unable to look at anything except Jadon's soft blue eyes, she didn't know what to say. Instead, she wanted only to shrink the space that separated the two of them. She wanted to take her hands and hold his face, run her fingers through his hair, and place her lips against his. *Would that be so bad?* Meg questioned, forcing her eyes to look at the ceiling of the elevator. Unable to resist the temptation to do so, she looked back into Jadon's eyes.

Their gaze held so solid on the other, neither realized that the elevator doors had opened. Meg was oblivious to everything except Jadon. She watched as he slowly erased the space between the two of them. Swallowing hard, Meg felt Jadon's breath replace her own while he lingered in the delicate moment before losing himself completely within her lips. Feeling her body react to his lips as they softly touched hers, she lifted her hands, and ran her fingers up his neck, feeling his long blonde strands fall effortlessly between her fingers before burying her hands deep within his hair.

"Meg?" Devon's voice echoed through the elevator, causing both Jadon and Meg to jump.

"Where did *you* come from?" Jadon yelled, infuriated by the intrusion.

"Well, I live here," Devon bit back smoothly, clearing his throat to sound unaltered by the passionate embrace he had just broken up. "Meg, I was hoping to discuss with you your novel."

"My what?" Meg's mind flopped violently from the wicked turn of events. "I . . .uh . . we . . . were about to take Bob for a walk."

"I can see that. Well, I'm sure Jadon wouldn't mind doing that, would you?" Devon asked coolly. "It will only take a moment, Meg. Claire has some questions and I assured her I would cover them with you prior to your leaving tomorrow morning." Shifting his gaze toward Jadon, he added, "Surely *you* understand the importance of a deadline, Jadon."

Jadon felt his skin crawl as the words spilled like acid from Devon's mouth. "Anything for Meg," he said.

Looking at Jadon, Meg wanted a moment alone to apologize.

"Don't worry, Meg, I'll take care of Bob," Jadon added softly, snapping the dog's leash onto his collar and walking him out the door.

"What kind of issues?" Meg asked angrily, kicking off her heels as soon as they walked into her hotel suite.

"I'm sorry to have interrupted you. I had no idea . . ." Devon's voice subtly glazed with undertones that revealed a sinister side.

"I, I don't want to talk about it. Just tell me what Claire needs," Meg said, sitting on the edge of her bed.

"Fair enough," Devon offered smoothly, tossing Meg's novel down on the bed. "She has highlighted some things she feels are inconsistencies."

Meg stared at the printed pages, baffled by Devon's words, wanting to quickly wrap up things before Jadon returned, hoping to continue where they'd left off.

"Inconsistencies, all of these? I don't understand. This has never happened before," Meg said in disbelief, thumbing through the numerous flagged pages.

Calmly pouring himself a drink from the well-stocked bar, Devon slowly dropped each cube of ice into his glass, resolving to himself that before Meg whirled any further out of his grasp he was going to end Jadon's delusional desires once and for all.

Standing on the sidewalk bordering the Grand, Jadon surveyed the light dusting of snow that had settled onto its surface. His mind spun wildly from the moment he shared with Meg on the elevator, and his blood boiled from Devon's power trip obsession over her.

"He doesn't fucking own her," Jadon said, looking down at Bob for agreement.

Standing beside one of the trees lining the sidewalk, Jadon heard his name faintly in the distance. Not in the mood to make nice with anyone, he hesitated turning around until the voice grew too loud to ignore.

"Coco?" Jadon said slowly, shocked by the sight of her once he turned around.

He hated Coco. Despite her overt attempts to make him like her, Jadon couldn't stand the mere sight of her. Everything about her seemed plastic and fake, including her personality. In his opinion, her mind consisted of a ball of yarn, her face oddly resembled that of a Barbie doll, and her body was always dressed in a way to amplify her costly manufactured figure.

"Hey, Jay," Coco smiled, her face gushing at the sight of him.

Jadon stared in disbelief, shaking his head, wanting more than anything to make her go away. Once she had him in her sights though, she rarely left him alone.

"I was hoping to meet up with you guys after the show, but Erin, well, she's so jealous of me, she flew off the handle. Yelled, then stormed away. Some women are so insecure."

"Coco, I have to run. I have to take care of Bob," Jadon pointed at Bob, who was waiting patiently to get back inside the warm hotel.

"Oh. Well, I have your tour schedule. I had to beg Daddy to give it to me. Of course, he wouldn't so I had to sweet talk it out of Bernie. You remember how Bernie can't resist me?"

Jadon looked on in horror, wondering how he would ever make his escape. He also wondered if she would pop up at every show they were booked at while on tour. After all, money wasn't an issue for Coco. Her father owned the booking company the band used for all their overseas concerts.

"Hey, nice seeing you, Coco. I gotta run. I don't want Bob to get cold," Jadon said, darting away.

Scooting Bob through the brass revolving door that led to the lobby of the hotel, Jadon quickly ushered him onto the elevator. Standing outside Meg's hotel room, he waited patiently for her to open the door.

The door opened abruptly and standing there was Devon. "Oh, wonderful. I'll take it from here. Thank you, Jadon. Such a nice chap you are. Goodnight," Devon said, slamming shut the door once Bob was safely inside.

"Where is Jadon?" Meg asked, watching Bob trot over to her.

"I don't know. He seemed as though he were in a bit of a hurry. He asked if I would give you a message."

"Oh, and what was that?"

"Goodnight," Devon said, settling back onto the overstuffed chair next to Meg's bed, burying himself behind the many Post It notes adorning the pages of Meg's novel.

"Oh," Meg said, as a pang of hurt sprinkled across her skin. "I don't get it. I don't understand why Claire is having issues with these sections. Almost every section involving Jadon she said doesn't flow properly."

"Well, let's just breeze through them. If they still seem right to you, then that's how they'll remain. You know I support you one hundred percent." Devon smiled, content with the ease with which his efforts so easily foiled Jadon's plans of being alone with Meg. He knew, of course, that as soon as the band flew out the next morning she was open game again, a fact that ricocheted inside his mind as he slowly perused the pages of Meg's novel. But, if things went as planned, Meg would be safely back in his arms by the end of the tour, perhaps even before then.

"See this one? What the hell?" Meg yelled.

"Want a drink?" Devon offered, methodically dropping five more ice cubes into his glass.

"No. No, I don't. I want this to make sense. And it doesn't. I'm calling Claire. This flows; it's right. I can't change it. This is how this has to happen," Meg demanded, glancing at the clock.

"No, no, no, we don't need to bother Claire. It's hideously late," Devon pointed out, spinning around quickly and tossing Meg's cell phone onto the bed. "Put your head down dear. Just take a moment. Breathe."

Sliding herself higher onto the bed, Meg rested her head onto the pillow next to Bob. Closing her eyes for a moment, overtaken by the long day, it took only a few moments of silence before she felt her mind quickly slide to sleep. Her hand still holding a handful of pages that landed softly onto Bob's heavily breathing body.

Standing near the bed, Devon watched Meg sink deeper and deeper into a heavy slumber. Stooping forward he reached under the lamp, and pulled the chrome cord that dangled beneath its shade. Slipping off his loafers, he slid his body behind Meg's. He breathed in her delicate perfume, and ran his nose along her hair and down her neck. Pulling himself closer, he wrapped his arm around her waist, leaving his head gently rested next to hers, he granted himself the intoxicating moment of holding her in his arms again.

With only a few hours of rest, Devon opened his eyes softly. Smiling, he gently began kissing Meg's cheek.

"Soon, soon my beautiful Meg," he whispered, kissing Meg's ear, "you're not even going to remember his name."

Caught in the moment of desire, Devon ran his hand up Meg's sleeping body, touching the skin that lay bare revealed by her plunging neck line, before gliding his hand back down below her stomach.

"I love you," Devon whispered delicately. "Why can't you see that?"

"*What?* What time is it?" Meg jolted her body upright, searching the room wildly with her eyes. "What were you doing? Why are you . . . ?"

Startled by Meg's sudden resurrection from a dead sleep, Devon slipped his shoes back on, and ran his fingers through his hair, "Darling. Well, it seems we both were so tired . . ."

"Who could that be?" Meg interrupted, darting to the door and quickly opening it. "Erin! Wonderful. God, I need you."

"Devon?" Erin questioned.

"Wonderful to see you again, Erin, as always. Well. I must beg off, ladies," Devon said, grabbing his briefcase and suit jacket as he breezed out of Meg's suite.

"*Oh, God!*" Meg screamed, whipping her shoe across the room.

"Whoa, what the hell happened?"

"Devon. Devon happened," Meg answered angrily. "Undo my zipper?" She asked, backing herself up to Erin. "He just showed up, out of nowhere. *Nowhere*, last night, just when . . . *Ahhhh!*"

"Just when . . . ?"

"Well, when Jadon . . . he was . . . he was about to give me the most wonderful kiss. Oh, God. I don't think I've ever been so aware of every molecule in my body before, but at that moment Erin . . . ," Meg said, sticking her head out from behind the shower curtain. "I could have counted each one. I felt them all. Then *poof!* Devon shows up, rambling on about my novel. I finished my novel. It should be off getting ready for print. God."

"Ah. That explains the sad little blonde puppy dog sitting at our table this morning at breakfast."

Devon rested his briefcase on the mahogany table outside Jadon's hotel room. Popping it open, he grabbed the loose pages of Meg's novel and calmly smacked each one back into place. He aligned them carefully so that, once done, he had created a large white block of paper that he slid back into his briefcase before closing the lid.

"This should be quite enjoyable," Devon hummed to himself, knocking on Jadon's door.

Hoping it was Meg, Jadon opened the door before the knocks had a chance to silence themselves. Staring at Devon's tall, well composed body leaning against the door frame of his hotel room, Jadon felt his body ignite. He also couldn't help but notice how pleased Devon looked with himself as he whisked uninvited into his room.

"You might want to close that," Devon suggested, moving his eyes toward the door still held open by Jadon's frozen hand.

Jadon walked over to the plush green chair sitting alone in the corner of the room, kept company only by a small round mahogany table tucked neatly to its side. Drawing a cigarette from its pack, he casually lit it before propping his body back into the chair, pushing one foot against the small table.

"No need to look at me like that. I'm not the enemy here, regardless of what you might think. I'm actually here to help you. Consider yourself quite fortunate," Devon rolled the words from his mouth like a long red carpet. "I thought perhaps I should clue you in on a little tidbit, one I believe you will find most interesting. You see, it occurred to me that it'd be a shame really if you weren't told, lest you be hurt by allowing yourself to dream too big." His words dripped with poison as he continued. "Meg, most likely hasn't shared with you . . . ," Devon paused for a moment, soaking in the drama of what he was about to say. "Quite simply, she is using you. You see you are, whether you're aware of it or not, providing her with a great deal of fodder for her latest novel."

Relishing the moment, Devon threw Meg's novel down onto the table with an incredible thud.

"Read it. I think you'll find it quite fascinating. Oh, don't worry," he added with a twinkle in his eyes. "You don't have to read the entire thing. The main portions involving you have been helpfully flagged. That should make it quite easy," Devon said spitefully, snapping his briefcase closed, and slowly turning to walk out of Jadon's hotel room.

Stopping suddenly, Devon couldn't resist the opportunity to release more of the acid that burned inside of him for Jadon.

"You know, you *really* didn't think a woman like Meg would be interested in you, did you? She is . . . she is far beyond anything you and your simple little mind can comprehend, really. Think about it for a moment. You're a little monkey that beats on his drum all day. You and your little friends are . . . silly really. So if I ever see you trying to place your grungy lips on Meg's again, I will destroy you. Quite happily, I might add."

Pleased with himself, Devon offered a friendly nod in Jadon's direction before gliding gracefully out the door.

Bob barked as soon as the elevator doors opened, zeroing in on Stu and Bob, both of whom were on their knees, arms open wide, waiting for him to skitter across the slippery tiled lobby towards them.

Meg looked around for Jadon, wanting a moment with him before they were shoved in the confines of the chartered plane.

"Looks like almost everyone is here," Chick sighed, eager for his band to leave Devon's hotel.

Devon eased himself over to Meg and the band while they stood near the entrance to the lobby waiting for their car to take them to the airport.

"Wonderful, the gang's all here." Devon smiled with a twinkle in his eye reserved for Meg.

"Yeah. We need to go. Hey. I can't find my book, did you . . ."

"Yes. Yes, dear. I was thinking, and as always, you're right. I don't want to change *anything*. It's *perfect*. I must run. You enjoy yourself." Leaning over, Devon gave Meg an unexpected kiss on the lips. Then turning quickly, he made a point to push Jadon aside with the strong brush of his arm as he walked away.

"What has gotten into him lately? He's really off his rocker," Meg joked, trying to find a happier place to put the sinking feeling she had in her stomach regarding him.

Standing by himself, Jadon kept his hands firmly shoved in his pockets, the backpack carrying Meg's novel resting heavily over his shoulder while Devon's words circulated inside his mind. He didn't want to read Meg's novel. He didn't want to find any truth behind the words Devon so easily threw at him. But the one memory that kept stopping dead center in the middle of his mind was of the morning after the video shoot, when he had listened while Meg poured her heart out to Bobby below his balcony. Although he was able to hear only bits and pieces, the words that stuck like sharp thorns were, *"I couldn't have found a better person for my novel."*

Chapter 21

Standing on the stage of the Monocle Theatre, Meg felt the hurried pace of doing a sound check and preparing for that night's performance buzz through her body. But that wasn't what had her upset. As often as she tried to make eye contact with Jadon during their short flight to Copenhagen from London that morning, she was never successful. It was a realization that made her tremble softly.

What the hell is going on? Meg wondered, grabbing her violin from its case. Within the course of a day, the energy surrounding Jadon changed, turning him cold and distant. It was a change that caused Meg's mind to twist with confusion and anger.

"This is it, isn't it? You allow yourself to feel something wonderful, then it's suddenly yanked away. God. This world . . . It has such a cruel sense of humor," Meg said coldly under her breath.

"How are you doing?" Erin asked, walking up behind Meg.

Seeing the obvious change between the two, Erin watched as Meg struggled to make sense out of Jadon's sudden withdrawal. Erin had never seen him crawl so far back into a corner. He wasn't talking with anyone. His eyes were filled with pain and sadness, while his face wore no expression at all. It was apparent he was suffering, but she had no idea why. But in the back of her mind something made her wonder if Devon was at the base of it.

"I'm great. Just great," Meg answered after a long pause.

"Of course you are," Erin sighed, knowing Meg was quickly retreating back into her corner, too. Backing away from Meg, Erin walked suspiciously over to Jadon, who stared blankly at her as she approached him.

"I don't want to fuckin' talk about it, Erin," Jadon shot out quickly.

"Talk about what?"

"Don't mess with me. I'm not doing so great at the moment. So, just leave me alone," Jadon said as he shook his head slowly, thinking about the words he saw beautifully written in Meg's novel. He saw how she had taken the most wonderful, passionate moments of his life thus far and crafted them into a story. *A story*, he mused. *A fucking story.* Holding back the tears that kept forcing their way into his eyes, Jadon tried to grow angrier with Meg. He was angry that she would use him, angry that she would take his feelings for her and scribble them across the pages of her book. Hardly able to breath after reading section after section of her novel, Jadon tossed it in the trash once they walked off the plane in Copenhagen. He didn't want to ever see the words again. Forbidding himself to look at her, he kept his eyes pulled away.

If Love were allowed to be described in only two words, without question these words would be Beauty and Tragedy. My mother was the embodiment of those two very telling words. Her life, her soul, her mind and all that she created were both beautiful and tragic.

This is the journey of a beautiful bird that flew radiantly above the ground, swooping down occasionally to gather the essence of others and to decide where she wanted to travel next. Her wings were iridescent blue, changing color as she shifted her body through the air. My mother was that bird, that beautiful bird that few get the privilege of watching fly. She was at her most divine when she flew freely in the sky. She was happy then. And isn't that the purpose for owning wings? To fly?

"Come on, Meggie Peggie," Bob begged, tapping on Meg's shoulder while she hammered hard on her laptop in the hotel lobby after the show. "Come on, it's almost Christmas. You just finished your first show on tour. All is good. We're all getting together up in my room. We're gonna relax a bit. Flo is there. She asked where you were. I told her you've had your nose stuck in your laptop since we got back from the theater."

"I'm. . ." Meg wiped under her eyes with the back of her hand. "I don't want to be a wet blanket. I'm just not myself."

"Well, we're all not ourselves sometimes. But that's what family is for. We force you to remember," Bob wiped away the tear that cascaded down Meg's cheek. "Remember that there are people who love you. And always will, even when you aren't yourself."

Meg bit her lip, not wanting to break down any more than she already was. "You're pretty good," she smiled softly, giving Bob a soft look through blurry eyes.

"Well, the troupe sent me. They said I can't come back until I convince you to come with me. Come on . . . and, if you decide you need a strong handsome ear, well, I've got two, so I'm well prepared and always available," Bob said, throwing an arm around Meg's shoulder, ushering her toward the elevator and up to his room.

"*Yeah!*" Stu shouted as Meg walked through the door. "Where the hell have ya been?" he grumbled, not pleased with the cold chill sweeping through the air lately. Convinced Devon was at the root of it, Stu wanted to pummel him. Or worse.

Meg waved at Flora, who sat on the arm of the sofa that was nestled in the corner of the room.

"There you are," Erin chimed. "I was starting to get worried. I really am getting upset. I just don't care for how things . . ."

"I took your advice and started that book you suggested I write."

Throwing her arms around Meg, Erin hugged her tight, knowing that Meg was starting down a very painful but necessary road.

Looking at Jadon, Erin couldn't help but wonder again why he had instantly pulled away from Meg. Within the course of two days he changed from excited and hopeful to slowly dying inside, a change that was clearly visible from the outside. Grabbing Meg's hand, Erin pulled her over to the love seat. A coffee table sat between it and the sofa that held Flora, Kofi, Bob, furry Bob and Stu. Chick sat reclined in a chair next to the love seat. Jadon's chair was next to his, but slightly removed.

"We need to fuckin' cleanse the air in the room," Stu said as he took a hit off the thick joint held between his thumb and finger.

"Yeah, God. Ain't that the truth," Bob agreed, rolling his eyes as he took the joint from Stu's hand.

"I couldn't agree more," Chick said. "Things have gotten a bit heavy." He turned and looked at Jadon.

After taking a hit, Meg handed the joint to Flora, who accepted it with a warm smile while looking deep into Meg's eyes. Meg didn't care. There wasn't anything left in there to see. All her delusions, all her fantasies, were just that. Things to write about. Not real. *Life sucks*, Meg mused while holding her breath, *and if Flora sees that inside of me, so be it.*

Shortly after the second hit, Meg felt her body creep subtly into numbness. Not the normal wave of numbness she was use to when drinking. This was different. Her mind felt calm but quite coherent.

"We need some fuckin' snacks," Stu grumbled, wondering if they had remembered to bring any from the theater.

"Doritos. That would be good. We got any?" Bob shot a look over to Erin, who didn't know and showed it by raising both her palms. "Chick?"

"Yeah. I think we grabbed some stuff," Chick said, rooting through the duffel bag full of loot. "Pirates' booty. Doritos . . . let's see . . . where'd we get these?" Chick eyed the box of Goldfish crackers.

"Yeah, throw me the fish!" Erin yelled, swinging her arms over her head.

"I like Cheez-Its better," Stu moaned.

"Goldfish are better than Cheez-Its. Hands down," Bob stated flatly while slowly letting the smoke empty from his lungs.

"No fuckin' way," Stu argued.

"Yes way," Bob stretched his words as he said them.

"I like Goldfish," Meg offered softly, staring at the little, orange, puffy fish-shaped cracker she held between her fingers.

"What?" Stu barked.

"These smile at me," Meg said, pointing to the tiny smile baked into the face of the fish. "Smiles are handy sometimes. Sustenance that smiles," she said, feeling too philosophical even for her own reflective mind.

Sitting quietly, Meg was no longer able to silence the question begging to be asked. "Who do you think . . . ?" She paused, needing the extra minute to pull the words from the shelves in her mind. "Who decided some cans don't need to be stackable?"

Hearing the question, the room fell under the silence of deep consideration.

"Those damn cans. I know what you're talkin' about," Stu moaned. "It's like, you buy some soup. You get home. You stack them neatly in the cupboard. Done. All is good. Then next time, without realizing it. You buy these damn cans that don't stack. So where the hell are they supposed to go?"

"So, Meg, were you able to finish your book? I know you were working on it," Flora asked, wanting to bring some simple facts to the light. Facts she felt certain needed to be revealed.

Within seconds of seeing Jadon walking into the room, Flora sensed his struggle. She saw his intense love for Meg, but also that it was buried under something. She was able to grab on to only bits and pieces, especially as he made an obvious point not to look her in the eye. Eyes were always the easiest portal to see the soul's torment, but not the only one.

"Yup. Off to the presses!" Meg answered, taking another hit from the joint that had been handed to her.

"Did it turn out as you had hoped?"

"It, it . . . turned out as it needed to," Meg said.

"What does that mean?" Bob asked.

"Oh . . . well . . . I hardly know how a book will end when I begin it. I just begin. I jump, and hope to God I land in one piece."

"That sounds cool. How do you know what to write about?" Bob continued, handing the roach clip to Jadon, who was sitting up in his seat, leaning forward to hear Meg's every word, hoping somewhere within them she would be able to undo what she had done to him.

"Ha!" Meg laughed. "This stuff isn't going to be interesting to you guys, trust me."

"I want to know. I really want to know," Chick said, hoping it would coax Meg out of the reclusive hole she recently jumped into.

"Okay. Well, I . . . uh . . . I just have a blip of a thought. An image. I close my eyes, I listen to music, I stare out the window, and let my fingers flow across the keyboard. Sometimes I try to write something different than what is naturally flowing out of me, and I can't. It screams to be removed from the page."

"So people like your books?" Stu asked, already knowing the answer.

"They seem to."

"You write under an alias, why is that, sweetheart?" Flora asked.

"Well. I guess. I . . . ," Meg paused, trying to find words that summed up a multitude of insecurities. "I guess I don't want anyone to know it's me. I don't want them to connect the dots and judge me. Yeah. I don't want to be judged. I don't want people reading my words, which come from someplace buried deep inside, and decide they don't like it."

Jadon closed his eyes, trying to remember that Meg used him, used his love for her, used it for inspiration for her book. Instead, he wanted to go to her. He wanted to hold her. He wanted to wipe away her tears, and let her know he liked everything about her.

"Hey, Flora just read a great book. Maybe you know the author?" Kofi asked, excited at the possibility. "What was the name of it Flo?"

"*Safe People*," Flora answered, already knowing there was an undeniable connection between the book and Meg.

"Me. That's me," Meg answered, staring at a dot on the table in front of her.

"Oh, my God, Meg, I can't believe that you never told me before. That book is like huge!" Erin shrieked, causing Chick to wince. "You never told me. And now you spit it out, like it's nothing. It's huge."

"I'm sufficiently stoned, Erin. And I'm tired. I'm tired of many, many things currently," Meg said, reaching forward to see if the dot on the table was movable.

"It's a beautiful story, Meg. Why not publish it under your own name?" Flora asked.

"It's that scared thing. Scared. Scared. Scared. A lot of people don't like that book, might I add," Meg sighed.

"You know," Chick interjected, "a lot a people don't like the songs I write, but I just have to keep writing them. I'll die if I don't. Fuck anyone who doesn't like them. Who cares?"

"Yeah. You're right. Just fuck it. Just fuck everyone who doesn't like me." Meg shot a glance in Jadon's direction. "I'm just me. Flaws and all. Even when I don't know what the flaw is."

"Mmm . . . you know what I'm in the mood for?" Flora said.

"Nooo!" Chick smiled, squirming in his seat. "Don't say it!"

"And you're first up. Get your handsome booty over here," Flora said, motioning for him to sit across the table from her.

"She fuckin' freaks me out with this shit. I love it, though. I can't help it. It's addictive, too," Chick said, smacking his gum nervously, taking the seat across from Flora.

"Shhh," Flora whispered, causing Chick to become instantly still.

Meg sat frozen, watching how willing Chick was to subject himself to Flora's gift. After all, he was the one who always seemed most put off by Flora's abilities. And now here he was, fully trusting and happy, his body relaxed while Flora held his hands in her own.

Meg's eyes scanned Flora's face and watched as she closed her eyes and nodded her head, as if gathering information from some faraway place. Flora smirked softly, then nodded again.

"Everyone will be okay. It won't be easy. There will be a storm, and it will be scary," Flora continued. "Just know that it will be okay. All hearts will be whole in the end, and happy." Flora released Chick's hands.

Chick sat motionless and stared at Flora like a small child.

"I don't know if I like the sound of that, Flo . . . ," Chick said slowly.

"Remember, everything will end well," Flora said. "Promise you won't forget that." She rubbed her fingers across his fingers. "If it were otherwise, I would tell you," she added, looking him directly in the eye.

"Looks like I'm not winning the lottery today, folks," Chick said, trying to chuckle.

"Erin," Flora said, extending her hand in her direction.

Meg watched as Flora settled into the same routine, closing her eyes as she held Erin's hands in her hands. Her head nodded again, and then she smiled. Evidently something seemed positive, or at least from Meg's perspective.

"You're sunshine, my dear," Flora said in a warm tone. "Whenever I read your energy, I see the sun. Yes. Yes. Keep pursuing your suspicions. Your answers are buried within your desire to find the truth. You will find those answers. Keep looking. They are right in front of you. You are on the right path." Finished, she released Erin's hands and motioned for Jadon.

Meg sat quietly, bewildered by the puzzling sentences that didn't seem to reveal much of anything. Meg watched as Erin gave Flora a relieved smile, then glanced at Jadon.

"Hey, babe, you're not suspicious of me, are you?" Chick said, looking up at Erin as she walked back to her seat next to him. "Jay, get your ass up there. You're not wondering about me, are you, babe?" Chick repeated, looking at Erin who sat confidently back in her seat, cherishing the words Flora shared with her.

Chick again looked at Jadon, expecting him to come forward.

"Nah, I'm good," Jadon said, lighting a cigarette.

"Boo!" Bob and Stu bellowed, waking Bobby who was sleeping peacefully between the two of them.

"Don't be a fuckin' chicken. Get up there," Stu said.

Reluctantly Jadon walked over to Flora. Unenthused, he sat down across from her, and tossed his hands on the table. Flora picked up Jadon's nervous hands and began to massage his fingers, trying to relax the energy that surrounded them. Pulling suddenly on his hands, Flora was able to snap Jadon out of his purposeful avoidance of her eyes. Once locked on, Flora stared deeply.

Meg turned her eyes away briefly to scan the room. Everyone, including furry Bob, was watching Flora and Jadon. Flora, sat motionless, her eyes now closed. Her head was not nodding, and her mouth was not smiling.

"I can't change what you're about to do," Flora said, her voice unwavering. "I would if I could. But it's your journey, and you are not choosing wisely."

"What the fuck?" Jadon said quietly, looking uncomfortably around the room.

"You will journey through a dangerous storm," Flora continued, her words hitting Jadon hard as she spoke them. "The storm will come. I don't see you avoiding it. No. Instead, you're suspended within its turbulent forces. Yes."

Flora let out a sad sigh that caused everyone to sit straighter in their seats. "I can't tell you the way. You'll decide this on your own. You'll decide wrong before you decide right. You're not alone in this storm." Flora opened her eyes, but didn't release her grip on Jadon's hands, instead staring at him for a moment longer. Flora added, "I don't know how the storm will end exactly, but it will end. Please. Please don't act impulsively."

Everyone remained silent, feeling the overall theme of the readings hover above them like a dense cloud. Jadon wanted to walk out; he wanted to clear his head, but he wanted to hear Meg's reading. He wanted to know what was going on inside of her heart — not that he would likely understand it once he heard it, anyway. As far as he was concerned, Flora spoke in another language. He hardly ever understood what she was trying to say when she gave readings.

"Meg," Flora said, extending her hand in Meg's direction.

Wiping her palms on her jeans, Meg slid off the love seat and sat across from Flora. Meg felt her hands get hot once Flora cradled them in her own. And as Flora moved her fingers across Meg's palms, she felt the heat in her hands move up her arms, sweeping gently throughout her body. Meg tried not to feel nervous. When Flora closed her eyes, Meg glanced across the room, noticing everyone firmly welded in their place, waiting and watching.

Flora nodded. Then slowly shook her head sideways. *Oh, God, that can't be good*, Meg thought. She stiffened when she felt Flora's grasp tighten. Meg watched while Flora tilted her head slowly to the right, smiled, then nodded again. She couldn't help but notice it was taking longer for Flora to read her than it took for her to read anyone else.

"Hello, sweetness," Flora said, her voice flowing like a plush velvet ribbon.

Meg sat stunned. Her widened eyes flooded instantly with tears. No one called her sweetness except her mother.

"Ch, ch, ch . . . ," Flora repeated in a luxurious whisper the sounds Meg's mother spoke to calm her when she was a small child. "Don't worry, sweetness. You're doing fine." Flora's voice churned through everyone in the room. "You're just getting a little ahead of yourself." She paused, nodding her head. "Ch, ch, ch . . .

it's all right . . . I'm here. Don't run from your darkness, my dear. Within that very darkness is the need for light. Beckoning and summoning it forth, to cast its bright glow upon the world only because there is a need, a place for it to go and explore. Little girl, don't be afraid to fly even when it hurts. Fly high . . . you won't fall. Your wings are too big to fail."

Slowly Flora opened her eyes and gazed at Meg. Holding Meg's hands for a moment longer, she finally released them.

Everyone sat in shock, frozen to their seats, their minds rocked by the magnitude of what just happened.

"Meg, hey . . . want some water . . . or maybe . . . uh . . ." Chick searched for a way to comfort her while she sat motionless in her chair, her mother's words etched into her mind.

Bob barked softly, jumping off the sofa and pushing his body into Meg's legs. Sliding down onto the floor, Meg hugged him tightly, wrapping her arms around his loving body. No one wanted to move, no one wanted to make any noise that would interrupt Meg as she sobbed, holding Bob snugly in her arms, pulling her face away for a moment to gaze into his loving eyes.

"I love you. Oh, I love you," Meg kissed his forehead before pulling herself onto her feet. "I need to go... be alone," she said, graciously making her way to the door with Bob.

Before opening the door, Meg turned slowly and looked at everyone in the room. She let her eyes fall on each distraught face, taking in their energy.

"Thank you. You most likely don't know how badly I needed to hear those words, and they never would have come to me if it weren't for you. All of you, I love you," Meg tapped her heart. "Very much."

Meg cracked open the window in her hotel room. Curling up on the windowsill, she let the frigid air sting at her skin, reminding her that she was still alive. Hugging her legs tightly to her chest, she listened repeatedly to her mother's words inside her mind.

"Oh, Mom," Meg whispered. "Help me fly. Please help me fly. Because I don't know what I'm doing."

Meg slid off the windowsill, grabbed her laptop and flipped it open, bringing it slowly out of its hibernation; her words appeared on the screen in front of her.

"If you weren't able to fly, Mom, how can I ever hope to?" Meg whispered, striking the keys on the keyboard.

Madelyne Maye Winchester walked gracefully and confidently into the small upstate New York town, her steps flowing beneath her as if she were an angel hovering above the ground. Her captivating smile dusted across the faces of the people who stopped to look. All were startled by her beauty. Glancing to her side, she noticed the young man stopping to offer her a nervous wave. Taken by his bright smile and vibrant eyes, Madelyne delicately returned the gesture.

Meg dug deep into her memories, trying to give her mother the life she had wanted. She tried to find the words that allowed her mother to spread her wings, twirling together both fiction and nonfiction. Creating a world where her mother bypassed the cage, and instead flew effortlessly next to it, landing on a tree branch, where she was able to look inside the cage but not be a prisoner of it.

"Here you go, Mom," Meg whispered. "Here you go. If I can watch you fly, maybe then I'll figure out how to do it, too."

Meg's fingers became a blur as they moved across her keyboard. She didn't want to break stride even to wipe her face; instead, she let the tears fall onto the head of Bobby, stretched across her lap.

Leaning against the door to Meg's hotel room, Jadon slowly slid his body down onto the floor. He so wanted to go to her, to kiss her softly, and to tell her how much he loved her. But he felt confused, far too confused to do anything. Meg was confusing, and Jadon now wished he had never read her novel. But he had, and he didn't know where to put everything that sat in his mind.

Erin rounded the corner of the hallway, heading toward Meg's room. She wanted to throw her arms around Meg and let her know everyone loved her. She stopped quickly when she saw Jadon sitting at the foot of Meg's door. Stepping back, Erin peered around the corner to watch him. Erin wanted desperately to put the puzzle pieces together. She watched as Jadon let his head rest against her door, his hands covering his face for a moment, before dropping his head down onto his knees. Erin wanted to scream at him; she wanted to throw him inside Meg's hotel room and lock the door, forcing him to work through whatever it was he was struggling with. But more than anything, Erin felt her heart breaking along with his. Wanting to allow him his time near Meg, Erin turned and walked back to her room.

Chapter 22

"Jesus Christ," Chick said, still suffering from the haunting effects from the previous night. Not able to move past the sheer size and gravity of everything, Chick stayed awake all night trying to make sense of everything Flora said. "Storm, what storm?" he asked Erin while tediously spreading a thin layer of Havarti cheese across his toast. "Christ, we arrange this low-key tour where we can hang out a little, not live on catered crap served in some back room hidden behind a stage . . . and here we are . . . *fucked*. We're all freaked out and miserable. This is the stuff I was worried about."

Chick continued grumbling until he noticed Jadon making his way toward their table.

"Are you finally going to eat?" Erin said, trying to get him to take the sweet roll from her hand.

Shaking his head no, Jadon leaned back in his chair, and looked around.

"She still hasn't come down," Stu offered. "Bob stopped by her room earlier to ask if he could take Bobby for a walk."

Stu nudged Bob to continue the story, noticing Jadon's eyes locked onto his as soon as he started to offer more information. Finishing his coffee with one big swig, Bob wiped his mouth with his napkin before continuing with the update.

"Yeah. I don't think she slept a wink. Jesus. She looked tired." Bob looked directly at Jadon. "All this fuckin' turmoil isn't good for

Bob or Meg . . . or anyone. Anyway, I noticed her bed hadn't been slept in, her laptop was out. I think she was writing all night. She looked beautiful. Tired, but beautiful. Amazing, considering everything she went through. You should have been there, Jay," Bob said, aiming his words carefully.

Feeling the direct hit, Jadon shook his head, taking a long drag off his cigarette. "I don't think Meg would have noticed if I was."

It was a statement that shocked everyone sitting at the table. Erin looked at Jadon, her mind taking a quick flip, trying to figure out what magical spell he was under.

"What the fuck does that mean? God!" Chick yelled at Jadon, irate and exasperated with the heaviness and secrecy that blanketed everyone. "It's like all the sudden we're livin' in some fucked up bizarro world. Cut the crap, Jay. What the hell?"

Jadon shook his head as he slid his chair away from the table. "It doesn't fuckin' mean anything . . . it doesn't mean anything."

"I'm about to fuckin' crack. I really am about to crack," Chick said.

Noticing Vince walk into the restaurant, Chick motioned for him to join them at their table.

"Good morning, don't we all look bright eyed?" Vince gave a nod to everyone finishing their breakfasts. "Hello, Flora. God, it's great to see you here. You keeping these boys in line?"

"Oh, they don't need me for that. They're finding their way just fine."

"I don't believe that for a second," Vince smiled. Not able to shake the gloominess that seemed to be mutually plastered onto everyone's faces. "Jesus," Vince said, "who just died?"

"Christ, Vinnie, we're just tired," Bob offered, not wanting to explain any more than that.

"Tired? What? This tour is a trip to the spa compared to your other tours. All right, keep it to yourselves. Fine with me. Probably better that way. As your manager, I'd just try to fix it anyway," Vince said, flipping over the small porcelain cup that sat in front of him, letting the waiter know he wanted it filled.

"When did you get in?" Chick asked, stretching his arms into the air before resting his hands behind his head.

"This morning. I just walked off the plane." Vince rolled his eyes from the recent plane hopping he had to do. "I have to wrap some things up here, then I'll meet with you guys after Christmas. I wanted to catch up with you this morning to let you know that Tom called. MTV wants you and the crew to do a little Christmas thing. Nothing big. It'll take just a few hours. It's actually quite funny. That's why I felt safe committing you to it."

Chick's interest was piqued. He appreciated all things funny. And right now, everyone needed a heavy dose of funny. "Continue," he said.

"They want to do a live feed from Vigeland Park in Oslo. The park is riddled with huge granite sculptures. That isn't the funny part. They want you guys to dress up and rattle off the Christmas Top Ten. It's cheesy, but . . . ," Vince said, once again rolling his vibrant blue eyes, "sometimes cheesy is needed. I thought it would be fun. They said they'd have the costumes and makeup people at the hotel."

"Sounds cool enough. What kind of costumes? It better be good," Chick warned.

"Oh, yeah. It's good. This is how they want you guys." Vince took a folded piece of paper from his briefcase. "I had them email it to me. I didn't want to get anyone mixed up." Putting on his reading glasses, Vince scanned the page with his finger. "Kofi," he said, looking over the top of his glasses across the table, "you're one of the elves. You know, Santa's helper. Bob . . . you're Jack Frost. I guess they thought that would be extra funny because you're so tan. Chick, you're Santa."

"I don't want to be just any ol' Santa. I gotta be all fat or super skinny . . . and I'm not super skinny, so . . ."

"Don't worry, the idea isn't to make you warm and cuddly. It's MTV, after all." Vince glanced back down at the paper propped against his coffee cup. "Stu . . . you're an elf, too." He chuckled as he read further down. "This part makes me laugh. They want Jadon and Meg to wear these big, *big* snowman suits. Look, they attached a picture of the costumes with the email," he said, passing the attachment around the table.

Puffing on his cigarette, Chick nodded his head slowly. "This is perfect. This is perfect. We need this. Yeah. Damn. Those are huge. I like the freakishly long nose they have for Bob, too. Yeah. This is good."

"Good. Well, once you land at Oslo, the cars will be waiting as usual. They'll whisk you over to the Ousland Inn. It's more of a grand hotel, but they call it an inn. Anyway, that's where you'll be camped out for two nights. Enjoy your Christmas, by the way." Vince snapped his briefcase closed, and slid his chair out from behind him. "I have to run. I'm meeting Cindy and the kids. Then I have a ten o'clock with Xaiver's people. God. I'm getting too old for this shit," he said, giving a warm wave to everyone at the table as he walked out of the restaurant.

"Yeah, right. You too old? Never," Chick yelled, making sure Vince could hear him. Scanning the costumes once again, Chick smiled. "This is good. This is very good."

Meg and Bobby stood outside the Ousland Inn waiting for everyone else to join them for a walk down the quaint city street that bordered their hotel. Bobby needed the exercise, even though Stu, Chick and Bob cheerfully grabbed him throughout the day and ran with him down the sidewalk, making sure he had plenty of fresh air.

Meg marveled at the old architecture that gave the Ousland Inn its shape. Admiring the grandeur of the inn, Meg smiled — a smile she purposely forced onto her face as the nine of them made their way leisurely down the sidewalk, peering into the various shops stacked tightly side by side along their way.

The snow danced slowly and landed lightly on their faces; the cold temperatures caused their eyes to turn to glass as they ambled along, and small clouds of hot breath to emerge in front of their faces as they spoke.

"It's goddamn cold out here," Chick said, pointing to the small tavern nestled between the historic buildings that colorfully lined the streets. "You coming, Jay?" he asked, looking back at Jadon, who was lagging behind.

His footsteps remaining slow, Jadon nodded his head. Flora's words from the other night pulled at his thoughts. *What if Meg hadn't really been using me? What if, somehow, everything we shared was real, not just a writer fishing for material for their latest book?* Jadon wondered, wanting to allow himself the hope. As his defeated body trudged past the small shops that lined the street, he blankly stared through their windows, thinking all the while about Meg.

Stopping suddenly, his eyes were drawn to a bracelet hanging from a black sculpted hand that dangled it precariously from its fingers. He pressed his head against the glass and instantly thought of Meg.

"That's her," he said. "That's her."

Stepping back to read the sign hanging over the door leading into the narrow artisan shop, Jadon smiled and walked inside.

"Let's just squeeze into this spot. I like it. It's by the window. This is the only window in the whole tavern and I like to see outside," Chick said, unwrapping the thick wool scarf that was curled snugly around his neck.

"See what?" Stu asked, peering out the window at the absence of light. "It's fuckin' dark out there."

"I know. I can hardly believe it's only four in the afternoon," Erin said.

"I kind of like it," Kofi smiled. "It's cozy. Very cozy. I can just picture all of us by a warm fire."

"Linie Akevitt," Chick said to the young lady patiently waiting for everyone to settle into their seats. "Everyone," Chick pointed his finger around the table.

"Whoa! That oughtta really get us in the Christmas spirit," Bob laughed.

"All we have is the MTV thing after this and then it's our time. We'll do the fire thing Kofi wants," Chick smiled.

"Sounds good," Stu lifted his glass. "Smooooth."

Meg couldn't help but wonder where Jadon had gone. He wasn't just distant with her, he was distant with everyone. *I should just corner him and ask him what's wrong. No. No. I want to know, but I don't want to know. I want to know that I'll wake up tomorrow, and everything will have gone right back to the way it was before Devon rudely interrupted us on the elevator,* Meg thought.

"Dude," Chick said, waving Jadon over to their table.

Bob stood and moved one chair away from Meg, leaving the only vacant seat the one next to her. It was a strategic move and one that Bob had planned as soon as the group first sat down.

Jadon squeezed his body between Bob and Meg, and breathlessly took a quick sip from the drink waiting for him. Smelling Meg's perfume, his eyes automatically scanned her face.

He didn't know what to say, so he finished his drink and signaled for another.

Meg felt as though she was going to literally die. Jadon was close enough that all she had to do was lean over an inch and her lips could be resting effortlessly on his face. The thought sizzled through her body as soon as she thought it.

"Where the hell did you run off to?" Chick asked, motioning for another drink for the rest of them.

"Just had to do something," Jadon said, still catching his breath after running through the piercing cold to catch up with them.

What a pathetic excuse for a self-respecting person I am, Meg mumbled in her head. But she couldn't help herself from getting carried away by the sounds of Jadon's breath moving heavily in and out of his body, having so many times imagined that very sound while dancing through her fantasy world over the past couple months. It was a fantasy world that revolved solely around Jadon. *The person who can't stand me anymore. Zip, in an instant. He lures me off my safe tree branch. So captivated by his trusting, beautiful eyes, I jump. I jump and fall. Splat*, Meg thought angrily. *Right on the ground. Broken wings, that's right. I've got broken wings now. And here I sit, still gooey eyed and pathetic, longing to have him in my bed.*

"God," Meg blurted, grabbing her drink.

The outburst startled not only Jadon and Stu, who were squeezed tightly next to her, but also everyone crammed around the tiny table.

"God is good," Chick stated, not sure what suddenly possessed Meg. "All in favor raise your glass!"

"*God is good!*" everyone except Jadon shouted.

"I can't believe that actually popped out," Meg said, startled by herself. "I was so engrossed in my thoughts . . ."

"There's nothing you can't say to us," Stu reminded her, shoving his cigarette butt into the overflowing ashtray.

"That's right," Chick said, checking the time on his cell phone. "Shit, we gotta run or we'll be late."

Chapter 23

Waddling out of the elevator, Meg held the oversized snowman head in front of her. She would have held it under her arm, but due to the width of the costume she was wearing, her thin, brown, spandex covered arms were forced to jut straight out, allowing her to either swing her arms to the side or straight in front. She chose to shoot them straight out in front, making it possible to grasp the snowman head in her hands.

The massive, white costume consisted of a body that was molded into one enormous piece, plus a head, both rounded to look like snowballs one on top of the other. Meg's slender legs, hidden under the same brown spandex that covered her arms and fingers, gave her limbs the appearance of twigs. On her feet were large black boots.

"Oh . . . that's so you," Erin said, breaking into laughter, causing Chick to spin his oversized Santa body briskly around so he could see Meg as she waddled closer to them.

Not able to wave, Meg just nodded her head as she smiled, enjoying the opportunity to hide behind the safety of a costume. Suddenly Bob slid across the lobby of the hotel, his feet adorned with giant slippers, extending a foot beyond where his toes ended. His well-tanned face was still deeply bronze, except now he had a long brown, pointed nose that darted out from his face like Pinocchio's. He wore a brilliant blue hat that formed a perfect point above his head. Both slippers and hat had bells dangling from their tips.

"Snazzy," Meg said, poking his stomach with her brown finger. Turning around, Meg watched as Kofi and Stu emerged from the elevator, both dressed as Santa's helpers. Their red striped outfits looked like the footed pajamas Meg use to wear when she was five years old. Except hers didn't have a trap door on the back that was open, revealing two large butt cheeks hanging out. Meg laughed at the sight of Stu, his golden curly hair covered by a bright red clown wig. Kofi grinned as he walked by Meg, his tall thin frame made even taller by the vibrant green clown wig resting on his narrow head.

"There's my happy little snow buddy!" Chick yelled, throwing his arms out wide to receive within them Jadon as he slowly stepped out of the elevator. His costume was the exact twin of Megs, except his snowman head was adorned with a large black top hat. He also had a corn cob pipe that dangled wearily beneath the soft carrot nose extending dangerously far from his large white rounded face.

Not realizing that her snowman head would be different, Meg immediately spun the large white head she was holding, so she could look at its face.

"I'll be damned," Meg mumbled, noticing that her snowman head had black eyelashes drawn around its button eyes, and pink circles on its cheeks.

Reaching over, Bob gently took the large snowman head from Meg's outstretched arms, and eased it onto her head. Meg's world turned dark except for the two peep holes, which allowed her to see only what was directly in front of her. Meg watched Chick shuffle after Jadon, who waddled out the door, not bothering to stop in the lobby.

"Hey, dude," Chick said, rubbing his large, red stomach while standing next to Jadon on the sidewalk. "Need help with your head?"

Jadon nodded, prompting Chick to slowly remove the large, smiling snowball head off Jadon and place it on the ground.

"Thanks. I don't think I can reach my mouth to have a smoke," Jadon said.

"I gotcha' covered buddy. I gotcha'," Chick giggled, fumbling in his pocket for a Lucky, which he quickly lit, and held in front of Jadon. Lighting another cigarette, Chick let it dangle from his mouth while he stuffed his lighter back in the large red pocket that sat under his thick, black belt.

"You know you can tell me anything, right?" Chick said, holding the cigarette back in front of Jadon's mouth.

"I know."

"This is . . . this is the farthest apart I have ever felt from you. And I don't like it. I don't like it. It's messin' with me," Chick said, standing with a burning cigarette in each hand."

"I don't know where to even fuckin' begin. I don't even want to. I'm just messed up."

"Is it Meg?" Chick asked.

"Yes."

The eight of them stopped traffic as they walked through the tall gates leading into Vigeland Park. Walking through the large wrought iron entryway, Meg looked around in wonder. Unable to take in her surroundings as she normally would, she instead viewed the world as if looking through the wrong end of a pair of binoculars. The view was narrow, but Meg didn't care. She was awed by the park's beauty. As she strained to see more of it, various crew members jockeyed her into one spot after another before deciding they liked her best next to Bob, who they had standing next to a statue of a small child. In front of them stood Chick with Jadon by his side. Kofi and Stu were asked to run around. The crew similarly asked Meg and Bob to frolic. Meg stood and watched as the young director handed Chick a microphone and pointed to the large white board in front of him on which were listed the top ten songs he was to recite.

"Hey, everybody, we're Equinox. We're on tour in Oslo, Norway. And we're here to wish you a Merry Christmas," Chick said, tapping his hand on his rounded stomach.

Not wanting to let go of the feeling her drinks had so graciously given her, Meg started to dance her oversized body around. The sight caused Bob to break into a uncontrolled laugh. Bending over to catch his breath, Bob watched Meg bounce her massive body around in the snow, twirling and spinning it behind Chick and Jadon. As she passed Jadon, she bumped him purposefully, causing his corn cob pipe to bounce up and down as he caught himself before falling over.

Chick turned his head over his shoulder to watch Meg twirl herself back toward Bob, her stick like arms swiping around at the side of her large snowball head. All she could hear was the song playing through her mind and Bob laughing hysterically, as well as the distant murmur of Chick as he read the top ten songs.

Slowly she spun herself around, crashing her rounded body against Jadon once more, enjoying the aggressive outburst for a moment before spinning herself back toward Bob. She danced in place momentarily to allow Kofi and Stu to pass by as they wiggled their backsides in front of the camera.

Bouncing next to Bob, Meg turned her bobbing head to look at him directly. The mere act made Bob laugh even harder. Enjoying the feeling that releasing some of her anger toward Jadon was providing, Meg asked for a snowball.

Not breaking from her rhythmic bounce, she held her hand out while waiting for Bob to pack a rounded snowball together between his hands. Once the snowball was placed in Meg's palm she bounced and swayed her enormous body slowly up behind Jadon, smiling inside her rounded head, she pulled back her right arm, and whipped the snowball directly at him.

Having made direct contact, Meg threw her spindly arms victoriously into the air as she shuffled back toward Bob, and extended her hand once more. Loving the small amount of retaliation the moment was providing, Meg replicated her first act of combat, once again achieving perfect contact, causing Jadon's black top hat to whiten with snow.

Dancing back toward Bob, Meg moved her arms in front of her like a clumsy hula dancer, swaying them back and forth, enjoying herself immensely. Suddenly Meg felt something slam against her body. She'd been hit. Spinning her large body around, Meg watched through her peep holes as Jadon struggled to gather more snow between his hands.

Quickly, Bob handed Meg two more perfectly packed and rounded snowballs. Like a boxer suddenly thrust into the ring, Meg began to move quickly to the right, then to the left, her feet shuffling through the snow as she danced her massive body in front of Jadon, waiting for him to prepare himself.

He had one poorly shaped snowball in his hand while she was equipped with not one but two perfectly constructed snow grenades.

"Come on . . . come on . . . ," Meg sang. "Wanna dance, huh? Wanna dance?"

Meg felt Jadon's snowball crash against her huge middle. Firing off her two snowballs like a semiautomatic pistol, Meg hit

Jadon first directly between his large button eyes; the other ricocheted off his left stick-like arm.

To the surprise of everyone, Meg raced toward Jadon with wild abandon, causing him to panic and run. Holding her arms straight in front of her, Meg kept him in her sights. Racing frantically through the snow, tripping over his large boots, Jadon began his bouncy decent to the ground. Overcome with anger, Meg seized the opportunity and launched her mammoth snowball body onto his. The weight of her costume pushed his costume deeper into the snow, before her rounded body bounced off of his, sending her hurling in the other direction.

"We're Equinox," Chick said evenly, holding the microphone as he watched the unscripted escapades play out behind him. "Merry Christmas."

Chapter 24

"Sir, I don't believe I am clear on what you're asking," the middle-aged, blond woman behind the counter at the Ousland Inn said.

"Okay. Let me try again. I need you to give this package to Meg Scott," Jadon said slowly. "I don't want her to know it's from me. I want you to say it arrived in the mail for her today."

Sighing suspiciously, the concierge finally nodded her head in agreement. Pausing for a moment, not sure if he had the stranger's trust, Jadon cautiously slid the small brown package across the counter.

"Thank you. It means the world to me," Jadon said quietly.

Feeling as though there was nothing else he could do to ensure that the concierge followed his directions, Jadon made his way over to the lounge just off the lobby. Gathered around the large fireplace was everyone except Meg. Taking a seat on the floor next to Bobby in front of the fireplace, Jadon began to run his fingers through his wavy red fur.

Standing in the elevator, Meg felt slightly embarrassed but also good. She felt more good than embarrassed. She was happy that she finally chose not to hide her feelings. Taking a deep sigh, she walked out of the elevator, and made her way toward the lounge.

"Ma'am?" The lady behind the counter called. "Ms. Scott."

"Yes. That's me."

"This came for you today," The concierge said, sliding the small package across the counter toward Meg.

"Oh, thank you," Meg said with surprise, trying to read the handwriting on the box as she walked toward the lounge. "Mandalay Bay?" she mumbled. Instantly, the address clicked inside Meg's mind: her mysterious neighbor.

"Watcha' got Meggie?" Bob asked, tapping at the open spot next to him on the sofa. "We've got more Linie Akevitt."

"I . . . I don't know what it is."

"Well, who's it from?" Chick asked suspiciously.

"It's . . . ," Meg slowly looked up at him. "It's from my neighbor, back in Mandalay Bay. It must have gotten forwarded to the Inn…"

"Neighbor!" Stu said. "I didn't know you even knew your neighbor."

"Well, I don't really. Not like you would think. I've never even seem him," Meg said, carefully unwrapping the package, revealing a small box with a note inside that floated down to the floor when she removed the brown paper.

"Here you go," Flora said, grabbing the piece of paper that landed next to her feet. Handing it back to Meg, Flora turned her head toward Jadon.

Staring at the small, handwritten note, Meg ran her finger across the words as she read them. *I saw this and thought of you. I miss you. ~ Your Piano Man*

Taking the lid off, Meg removed the delicate silver bracelet from its box. Her eyes poured over every intricate piece of silver that had been gently formed into numerous infinity symbols. Connecting each rounded symbol spanning the length of the bracelet was a brilliant, polished stone. From what Meg could tell, there were hematite and quartz as well as tourmaline, among others.

"*Infinity — without end,*" Meg whispered under her breath, reading the description written by the artisan that crafted the bracelet.

Jadon kept his legs curled in front of him as he watched Meg examine the gift. He watched her face brightened with happiness as she looked at it, and her eyes fill with tears.

"God, Meg. That's beautiful," Erin said, peering over Meg's shoulder.

"Well, he's . . . he's beautiful," Meg said, easing it onto her small wrist.

Jadon rubbed his hands over his face, more confused now than ever before. Buying Meg the bracelet was never part of the plan. His plan was to try to hate her. Hate her for not telling him the truth about why she acted like she wanted to be close to him. Instead he couldn't hate her, and pulling himself away from her was virtually impossible.

"Mandalay Bay," Bob said out loud as he read the brown wrapper the box was packaged in. "Hey . . . Jay?" he began to say, remembering Jadon lived on the same road. "Don't you . . ."

"Bob. Would you pour me another glass?" Erin interrupted. She wanted nothing to complicate Meg's wonderful moment.

"Sure," he said, startled by the sudden request to fill an already half full glass.

"Meg, what gives with this neighbor?" Bob asked, keying into Erin's desire for secrecy.

"Well, it's odd, sort of," Meg said.

"We like odd, if you couldn't tell already," Flora smiled.

"Well . . . lately, things have been so . . . strange. But during it all, there's been this constant current of radiant beauty flowing through my life — even when I have felt so empty and alone. All we do is play music together. That's the funny part," she said, letting out an awkward laugh. "But that music, those moments . . . they've really moved me. It's like through music he holds my hand. More than that really."

"That sounds beautiful, Meg," Flora said.

"Jesus Christ. I want to meet this guy. If we don't approve . . . ," Bob winked.

"Well, maybe it's best if I don't meet him," Meg said sadly.

"How so?" Chick asked.

"Beautiful things don't last long. Or at least around me they don't."

Erin glanced at Jadon, finding him still frozen in the same position, his head tilted behind him, his eyes closed with the same emotionally overwhelmed look on his face.

"Come on. This is Christmas," Chick said. "Tell us your favorite Christmas memory. That oughtta get us in the mood."

Meg stared over Jadon's shoulder at the flames dancing above the logs. "First, you should know: I hate Christmas."

"*Whoa!* You can't hate Christmas!" Stu bellowed. "What for?"

"My parents died right before Christmas," Meg said flatly, watching the ice cubes float around in her glass.

"Sorry, Meg," Chick said. "Let's not celebrate Christmas. Let's just start celebrating New Year. Yeah . . . we need noise makers."

"No, that's okay," Meg gave him a sweet smile. "You know. This year, I can handle it. You guys are the most family I've had since my parents left. I only remember a few Christmases really. But I remember one gift in particular that really stuck out. It was a normal Christmas. My mother handed me something. I could tell it was one of her paintings. But this one, it was all mine. Not done for an exhibit or a gallery. This one she painted just for me. The painting was in beautiful shades of pink, with a flurry of little blue birds flying around in the distance, except for one, one gorgeous blue bird that was painted in the foreground. And the way she painted it, you could tell it was just about to take flight. The thing that stood out, beyond the amazing beauty of the painting was . . . the birds didn't have eyes. And I know that sounds creepy," Meg chuckled. "But you hardly noticed until you looked closer at it.

"Later that night as Mom gave me a goodnight kiss, I asked her about it. And she said, well, baby, I thought about it for a long time. And my hope is that you will always have that painting hanging somewhere near you, and if you do, I want you to live without being watched. Eyes are funny things. When you look into certain eyes, you see love and acceptance. But often, eyes carry judgment. They watch and calculate. So, my dear girl, I want the only eyes that look at you to be ones that bring you divine joy. Never settle for less than that. Goodnight."

"Sounds like your mom and Flora would have made quite the team," Chick laughed warmly.

"I will take that as a huge compliment," Flora said.

"Well it was a compliment," Chick added.

"Okay. Who's next?" Meg said, soaking in the moment.

Glancing at the fire and around the room, Meg listened and enjoyed the vivid memories being told by everyone. Each story held a tender sweetness that for whatever reason caused the memory to hold a sacred place within the heart of the one who lived it.

"Looks like you're the only one left, Jay," Chick said, causing everyone to turn in Jadon's direction.

With a smile easing onto his face, Jadon simply said, "A piano. My dad gave me a piano."

A bolt of surprise darted through Meg's body. Picturing Jadon playing the piano messed with her thoughts of her neighbor. It played with her fantasy that somehow in some twist of fate, her neighbor would ultimately turn out to be Jadon. It was a fantasy that she allowed herself only because she knew it could never come true.

As the night drew to its natural close, everyone began to yawn, their eyelids heavy from a night spent surrounded by the uncomplicated love found between good friends.

"My mother would have loved this, this night surrounded by each of you," Meg said.

"I have a feeling she did," Flora said, standing to give Meg a hug before continuing to give everyone else a hug goodnight.

Embracing everyone, Meg gave each one an extra tight squeeze. Moving around the room, she hesitated, if she proceeded any further, she would be standing in front of Jadon.

"Christ. It's Christmas," Stu yelled, taking his hand, and pushing Jadon and Meg together.

Caught in an instant embrace, Meg slowly slid her hands around Jadon's back, and pulled herself closer to him. With her head against his, she closed her eyes and tried to remain still, giving herself the moment of holding him in her arms. Even if he didn't want it.

Jadon's head spun with the same confused thoughts that had marched through his mind all evening. Wanting to hold Meg, he pushed the thoughts aside for the moment; sliding his hands up her back, he gently pulled her into him. Trying not to let his thoughts go any further than recording the feeling of her body in his arms, he closed his eyes. Forgetting the pain she caused, he dug his nose into her hair, and took a deep breath of her perfume. As if boulders waiting their moment to fall off a cliff, the words from Meg's novel tumbled through his head. Unable to stand in front of her any longer, he suddenly released her, and walked out the door.

Chapter 25

If I'm right, that pain always precedes the birthing of something beautiful, then my performance tonight will be a glorious one, Meg thought, holding her violin in her left arm, her right arm poised and ready. Finding balance on the thin edge that separated her from a very dark place and the hope for something better, Meg reached out and struck her first riveting chord. She was handing over her struggle to the only canvas she knew how to paint on, her violin. In an attempt to release everything that clung inside of her, Meg sent her tormented emotions spiraling out into the packed audience at the Johan Auditorium. She dove headlong into every note, bending her back, swaying effortlessly through song after song, her hair whipping around her face like a temperamental fire. It was a performance that captivated everyone watching it.

Unable to resist the beautiful sight before him, Jadon watched as Meg moved through series after series of notes and melodies. He watched as she made the violin sound almost exactly as it did the first night he heard it. During her solo, he couldn't stop himself from giving her a gentle rhythm to bounce her music off of. He wanted to be with her. He wanted to forget the past. He wanted to feel her with him.

Meg waited all night to play the last song, *Longing*. She still loved her part in it and how it dug at her soul, in the process cultivating a myriad of emotions. But tonight Meg wanted to break through the emotions. Standing tall and resolute within herself, looking each emotion in the eye, Meg had no plans of backing down. Her body anxiously moved to the beat of the song as it thundered along. Turning her head she looked at Jadon. She watched as his beautiful body and face poured themselves into the song. Her eyes followed his long blonde hair as it flew erratically around his head. His eyes locked onto hers for moments at a time. These were moments she absorbed, grabbing them like a thief who wants to selfishly own something that isn't hers.

Feeling her heart beat wildly, Meg drew back her arm and sent a piercing note echoing through the building, holding it she harnessed its sound, extending it as far as it would reach before dropping down into her next rapid succession of notes. Listening to Jadon's drumbeats dance along with her, Meg allowed her heart to scream anonymously through her violin, releasing a million angry voices.

As Roach and his team swarmed the stage like worker bees collecting pollen once the show was over, Meg nestled her violin back into its case. Taking a moment she drifted her finger across the beautifully detailed etching that spanned the length of her bow. Closing the case, she couldn't help but remember when Jadon asked if he could show her how to play the drums.

"Oh, God. I'm never going to get him out of my system," Meg sighed. "Maybe I don't want to."

"Ready, Freddie?" Bob asked walking up behind Meg.

"Ready."

Sitting next to Stu in the small bar fittingly named Hyggly that was adjacent to their hotel, Meg tried to wash the images of Jadon out of her mind.

"You want another, Meg?" Chick motioned to the bartender to give everyone another round.

Meg knew it wasn't right to submerge her woes with a stiff drink, but for the moment it seemed like the best approach. The alcohol didn't help her confusion, but it at least distracted her. Staring across the table, Meg noticed that Jadon wasn't hesitating before finishing his drink either.

Lifting his glass of Linie Akevitt, Chick beamed at everyone at the table. "Skål!" In unison everyone took a sip. "Yeah! I'm likin' this stuff. We need some of this at the studio."

"Jadon?" Coco's voice rocketed across the bar.

Jadon's eyes held a position of defeated disbelief as he watched Coco move briskly over to their table.

"There you are. I'm in town with some of my friends, and I asked around where you were hiding while you were here," Coco said.

Forcing her way past Bob, she wiggled next to Jadon, and motioned for the bartender to include her on the next round.

"I was looking for you in London at your hotel, but you'd already left. I would've come sooner to meet with you but . . . ," Coco continued after taking a small sip from her drink, "but I had a photo shoot."

"What?" Jadon shrieked. "What are you talking about?"

Coco smiled blissfully at everyone, her gaze settling onto Meg who sat baffled on the other side of the table.

"Coco, what the hell are you doing here?" Chick finally barked. "What fuckin' brainless Barbie doll plane did you get dropped out of?"

"That's not nice, Chick, and you know it. I'm here because your friend asked me to meet up with him."

"Coco . . . I never . . . ," Jadon started to say, visibly mystified.

"You must be Meg," Coco interrupted, "Oh, there's that dog again," she said looking under the table to see Bob curled on top of Stu's large feet.

"How do you know . . . ," Stu started to ask.

"Jadon introduced me to him. He's a sweet looking thing isn't he? Although I don't quite get it."

"Get what?" Erin said, angered that Coco was sitting there. Angered that she was saying the things she was saying.

"The dog thing. I just . . . ," Coco laughed, "I mean. I like the little ones that you stuff in your bag. I mean those are fine. But a big one?" she added looking once again under the table. "I just don't quite see the attraction."

"How do you know Meg?" Bob said in disgust.

"Well, duh, she's in all the papers lately. And, Devon told me all about her," Coco answered, loving the moment when she could drop Devon's name like gasoline on an open flame.

"You know Devon?" Meg asked.

"I *always* stay at his hotel whenever I am in London, which is most of the time. Well, after all of you left he stopped and filled me in on all the latest details. Congratulations by the way."

"Oh, thank you," Meg answered, wondering why Devon would take the time to talk to Coco about her latest book.

"Devon said *not* to let the cat out of the bag." Coco reached up to her face and turned an invisible key to lock her mouth shut. "I promised him I wouldn't. I won't spoil your fun. Jadon? Walk me to my room again?"

Again, Meg wondered. *I am such a fool.*

"Really. I need to speak with you," Coco said giving Jadon a final pull, dislodging him from the table.

Standing outside the bar, Jadon lit a cigarette and tried to collect his thoughts.

"Coco. What the hell are you doing here? And what the hell was all that crap you just said? I never said that stuff. Coco, I don't want to hurt you, but I don't like you in that way."

"I know. I wish you did though. And I think if you gave us a chance . . ."

"No. Not going to happen. I'm in . . ."

"I know. Meg. Devon told me."

"Devon told you what?" Jadon said.

"Well, I had a really long talk with him. And, well. I just don't like that she's keeping so much from you. It's not right."

"You don't know what you're fuckin' talking about." Jadon tossed his cigarette on the ground as he turned to walk back in the bar.

"She's engaged."

The words stopped Jadon before he could open the door. "What? No she isn't."

"It's very private. Devon said that I can *not* tell anyone. But, I felt you needed to know. Especially once Devon shared his suspicions that you might be attracted to her," Coco said, sliding her body next to his. "You heard her. I told her congratulations, and she said thank you. Without evening blinking an eye, she knew what I was talking about. He said they're holding off until after the tour."

"Well, I suppose we could just go ask her," Jadon said.

"Dev said she would just deny it. He said Meg is a master at secrets, and this one she didn't want anyone to know about." Remembering another morsel Devon told her to drop, Coco added, "Devon told me how one time . . . she was doing research for a novel, so she traveled on and off for years with some of the biggest names in the music business . . ."

Inside the bar, Meg ordered another drink, this time not waiting for Chick to start another round before pouring hers down her throat in an effort to wash away the pieces of the puzzle that were brutally falling into place. *I'm such a fool*. Meg kept repeating in her mind.

"I don't have a very good feeling about this Coco character," Flora said, watching Jadon through the glass doors of the bar.

"Well," Erin began, her voice full of exasperation, "she isn't good. I don't think any of what she said is true."

Completing her fifth, frosted glass of Akevitt, Meg pushed her chair out from behind her. "I think Bobby and I need to go for a walk."

Standing up, Meg motioned for Bob to follow her as she slowly made her way out the back door.

"Maybe one of us should go help her with Bobby," Stu offered.

Not sure what to do, everyone sat quiet, shocked by Coco. Shocked more by the small potent drops of information Coco glibly tossed on the table.

"I know him. He's not messin' around with Coco. No way in hell," Chick said, putting his hands over his face. "No way in hell. I don't know what the fuck is going on. He's not talkin'. I can't get him to open up," he said loudly, fed up with everything. "Let's all go."

Meg stepped off the elevator, ready to put an end to the day. Taking her key card from her pocket, she swiped it through the lock and slowly opened her door. As she stepped into her room, she noticed Coco stepping out of Jadon's. Walking by Meg, Coco gave her a wave and a very bright smile.

"Bitch," Meg said under her breath, slamming her door shut. "No. No. Bitches tend to at least have a brain. What doesn't have a brain?"

Sliding onto the bed, Meg curled herself next to Bobby. "Oh, Mom, please help me. Show me the way. You're here. You can do it. You talked through Flora. Talk to me. Tell me I'll live through this. Tell me this pain will go away," she begged softly until finally her eyes closed, and she was no longer held captive to the moment.

Jadon sat in a chair in the corner of his room, his mind mulling over Coco's words while he tried to get a handle on the new level of pain that was busy layering itself over his heart. Laughing bitterly, he shook his head, amazed by how clueless he was.

"I fell so hard for her," Jadon mumbled into the empty room. "First I think she's married, and it drives me insane. God. That seems so small in comparison. I would rather she loved me, honestly loved me and wanted me, but was married, than this. To be used liked this. Fuckin' Devon. God. What does she see in him? Doesn't matter. None of it matters."

"Meg?" Erin said softly, trying to wake her from a drunken sleep. "Meggie. Morning is here whether you like it or not. Hey, girlfriend, we have to leave soon, you better get up."

Meg didn't open an eye. Her face and body didn't move.

"Okay. Now you're getting me worried. I knew you drank too much last night. Come on," Erin pushed Meg's body back and forth, causing Bob to bark. "Meg! God damn it. Don't scare me like this. I swear to God I'll get Jadon in here if I have to."

"Fuck Jadon!" Meg yelled, her mouth and face still pressed into her pillow. "Fuck him, Erin."

"Thank God. Christ. Don't do that to me," Erin ordered, relieved Meg was still alive. Sitting on Meg's bed, Erin began to pet

Bob. "Hate to break it to you, but we have to hit the road. You and Jadon are the only two no-shows."

Pulling her head off the pillow, Meg squinted and looked around the room. "That's because he was busy with Cooocooo last night."

"I doubt that," Erin said, walking to the door and opening it. "She's okay," she said to Chick. "Here's Bobby," she whispered, letting the dog out the door so Chick could take him for a walk.

"Well, I don't," Meg said. "I know. I watched the little skunk scamper out of his room last night. How about them apples?" she asked, throwing on a pair of ripped and faded jeans.

"I know Jadon. He wouldn't touch Coco with a ten-foot pole. I know he wouldn't."

"Oh. Ohhhh, I doubt that. I think he more than touched her last night, Erin," Meg said, plopping her body on the corner of the bed. "But . . . what's it matter? I mean, sometimes I get this fantasy thing going. Maybe because I'm a writer. Yeah. That's it. I just let my mind loose to run around and play. Then I can't tell what is fantasy and what isn't anymore. He isn't even anything like what I thought. And I am so not his type. I'm nothing like Coco. Thank God! Erin, the girl looks like she's been squeezed from a tube of tan putty. I don't know what that stuff was on the elevator between Jadon and me. I don't know. Maybe he just wanted to see if he could. You know?" she asked, standing up to march into the bathroom. "Guys are like that, Erin. Sometimes they do things just to see if they can. I was such a fool."

Chapter 26

"No, I'm good. Really. No, everything's fine. Why do you keep asking me that?" Meg demanded, irritated that Devon not only continually called but also kept asking if she were all right. "It's going fine. Great time. Great," she said, waiting for Devon to finish his next series of questions. "Spring. No, that's still fine. I think it should happen before then, though. I don't know what the holdup is. I don't want to postpone it any longer than that."

Normally the turnaround time to publish one of her books was far shorter than what Devon was proposing. Why this book had to have so many complications bewildered her. Despite the part that involved Devon, Meg was happy to be working on her latest book, the book about her mother. It was the first of what Meg hoped would be many to be published under her own name.

"Yup. Yup. No. No. I'm not angry. Do I sound angry? I'm not angry. I'm tired . . .No, Bob is good. I want him with me. Why in London?" Meg asked.

Jadon kept his eyes fixed on the buildings quickly flying past the window of the limousine while his ears were fixed on Meg's conversation. Her words were erasing the question mark of doubt he had after Coco told him about Meg's engagement.

"I want to do it in New York. That makes sense," she argued, angered that Devon wanted to release her mother's book in London before releasing it in the States. With every passing day

Meg wanted less and less to do with Devon. "No, Devon. Goddamn it, I'm not angry. Okay. Bye," Meg snapped her cell phone closed.

"You okay, Meggie?" Stu asked.

Meg stared at his scrubby rounded gentle face for a moment before offering a simple lie that would change the subject.

"Yeah, I'm good," Meg answered as the limousine pulled into the parking lot behind the Wagner Halle. Nestled in the heart of Duisburg, Germany, the large concert hall overlooked the Rhine River.

Meg looked through the dark lens of her large sunglasses, the ones that hopefully hid most of her face. She just wanted to get the sound check over so she could go back to the hotel room and collapse. And perhaps write a bit before the show and then collapse again. She was nurturing herself with the easy fix of sleep, so often sought after by the depressed.

Looking down at her bracelet, Meg began to think about her neighbor. She wondered where he was. What he was doing. If he was happy.

Finishing the sound check, Meg felt relieved knowing soon she would be able to hide away in her hotel room for a few hours. With Bob curled next to her feet, she could try to move some level of cleansing energy through her body.

"Meg," Chick motioned, "I want you to do the interview with us this afternoon. It's at three o'clock. Won't last long. Then I want us all to meet up for dinner and drinks before the show."

"Me?"

"Yeah. You're part of the band. You're the one whose name keeps popping up in the headlines on this tour. Can't keep hiding you away." Chick smiled, wishing in many ways he never tried to stop the attraction that was flowing between her and Jadon. As combustible as it was, it was at least alive; now, in contrast, both seemed barely breathing. Their pain was felt throughout the rest of the band. No one was happy. Not a single one of them.

"Sure. Sure. Anything you want."

"Great. I'll be knocking on your door around 2:30." Chick winked before walking over to Erin.

Alone in her hotel room, Meg sat on the floor of her shower, letting the water pour over her body before getting ready for the interview.

"Mom would want me to be tougher than this," she moaned, as the hot water slowly turned her fair skin pink. "She was tough. Why can't I be tough? I don't know if she forfeited her life, her hopes and dreams, or merely set them aside waiting for me to grow my wings so I could fly on my own. I'll never know. But she was tough. Somehow I need to be tough too."

"Sit next to me, Meg," Chick said, pointing to a space on the blue sofa inside the small room used for press interviews.

Looking around the room, flooded with light, Meg wondered why it was so bright. She smiled at Bob as he plopped his body next to hers and instantly felt safe. Chick and Bob felt like brothers, as did Stu.

Meg watched as Jadon walked in and anxiously sat in the chair pulled next to the sofa; his knees bounced like jack hammers. She noticed he looked tired. *Coco probably. He probably has her thin Barbie doll body laid out on his bed right now,* Meg thought. She winced at the thought; the pain associated with it was still too fresh in her heart to be approached with sarcasm.

"About ready?" Chick asked, watching the young interviewer shuffle his papers.

"One minute," said a producer sitting next to some broadcast equipment in a corner. A digital clock ticked off the seconds. A single TV camera focused on the young interviewer sitting at the table, next to an interpreter. Keeping her eyes on the young German journalist as he prepared himself for the live interview that had been arranged to help promote the newly remodeled Wagner Halle, Meg couldn't help but notice how his animated movements were in stark contrast to those of the band, including herself. Except for Jadon's ever bouncing knees, all five of them were nearly catatonic.

"Good afternoon," Thomas said in perfect English, something that surprised Meg right away. He continued looking into the camera. "We are coming to you live, from the Wagner Halle," he said slowly, waiting for the young woman seated next to him to translate his words into German. Then he turned to look at Chick and the others. "We would like to start by saying thank you. Thank you for taking the time to meet with us. We know you're busy getting ready for tonight's show."

Looking around Meg noticed both Jadon and Stu had their sunglasses on. She wondered if it was a rock star thing or because they knew it would be so incredibly bright in the room.

"Jadon," Thomas said, turning his body in Jadon's direction, "what was the motivation behind the scenes in your music video *Longing*?"

Meg suddenly sat up straight in her seat, waiting to hear how he would respond. *Was he thinking about Coco? Maybe*, she wondered, biting at her thumbnail.

Tapping his palms together in front of his face, Jadon paused and thought about his answer. There was no way he would ever disclose the truth about what he was feeling during the video shoot.

"Good directing," Jadon said, shooting off a quick smile that just as quickly faded back into nothing.

Thomas paused as Jadon's words were being translated, stunned by the flippant answer.

"I asked the director, Cameron Berkshire, and he said much of the video was . . .spontaneous, nothing planned," Thomas said.

Jadon's head jerked back, surprised that Cameron would be so forthcoming.

"Meg," Thomas said, taking advantage of Jadon's pause. "I notice you have a small scar on your cheek . . ."

"Whoa, dude," Chick protested. "Where's the police? It feels like we're getting interrogated. The video . . . ," Chick continued, downshifting his tone, "it was beautiful. It turned out exactly as we had hoped. It's got you talkin'."

"Okay, okay," Thomas said, realizing he was coming on too strong, but more convinced than ever he had stumbled upon something interesting. "There is talk of continuing with another album after your tour. Is this so?"

"I've been asked. I just don't know the answer yet," Chick said, leaning back into the sofa, his eyes fixed on Thomas, not yet feeling relaxed.

"Meg. What has been your favorite part of being with Equinox?"

"They . . . ," she said, looking at everyone except Jadon, "they feel like my family. So when I'm with them, when I get to make music with them, I feel whole."

Thomas stared at Meg, not expecting such a heartfelt answer. "Well, we feel that your energy, your talents, and what you bring to the music all add a spiritual energy that is phenomenal," he concluded with a smile, suddenly not feeling compelled to dig any further.

Walking back through the narrow hallway leading to her hotel room, Meg considered Thomas' words, and wondered what *spiritual energy* truly meant.

Meg sat down on her bed, flipped open her laptop and woke it from hibernation. Gazing around the room, she admired the simple design of her hotel room. She walked over to the window and ran her fingers down the long gray curtains and then stepped back to let her eyes explore the beautiful large blue flowers that formed a column on each gray panel. Hearing a knock at the door, Meg spun around to answer it.

"Hey, there," she smiled.

"Bob ready for his walk?" Chick asked, peeking his head into Meg's room.

"Sure is. Robert, your personal trainer is here," Meg smacked her leg signaling Bob to come over.

Closing the door Meg felt blessed she had the good fortune to meet such a wonderful group of people. She walked back to the window, sat on the tiled sill, and gazed down at the street.

Except for the ghostly halo under the large street lights, it was completely dark. Looking at the Wagner Halle, Meg admired its architecture and liked how it towered over the river. Something about its size made it seem impenetrable.

Looking at the sidewalk, Meg saw Jadon walk from beneath the canopy leading to the hotel's entrance. Startled by the sight of him, she watched as he knelt down and hugged Bob. Bob's tail wagged profusely as he sat and received Jadon's love. Peering down harder, Meg tried to see everything she could. She couldn't help but envy Bob again, envy how wonderfully he was being embraced by Jadon. She watched as he dug his head into Bob's warm neck, nuzzled his face, kissed his nose and then began to run with him down the sidewalk. Meg watched them both until she couldn't see either one once they passed the Halle.

"Lucky Bob," Meg grumbled, suddenly remembering how unhappy she was.

A half hour later, Bob ran happily through the door Meg held open for him, the cold outside air still clinging to his fur. Turning to look at Chick, Meg wanted to ask about Jadon but decided she didn't want to know. After a long pause, one in which she was sure revealed to Chick what was rolling around in her mind, she simply said thank you and told him she would be down shortly.

Turning to get dressed, Meg wondered what Bertie would do. *She would kick ass. She wouldn't allow anyone to mess with her heart. She would walk straight up to whomever, and lay it all out on the table,* Meg thought, smiling at the vision.

"Wouldn't that be wonderful to do?" She laughed out loud.

After wiggling herself into her gown, Meg stared at herself in the mirror. She liked how she looked, she liked how the thin satin gown flowed over her curves. Slipping on a pair of red stiletto heels, Meg ran her finger across the bracelet that danced on her wrist.

"What would Mom do right now?" Meg asked, looking in the mirror. "She would breeze past Jadon, give him her eyes, smile and let her energy do the rest. I like that."

Walking through the lobby, Meg noticed Erin sitting at the already full dinner table inside Schatz, the very upscale restaurant where they were meeting. Meg walked past the maitre d' and made her way over to Erin's table. Taking a deep breath, she wondered if her energy could carry such power. Whispering silently as she walked, Meg asked her mother to help swirl some of her magic into the air and give her the courage she needed to reach out to Jadon one more time.

"Be with me tonight, Mom."

Giving everyone a smile that lit the room, Meg felt better than she had for some while. She felt good inside. Something inside her felt stronger. Meg allowed Bob to pull her chair out as she graciously took the seat directly across from Jadon.

Not able to keep herself from smiling, comfortable between Bob and Flora, Meg took a deep breath, and let her eyes drift over in Jadon's direction. And tried not to panic when she noticed his eyes were locked onto hers. Searching his eyes with hers, Meg willed herself not to look away like a scared child, but instead kept her eyes steady.

"Your mother is with you tonight," Flora said, tapping Meg's hand.

"I hope so. I really could use her help," Meg said.

Scanning her menu, Meg finally found what she was looking for, and pointed to it so the waiter could take her order.

Paying careful attention, Meg noticed that Jadon's eyes were often resting on her. Not wanting to interfere with the flow of energy, Meg wasn't sure if she should allow herself to stare back or not. She looked once more at his face, her eyes stopping directly on his, and stared as long as possible, until he glanced away. *Thank you, Mom*, Meg said to herself.

Standing in the Wagner Halle Meg felt overjoyed with her playing and equally overjoyed with the people surrounding her. Her smile came effortlessly while she played. She felt her mother fly alongside her bow every time she grazed it across the strings of her violin. Wanting to live in the moment she was given, Meg swayed and allowed the music to move through her body, feeling every note and every one of Chick's soulful words cascade down her spine. Meg loved everything about where she was and was able to find contentment in the moment. Deeply moved, she turned and smiled at Chick, sending her love in his direction as he got ready to introduce her to the audience.

"Okay . . . so here's the deal. Many of you have heard," he began, using the moment as he always did to savor his words, "we adopted a new family member, a sister," holding his hand out in front of him signaling for the audience to stop applauding. "Now . . . before you guys out there get any bright ideas, you're goin' to have to make it past. . . ," Chick turned around to count Stu, Bob and Kofi, "four . . .," and then turning to look over his left shoulder at Jadon, "maybe five brothers, and we're tough. We'll beat the shit out of ya. All right, enough fun. I've left her hangin' over there for too long. This is, without a doubt, the best violinist I have ever had the pleasure of listening to, let alone make music with: Ms. Meg Scott."

Tapping her foot, Meg began to nod her head. Finding some rhythm, she turned and faced Jadon. Throwing all caution to the wind, she slowly began to walk in his direction as she drew back on her first chord. Looking him directly in the eye, Meg wanted him to feel her presence.

Jadon watched as Meg drifted her body closer to his, listening to her play the familiar notes he longed to hear every night, he couldn't help but smile. Forgetting for the moment all that separated them, he slowly joined her, giving her haunting melody a rhythmic beat that pulled and swung at the tail of her notes. Not wanting to let go of the moment, the two slowed down their song, then as if they'd practiced it for years, built it back into a thundering melody that pounded and soared through the music hall.

Meg stared at Jadon, her love for him flowing easily with every soft glance. Smiling a smile reserved only for him, she pulled the two of them toward a spine chilling ending. Breathing heavily, Meg dropped her arms, and stared into Jadon's eyes. Watching the dynamic energy soar between the two, Chick didn't want to say a word; instead he gave them their moment. At this point, he wanted to push the two of them together, not tear them apart.

Noticing the crowd was growing quiet, Meg slowly stepped back to her spot, and nodded toward Chick.

"Okay . . . our final song. It's real special," Chick said, deciding to share with everyone. "Someone really exceptional wrote this. It wasn't me. But someone real special to me . . . he wrote it about a woman, and I think he captured within the song something that although dangerous because of its power . . . ," Chick paused, "it's beautiful, and it's the stuff of life. Hope you like it."

Meg's mind froze, shocked by Chick's words. Simple deduction meant Jadon wrote the song. Shifting nervously on his stool, Jadon was noticeably uncomfortable by what Chick had said. Keeping her eyes in his direction, Meg waited for him to begin singing. She watched him intently, both unable and unwilling to pull herself away. Hating herself for it, she felt herself fall further in love with him.

Jadon leaned his head toward his mike and looked at Meg. The words poured from him, from his heart, directed only at her, still fueled by his love for her. He wanted to silence the thoughts that swung in front of his mind like a heavy pendulum, reminding him of his pain with every weighted swing, and so he did what he always did when he sang the song he wrote for her: he lived in the now. Not wanting to look away, he sang to Meg.

Meg raised her violin to her chin and waited for the moment to tell him how desperately she wanted him. Hitting her first chord, she sent the radiant sound of her passionate love sweeping across the audience. She kept her finger steady, and holding the note firmly in place she urged it to remain in the air a little longer, giving everyone who heard it the chance to reach out and grab it for themselves. As Meg fell into her third note, Jadon sent out a thundering boom that vibrated the floor under Meg's feet. She felt his commanding drum beats move through her body, and into her mind.

Striking the drums harder, Jadon felt his heart break while he looked into Meg's eyes. He wanted to turn back time; he wanted to erase the damage. He didn't care about Devon, he didn't care what Chick would think. He wanted to take her in his arms and pull her close. Hitting his last beat, Jadon held the cymbals, quickly turning the hall silent. And with that the curtain dropped to thunderous applause.

Looking at Jadon, Chick noticed he wasn't moving. "Dude, you okay?"

"Yeah," he answered, taking his hands off his cymbals.

"Let's scoot," Chick flipped his eyes toward the door. Chick wanted to get everyone out the door as soon as possible. "Come on. We're heading over to Tanz. We're all walking over right now. No time to clean up. Drop your sticks."

Arm in arm, Erin and Meg walked into Tanz, the dance club next to the hotel. Erin smiled with excitement when she spotted Chick and Jadon already seated around the large glass table perched on the second level, above the dance floor. Erin waved at everyone else already nestled into their spots.

"How did we get so far behind?" Erin questioned, surprised they were the last ones there. "Stu, did you let Bobby out?"

"Yup. He asked if he could come dancing tonight too, but I told him these places can get a little nutty," Stu chuckled, looking over his shoulder to peer down at the crowded dance floor.

"That was one of our fuckin' best shows," Bob said, spinning his empty beer bottle around on the table. "Man, Jadon, you and

Meg were on fire. Christ. I had to sit down and just watch. It was amazing."

"Yeah. Perfect. I couldn't have dreamt of it being any better," Chick agreed, anxious to start the mission he planned.

Throwing a newspaper down on the table, Stu slid it over to Chick. "Did you fuckin' read that? It's like Bob and I weren't even at the show we did in Copenhagen. Sounds like a report written by a doctor or some company CEO. Where's the spunk? Where's the heart?"

Chick ran his eyes over the article. Once again he noted how quickly the reviewer found a connection between Jadon and Meg, devoting two of the five paragraphs solely to them. There was one paragraph about him; the remaining two described the music and the band's tour.

"Who cares?" Chick said, tossing the newspaper back onto the glass table. "What the hell do they know?"

"Hey, you should write something about us, Meg," Stu said.

"Oh, well, a novelist is a very different animal from a music reporter, or any other reporter for that matter," Meg said, reaching over to grab the newspaper.

"Come on, give it a shot. Describe each of us or the music or something. Show us what you got," Stu prodded.

After eating the olive that was just moments ago, forced to drown at the bottom of her martini glass, Meg took another long sip and decided, *What the hell, turning over a new leaf means taking the chance to reveal a new side.*

"Okay. Let's see . . ." Meg paused. "When Stu Smith, bassist for Equinox, eases himself casually onto the stage, he also eases his low key, funky rhythm into the hearts and minds of everyone in the audience who can't resist moving their bodies in response to his perfectly blended sounds."

"See! We need more of that!" Stu yelled. "All right, how about Chickie down there?"

"Nahhh, Meg doesn't have to," Chick blushed.

"I'm on a roll, and as a writer you have to write while you're on a roll," Meg said. "Few get the privilege to bask under the radiant sun of musical genius, but for the audience at any Equinox concert, their bodies quickly glow from the brilliantly gifted front man, Kurt Holschick. His every word, song, shift of eye and strum of guitar melt away the cold edges that enslave the soul."

"Jesus. That was . . . wow, thank you. God. Write that down," Chick said, giving Meg a warm laugh. "I might need it when everyone says I suck."

"How about our man Jay?" Stu chimed.

Lifting his eyes from the still soggy beer label he was carefully spreading onto the table, Jadon looked at Meg, not sure if he really wanted to hear what she would say.

"Beautiful," Meg said softly, her heart flipping as the word unexpectedly leapt from her mouth. "I mean . . . let me think . . . that was just what popped into my mind . . . um," Meg closed her eyes. "To watch Jadon Hastings play the drums is to watch the human spirit fly freely, expressing itself in the most stunning way. With every commanding beat, he masterfully pulls your heart along with his," she said softly. "I suppose you might want something more rock star, Rolling Stone like."

"No, no," Jadon said, looking directly at Meg. "I like what you said. I really like it."

Feeling as though the moment was perfect, Chick grabbed Jadon's arm and pulled him abruptly from his seat.

"Time to dance. Come on everyone." Chick motioned for everyone to get up.

"Whoa! All rightie, we're dancin', we're dancin'," Stu said, remembering what Chick had told them to do: get Meg and Jadon together on the dance floor.

"Come on, Meg," Erin yelled.

Again with Meg on her arm, Erin made her way down the steps leading to the dance floor. Lost in the sea of dancers, Meg tried to relax into the song; something she always struggled to do when she didn't know the song or was still too sober. Meg slowly scanned everyone as they wiggled and bounced, letting the music move through them in whichever way it chose. As the song came to an end, Meg heard the band slow itself, settling casually into the romantic rhythm found in a love song.

"Stay out here, Meg!" Erin called, turning to find Chick, who had Jadon firmly in tow.

"We're staying out for this one, you two stay out, too," Chick said as he shoved Meg and Jadon together before turning to whisk Erin into his arms.

Jadon stood paralyzed. Taking a short second to let his mind catch up with the place his body now stood, he willingly slid his arms around Meg. He pulled her body next to his and delicately ran his hands along her bare back. Feeling her damp skin beneath his fingers, he moved her body tighter against his.

"Is this okay?" Jadon asked.

"Yes, yes, it is."

Offering her a warm smile, Jadon moved his head back beside hers, his nose resting next to her ear. He felt his body spiral nearly out of control, while he swayed them both to the music, and hoped the song would never end. Whether he would hate himself for it or not, he wanted the chance to be with her. He pushed aside every thought except the one that said how right the moment felt and ran his lips up Meg's neck and across her cheek, his lips searching for hers. Pressing his lips against hers, he eased her mouth open and gently began to kiss her. Opening his eyes softly to look into hers, he quickly got lost in the multitude of colors that made Meg's eyes sparkle. Running his hands farther up Meg's back, he slid his hand into her hair and held her head in his hand.

With his mouth gently glued to Meg's, both were lost in the moment and equally unaware that the dance floor was rapidly filling up with bodies that bounced to the quick beat of the next song.

Peering over the rail, Chick turned around and smiled at everyone seated at the table. "Jesus. Didn't think it would be *that* easy."

"Yeah, I kind of thought it would be a bit harder," Bob said, leaning over the railing.

"Oh, boy . . . ," Stu moaned with a mischievous smile, leaning his arms on the railing, watching Jadon lose himself to Meg. "That boy's got it bad. He's got it real bad."

"Chick?"

"Xavier? Small world," Chick said, quickly spinning around, "What the hell you doin' in Germany? Not just Germany, Jesus, what are you doin' in Duisburg?"

"You're not the only one on tour," Xavier reminded him, easing himself over to the railing. "I'm just here for the night. Actually, I have a show in Berlin."

"That's right, that's right," Chick said, remembering the world tour his old friend was on. "Those are some huge arenas you're playin' in."

Xavier nodded with a grin, taking a sip from the beer his assistant handed him. "It's good. It's all good. Full house, too. Each one," he said, peering over the railing to get a view of the dance floor. "Christ, no fucking way. Is that Meg?"

Not waiting for an answer, Xavier swept his small frame down the stairs that emptied out onto the dance floor.

Hoping for a moment to get lost in Meg's eyes, Jadon reluctantly ended their kiss, and slowly eased his head back.

"Oh, Meg," he whispered softly, bringing his lips back toward hers.

Lost in his delirium of desire, Jadon was slow to acknowledge the voice that was trying to interrupt them.

"I cannot believe this," Xavier said, standing next to Jadon and Meg.

"Xavier?" Meg said, feeling as though her life just came to a brutal end by the sight of him, or of anyone for that matter.

"This is such a small world," Xavier said warmly. "This makes me so happy. Come on, let's have a drink. I read that you were playing with Chick's band, but I never imagined I would run in to you. My God, this is wonderful," Xavier said, grabbing Meg's hand and dragging her up the stairs, and back to the table.

Standing above the dance floor, Chick and the rest of the band watched in horror as Xavier broke apart Jadon and Meg.

After slowly walking up the stairs, Jadon made his way to the table. Finding an empty chair next to Chick's, he sat down, his mind numb from the passionate moment he shared with Meg, but also by the cruel way it ended. Looking across the table he watched Xavier pull his seat closer to Meg.

"Hey, how do you know our Meg?" Chick asked, taken back by how quickly Xavier zeroed in on Meg and snatched her off the dance floor.

Xavier looked at Chick for a moment and then turned his small but muscular body back toward Meg. Running his fingers through his short black hair, he offered Meg a wink.

"Are you doing research with these guys too?" he asked.

"No," Meg said. "No. Absolutely not. This, this is all me."

Turning to look back at Chick, Xavier finally answered his question.

"Meg traveled with me while I was on tour in the states a couple years ago. She's been trying to elude me ever since."

"So . . . you probably have to get going. I think we do, too," Chick said, searching for a way to make Xavier disappear as suddenly as he had appeared.

"No. I'm good." Xavier answered. "I'm just trying to think of a way to finally convince this woman to run away with me. Or at least get her into my bed."

Stunned by his words, Meg began to feel ill.

"Come play with me when I'm done with this tour. We'll make beautiful music together. God, I can't even imagine how wonderful that would be," Xavier said.

"No, I'm happy here," Meg said, shaking her head. "Thank you, though."

"No. Really, Meg, I mean it," he said, pulling a cigarette out of its pack. "This spring. I'm going to find you and take you away."

"No! I'm busy. I'm engage . . . ," Meg paused, shaking her head, her tongue getting tied with frustration. "I have an engagement already. It's important."

Meg's eyes moved quickly from the drink in front of her and onto Jadon as he slid his chair back and walked out of the club.

"What the hell is so damn important that it can't be changed?" Xavier asked, not pleased with Meg's obstinacy.

Pushing his chair away from the table, Chick grabbed his coat and walked after Jadon. As the door to the club swung closed behind him, he saw Jadon walking toward the hotel.

Looking around the table, Meg tried to ignore Xavier's presence. "I was hoping for a much nicer time to tell you all this," she said to Stu, Bob, Kofi, Erin and Flora. "This spring, when my novel about my mother is done, I'm publishing it under my name. So, it's sort of a big deal. Or at least to me it is. I want you guys to be there. I know it's not something you would normally go to, but it's because of you that I'm finally finding the strength, my own voice, or at least a voice that I want to claim as my own."

"I'm so proud of you," Flora said. "This is good. This is good, Meg. Don't worry, dear. Remember what your mother said — you can't fall."

"I feel like I'm falling. I feel like everything is so uncontrollable. Nothing makes sense. I don't make sense. I don't know how I'm even going to finish this book in time. But I will. I owe it to my mother."

"And you owe it to you," Flora added.

"Meggie Peggie, you're such a beautiful person. There's *no* place we would rather be than with you when your book is released. I can't wait," Stu said proudly.

"That's right. You're stuck with us. Like Gorilla Glue, baby. Stuck," Bob winked. "Come on, let me walk you back to your room."

"What?" Xavier shouted, breaking from the conversation he was having with his assistant. "No, no, no. I'll be the one to do that."

"*No!*" Meg said. "Now stop it. Maybe the world loves you, but I don't."

"I can't take this," Jadon said, letting out a long tortured breath. "I can't fucking compete with Devon and Xavier. Xavier? What is that? I mean. Jesus Christ. He has to be the biggest name in the business, and there he is, running his paws all over Meg like he owns her."

"Dude, one, you can tell Meg can't stand him. Two, I don't know if you happened to catch it or not, but I watched her kiss you on the dance floor. That was more than a kiss," Chick said.

Looking hard at Chick, Jadon threw himself onto the low brick wall bordering the tree they were standing under. "God. She's engaged. What am I fuckin' doing? She's already engaged to Devon."

"What? Dude, I don't know where . . ."

"Coco."

"Well, uh . . ."

"No. I told her I don't want anything to do with her. I told her I don't want to ever fuckin' see her again. No. She said she was talking with Devie and *he* told *her* that he and Meg have been engaged for quite some time. She's just waiting for the tour to get over. Late this spring they're tying the knot, and he is whisking her away."

"That don't sound right," Chick said, shaking his head as he began to pace. "I don't think Meg would dick around with you. I really don't. I've been watching this whole thing go down . . . there's no way in hell. I won't believe it. You shouldn't, either."

"I gotta stop doing this," Jadon said. "I gotta stop feeling this way. Letting myself get carried away. Why? Just so she can put it in one of her books?"

"She wouldn't do that."

"Well she would, and she did. Thanks to wonderful Devie, who couldn't wait to share with me Meg's latest novel, I was able to read it for myself. Right there, spelled out beautifully. It sounds good. God. It sounds amazing . . . but it's me. It's my heart. She used it, and shaped it into her book."

"Let's seriously question *anything* Devon has his hands on. I don't trust him. I don't like him. I think he's *bad* news, and that guy *hates* you," Chick said, trying to sort through what he was hearing. "Did you ever think he just created it, or faked her book or something? It's probably not even her book you read."

"How the hell would Devon know those intimate details?"

"Well, I don't know. Fuck. I just know I don't trust him. I don't trust Coco. I double don't trust the two of them together. You *know* that is a fucked situation if you ever saw one. I think that dude would do anything to remove you from the planet. Don't go down this road man. Don't fall for it. Let's just figure this out. Let's just cool it for a moment."

"I can't just cool it. I can hardly breathe."

"Hell, I'll just ask Meg what the hell is going on."

Jadon shook his head no. "I already told Coco I would do that. She said Devon told her Meg would just deny it."

"We'd know. We'd know if she was lying. I don't think Meg would lie to us. I *know* she wouldn't lie to us. She wouldn't lie to you. No way. Don't forget the players involved. You're letting your insecurities get the best of you, Jay. Step back. You got the girl . . ."

"I don't fucking have anything. I can't even hold her in my arms without something horrible happening to pull us apart. And then sometimes I think, I can't even handle all of this. It's so . . . intense."

"Fuck Xavier. He's so full of himself. Meg doesn't like him. Don't worry. Move past that. The fish we need to fry is Devon. I don't think they're engaged. And so what if they were? Who cares if she were married? She loves you. Plain and simple."

Chapter 27

Madelyne's eyes glazed over as she watched her husband rifle through her bureau drawer. From a hidden distance, she silently observed his large, muscular frame mutate into the vision of a man made small — the outward result of his spirit being reduced from the crushing effects of his insecurities slowly taking over his mind.

Tired of trying to convince him of her love, she no longer made the attempt. Sadly, Madelyne knew, the words she would offer would no longer be true. It was that truth he saw resting patiently behind her eyes each time he looked at her. For that, she was sorry.

With no consideration for time, Madelyne stood and watched him carefully run his eyes over the pages of her magazines in the same way he looked too deeply into her paintings, trying to discover the things that beckoned her away from him. He hoped that if he knew, he would be able to offer it, magically turning her internal compass back toward him.

There is no thing, no person, no object that pulls me toward it, Madelyne said to herself. And that seemingly simple thing was what separated them. His mind rested forever in a different world from hers. Not a place that was better or worse, just different.

Feeling nothing, she slowly turned, and walked out onto the large porch that rested gracefully behind their house. Sitting down, Madelyne withdrew a cigarette from its pack. Her statuesque slender body unmoving, deep in thought she exhaled slowly, sending a long white cloud of smoke to swirl in front of her face before dissipating into the sky.

Meg pushed aside her laptop, and walked to the window overlooking the dimly lit buildings lining the streets of London. The only words she wanted to speak were the ones she privately and silently wove into her novel. She felt the pain of Jadon's distance during their last few shows and so she pushed herself harder, pouring her feelings into her music like an angry thunderstorm of emotions. Deciding to walk off her tension, Meg slipped on her Vans and walked down to the bar that Stu had said some of them were planning to check out. She smiled when she saw Bob's well tanned face beam as soon as he saw her. Meg swayed her body between the chairs, making her way over to their table.

"Hey, guys," Meg said, looking around the dark wooden table, relieved to find Jadon wasn't there.

"You sounded great tonight, Meggie," Stu offered.

"Jesus Christ," Stu said in disgust, looking over Meg's head, fixing his eyes toward the door to the pub.

"There you are," Devon said breathlessly. "I've been looking all over for you. I went to your room. Which I hope is to your liking, by the way. And you were gone. I did get a nice moment alone with Bobby however."

"You were in my . . . ," Meg began to say, uneasy at the idea that Devon made himself so welcomed in her private space.

"Well, of course, dear. How was I to know you weren't in there, unless I actually went in?" He answered, his tone indicating how silly her question was. "You look tired. You look unhappy. I knew this tour would be too much for you. God only knows what it's doing to Bob."

"No, I'm not tired. Neither is Bob. I've just been working out a few things, that's all. I've been working on my book, and other things."

"What other things?" Devon asked, pulling a chair next to Meg. "Darling, you tell me everything. What is it?"

Meg sat silently thinking, knowing she didn't tell him everything.

"Stuff. Just stuff."

"Well, let's talk about it shall we?" Devon said, running the back of his fingers down Meg's cheek.

"I don't want to talk to anyone. About anything," Meg said, with a tone of resolve settling into her voice.

"We need to discuss some things. I need you to come with me. We can go over whatever it is that's bothering you."

Chick sat with the others, watching Meg's body stiffen every time Devon tried touching her.

"No. No, thank you, Devon. I'm where I want to be."

Startled by Meg's response, Devon paused a moment. Burning his eyes deep into her face, he tried to coax her again.

"Surely you don't mean that. I can tell you're quite tired . . ."

"I'm tired. I am tired . . . and I'm thoroughly pissed. No, no, that's not quite accurate," Meg said, turning to look Devon directly in the eye. "I'm fucking pissed. And if you try to fucking mess with me anymore, you will be fucking sorry. So back the fuck off!"

Standing slowly, Devon slid his chair back under the table. He looked down at Meg, keeping his composure in check. He bent down and said gently, "I'll be back." Then turned slowly, and walked away.

"I hope he never fuckin' comes back," Stu said.

"You and me both," Bob agreed.

"I so don't like that guy, Meg," Chick said, putting his palms together in front of his face.

Staring at her bottle of beer, Meg offered confidently, "I'm not sure I do either. That's one of the reasons why I'm going to switch publishers. He doesn't know that yet. And I can't believe it will go over well. But, the thought feels . . . downstream."

"Meg," Flora said gently. "You're doing the right thing."

"Yup," Bob added.

"If you need any help when you break it to him . . . ," Stu offered, feeling his protectiveness of Meg rise into his eyes.

"Yeah. You want us there, we're there. Don't even hesitate. In fact, I think we *should* be there," Chick said, plunking his finger down hard on the glossy wood table. "Cuz' I don't think he'll ever walk away from you."

Meg smirked. "Wish others had that same kind of tenacious determination toward me. Doesn't matter. I feel good. I know I'm doing the right thing. He can't change my mind. Thank you, though. Is it too sappy to tell you guys how much I really care about you?" Meg asked, surprising herself with a quick laugh followed with tears.

"We love you too," Flora said.

"Yes, we do," Bob added.

"You know we do. Hell, we fell in love with ya the moment you smiled at us," Stu grinned.

Rubbing his face, Chick wanted to make the world stop spinning. He wanted to push his finger down on the globe, bringing it to an instant halt. Then he could turn it back slowly, trying to find the place where everything began spiraling out of control.

"You know we do. All of us," Chick said, wishing he could tell her how his closest friend was going out of his mind with love for her. "Hey, Meg," he continued, "what's your thought on marriage? You ever plan on getting married?"

"I don't plan to ever marry. I don't like it. Nothing good comes of it."

Everyone sat silently, surprised by Meg's answer and her lack of hesitation in which she offered it.

"Aw, gee . . . it's not *that* bad," Bob blurted.

"No. It's not that. I think it works for some people. Not for me," Meg said flatly. "I watched what it did to my mom. Nope. Not me."

"What did it do to your mother?" Flora asked.

"I just think for some people, like my mother . . . ," Meg continued. "It's an ill-fitting coat. Nothing about it feels right. My mom just wanted a life without eyes watching over her. Beautiful, passionate eyes, yes. Fearful eyes that hate so easily, *that* she could live without."

"Well, what the hell. What if *you* met the right guy? And he had the right kind of eyes?" Stu said, throwing the idea out on the table.

"The right kind of eyes," Meg smiled, seeing Jadon's eyes in her mind, thinking how delicious that would be, whether she believed it to be possible or not. "Well, I guess he would just have to agree to live with me as long as he felt that way. But, no, I don't see the need in legally binding myself to anyone."

"Okay. Shit, I'm just going to say it," Chick blurted, unable to contain himself any longer. "What about Devon?"

Meg stared at Chick, waiting for him to continue. "What about him?"

"Supposedly you two are fuckin' engaged!"

"*What?*" Meg burst into a deep laugh, not realizing the implications of Chick's words. "That's funny. You're funny."

"I think *he* would like being engaged to you," Chick said.

"Well, I think that Devon, like my father, is, or at least was, a good person. I don't know what has come over him lately. But awhile back I could safely say he was a truly good person. But, no, I just don't feel that way towards him. Never have. Enough Devon talk. Anyone want to go for a walk?"

"Let's go!" Bob shouted, ushering everyone up from the table.

Giving everyone a moment to bury themselves under their coats, hats and the time to carefully wrap their wool scarves around their necks, Meg watched her new family follow her out the door. She felt nothing but love as she ran out onto the empty snowy street bordering the pub and their hotel. Throwing her arms out into the air, she attempted to catch the snowflakes on her tongue while twirling her body on the dimly lit street.

Reaching down to grab some snow, Chick couldn't resist the urge to blast someone with a snowball. Stu let out a roar of laughter as he was hit. Fumbling his hands through the cold snow, Stu quickly armed himself with one misshaped snowball, and retaliated.

"Nail him!" Meg yelled.

"*Noooo!*" Stu yelled, darting behind a car parked on the street. Accidentally hitting the car with the snowball, Chick set off its car alarm. As the horn howled in distress, all seven of them scurried down the empty street. Reaching down into the snow, everyone tried to form snowballs to throw at one another. Flora nailed Chick right between the eyes, sending him staggering backward.

"You know what? Tonight's the night. Tonight's the night," Meg yelled, running down the middle of the road, heading back toward the hotel.

"Where the hell ya goin'?" Stu yelled.

Turning around while she was running, Meg smiled and yelled, "Devon! Devon! It's over!"

Running into the hotel, Meg breathlessly looked around for Devon, wondering if he would be waiting for her. She glanced into the lounge that was off the main lobby, peering cautiously past the dark mahogany door frame that separated the open space of the lobby from the intimate setting of the lounge. Instead of seeing

Devon, Meg's heart slipped from her body as she watched Coco lean in closer to Jadon. Stepping back, she tried to ignore the hurt that vibrated through her bones. Glancing back at the lobby once more, Meg made her way up to Devon's suite.

Staring at the floor in the lounge, Jadon said in a low growl, "If you ever touch me again, I will break your fingers like the thin little sticks they are."

"Well," Coco said, "that's not nice. You know, Jadon, men are waiting in line to be with me, so I don't know what your problem is."

"You. Simply put, you. You are the problem. I've asked nice. But I'm not in the mood to be nice about it anymore. So just go away. Go away, Coco, and don't ever get within a hundred feet of me ever again."

"Darling!" Devon beamed, opening the door to his suite. "I was just going to go look for you. But then, I realized something. Meg, I need to talk with you."

Walking over to the sofa near the window that spanned the length of the wall and afforded a panoramic view of the city, Devon slowly sat down, crossing his long legs in one graceful movement.

"Please. Allow me this. Allow me to go first. I . . . ," Devon paused, waiting for Meg to sit next to him. "I think we need to make some changes. I think it's excellent that you want to begin writing under your own name, and although I was taken aback by it initially, I think it's good. It's what you need. And I also think you need to take this moment in your life to begin this new journey with an entirely new publisher."

Wanting desperately to derail any attempts Meg might have had of separating herself from him out of anger, Devon wanted to reshape the picture she had of him in her mind.

"I have a few publishers that I believe you should consider, but of course, the decision is ultimately yours. I can guide you if you wish. I . . . just want you to be happy. And if I can still be a part of that, then . . . well . . . my world will be a much, much better place. Darling?"

All the thoughts and sentences that Meg had carefully crafted in preparation for this moment shuffled in front of her mind like a deck of cards. Replaying Devon's words slowly, she considered carefully how to respond, only to realize she didn't possess one word or expressible thought. Tears flowed from her eyes as she sat motionless. Overcome by how incomprehensible everything had become, Meg wasn't able to tell if Devon was good or bad anymore.

Putting his arm around Meg's shoulder, Devon pulled her in to him. Resting his mouth on her head, he kissed her hair softly.

"I know, I know. You've been through a great deal lately. I'm here. You'll be all right. You'll be all right," he whispered.

Giving Meg the time she needed, Devon held her close, occasionally wiping her tears away with a gentle finger.

"It's okay. It's okay. I know you've been hurt lately. I wish I could have protected you from it. From him." Devon let his last two words barely fall from his lips.

"It's not . . . ," Meg struggled to say.

"Meg, I know you felt a great deal for him. I know you. Remember?" He smiled warmly. "And it's okay. Except that he hurt you. I want you to be with whomever makes you happy. And if that would have been he, then . . ." Devon said scanning her face. "I just wish I could somehow find the way to take away the pain he caused you. Tell me, how I can make you feel better?" Looking at the tears covering Meg's cheeks, Devon felt the need to softly kiss her face.

Closing her eyes, Meg tried to forget about Jadon while feeling Devon's lips seductively gaze across the surface of her skin. Despite her attempts, she pictured Jadon's soft eyes while Devon kissed her on the cheek.

Devon felt his mind cloud over as he moved his mouth across Meg's face. He wanted intensely for her to have the same look in her eyes for him that he saw in her eyes when she was about to kiss Jadon on the elevator. Keeping his movements slow but steady, Devon patiently tried to coax Meg into loving him.

Delicately moving his lips onto Meg's, almost immobilized from the fear of ruining the moment, he kept his kisses soft, easing each one gently onto Meg's delicate mouth, making sure she never felt overwhelmed. Finally allowing his eyes to close, he lost himself within her kiss.

Tilting her face up softly, Meg shook her head, confused by everything that was taking place. Her feelings, her judgments, her desires, everything that pulled at her heart seemed to carry a level of confusion and pain that made life almost unbearable.

Devon pulled back, not wanting Meg to question the moment. Sitting next to her, he once again put his arm around her, and pulled her close. His heart beating rapidly from its acute longing for her.

"You know . . . ," Devon said, playing with his words softly, letting them linger on his tongue before sending them in Meg's direction. "I think about our night together. You're so beautiful, Meg. Don't ever let anyone make you feel like less than the radiant woman you are."

"I don't even know what beautiful is anymore."

"Well . . . ," Devon laughed lightly. "My dear, you're it. You have always been it. For me you have. There has never been another woman, not since my eyes had the rare privilege of gazing upon you."

Meg felt the sincerity of Devon's words seep into her mind. Lifting her wet eyes onto his, her mother's words fluttered into her mind: *Sometimes the cage looks quite lovely*. Turning away, she tried to focus on the oversized painting positioned artfully low on the wall in front of them. Moving her eyes over the painting, she noticed the simple beauty of the giant white open petals of the rose flowing outward from the right side of the canvas. When painting it, the artist made a conscious effort to leave a large open space of black canvas on the left, and beyond the midpoint of the painting, giving it perfect balance. Not confined, the rose was allowed to expand into its full splendor, even if its ability to do so was only within the mind of the one viewing it.

Turning to look at Devon, Meg watched his face soften as he studied her. His eyes wanted to find love within her eyes as she looked at him. Devon felt his heart beat painfully. Wanting to erase Jadon from her mind, he leaned over and kissed her softly. Cupping her face in his hands, he pulled her face closer, sinking deeper into the kiss. Seeing nothing past his passion, he ran his hands deep into Meg's hair as he eased her body down onto the sofa.

"I love you," he whispered looking into her eyes. "Marry me, Meg." The words fell from his tongue before he could restrain them. "No. I mean . . . I know you don't like marriage. I didn't mean to say that really. I just mean . . . be with me . . . here."

Meg felt Devon's body resting on hers, his chest moving heavily while his body desperately tried to catch up with his accelerated mind. Looking at his face, she ran her fingertips around his dark chocolate eyes, and across his perfectly shaped lips. As she did she watched Devon kiss her fingertips. Easing her hand away from his mouth, Meg rested her fingers on her own mouth, pausing for a moment.

"This . . . as beautiful and as tempting as it appears, isn't where I should be," Meg said delicately. Feeling his body tense to the sound of her words, she began to slide her body out from under his.

"No." Devon said, gently tucking her back under him. "No. You're just confused, darling."

"No," Meg said, her thoughts landing in her mind in a coherent orderly fashion, the first in a long time to land that way. "No, I'm actually not confused at all. I love him. I do. I hate myself for it. But I love him."

"Don't do this. You're being unreasonable."

"Unreasonable," Meg said, trying again to slide her body off the sofa. Once successful, she slowly started toward the door. "Unreasonable. There's nothing reasonable about love. It just is."

"He's . . ." Devon stopped Meg from opening the door. "He's just using you, Meg."

"It doesn't matter. It's done. But it doesn't change what's in my heart. Maybe I'm damaged goods now. I don't know. I don't care. He's all I see."

"He's probably slithering around with another one of those disgusting women right now. What do you see in him? God, Meg." Devon's voice started to amplify.

"I see everything. But, you know, it doesn't matter. It's over. And it kills. I would almost . . . almost rather die than live without the chance to look into his eyes," Meg said angrily, angry at herself, angry at Jadon, angry that she had to explain her feelings to Devon.

"Oh, yes. Yes. I know. I *read* every last bloody word of it. God, how I know."

Walking closer to Devon, Meg looked directly into his eyes. "You. You made sure of it didn't you? You made sure my heart would break. I was such a fool," she said, slowly putting the pieces together as she formed the sentences in her head. "I called Claire. I called her, Devon. And while I was talking with her, I asked her about *all* the chapters she flagged and said were inconsistent. She said she never flagged anything. Nothing. She thought it was perfect and beautiful. *You.* You did it. I don't know why . . . why I never made the connection before. You wanted to find a way to keep me from him. A little something to sidetrack me for the night. Well, you succeeded. You were the first horrible crack in a full blown avalanche. An avalanche I don't even fully understand. But because of it, I feel like I'm smothering to death. I feel like I'm not going to make it. Do you hear me? I feel like I'm literally dying while I'm still breathing. You, you didn't care. All your words about wanting me to be happy. They were lies. What kind of love is that? The kind that plays games. The kind that so easily mutates into jealousy and hatred. Hatred that I love you differently than I love him. I don't want that kind of love," Meg said, her voice cracking from her volume.

Walking out the door, Meg turned and looked at Devon, unable to decipher who or what he was anymore.

Chapter 28

Poised like a statue, Madelyne sat and watched as her husband hurled venomous words in her direction. Carefully positioning himself, making sure his sights were set directly on his target, he ensured a direct hit each time. Her mind was now void of the feelings and joy that first drew her to him; she simply absorbed one wicked word after the other.

Despite the monstrous picture he tried to paint of her, the only monster she knew was the one that crept through her own mind. Its malicious voice convinced her and finally forced her to believe she would destroy her daughter's life if she reclaimed her own. She looked blankly into the distance as the accusatory thief tried to burglarize her mind. Madelyne began to realize that her world, her thoughts, the darkness that dwelt inside of her — all of this was what made her who she was, and thus made her beautiful daughter as well. The darkness is what gives the light a reason to shine. And in doing so, enlightening the deepest parts of the soul.

Within those darkened spaces, she found her inspiration to paint. From those places came the visions she carefully brushed onto the blank canvas. But it was also that darkness that kept her mind in a different place, a place that separated her from her husband and from the things he desired.

It only took a short time for Madelyne to recognize she could not share that different place with him, because he couldn't and didn't want to understand it. But it was that different space, that uniquely different world that constantly lulled her. Called her name and kept her company. He was *not at fault for not grasping what she could barely understand herself. But the draw to explore that different world was pulling her apart inside.*

Love, Madelyne realized, is a unique thing. So thinly is it separated from hate that it, or at least certain versions of it, are meaningless. And with that she concluded that the shade of love currently painting her world, she could forever live without.

Meg hit *save* and closed her laptop. Stretching her body across the luxurious black bedspread that draped her bed, she rested her head on Bob and let the peculiar feeling of leaving something she thought she trusted behind, mixed with the nervous excitement of starting something new settle over her.

She rolled off her bed when she heard the knock on her door. Swinging it open wide, Meg was pleased to see it was Erin and Bob.

"I'll just be a minute," Meg said, walking over to grab her leather jacket before walking with Bob and Erin to the elevator.

"You know we're dying to know," Bob finally said, as they stepped into the elevator.

"We've been waiting all day for you to show your face. Nothing. You didn't show at breakfast, lunch or dinner," Erin added, pushing hard on the button marked *Lobby*.

"I needed to get some things off my chest, so I've been writing since I walked back into my room last night. And to be honest, I didn't want to see . . . Jadon."

"Well, *he* hasn't been around either. It's like you two are troglodytes. Hermits or something," Bob said sadly.

"Back to the *other* big deal, Devon. We saw him glide through the restaurant this morning. He didn't look happy. Amazing though . . . ," Erin offered reflectively, "he was still quite handsome."

"Yeah," Meg said with a light laugh. "He's gifted that way."

The elevator slowed and stopped, and the doors opened.

"Christ!" Bob stopped quick, shocked by the sight of Devon standing directly in front of them.

"Meg, I really feel we should talk again." Devon explained.

"You're right. We should. Come and watch the show tonight. I think you won't have any questions afterward," Meg said.

Following Meg's lead, Erin and Bob pushed past Devon and walked with her across the street to the Ashby.

Feeling liberated, Meg held her head high as she waited for the show to begin. Having loved and lost, she shook her head with the simplicity of the words as they snaked across her mind. She stole a glance at Jadon and winced when his eyes briefly met hers. *Well*, Meg said to herself, *he is still the most beautiful shade of love.*

Meg watched as Chick eased himself easily into his first song of the night, his soulful eyes dancing across the audience, giving them his heartfelt smile that somehow made everyone feel as though they'd be all right, despite how everything may seem. She smiled watching Stu recline in his chair, casually strumming his guitar. Not rushed or hurried but living in the moment contained within each song. Then Bob, giving the songs their intricate detail, hitting his notes perfectly, and with mesmerizing skill. Looking beyond Bob, Meg watched as Kofi swayed his tall thin body back and forth, brushing his fingers across the keys, content and happy with the sounds he was creating. Looking at that small cluster of people, Meg smiled, enjoying the warm feeling of knowing they had her back, if ever she needed them.

Even though she knew she still was drifting in the middle of an ocean of mixed emotions, Meg turned and again looked at Jadon. She refused to let go of the warmth of having people who love her without question, without motive, without judgment or personal motives. Letting that good feeling wrap around the pain that was now her heart, she watched Jadon move his body behind his drums. Taking advantage of the one song she didn't have a small part in, she soaked them all in. Pain and all, she decided there was no place else she would rather be.

Turning slowly to look down and across the audience, Meg felt her heart strike hard against her chest once her eyes met Devon's. Turning her head, she smiled at Chick, who was already smiling back at her.

Ready to fly, Mom? Meg asked silently in her mind.

In an instant Meg lit the room with the intensity of her sound. Sliding her bow across the strings, she pushed her energy out into the audience. Smiling as she walked closer to Chick, making a point not to hide in the corner, she stood alongside him.

Once the song drew to a close, Meg continued to play, skyrocketing her first note into the hearts of the audience, filling their chests with startled excitement. Moving her fingers with speed and perfection, she flew through a flurry of notes, giving the invisible energy of life a tangible beauty felt by everyone in the room. Wanting everyone to feel the tumultuous feelings she held within her soul, Meg drew her bow harder on the strings, giving flight to all the anger she felt.

Anger that her parents were ripped from her life so quickly one snowy night. Anger that their lives, while they had them, were filled with pain. Anger that she spent years of her life hidden away, too afraid to even try. Anger that once she tried to fly toward love, it turned its back on her.

Listening carefully, Chick found the same melody Meg kept repeating, and strumming his guitar he found his place next to her. Within moments Bob added his sound, giving her melody its pitch. With the sounds of his steel guitar, he was able to make Meg's notes stand out, stamping them perfectly in place. Stu casually eased himself into the mix, giving Meg's sound the body it needed by filling it with a low repetitive rhythm. Kofi waited until Meg hit her low notes, and within them he dusted his fingers across the keyboard, adding dimension to her sound.

Jadon watched as the new song created itself on the stage, finding its perpetual rhythm and harmonies between the different instruments, he crept his way in. Hardly wanting to be noticed, but not wanting to be without her, he added his own texture to the song, giving it a vibration that caught the body and summoned it to move forward.

Allowing this new song ample time to express itself, Meg smiled, her heart enraptured by the wholeness of being surrounded by love. As she brought the song to a close, the band took her lead and turned silent. Not having the words to describe it, Chick tried to keep his composure. Putting his guitar down, he walked over to Meg and wrapped his arms around her.

With a smile and tearful eyes, Chick bowed in front of Meg. Having the same mutual respect, Meg bowed before him, then turned to give the same bow to Stu, Bob and Kofi, nodding her head at each of them. Turning to look at Jadon, Meg nodded her head before turning and giving the audience a final, grateful bow.

Standing tall she brought her palms together in front of her face. "Namaste," she whispered, appreciating the divine presence of everyone surrounding her.

Content that her voice was heard, Meg walked over to her stool. Glancing down, she nodded at Devon, knowing that in fate's wicked way, without him she never would have been given this new life.

Chapter 29

Madelyne held her daughter's hand as they walked out the door, eager to begin a life without the threat of watchful eyes. Filling her lungs with the fresh air of new possibilities, Madelyne looked down at her daughter and smiled. It was a smile that lit the world and the galaxies that lay far beyond.

"Time to fly," she whispered to her daughter, her eyes full of hope and promise.

Carefully crafting a life that held freedom firmly as its foundation, Madelyne stretched her large wings, spreading them across the world that now was hers. Living with the pain of the past, she stepped off the branch and let the energy that is life carry her across the clouds. She turned back only to smile, watching her daughter gracefully catch up with her. Together they swooped and danced as the brilliance of the sun swept across their beautiful wings. Content with what is and eager for what lies ahead.

That is the ending that should have belonged to my mother. Perhaps somewhere, in another lifetime, she is still flying beautifully, living the life that should have been hers. I will never know. I can only, when I am at my best, allow myself to dream that wishful dream.

~ Meg Kathryn Scott

Meg reread her words once more, again concluding that they were as perfect as she had the ability to create them. Taking a long deep breath, she stepped out onto her balcony and welcomed the barely warm ocean breeze that swept across her face, feeling confident she had given her mother a taste of something wonderful. It was Meg's shortest novel, but her most delicately worded. Yet her new publishing house eagerly accepted it.

Rubbing Bob's head as he stood next to her, Meg looked down and reminded him how wonderful he was. Since they arrived back in Mandalay Bay a few weeks ago, Bob had constantly been whisked away. Treated to walks on the beach, afternoons at the dog park, or just time to chill at the studio. *He has people now, good people,* Meg thought, smiling at his gentle face.

"Are you still stealing away afternoons with Jadon?" Meg asked, trying to look Bob in the eye. She couldn't help but wonder. Erin alluded to it the other day when they went for a walk along the beach. "Why does he want to be with you and not me?" Meg wondered.

Making her way over to her laptop, Meg looked at her words once more before confidently emailing her last chapters to Trish at Handle House Publishing. Closing her laptop, she thought about Devon. He still called. She still didn't answer. Looking at her calendar, Meg noticed that her book *Love's End*, with Elle and Jadon, would be released in a few short days by Hathaway Publishing. It would mark an end to a long and very successful commercial relationship. She sat down and lowered her head onto her desk, resting it softly on her arms. Meg thought about Jadon and the scenes she so carefully wrote trying to capture his beauty and how he made her feel. She wanted to own it. She wanted to find a way to keep it with her forever.

Erin told her Jadon barely spoke to anyone, and from what Erin could tell he wasn't sleeping or eating much. Erin explained how upset Chick was, practically going out of his mind with worry. All the more reason for him to take them all on the camping trip he had painstakingly planned. Meg didn't think camping sounded like fun, but she would do anything for Chick. And the thought of being surrounded by the band felt good.

Walking back to the kitchen, Meg poured a glass of wine and took it out onto the balcony, where she let the ocean air push her hair around.

Taking the pillow off of his head, Jadon rolled out of bed, his body and mind too tired to sleep. Sighing from exhaustion brought on by months of limited sleep, he walked across his living room and stood on the balcony, trying to appreciate the sunset that was quickly fading in front of him. But instead, Chick's words tumbled through his mind, repeatedly telling him that Meg not only wasn't engaged but she didn't even believe in the concept of marriage. This stood in bright contrast to what Coco had told him. Rubbing his face, Jadon didn't know where the truth rested.

"Even if she wasn't engaged, she still used my feelings for her. God, Meg," Jadon whispered.

Turning around, he looked at his piano. He eased himself onto the bench and stared at the new song he had written just prior to leaving on the European tour. Gently placing his hands on the keyboard, he began to play softly the song he wrote for Meg.

Meg's heart jumped as soon as she heard the sounds of her neighbor's piano. Standing and listening, Meg noticed it was different in that it wasn't softly tapping for her to join him; instead her neighbor was in the midst of a beautiful song. One she'd never heard before. Curling up on a chaise lounge next to the railing of her balcony, Meg enjoyed the sounds emanating from her neighbor's home. In her mind's eye she saw Jadon sitting behind the piano. Shaking her head, she quickly pushed the image away.

Running his fingers over the keys, Jadon couldn't help himself but to call out for Meg. Tapping lightly on the keys, he tried to summon her sound, all the while hating himself for being so vulnerable to her.

Meg's eyes shot open when she heard the familiar tapping radiating from her neighbor's piano. Springing to her feet, she rushed indoors to retrieve her violin. Quickly throwing open the lid of the case, she hastily grabbed her violin and bow and ran back to her balcony. Shifting her body quickly around her sofa, she felt her body come to a crushing thud against her floor. Not wanting to injure her violin, Meg wasn't able to catch herself when her foot caught on Bob who was laying in the narrow passageway between the sofa and the kitchen island.

"I'm here, I'm here," Meg said softly, struggling to pull her body off the floor.

Not hearing the sound of Meg's violin, disappointment quickly settled over Jadon. Normally, within a few notes she always answered. That was only possible, he reasoned, because each was always waiting for the other to play. He regretfully took his hands off the keys, and slid the bench out from under him.

With every movement, and every attempt to breathe, pain radiated from her ribs.

"Jesus Christ, Bob. Did you have to pick *that* spot?" Meg struggled to say as she willed herself to move toward the balcony. "Don't go anywhere, please don't go . . ."

Holding her breathe in an attempt to ease the pain that skyrocketed through her body, Meg gave a quick hit to the strings on her violin, letting him know she was there.

"I'm here. I'm here," she whispered.

Halted by the sound, Jadon turned quickly. "She's there." Rushing to the piano, he threw his hands across the keys, sending her a musical kiss with every touch of the key.

Biting her lip, Meg pushed past the pain riveting through her body as she sent her music his way. Within the resonance of every note she shared how much she missed him.

"Oh, I've missed you," Meg whispered.

Refusing to give in to the pain, Meg continued to make music, giving her neighbor a piece of her heart; so hoping he still wanted it.

"Oh, Meg," Jadon whispered.

Hitting the keys harder, Jadon felt his body urge him to go to her, to charge through her door and forget the past. Forget everything except the look in her eyes.

As she felt his notes push harder through her body, Meg found the strength to match his intensity. She did not want to let go of the moment. Insisting that her body allow her the chance to feel the love of her neighbor, Meg bit down hard on her lip, trying to shift her focus off the pain that was rapidly making her knees weak. Leaning against the railing, Meg enjoyed every second, every note that radiated from her neighbor's balcony. As the music came to its natural sad ending, she tried to breathe.

With each painful step, Meg made her way slowly back into her house. Nodding her head, she felt confident with the decision she just made. Forcing her movements, Meg slowly made her way out the door. Bob followed her as she slowly walked to her neighbor's house. Determined not to let him slip away also, Meg demanded from herself that she meet the man who seemed to know and share the most private places within her soul.

Knocking on the door, Meg pushed herself to remain upright, standing in front of his door for as long as her body would permit. She felt her world collapse when he refused to answer. She stared down at her bracelet and felt like a fool. Having given her neighbor enough time to answer if he had truly wanted to, Meg slowly turned away.

Bob barked softly while looking at Meg, watching her take small painful steps back to their house. Lowering her body onto her front step, she began to cry. Dropping her head in her hands, she sobbed. Sitting next to her, Bob kissed her face. With each tear, each breath of air, pain shot through Meg's body like exploding dynamite.

Pulling herself back up, Meg slowly walked over to her neighbor's house once more. Slipping the bracelet off her wrist, she tossed it at the base of his front door. Hardly able to breathe, she turned around and made her way into her house and opened her garage door. Holding the car door open for Bob to jump in, she slid her body onto the leather seat, and brought her car to a roaring start. Wiping the tears from her face, she pulled onto the street, and headed to the hospital.

Opening his door cautiously, Jadon felt his heart sink when he looked down and saw the bracelet he had given Meg. He reached down and held it in his hand. He now hated himself for being too afraid to open the door; instead he had stood motionless while she knocked. He wanted to go to her. But he couldn't step beyond the fear that her anxious smile would quickly disappear once she saw it was he standing on the other side of the door. He forcefully wiped the tears away from his face, wishing he had the courage to make it up to her. Walking back into his house Jadon wished for her return. Keeping his lights off, he waited.

Meg didn't want to follow the advice of the doctor who treated her. She didn't want to wait until she got home before taking the pain medication he had given her. Instead, she wanted the pain to go away as quickly as possible. Knowing she was trying to numb more than the pain from three broken ribs, Meg opened the bottle as soon as she closed the door of her car. Sitting next to Bob, and without the aid of water, she swallowed hard, forcefully moving each large capsule down her throat.

Leaning her head back onto the head rest, Meg waited for some level of numbness to settle over her body, eager for the medication to take effect. Taking shallow breaths, she tried to be patient as the painkillers began to carry out their task.

Turning on the radio, Meg cringed from the pain. Looking at Bob, she reached over and rubbed his head. She saw the worry in his eyes and wanted to let him know she was all right.

She tilted back the car seat, closed her eyes and pondered the lyrics of the songs she listened to. As a writer, her words needed to paint the picture, walking a fine line between painting too vividly, which would give the readers no freedom to roam or imagine, and too vaguely, which would leave the readers wondering where they were or what direction to go in next. But within a song, a song writer could dance freely, being as abstract as desired and leaving it entirely up to the listeners to form their own stories, paint their own pictures of what the song meant to them. Meg liked that.

Without thought, Meg's body took a deep breath, her first since her fall.

"Thank God," she smiled, in awe of the power of pharmaceuticals as she carefully leaned forward to hit the ignition.

Jadon's sleepy eyes sprang open when he heard Meg's car pull into her driveway. Jumping to his feet he watched as the lights went on first in the living room and then in the kitchen.

Standing before the sink, Meg tossed two more pills into her hand and quickly washed them down with a large drink of water. She didn't care that she was suppose to wait until the next morning before taking them. Meg was eager to feel nothing, in both her body and her heart. Sitting down on her sofa, Meg slipped off her Vans, and carefully eased her body down on its non-injured side.

Breathing steadily, she tried to buy her time. She didn't want to think about Jadon. She didn't want to think about her neighbor. She didn't want to think about her parents or Devon, and she didn't want to feel any more pain of any kind. Instead Meg stared at Bob who sat in front of her, watching her intently.

Sitting down behind the piano, Jadon hoped to entice Meg to come back onto her balcony and give him one more chance. He wanted to hear her again. He wanted her to forgive him . . . to forgive the part of him that was scared to death that she loved the anonymous neighbor, but not him. Tapping at the keys softly he tried to call out her name.

Meg remained motionless listening to the sounds of the piano in the distance.

"Right. Sure. You don't want me. You want some distant version of me that's tucked behind a wall," Meg mumbled, reaching behind her back to grab the black pillow wedged behind her. Pushing it onto her head she tried to mute out the sound.

Meg felt her body grow heavy as the effect of the pain pills melted over her. Closing her eyes, she let her body sink deeper into the sofa. She welcomed the darkness that slowly engulfed her mind, and as soon as it became possible, she pulled her head under the warm drowning waves of a narcotic-induced sleep.

Bob barked at the door, wagging his tail profusely. The repetitive knocking caused him to anxiously scratch the wood surface of Meg's front door in an attempt to get to the other side.

Jadon stood apprehensively outside Meg's front door, and tried to prepare himself for whatever reaction he might encounter, fully understanding why she refused to play music with him. He knew it was his own fear that pushed her away. He felt his heart sink as he waited. Pounding on the door, he repeatedly yelled her name. Peering through the windows on either side of the door, he was unable to see anyone except Bob, who was frantically scratching at the door. His mind and heart lost their ability to stay intact as he waited. He came to the smothering conclusion that she had already looked out the window, saw him standing there, and — because of that, because it was he — she didn't want to open the door.

Jadon turned and sat down on Meg's front step. Gazing across the street, he leaned his body against the thick white post of her stair railing. Not wanting to move any further away from her than that, he closed his eyes. Rudely awakened early the next morning by a garbage truck slowly making its rounds on the street, Jadon pulled himself off her front step, and walked home.

Chapter 30

"Thank God we're *all* finally out here. Smell the air!" Chick said, turning to watch everyone drag their feet behind him up the narrow hiking path leading to his favorite camping spot, nestled beyond the Kern River, many miles from Bay City.

Chick sighed with relief at the above normal temps that helped the snowy mountains thaw earlier and faster that spring. There was still a considerable chill in the air even at the low elevation area where his favorite spot was located, but it was invigorating, he told himself and everyone else as they grumbled sluggishly up the dirt trail.

Meg's head felt the effects from her pain pills, while giving Chick the thumbs up when he darted his head around the others to make sure she was still following along.

"You know, people get lost out here guys, so keep it tight. Let's stay together!" Chick yelled, excited at the chance to rally his troops.

"Jesus Christ, Chick. We've done this every year since we've been touring," Stu barked, his stout body already exhausted from the hike. "Who the hell's going to wander off?"

"That's my guy. That's my guy," Chick said, throwing a hand down onto Bob's furry head. "See, Bob knows how to stay together," Chick tossed his words back toward the others, happy for the opportunity to clear the air. *Do or die*, he mused, *the air will be cleaned by the time we hike out of here.*

"I always forget how goddamn long this hike is," Bob huffed.

"Oh, Mr. Fitness is getting tired?" Erin said walking by him, easing herself next to Meg. "How are you doing? If you were any quieter you would disappear."

"I'm good. I'm good. I've just never been hiking and I've never been camping. I sort of fell down last night, too . . . ," Meg said, dismissing her words shortly after she said them.

"Are you okay?"

"Oh, I will be. In a few weeks, or months. I can't remember exactly what the doctor said. It's all a blur."

"Doctor!" Erin yelled, causing Chick to stop abruptly.

"Meg? You okay? You need a doctor?" Chick said, rushing to make sure Meg was all right.

"No, no. I . . . I just busted three ribs last night. I'm good. With the help of my little friends that live in this bottle, I'll be fine."

"Jesus Christ, Meg. You sure as hell shouldn't be carrying a backpack!" Bob said, trying to delicately but quickly remove Meg's backpack from her back.

"You don't have to do that. Really I'm good. The pain. It's helpful. It sort of numbs my mind."

"Meg. Christ. Bob, carry her backpack. Once we're at the site, you're relaxing. How the hell did you fall? Three ribs? Broken or cracked? Cracked is one thing, broken is another. Broken ribs are fucked up. They take forever to heal," Chick began to blather with worry.

"Broken. Three of them. Boom. Down I went. It's embarrassing. I'll tell you once we're huddled drunk around a campfire. That way none of you will remember it in the morning," Meg said, pointing her finger down the trail.

Walking along, Jadon watched Meg struggle to keep up. Not wanting her to fall behind, he made sure to stay in the back, making it appear as though he was naturally a very slow hiker. *When did she break her ribs? After we made music together? Before? After she left the bracelet on my front door, or before?* Jadon wondered.

Meg felt as if her body were going to collapse when the three-hour hike came to an end. They had veered off the trail and then back on before heading back off again. Finally Chick shouted excitedly that they'd arrived at their perfect destination. Looking around, Meg couldn't quite tell how the spot they were standing in was any different from the other spots she'd seen along the way. It didn't matter. All that mattered was that she was able to sit, even if sitting hurt worse than standing.

"Holy fuck, that was a long walk," Stu bellowed, throwing his backpack down on the ground.

"Hike. It was a hike. Same one we take every year," Chick reminded him, shuffling the leaves out of the way with his foot to build a fire.

Resting her arm on Bob's warm furry head, Meg watched as Jadon strolled along, not saying a word to anyone. She watched as he put his backpack down and walked into the woods to gather scraps of dead wood for the fire.

"We're goin' to get you all warmed up, Meg," Chick assured her with a caring smile.

"Your warm smiles are all I need," Meg said.

"Don't move, Meg, I'm going to put your tent up," Bob told her.

With one magical strike of a match, Chick created fire. Waiting and making sure the small pieces of wood were positioned just right, he kept his eyes glued to the small promising flame jumping beneath his teepee of sticks.

"It's going to be an impressive fire. I can just tell," Chick said.

Meg watched as everyone scurried around, carrying out their well-rehearsed duties. Each one was doing something different.

And within what seemed like minutes, they had created a miniature camping utopia before her eyes.

"The bear's gettin' hungry," Stu growled, while rubbing his stomach.

"Well, the bear better cool it. First things first," Chick snapped, struggling to set up the folding green table. "You're not the one who had to drag the fuckin' cooler for three goddamn hours."

Trying to appreciate the simple joys of what appeared to be the not so simple task of camping, Meg stretched her back, easing the pressure off her ribs.

"You know, I could do *something*. Give me something to do, please?" Meg begged.

"Almost done, you just sit tight," Chick said, rummaging through the cooler and pulling out a package of hotdogs. "Where the hell are the tofu dogs?" he mumbled, digging his hand further down into the ice. "Got it. Okay. Dinner's comin' up.

"Don't worry, I don't bite," Stu said, opening his camping chair next to Meg's. "Well. I do. But I won't bite you."

"Dos Equis, Red Stripe or Coors?" Stu said, pulling out a few cans and handing them around as everyone relaxed and sat down, warming themselves in front of the fire.

"Can you have one? Erin, can Meg have a beer?" Stu yelled.

"I dunno. If she wants one, I guess," Erin answered. "What pills do they have you on anyway?" Meg handed her the pill bottle. "Oh, boy, these are potent little suckers," Erin remarked, staring at the label: "750 milligram Vicodin. You'd better take it easy."

Stabbing a hot dog with a long metal fork, Chick added, "Well, broken ribs are not pretty. Christ. Remember when I broke three of mine? Remember? God. I was flying down the street on that damned scooter, hit the ramp and the goddamned handle bars flew off. Christ. I fell right on the curb. I could have sued, you know. I almost skewered myself to death. That was a fucked up scooter."

Handing Meg one of the grill forks, Bob took his seat by the fire. "So . . . ," he said, looking at Meg while he dangled his hotdog over the flame, "how the hell did you not just crack but manage to break three ribs?"

Having dreaded the arrival of this moment, Meg rocked her head gently back and forth, debating how detailed she should be.

"Well, I . . . God. This is sort of embarrassing," Meg stopped to glance across the fire at Jadon, relieved to see that he was preoccupied trying to coat his hotdog with an even layer of charred blackness on each side. "Well, I was sitting on my balcony, staring at the ocean and heard the *most* beautiful song coming from my neighbor's house."

"Oh . . . ," Stu moaned, "the infamous bracelet-giving, piano-playing neighbor guy."

"Yeah. Him," Meg nodded. "This song, was. . . . well, I've only heard one other song so beautiful. Anyway. That wasn't what did it. Shortly after the song ended, and I was still completely entranced by it, I heard him tickle at the keys sending out his little invitation to me. I was so damn startled I ran to get my violin, hastily ran back out onto the balcony and tripped over Bob in the process. I fell like a huge tree hit with lighting. Instantaneous."

"So . . ." Erin let her words crawl from her tongue, glancing over at Jadon. "So you weren't able to join your neighbor then?"

"Oh, no. God. It took everything I had, but I pulled myself up and stumbled onto the balcony, I was in so much pain. But I leaned against the railing, and I played. I played and played and it was . . . wonderful," Meg smirked, not wanting to include the grim details that followed.

"Oh. So your neighbor knows you still like . . . .or whatever we call it . . . him?" Erin asked.

"I don't know what he knows."

"Hey, where the hell is your bracelet?" Chick asked, eating the hotdog still dangling on the end of his fork. "It was probably a good idea not to wear it. You might have lost it out here."

Relieved he had inadvertently given her an out, Meg nodded in agreement. "Yeah. I wouldn't want to lose it."

"Look how Flo's tofu dog is getting all weird and wrinkly," Chick said with a laugh.

"How ya doin', Jay?" Stu shot out unexpectedly. "You look like hell. You really do. Did you even sleep last night?"

"Yeah. I got a couple hours in before the garbage truck woke me up," Jadon said quietly.

"Garbage truck? Jesus. You're a light sleeper," Stu said.

"Finish up, Meg. It's almost marshmallow time," Chick ordered, his eyes shining like a small boy.

"Tell us about your book that's coming out in a few days," Bob said, his eyes mesmerized by the flickering flames dancing in front of him.

Noticing Bob's zombie like stare, Meg turned her gaze onto the flame as well.

Wanting to focus on Meg, Jadon took advantage of the fire that separated them. He wanted to hear her talk about the book, the book Devon heinously tossed in front of him, breaking his heart with one quick thump from its heavy pages.

"Oh, it's just a love story I suppose," Meg mumbled, every fiber of her being not wanting to discuss it in front of Jadon.

"Well, you know we're *all* going to buy the damn thing, so just tell us about it. It would make a nice campfire story," Bob suggested, oblivious to the complications hidden within the book's contents.

"Who are the characters?" Erin asked.

"Uh. Well," Meg tried to begin, her throat getting tighter in the process. "I guess you could say it's centered on this woman. She owns an art gallery in Manhattan."

"What are their names?" Jadon asked directly, startling everyone who sat around the fire. His silence all day, making the sound of his voice shoot across the fire like a rocket launched unexpectedly at Meg.

"Elle, and . . . uh . . . and, uh . . . Jadon," Meg said sheepishly.

Jadon tilted his head slowly to the side and looked at Chick.

"I like the name, I guess," Meg said.

"Sure. Sure. We all do," Stu said, lighting his cigarette. "It's just a fuckin' name Jay...," he growled, giving Jadon a look of disapproval.

"You have to tell us more than that. All we have are two people, one of which is Elle and she owns an art gallery. Is it juicy?" Erin teased.

"It's nice. It's real nice," Meg said uncomfortably.

"Nice?" Jadon chimed. "That's it?"

Chick's eyes darted from Jadon to Meg and back again, taking notice of the combustible situation that was forming.

"I would think it would have been a little better than just nice." Jadon asked.

"Jesus, Jay," Bob said, looking over at Jadon. "How the hell would you know? Dude, you really need to get some sleep or something."

"It was more than nice. It was . . . the stuff you dream about," Meg said.

Not sure that Meg's answer calmed down Jadon, Chick wanted to change the subject, but before he could Erin innocently asked another question.

"Does it have a happy ending?"

"I guess. It's fiction, so anything's possible."

"Meg?" Flora said.

"Happy endings are relative. Who knows what makes anyone happy?" Meg said with a hint of sarcasm.

"You know, I like the smell of fresh cut grass," Stu offered kindly, trying to rescue Meg and change the subject at the same time.

"Me, too," Chick agreed, appreciating the quick shift.

"How's Devon?" Jadon shot out quickly.

"How's Coco?" Meg countered.

The two questions launched rapidly across the fire like two torpedoes, released one right after the other. Jadon didn't want to drop anything. He didn't want to talk about grass or any other subject. He wanted to talk about Meg, and how she used his love for her, reducing it down into the pages of a book.

Meg felt the hit from Jadon's question. Wanting to leap across the fire and strangle him, she gave him a friendly nod instead. Looking back at Meg, Jadon offered the same gesture she gave him.

As Chick watched things heat up, his mind began to race trying to find a way to unite the two. Deciding to hit it head on, Chick shifted gears.

"Hey, Meg, so how'd Devon handle it when you told him you wanted to drop him?" Chick asked, choosing his words carefully.

Taking a painful sigh, Meg softened her face. "It didn't go real well. But it's done. And I couldn't be happier. I really owe it to you guys. I do. I feel liberated."

"Did he get mad?" Bob asked.

"Oh, yes. He has so much poise though, it takes a lot to get him upset, but, yes. He actually grew quite vicious. He said some pretty hurtful things."

"He didn't doubt your ability to publish under your own name, did he?" Kofi asked.

"No. Actually he came at me from an entirely different angle. It was a hard night, but a necessary one."

Chick purposefully and slowly turned his head in Jadon's direction while taking a long drink from his beer in an effort to see if Jadon's steely glare had softened any.

Rubbing his fingers on his forehead, Jadon felt tired, his confusion was subtly displayed on his face as he glanced at everyone.

"You okay?" Bob asked, breaking his trance long enough to notice Jadon staring at him.

"Yeah," Jadon said softly.

"No wrong answers. Just answers," Stu broke in. "Letterman or Leno?"

"Letterman," Meg answered without hesitation.

"Letterman," Chick shot out right on the heels of Meg's answer.

"Um, Christ, depends who's on," Bob said. "Overall, I gotta say Leno."

"Letterman. All the way," Stu added.

"I like them both. I really don't prefer one or the other," Flora said.

"Yeah. At times I like Letterman better, but then I'll flip on Leno and I'm liking him too. It's a crap shoot," Kofi said.

Turning to look at Jadon, Stu put his hand out to show he was waiting for a response.

"Letterman. I don't know. Yeah, Letterman," Jadon answered.

"Erin?" Stu asked.

"I'm a Leno gal," she answered.

"Okay, let me think . . . ," Stu continued, rubbing his stubby face. "Hot dogs or hamburgers?"

"Nah, do something else, Christ, we all just ate hot dogs. We're tainted," Chick said.

"This is good one . . . lake, river or ocean?" Stu asked.

"Oh, that is a good one," Flora said.

"Mmm . . . yeah, boy, that's a hard one," Erin said.

"Ocean. Yes. Again, no question," Meg said.

"Well, you can't just give your answer without an explanation, Meg," Chick insisted.

"I like that it appears to be without limits," Meg answered.

"I think they're all quite nice," Flora finally added.

"Yeah, I don't know. I guess it depends," Chick offered.

"I like the ocean," Jadon answered softly.

"Why?" Chick asked, drawing the word out as he said it.

"It's . . . big. It's overwhelmingly big. It kind of takes my breath away," Jadon said.

Like I needed one more reason to think he was beautiful, Meg grumbled inside her mind.

"Okay, this is my last question then it's lights out for this ol' bear," Stu growled. "Reincarnation or not? Heaven or not?"

"Whoa, that's a big one," Chick said.

"Yeah, what are you tryin' to do to us?" Bob asked.

"Well, we know Flora has something to say about this one."

"Yeah, lay it on us, mama," Chick teased.

"I'd like to hear what Meg has to say," Flora answered.

"Oh, boy. Uh . . . I don't know for sure what I believe. But, I know at times when I'm struggling my hardest, I think about my mom. She always seemed so in tune with the spiritual world. I remember this one time, when I watched my mother carry the lifeless body of our dog from the road in front of our house. I don't know why he was out there, but he was, and he got hit. Just like that he was gone," Meg snapped her fingers. "There I stood, watching my mom scoop him up and carry him to the backyard. Now, my mom hated any kind of physical labor, but she dug and dug and dug until she was satisfied with the depth of the grave she made for him. Then I watched as she made him disappear under the dirt. Well, I fell apart. I lost it. My mom took off her gloves, and sat down on the grass next to Stinky's grave. He always stunk. He just did. He was clean, too. He just stunk. So we named him Stinky," Meg interjected. "She put her arm around me while I looked at the mound of dark dirt that covered him and sobbed. Once I was quiet, my mom told me, Stinky is just as happy now as he was when he used to curl up next to me in bed. His spirit remains. The same energy that made him wag his tail, that made him wake out of a sound sleep so he could meet you at the door after school every day, is the same energy he has with him now. He is still here, sweetness. But now, he just needs you to notice him living among all the things that bring you joy." Meg wiped the tears from under her eyes as she reached down to run her fingers across Bob's silky fur.

"That was lovely, Meg," Flora said.

"So, what do you think?" Chick asked softly.

"I don't know what I believe. But, I *feel* my parents. I feel them around me. And I know, I know she spoke through you Flora," Meg said.

"I have only had one other person move through me so forcefully. Only one other person," Flora revealed with certainty. "Your mother has a very strong spirit. And she's around you almost every time I'm near you."

Jadon felt his chest tighten while Meg talked about her mother. Running his hands through his hair in frustration, he forced himself not to go to her.

"How about you, Jay?" Chick asked quickly.

"Uh. . . ," Jadon hesitated, not prepared to answer. "I, uh, well. When my mom died, well, it was real rough. And, uh, my dad never seemed to recover. He changed. But, I guess, I feel, I know, I know there's something going on. I don't know what to call it, but it's real."

"Yeah," Chick said, "it's real. Sometimes I just wish the two meshed better. Not such a jump from one to the other." Chick paused and looked at Meg. "If we want to do another album, and keep doing this acoustic thing for a bit . . . you still with us?"

"As long as you will have me," Meg said without hesitating.

"Sounds good to me," Stu yawned. "On that very, very promising note, I'm out of here, folks."

"Me, too. That walk was enough to kill anyone," Bob agreed.

"Hike. It was a hike," Chick corrected him.

"I'm exhausted too," Flora said, grabbing Kofi's hand.

"Night folks," Kofi said.

Sitting quietly, Chick tried to figure out the best thing to do. Leave, and allow Jadon to be alone with Meg. Or stay by the fire, to prevent them from killing each other.

"Let's hit the hay," Erin suggested.

"All right," Chick gave Meg a quick wink. "You want me to help you to your tent?"

"No. I'm good. I'm going to watch the fire die out then take Bob for a walk. I'm good."

"Jay . . . need me to walk you to your tent?" Chick laughed.

"I'm good, right where I'm at," Jadon answered.

Hesitantly, Chick followed Erin to their tent. Pushing him inside, Erin zipped up the tent flap behind them.

Meg tried to relax and enjoy the fire, watching it consume each piece of wood carefully stacked and mingled into its burning flame. Occasionally she let her eyes drift onto Jadon before returning her gaze to the fire.

Jadon kept his eyes fixed on the fire, trying to find a way to say what he was feeling inside.

"Why'd you do it?" Jadon worked up the courage to ask.

Startled by the sound of his voice, Meg jumped. Tilting her head to one side, she turned to look at him directly. "Do what?"

"Why did you do it?" Jadon repeated.

"Do what?"

"I know all about the book, Meg."

Meg felt her hands begin to tremble. "I don't understand."

"I read your book."

"How could you . . . have?"

"Your fiancé gave it to me. He threw it down in front of me. He said he carefully marked each page where you used me. I think he called me . . . inspiration." Jadon's voice cracked.

"My what? I don't have a fiancé. I don't . . . He . . . he gave you my novel? How could he do that?" Meg said, standing up, getting sick from the thought.

"Well, he did. He loved every minute of it too. He's a real peach," Jadon said, watching Meg pace by the fire.

"Why would he . . . *That's* why he had all those passages marked . . . ," Meg whispered, realizing Devon's betrayal went far deeper than she had realized.

"I think he said he wanted to spare me from getting hurt. He loved telling me how you used me. He loved calling me a little monkey that beats on a drum all day. He loved every minute of it.

He told Coco how you two were getting married this spring," Jadon said, rattling off the painful words Devon threw at him.

Trying to get her attention, Bob pranced around Meg's legs while she paced back and forth next to the fire.

"I've never been engaged," Meg offered softly.

"He said you'd deny it."

"Well, I guess after everything else he said, it would make sense he'd say that too. Bob, just a minute," Meg said looking down at his urgent face.

"Why would you do that to me?"

"I didn't do anything to you. Bob!" Meg shouted quickly, watching the dog run down the trail. "I didn't do anything to you. Why do you even care what I wrote? God," she yelled, running down the path to catch up to Bob.

Finally catching up, Meg stood near Bobby, painfully holding her arms around her ribs, while keeping a watchful eye on him as he explored the trail leading away from the campsite.

Running up behind Meg, Jadon breathlessly asked, "Why did you write about me?"

Shaking her head, Meg felt herself get angry. Angry that he even had the nerve to ask her anything. "Did you share my novel with Coco?"

"Coco? This isn't about Coco."

"Oh," Meg nodded her head, glancing quickly at him, before returning her eyes onto Bob. "In my world, it has everything to do with Coco."

"Why . . . did you . . ."

"I don't know why Devon did that. Other than he has a real twisted way of trying to shape his world. But those words meant the world to me. So you standing here acting all upset about the fact that I put them in my novel infuriates me."

"Meg. Those moments . . . God. They changed my life and you just used me, you used me like a puppet in your show. I gave you precious pieces of myself, and you took them and threw them into your novel, like all the other research you collected along the way."

"Used you? Let's talk about using for a moment. You hop yourself around, in and out. Ricocheting yourself through my life. Breaking and destroying parts of me as you move along," Meg said, her eyes filling with painful tears that matched his.

"Destroying you? Destroying you? There's nothing left of me because of you!" Jadon's voice cracked with emotion.

"Oh, really? Well there's enough of you to keep Coco busy."

"God, Meg. You just don't get it, do you? There has never been a Coco. There's only you. You. You're all I think about. From the moment I first saw you, you've been the constant picture that sits in my mind. You're all I see. You're all I want to see. I wrote that song about you. You, Meg. And how I feel about you. Who do you think gave you that bracelet? Me. Me, Meg. I'm him . . . me," Jadon's voice strained from the intensity. "I'm so fucking in love with you. Even though I've meant nothing to you. Just some fictional character for one of your bestsellers. I still can't stop myself. God. I've tried. I've tried and tried. But I can't let go. I bought the bracelet in Norway. I wanted to reach out to you somehow, even though I felt like I was dying inside because I meant nothing to you. I had to nearly bribe that damn concierge at the hotel to lie and say that it came in the mail. I wanted . . . I wanted you to know that, *that* guy . . . that part of me . . . the deepest part of me, loved you and still needed you. God. I can't stop myself even though it's meant nothing to you. I can't stop all this . . . this pull, this unstoppable pull to love you."

"You're my . . . all this time . . . it was you? And you never . . . told me?" Meg felt her mind explode into a million tiny pieces.

"But, I came to you last night. I . . . I came to your house, and you turned your back on me."

"I didn't think you'd want to know your neighbor was me. I'm just that monkey . . . that meaningless guy who gave you something to write about. From the day I first saw you, I've been scared out of my mind. I've been scared to death, scared of how little control I have over my own thoughts. I finally get the courage to do something. To show you how much I want you, how much I love you, and in one quick thud, your novel is tossed in front of me. Showing me that I was just . . . I was . . ."

"You're my world," Meg said softly. "I wrote those words because it was the only way I could keep them. Make them mine. By putting them down on paper I could own them. I could keep replaying them. I could give them a life beyond myself. They were too beautiful not to express. I worked and worked to find words to describe something that was far beyond what any word could ever describe. That was my heart, and my love for you, my stupid love that I couldn't control or stop. Those words were my song. I put my soul into those words, just like I put my soul into playing the violin. I didn't want to lose the most precious thing I had ever experienced. I love you. I can't breathe. I can hardly think. I just think about you. And looking into your eyes and wanting to touch you. Hoping you feel the same for me. I love you. With every fiber in my body, I love you," Meg yelled, turning to run after Bob who had already run out of her sight.

Yelling Bob's name, Meg moved as fast as her feet would allow. Hearing Jadon run after her, she kept moving forward, trying to find Bob, trying to listen for any sign of him.

"Bob! Where are you?" Meg's voice broke through her tears.

Running through the woods bordering the river she heard the sound of splashing. Barely able to see under the light of the moon, Meg saw the silhouette of Bob struggling in the river.

"God! Bob!" She screamed, throwing her body into the river. Forcing her body through the strong current, Meg dipped her head under the ice cold water trying to break free his hind foot that was trapped in a thick nest of branches from a fallen tree.

"Be still! Be still!" she commanded, as he thrashed his legs violently, hitting Meg and sending her under the water. Pulling herself back up, she worked to calm him and give her a chance to release his foot. Thrashing his limbs, Bob kicked Meg harder under the water.

"Meg!" Jadon shouted, desperate to find her. Hearing Bob thrash in the water, he ran toward the river. Barely able to make out Bob's shadowy figure, he screamed for Meg. Then he noticed her body floating above the surface of the water.

"No, no, no! Meg!" he yelled, plunging his body into the water toward her, then quickly lifting her out and onto the bank of the river.

Making sure she had a pulse, Jadon dove back into the river, and wrestled to set Bob free. In his panic Bob kicked Jadon, striking his head hard against the large stone the fallen tree was resting on. Feeling his world suddenly go black for a moment, Jadon pulled himself back into consciousness. Focusing on Bob, he ripped his foot free and dragged his heavy body onto the river bank next to Meg.

Finding an open area, Jadon carried each of them onto the level ground under two large trees. Unable to focus his eyes any longer, Jadon rested his body next to Meg's as his world shifted swiftly from gray to black.

Chapter 31

Forcing her eyes open, Meg struggled to make out the world around her. The pain in her head and chest made it almost unbearable to move. Moving her eyes slowly, Meg tried to get a sense of where she was. Seeing nothing but tall trees, she turned her head slowly in the other direction. Staring at Jadon, she tried to understand why he was lying on his side facing her, his eyes closed, his body void of any visible signs of life.

With the awkward almost painful feeling of heavy thoughts jumping into place, Meg remembered her head going under in the river while trying to set Bob free. Scanning Jadon's face, Meg hastily moved her hands over his body trying to wake him. Looking behind Jadon, Meg saw Bob lying as quietly and motionless as Jadon.

"Oh, God. Oh, God. *No! No!* You *can not* do this to me!" Meg yelled, her rage kick- starting her lagging mind. "Not again. Not again. No. No."

Meg quickly ran her hand over Jadon's neck, trying to find a pulse.

"Oh, thank God. Thank God," she cried, looking over at Bob. "Bobby? Mama's here. Mama's here. Don't move. You're doing fine." Meg pulled herself over to Bob. Running her hands over his body, she struggled to find any sign of life. "Bobby? Come on, honey." Lifting his leg, she watched it fall hard to the ground once she released it. Sitting on her knees, Meg threw her hands over her face.

"No! *Goddamn it, no!*" she screamed. "You can't leave me. You can't. I love you. I love you."

"Meg?" Jadon whispered, silencing Meg instantly.

Shuffling her body in front of his, Meg ran her hands over his face and searched his face with her eyes.

"I'm right here. I'm right here."

His eyes closed, Jadon smiled with relief. "Are you okay? Are you okay? Tell me you're okay."

"I'm perfect. I'm perfect. Look at me. I need you to look at me."

Barely able to open his eyelids, Jadon looked into Meg's eyes.

"There's those eyes. There's those eyes I needed to see," Meg cried, touching his face frantically, trying to make sense of his semiconscious state. Running her hands along the side of his head, Meg's fingers were stopped by the discovery of a large gash.

"You were floating in the water, Meg. I . . . I thought you were gone. I thought you were gone. I thought you drowned. In an instant I saw everything I ever wanted flash in front of my eyes. I was so scared," Jadon whispered, trying to keep his eyes on hers. "I pulled you out. Then I had to get Bob; he was still caught. He was kicking his legs trying to free himself. I think he kicked you. He was so panicked, he kicked me against the rock. How is he?" He asked, moving his arm behind him trying to feel Bob's body behind his. "He's okay, isn't he, Meg?"

"Yeah . . . he's good. He's good," Meg assured him, choking back the heartbreaking loss. "I need to make sure you're okay. I need to get help. I can't even see anything, it's so damn dark." Looking around Meg could barely make out the river snaking its way a few yards away from them. "Oh, God. I need to somehow get on the other side again. I have to . . ." Meg felt her voice break. "I have to get help. You hit your head. I need to make sure you're okay. I can't lose you. I can't lose you."

"No. No," Jadon whispered, pulling Meg's arm. "I want you right beside me. I don't want you getting lost. I need you right here. Don't leave. Don't ever leave."

"You're freezing. I have to get you warm. Oh God. I can't make a fire. I don't have any way of making a fire. Oh, wait. Oh, wait," Meg said quickly, fumbling her hands into the waterproof side pocket of her hiking pants. "Matches. I've got matches. I'm going to make a fire. I'll be right back. Don't try to get up. Stay right there. I need to get you warm."

Meg watched Jadon's eyes close again. Pushing herself up, she ran through the trees, searching for small pieces of wood.

"*Damn it!*" Meg yelled as she fell hard onto the ground, causing her world to instantly turn black. "Christ," she said, trying to put a stop to her spiraling mind.

Leaning against a tree, Meg tried to stare down the stars floating in front of her eyes until each one faded and she was able to find her way back to Jadon.

"Okay. Okay. Oh, God. I'm so goddamn scared. I need to keep him warm. I don't care about me. I just need to make sure he's okay," Meg's voice echoed through the forest as she plunged her body down onto its knees, her hands rapidly clearing an open space near Jadon. "I need something that'll burn real quick. Dry stuff. Dry stuff," her words raced from her mouth while gathering a hand full of leaves in her hands. "Stay with me, Jadon! Stay with me. If you love me like you say you do, you can't leave me!"

Trying to steady her hands, Meg ran the match across the rough brown surface of the box it came from.

"Fuck," she screamed, watching the flame quickly disappear. Striking the next match, Meg found success. "Thank God. Thank

God. Okay. I need some more wood. I need to get some wood. Open your eyes. Please. Stay with me. I know it hurts. I know it hurts," Meg said, sliding her body next to Jadon's again.

"I'm here. I'm here," Jadon said, opening his eyes to look at Meg's frightened face. "I'm not going anywhere. I can't move my head, Meg. I'm so cold I can hardly feel anything. Everything just keeps getting real dark."

"Oh, God. Oh, God. I know, I know. Just . . . try. For me. Please. When it gets dark, focus on me. I made a fire. I'm going to get some more wood. Then I'm coming right back. I'm going to hold you until I figure out how to get help."

"Kiss me," Jadon whispered.

As the tears flooded Meg's eyes, she brought herself closer to him, and gently kissed his lips. With every kiss, she felt her chest tighten, the pain of watching him fade away choked the life from her own body.

"I love you. I have always loved you. I loved you from the moment I saw you standing in your driveway. It hurt, I loved you so much. It scared the hell out of me Meg," Jadon confided.

"I thought you hated me. I thought you couldn't stand the sight of me. And . . . it hurt so much. Because you took my breath away. From the moment I saw you, you took my breath away," Meg whispered. "I need to make sure you're warm. I need to get some more wood. I'll be just a second."

"Okay. But just a second. No more, Meg, you're freezing too. Are you okay?"

"I'm perfect. I'm perfect. Bobby's going to keep you warm while I get more wood," Meg said, forcing the words through the painful truth, while delicately sliding Bob's lifeless body tight against Jadon. "He loves you. He loves you so much. Okay . . . he's going to help keep you warm until I can figure out how to get you out of here."

Struggling to pull herself up Meg stumbled back into the woods, scavenging for any piece of wood she could find, quickly gathering them in her arms, she moved in between the trees. Stopping to balance herself against a tree, Meg felt her mind violently spin again, sending tiny white stars shooting rapidly in front of her eyes.

Lowering herself close to the fire, Meg tried positioning two large sticks over the small fire burning brightly next to Jadon. She paused, holding her head in her hands to give her body the time it needed to purge itself of its pain.

"Meg?" Jadon whispered, opening his eyes wider than before. "Good. You're back. Don't go away again. I want you next to me."

Sliding her body tight against his, Meg pushed his body closer to Bob's.

"I want to tell you I love you again . . . just in case . . . ," Jadon said softly.

"No. No just-in-cases. You're going to be fine. You're going to be better than fine. God can't be that cruel to take you away from me, too. He can't. He can't. So just forget it."

"You know . . . holding you in my arms . . . I feel so content. I feel like, like I'm holding heaven."

"I don't want to be here," Meg cried, "if you're not here."

"I love you so much. Every time I breathe I feel you. Every time I dream I see you. You are my dreams. You're the thoughts in my head. You're the notes I play on the piano."

"You're the one that holds my hand, whether you knew it or not all those nights. You held my hand as we traveled together deep within my soul. That's what those moments were to me on the balcony. God, I fell in love with you instantly. And I didn't know who you were. I didn't know what to do. I didn't want to ruin anything. Then I met *you*. And I felt like my world was torn in two. I wanted this man that was able to move me like no other with his music. Then there was this person. The most beautiful thing I had ever seen. The most beautiful color . . . and . . . I wanted desperately to paint my life with it, with you. Brushing your color all over my world."

Resting her head slowly next to his, Meg felt her world go black again.

"Meg . . . ," Jadon said softly. "Meg . . ." Staring at her face, he couldn't get Meg to open her eyes, realizing that every bit of movement had suddenly left her body. "No. Oh, God. Oh, God. Meg. Come on. Come on. Wake up. God, no. No."

Holding her tight next to him, Jadon rested his head next to hers. Not wanting to be a part of this world if Meg wasn't in it, Jadon gave in to the call of sleep, yelling within his mind.

Chapter 32

"Something's not right," Flora said, shaking Kofi out of his sleep.

"What?"

"Something's happened. Something's wrong with Meg. Something's happened!" Flora said, her mind filled with the images that had been carefully placed in her dreams while she slept.

"All right, all right. Let's go see what's going on," Kofi said, unzipping their tent and slowly making his way over to Meg's tent.

"What's going on?" Chick asked, walking over from his tent. Not able to rest, Chick kept rolling from side to side, his mind tossed viciously from rampant nightmares all night. Now, he stood next to Kofi, wide-eyed and wide awake.

"Flora says something's wrong. She's almost paralyzed with fear," Kofi whispered, trying not to wake the others as he peered inside Meg's tent. "Well, she's not here. Where's Bobby?" He scanned the inside of her tent with the narrow beam of his flashlight. "I don't think she's even slept in her sleeping bag."

"Oh, God. Oh, God," Chick spun around on his feet.

"Jadon's gone too. I don't think he's slept in his, either," Kofi yelled.

"Christ. I knew it. I knew it. Flora!" Chick screamed, rummaging through his backpack for his cell phone. "Fuck. Fuck. Double Fuck. No signal. I gotta find a signal somewhere!"

"What the hell is going on?" Bob asked, trying to make sense of what was going on.

"It's Meg," Flora cried. "I think Jadon, too. Something's happened. I can't make sense of what's in my head. It's not good. It's not good."

"Let's go," Stu said as he handed Bob a flashlight. "We're going to find them somewhere. They can't be far."

"Oh, God. What's going on? What could have happened? Give me one too. Give me one!" Erin yelled, throwing on her jacket.

"*I got a signal!*" Chick yelled, frozen in place, pushing his trembling fingers across the surface of his cell phone to dial 911.

"They're by water. They're by water!" Flora shouted.

"We need help. We have two lost hikers. I don't know how long they've been gone. I don't know what happened," Chick said, carefully trying to explain the unexplainable.

Flora listened as Chick gave as much information as possible to the dispatcher on the other end of the phone. Closing her eyes, Flora fell abruptly to the ground.

"They're cold. They're very, very cold. Someone keeps blacking out. *Someone keeps blacking out!*" Flora screamed. "Someone's dead . . . I don't know who . . . ," she whispered to herself, running past everyone, swiftly making her way down the trail.

Darting after her, Chick kept two paces behind as Flora lunged her body back and forth, stopping abruptly to close her eyes, before running in a different direction again. Helped by the flashlights held behind her, Flora leaned next to a tree, running her hands slowly over its bumpy, dry surface she closed her eyes. Trying to find clarity within the images exploding through her mind, Flora asked for guidance. Seeing an image of the river, she remained silent, giving the image time to explain itself. As the river broadened within her mind, Flora watched as her view of it withdrew, giving a clear view of the three motionless bodies lying next to it.

"Show me. Take me. You can do that. I'll follow," Flora patiently waited, while trying to silence the panicked mumblings of everyone standing behind her. Within moments the air in front of Flora became dense and powerful, just as it did the day it moved through her to speak to its daughter.

"Let's go find her . . . just take me to her. I feel you. I feel you," Flora said.

Chick tried to balance Flora as she was guided through the woods. As her feet were pulled closer to the river, the glow of the flashlights darted across the water, allowing everyone to see Jadon and Meg huddled together near a cluster of red embers. Next to Jadon, Flora saw Bob lying as motionlessly as the two people he most loved.

"*Meg! Jadon!*" Chick screamed, rushing past Flora. "*Oh, God! Oh, God!*" This don't look good. No one's moving."

"Bob should be wagging his tail. I know he hears us. Why isn't he moving? No one's moving. I'm coming with you," Stu yelled, launching his body into the water. Locking arms with Chick, the two steadily made their way through the forceful current.

"I'm going across," Flora said, plunging her feet into the icy water.

"Let's all go together, we'll hold hands," Bob said.

"Wake up, Jay. Wake up. Come on," Chick's voice growled as he tried to shake Jadon awake, "Come on man. You can't leave me, dude. Wake up. Wake up. Come on, you've got a pulse, dude. Come on. Goddamn it, Jay!"

"She has a pulse too. She's not moving. Her eyes don't look good," Stu said, flashing the light in front of Meg's eyes.

"Oh, God. This doesn't look good. He's got a big cut on his head. Christ. What the hell happened? God!" Chick screamed. "Bob's not moving Stu. He hasn't moved since we got over here."

Running his hands over Bob's body, Chick couldn't find any signs of life buried under the soft red fur.

"Oh, fuck. Oh, fuck. I think he's gone. He's not moving, Stu!" Chick yelled.

"Meg," Jadon whispered quietly.

"Dude. Open your eyes. Open your eyes," Chick said steadily.

Slowly Jadon opened his eyes, trying to focus them on Chick's face while it hovered over his.

"Thank God, thank God," Chick repeated.

"Meg. Meg won't open her eyes. She won't open her eyes anymore," Jadon cried softly. "I keep trying to get her to open her eyes. Is she okay?"

"She has a pulse. She has a pulse. Right, Stu. Right?" Chick said frantically.

"Yes, she does, Jay. You better open those eyes," Stu answered.

"But she won't look at me anymore, and she doesn't move anymore . . . ," Jadon's voice cracked. "I don't know why. I don't know why she won't look at me. I found her floating in the water. I pulled her out. I pulled her out. Then Bob. God. Is Bob okay? She said he was good. She said he was fine. He's right behind me. She said he was keeping me warm."

Chick put his hand over his mouth, trying not to let Jadon hear the mournful cries erupting from his chest.

"Bob's good, man. Don't worry. He's right here," Chick glanced across Bob's faithful body.

Throwing her body next to Meg's, Flora scanned Meg's body, trying to assess her condition. Slowly Flora moved her hands over Meg's head.

"Flora," Jadon whispered through his tears. "She's going to be okay. Right? Tell me she's going to be okay. I can't lose her, Flora. I can't. I can't lose her. You know. You know more than anyone. I can't lose her. She's just tired. Right?"

Holding her hands on Meg's head Flora felt her hands burn with pain. Unable to control her emotions, Flora sobbed. Watching Flora break down holding Meg's head in her hands, everyone began to crumble at the prospect of losing Meg.

Hastily shoving wood on the fire, Stu brought it back to life. Trying to busy himself, he also hoped to keep Jadon and Meg safe from the cold air that surrounded them.

"They're getting close. They're getting close," Bob repeated, listening to the 911 operator on the other end of the phone. "Hang in there. Hang in there."

"Flora. Tell me she's okay," Jadon said softly, his blue eyes silently begging her to give him the answer he wanted to hear. "Flora . . . I don't want to be here if she's not here. So, tell me she's okay. Or I'm going to close my eyes, and try to be with her wherever she is."

"I don't know, baby. I don't know for sure. But what I do know is love is a very strong thing. And this girl loves you. I know she'd move heaven aside to be with you. You make sure you're ready for her once she's had the chance to do that."

"I will. I will. I'll be here. Tell her that. Tell her for me. You can do that. You can still talk to her," Jadon cried.

"You tell her. She can hear you, baby. You make sure she knows," Flora said, rubbing her hand across Jadon's gentle face.

Delicately letting go of Meg's head so Jadon could once again cradle her in his arms, Flora stepped away. Her heart tight with pain, she watched as he fell apart, his love for Meg flowing from his eyes as he searched for signs of life from within hers.

"I love you. Oh, God, how I love you. I love everything about you, Meg. I love all the stuff you try to hide. I want it. I want every part of you . . . Come back. Please," Jadon cried desperately.

Slowly reaching into his pocket he pulled out the bracelet he had given her. Lifting her hand, he slid it back onto her wrist.

Chapter 33

"Mr. Hastings, Mr. and Mrs. Holschick," Dr. Solomon, head of the Neurological Surgery Center at Bay City Medical Center said, stepping out of the intensive care unit. Scanning the hall quickly, Dr. Solomon nodded at the other faces eagerly waiting for him to say something. "Ms. Scott is not responsive, as you're all aware. We have her stable, at the moment. Her heart rate keeps elevating. We aren't sure why."

"What? What do you mean you don't know why?" Jadon asked. "She's here. You've run your scans. You should be able to fix her."

"I know. I know it seems that simple. I wish it were that simple, Mr. Hastings. Unfortunately, Ms. Scott suffered considerable head trauma. She has an intracranial hemorrhage. The bleeding is causing a significant amount of intracranial pressure. Because of the amount of pressure, she isn't able to respond. At this point all we can do is stabilize her breathing. It's imperative we keep her blood pressure monitored. If the pressure increases . . . ," he said, looking down briefly. "We've given her all the drugs we can to reduce the swelling. If we get the swelling down then the pressure is reduced. Reduce the pressure and maybe . . . maybe she has a chance."

"What?" Jadon cried. "Oh, my God. Oh, my God. How did this happen? How did this . . . happen? She said she was okay. She was so worried about me."

"Mr. Hastings, she most likely didn't know, although honestly with the level of hemorrhaging that occurred, I think she was struggling. She must have been blacking out. I don't really know how she managed to walk, let alone build a fire. She's a fighter. So whatever it was that made her fight last night, let's hope it keeps her fighting. Mr. Hastings, Ms. Scott would want you to be taking care of yourself right now too. You shouldn't be out of your bed."

"No. I'm not going anywhere. I want to sit with her. I want to go in there. Can I go in there?" Jadon asked.

Feeling Jadon's desperation, Dr. Solomon agreed, opening the door behind him leading to Meg. Slipping his body through the door, Jadon quickly pulled a chair next to Meg. Staring at her face, he felt the floor beneath his feet disappear.

"Dr. Solomon," Chick said, finding it almost impossible to breathe, "I don't mean to be dense but . . . I'm not real sure if you're saying she'll be okay."

"Mr. Holschick, I won't lie. Ms. Scott will need to fight real hard. We've done all we can at this point. If the swelling continues we might consider surgery, but because of the location of the hemorrhage, it would be risky. I wish I could tell you something different. In addition to Ms. Scott, your friend is recovering from stage three hypothermia, which is nothing to be taken lightly. His head is fine. But his body will need time to recover from his body temperature falling so low. We need to watch him to make sure none of his organs were injured as a result."

"Well . . . I don't think we'll be able to keep him on an entirely different wing of this hospital. He's losing it. And . . . if he loses Meg . . . you know . . ." Chick had to stop.

"Dr. Solomon," Erin asked, "is there anything else we can do?"

"I'm sorry, Mrs. Holschick, no, there isn't. Just keep talking to her. If Mr. Hastings is what she needs, maybe . . . I'll let them know he'll be staying over here," Dr. Solomon conceded, trying to muster a smile onto his well-seasoned face, before walking toward the nurses' station at the end of the hall.

Chick peered into Meg's room. Standing still for a moment, he watched Jadon slide onto Meg's bed, gently resting his body next to hers.

"Meg," Jadon whispered. "You're going to be okay. Just keep fighting to come back. I'll be right here when you do. I want to be the first thing you see when you open those magnificent eyes of yours. I love your eyes so much. Please give me the chance to stare into them."

In the corridor outside the ICU, Chick paced back and forth. "How the hell are we going to tell him Bob is gone?"

"Maybe we don't," Stu offered gently.

"Yeah. Maybe we just don't tell him. I don't know," Bob shook his head.

"He'll need to know," Kofi reminded them. "Did they take him to Dr. Banard's office."

"Yeah. Yeah. I told them I was going to pick him up. I want to bury him like Meg's mom buried Stinky. Right in my back yard. That way we can all say goodbye. You know . . ." Chick buried his face in his hands. "What a fuckin' nightmare."

"Mr. Hastings? We need to take Meg's vitals." The young nurse reminded him again. Jadon slid himself off the bed the same way he had every half hour for the last nine hours he had been curled up next to Meg. "You should really take a moment to rest. Maybe eat something. You need to take care of yourself, too."

"No," Jadon shook his head adamantly. "No."

"Okay. Okay. That's okay. Her blood pressure seems to calm down when you're next to her. You're like medicine to her. That's a good thing. Would you like me to get you anything?"

"Yeah. Bring Meg back," Jadon said quietly, crawling back onto Meg's bed.

Waking the next morning to the soft noises that filled the room, Jadon watched as Erin took a seat next to Meg's bed.

"I'm not moving," he said, gently kissing Meg's head.

"I know. I thought you might like company. We . . . none of us know what to do with ourselves."

"Excuse me," the nurse said, opening Meg's door. "We have to take Ms. Scott down for another scan. Dr. Solomon wants to make sure the hemorrhage isn't traveling."

"Traveling?" Erin asked.

"Yes. We'll bring her right back. It should only take about a half an hour."

Kissing Meg's cheek, Jadon slid off her bed again.

"I brought you some fresh clothes," Erin said, grabbing the canvas bag resting next to Chick in the hallway.

"Take this time to wash up. Try to clear your head. I wanted to get you something to eat. Okay? So, Bob and Stu went down to the cafeteria to find something for you," Erin said.

Nodding his head, Jadon silently took the bag, and walked down the hall.

"I've got to tell him about Bob. Now is the time," Chick said, keeping his palms together in front of his face.

"Dr. Banard said Bob died shortly after he was taken out of the water. Meg must have known. I can't imagine what she must have gone through," Erin sighed. "I'm pretty sure Meg told him Bob was okay because she didn't want to upset him."

"I know. I am, too. God!" Chick cried.

"Were you able to . . . to take care of him like you wanted?" Erin asked softly.

"Yeah. Yeah. Kofi helped. Stu and Bob did, too. He overlooks the ocean now. Nobody saw us, so we should be all right," Chick said, watching Jadon walk back toward them.

"You look better. I hope you feel a little bit better. I put your cologne in there, too. I thought Meg would appreciate it," Erin smiled, motioning for him to sit next to her in the hall outside of Meg's room.

"Yeah. I don't know. Maybe," Jadon said.

Pacing back and forth, Chick finally stopped and sat down next to Jadon. Staring at him, then back across the hall, Chick shook his head slowly.

"Bob. Bob didn't make it, Jay," Chick finally said.

"What?" Jadon asked. "No. No. There's a mistake. Meg said he was okay."

"I know. I know. But I talked with Dr. Banard and he said Bob passed away probably shortly after you pulled him out of the water. We think Meg knew. We think she was so worried about keeping you calm that she told you he was okay. She moved him up next to you, so his heat would help keep you warm," Chick struggled to give voice to the words as he said them.

"She . . . she had to handle that alone. She . . . ," Jadon stammered.

"She didn't want to upset you, we think. I can't imagine what she went through in that moment. Seeing the two of you lying there. God," Erin dropped her head into her hands.

"What the fuck?" Chick said in disbelief as he watched Devon stride down the hallway, quickly making his way into Meg's room.

"Where is she?" Devon asked with contempt, after looking in Meg's room. "What have you done to her?"

"Get the hell out of here," Chick ordered.

"No. No. I don't intend on doing anything of the sort. I want to see Meg. I think you people, *you* especially," he said bitterly, pointing at Jadon, "have done quite enough."

Without thinking Jadon hurled himself across the hall, throwing his body into Devon and knocking him against the wall.

"Get the fuck out of here!" Jadon yelled. "Get the fuck out of here. You have caused so much hurt and pain. You're so messed up."

"Me? Really," Devon said, moving away from Jadon. "From what I'm told, Meg might not live. Whose fault is that?" he asked angrily.

"If you care for her, like you say you do, leave," Jadon said.

"Get the hell out of here. *Now!*" Chick yelled. "If you don't remove yourself, I'll fucking do it with my own two hands."

"Not just *his* hands. The rest of us are ready to kick your ass out of here," Bob said.

"And don't ever come around our Meg again," Stu said steadily.

"Brilliant," Devon said, "just brilliant. Well. I'll go. For now. But I will be back. And when I do, I'm sure Meg will come to her senses. So . . . your days with Meg" — Devon gave a hateful look toward Jadon — "are over."

Chapter 34

Jadon woke early. He opened his eyes to look at Meg, then glanced above her head to scan her monitors. Rubbing his head gently on hers, he struggled to clear the dense clouds that filled his mind. Spending every minute given to him over the past two days lying next to Meg, he felt as though he were living in a bubble.

"Hey," Chick said in a low whisper, walking into Meg's room, "were you able to get any sleep?"

"A little. A little. I hardly want to. I don't want to be asleep when she wakes up."

"You want to get a little sleep now? You can doze off there. I'll just sit here and watch. As soon as I see any movement, I'll wake you. Promise. If there's a blip on that monitor, I'll make sure you're awake."

"I don't know. Thanks. But the nightmares are almost too much," Jadon said. "I . . . I keep seeing her . . . floating there. I keep seeing her trying to take care of me. I keep seeing so many things. I can't get them to stop."

"Maybe Dr. Solomon can give you something. You need your sleep. She's going to need you to be strong. You're falling apart at the seams."

"No. No. I don't want to be out so hard I can't wake up for her. She's going to wake up. I know it. I know she is." Looking above Meg, Jadon carefully took note of her vitals again.

"I stopped by your place. I stopped by Meg's, too. I wanted to put Bob's . . . things away. I didn't want her dealing with that. I didn't want you dealing with that."

"Thank you. That means a lot. Thank you."

"I grabbed your mail, and hers. This was in yours," Chick said, handing a package to Jadon. "I sorted through the other things; there wasn't anything important in there. But I noticed the return address on this said Hathaway Publishing. I thought I'd made a mistake and it was for Meg. But it's addressed to you, so I thought maybe you'd want it right away."

Staring at the package, Jadon pulled on the tab, allowing it to open. Tipping the box, Meg's novel and a small handwritten note slid out:

Dear Mr. Hastings:

I was contacted by Ms. Scott shortly after she submitted her novel for publishing. She advised that she would not consent to its release unless its dedication was printed exactly as she had written it. Please note the dedication is per her exact words. Following her other request, I have sent you, Mr. Hastings, this first edition copy.

Sincerely ~ Claire Hanover, Hathaway Publishing

Removing his eyes slowly from the note, Jadon contemplated the words he just read. Meg had contacted her publisher while they were still in Europe on tour.

"What is it?" Chick asked anxiously.

"It's . . . Meg's book . . . the one she just published, the one that . . ." Jadon's words faded as he eased open the hard cover from her novel. Turning the dedication page, he read the words she had written exclusively for him.

To Jadon,

Who, without his knowing, inspired the passion filling the many pages you're now holding in your hands. Because of him, I

*will live happier, having experienced what love in its most
exquisite form feels like. I only wish that during those most
precious moments, when my world stood still as I gazed into his
eyes, I had the courage to tell him how I felt. So now, now that it's
perhaps too late, I will say without hesitation or regret, he is the
most beautiful color of love.*

> *~ Meg*

Dropping the book on his lap, Jadon threw his face into his
hands and cried.

"I was so wrong. I messed up everything," Jadon whispered
through his hands. "I was so angry. I was mad at her because I
thought she used me. I can't believe how wrong I was. I . . . was so
scared of how I felt."

Reaching onto the bed, Chick grabbed the book once Jadon slid
his body tight against Meg's. Chick sighed heavily after reading
Meg's dedication to Jadon.

"I could just kill that bastard. I could kill Devon for what he did.
Everything was good. Everything was good. Both of you
were . . . ," Chick's voice cracked with anger, "so alive, and in love. I
was the only fuckin' obstacle. And I was quickly losing ground to
you guys. I knew it. I knew it. And . . . you know . . . I was starting
to not care. I just wanted to see you happy. I wanted to see Meg
happy. Then that fucker showed up and in one clean sweep of hate
and jealousy he took both of you guys right out of the game."

"No, no," Jadon protested. "I should've just talked to her. I
should've asked her. I should've had the courage to put myself out
there. I didn't. I was too goddamn scared."

"Mr. Hastings?" The nurse said quietly, poking her head in the
room. "Dr. Solomon has ordered more tests. We need to get her
prepped and ready."

"Oh, okay. What tests? I thought they just did another scan. I mean . . . ," Jadon said nervously.

"Well, Dr. Solomon is concerned, he . . . ," she said carefully looking at both Jadon and Chick, "he feels the pressure should be lessening. Instead, from the scans we've done, it appears to be rising. If it continues . . . it could lead to . . . We need to run more tests. To see if there is anything else that can be done."

"What about surgery? Dr. Solomon said something about surgery," Chick reminded her.

"I know, Mr. Holschick, but because of the placement of the hemorrhage, surgery would be . . . the last resort. The very last resort. Please know if that does become necessary, Dr. Solomon is a remarkable surgeon. Meg is in very good hands. Let's run these tests," she said, motioning for them to leave the room.

"Oh, God." Jadon leaned against the wall next to Meg's door. "I . . . Chick . . . I can't lose her. And I can't do anything to save her. God. *God*, this is unreal!"

"I think you're doing something. I think Meg is fighting right now. I don't know where or how, but she isn't gone. You know she isn't gone."

"I know. I know. I feel her."

"Let's go. Let's get some fresh air. I know where I want to take you."

"I don't want to leave. What if something happens while I am gone."

"You need fresh air. You need to breathe. Meg needs you as strong as possible. I won't take no for an answer. So come on. We'll be right back. Promise. It's just a couple miles away."

His head resting hard against the headrest of Chick's BMW, Jadon watched the immense cliffs come into focus as they quickly drove up the winding dirt road to the open space overlooking the ocean, the same place where part of the video for his song was filmed. The same place Sidney photographed them sitting next to one another, overlooking the vast ocean that sat before them.

A slight look of panic flashed across Jadon's face. He glanced at Chick. The emotional significance of this place was almost too much for him to handle at the moment.

"I know, I know," Chick said, turning in his seat to look at Jadon. "But hear me out. I think this is the perfect place to collect your thoughts. I don't know, but that day we filmed the video . . . watching Meg standing on the cliff. I don't know. This place, it just feels like she's in the air here. There's something about it . . ."

"I know," Jadon responded weakly. "That's why . . . I almost feel like I can't quite be here. I'm afraid something . . . something in the air will tell me she's gone. I don't know if I'm strong enough. I know that sounds strange, but . . ."

"Nothing sounds strange anymore. Let's just do this and . . . and get right back to the hospital," Chick said, stepping out of the car.

After walking slowly to the cliff, Jadon stood motionless. Resting his feet on the edge, he stood in the same place he saw Meg stand months before. Closing his eyes, he stood just as he had watched Meg stand months before. He stretched his arms into the air, just as Meg had done, and felt the ocean wind sweep hard across his body. Surrendering to the wind, he felt it return his trust by pushing against him. Although he still saw all the images that constantly plagued his mind, Jadon also saw a window of space. Focusing on the small space emerging within the center of his mind, the space expanded. Within that space he recognized the faint image of Meg spinning her radiant body around in circles, with a tranquil, luminous smile on her face. In his vision, Jadon saw

Meg's soulful eyes opening long enough to see him staring back at her. He watched within his mind as Meg danced to the music of life. Straining to catch his breath, Jadon allowed his tears to fall freely while watching Meg. He felt her energy move throughout his body, and he tried to absorb everything about her heavenly presence, wanting to join her wherever she was.

With this blissful image in his mind, Jadon felt his body push slightly forward. He was not frightened by the movement. Instead he chose to give himself the courage to trust, to trust that if he was meant to stand he would be firmly supported. Feeling his body tense slightly, Jadon tried harder to focus on Meg's image, but it quickly became transparent, then swiftly and harshly was pulled from his mind.

Jadon opened his eyes, startled by the vigorous push he felt from the wind. Staring out at the immense ocean, Jadon felt his body tighten with pain.

"Meg. Meg. It's Meg. Something's wrong. I think. I think . . . something's happened!" Jadon yelled, throwing his body into Chick's car.

Sending a plume of dust and gravel behind them, Chick sped the car down the curving road and back onto the street leading back to Bay City.

"What the hell happened?" Chick screamed.

"I think. *God! I don't know!* I saw her. She was dancing. And then, it was like something ripped her right out of my mind. It hurt. It hurt the way she was pulled out of my mind! That's why the wind pushed me back. I know it. It was like it told me to go."

"That's what we're doin' . . . don't worry . . . ," Chick yelled, bring the car to a shuddering stop in front of the hospital's main entrance.

With no sensation of breath, one of the many things innately belonging to each human, Meg felt herself long for an understanding of where she was. Surrounded by the absence of color, and the absence of all things, with only nothingness that seemed to span without ever reaching an end. Not frightened, Meg had only the awareness of *being* — fully experiencing herself in its eternal form.

Within this spaceless area, Meg felt something larger than herself shift, and rebalance itself. With an unapologetic commanding strength, she felt the force of life emerging back into her body. Opening her eyes slightly, she tried to discern the images surrounding her. She slid her fingers over the soft blanket spread across her body and tried to take a deep breath.

Too tired to move, Meg closed her eyes and sank into a celestial dream. Within the ethereal space of her dreaming mind, Meg felt her body move and sway to the warm wind that travels the world. As if her partner, the breeze danced and moved her body with its gentle rhythm. Opening her eyes within the dream, Meg saw her mother in the distance walking through an open field of wildflowers, her long chestnut colored hair flowing behind her. She turned and smiled at Meg.

Meg watched as her mother silently mouthed the words, *My heart sweetness*, the very words she had spoken every night when tucking her into bed as a child. Wanting to follow her, Meg started to walk in her direction, stopping to watch her mother smile and lovingly shake her head no.

Standing within her dream, Meg watched her mother turn and peacefully walk through the wildflowers, stopping occasionally to pick one. Waving a bunch of them lightly under her nose, Meg's mother turned to wave it playfully in front of Bob's long auburn snout before bouncing it off of the scrappy head of Stinky, who wiggled his body happily alongside of Bob's. Meg watched as her mother continued on, followed not only by Bob and Stinky but also two other dogs she could only faintly remember from photographs taken of her mother before Meg was born. Not wanting to miss a moment, Meg looked intently at her mother until her image faded, then finally disappeared.

Overcome with joy, Meg spread her arms wide and twirled her body, happily giving in to the life force that flowed through her dream. As she spun her body, dancing from deep within her soul, Meg felt her longing for Jadon rise within her. She saw him standing before her, standing on the cliff overlooking the bay, staring back at her. Reaching her hand out, Meg wanted to touch his face. She wanted to tell him she loved him. She wanted to carefully wipe away the tears she watched stream down from his beautiful, soft eyes. *Let me go to him,* Meg said silently to herself.

"Mr. Hastings, wait!" the nurse said, trying to catch up to Jadon as he ran toward Meg's room. "Mr. Hastings, *Mr. Hastings!*" she yelled, pushing her body in front of his in an attempt to stop him. "Wait, Mr. Hastings, I need you to wait. Ms. Scott is about to be prepped for surgery."

"What?" Jadon screamed. "No, no. Let me see her. I have to see her." Jadon shifted his body around the nurse, opened the door to Meg's room, and looked at the monitor, which alerted everyone to Meg's elevated heart rate and blood pressure.

"Mr. Hastings, we need to get Ms. Scott ready for surgery," the nurse repeated, attempting to stop Jadon from sliding onto Meg's bed.

"Oh, my God. I knew it. I knew it. I shouldn't have left. I shouldn't have left," Jadon cried, pushing his body tightly against hers.

With her eyes still closed and heavy from sleep, Meg smiled and wrapped her fingers around Jadon's and in a soft whisper said, "Is that my piano man?"

Hearing her voice, Jadon's face softened with relief then crumbled into a soulful cry. Turning his body towards hers, Jadon delicately held Meg's face in his hands, staring hard into her eyes, needing to erase any doubt that he was dreaming.

"I love you Meg. God. I love you. With everything in me . . ."

Closing her eyes, Meg felt his lips on her own.

Chapter 35

"Mr. Hastings, I need you to make certain Meg does not in any way exert herself," Dr. Solomon repeated slowly, keeping purposeful eye contact with Jadon yet unable to determine if Jadon was absorbing the seriousness of what he was trying to carefully explain to him.

"But . . . it's been four days since she woke up, and her tests are good, right?" Jadon asked hesitantly.

"Let's sit down," Dr. Solomon said, motioning to the two chairs across the hall from Meg's room.

Taking a deep breath, Dr. Solomon turned his head to look at Jadon, giving him a paternal look of patience and compassion.

"Yes. Her tests show great improvement. If they didn't, I wouldn't allow her to go home today. But, as I explained to both of you earlier, there's still a great deal of blood in her brain that hasn't yet been absorbed by her body. We're hoping that in time it will. Until then . . . what's left . . . ," Dr. Solomon sighed, trying to keep his words easily understandable. "We don't want any of that blood to clot. We don't want anything to happen that might cause an increase in her blood pressure or heart rate, no lifting or unnecessary exertion."

"And . . . if it does?"

"Well, she might still be okay, especially if we're able to dissolve the clot quickly. My concern, Jadon, is that a clot develops and then breaks free. Once a clot is moving around inside the body, especially in the brain, it can lead to complications. My main concern is that it would cause her to have a stroke. A stroke, if not treated in time, could cause permanent neurological damage or complications . . . or death."

"But . . . how do I know . . . if . . . ," Jadon cautiously started to say.

"Well, if she feels dizzy, blacks out, or suffers tingling sensations . . . get her here right away."

"Okay. Okay. I can do that," Jadon nodded his head.

"But . . . it's vitally important that until all the blood that's left in her brain is fully absorbed, she remains calm. And as I told Meg privately . . . ," Dr. Solomon looked down at Jadon's sensitive face, much like he would his own son, "it's important that . . .you two wait on certain things."

Glancing up at Dr. Solomon, Jadon felt his face flush instantly once his mind registered what Dr. Solomon was referring to. "Oh, uh . . . of course."

"I can tell you feel a great deal for Meg, and she for you. So just keep things very low key. Abstaining from sex is my main . . . concern."

"Oh, God . . . Yes. No. I wouldn't do anything, anything that would hurt Meg."

"I never once doubted that. I know Meg is very important to you. I also can tell . . .well . . . all right. Have her back the day after tomorrow for her next MRI. The nurse should have given you the information in Meg's discharge papers," Dr. Solomon concluded, pointing down at the thick stack of papers Jadon held in his hands.

"Yeah. It's in here . . . somewhere."

"She's fortunate to have you."

"Oh, no. No. I'm the lucky one. Trust me," Jadon said, standing up. "Thank you."

Reassuring Jadon once again that she was strong enough to stand on her balcony, Meg rested her hands on the thick white railing and closed her eyes. She had longed for the moment when she could stand in that very spot, smelling the salty ocean air again.

Before her second breath had the chance to enter her body, she felt the pain of Bob's absence. Pushing back the tears, Meg settled her thoughts on his image, walking peacefully behind her mother in whatever place they were in.

Meg watched as Jadon slid his body beside hers, edging his hand next to hers on the railing. She eased her eyes onto his face. Meg soaked in his beauty, confident that every time she would look at him, for as long as she was blessed to do so, he would, without knowing, take her breath away.

Wanting to look into her eyes, Jadon turned toward Meg, causing her to gently turn her body to face his. Not knowing how to start, Jadon gently held Meg's hands in his and looked into her eyes.

"I . . . I never thought I would ever fall in love. I mean . . . ," Jadon glanced at the ocean before returning his eyes back onto Meg's. "It didn't even interest me. And now, I stand here, and when I look at you, and try to find words to describe how I feel about you . . . *I love you* doesn't even begin to describe it. It doesn't even graze the surface of all that I feel. I don't even know the world exists when I look into your eyes. And I don't care if it does. I only want to keep looking. Part of me is scared to death, Meg. Because you're all I think about. All I want. I want to lose myself in you . . . and . . . if you . . . I hope you feel . . ."

Meg put her finger softly on Jadon's lips. "I'm so in love with you. And it's the most delicious feeling. I'm out of my mind with love, passion, shameless lust . . . fear and joy. There isn't one thing about you and your beautiful mind that I don't yearn to get lost in. Wonderfully lost. And, if I'm lucky, if the heavens will allow me, I'll never find my way out again. Because I won't be looking. I won't bother to make my way back out. Instead I just want to walk deeper within the amazing soul that rests behind your eyes."

Pulling her close, Jadon pressed his lips against hers, consuming every passionate kiss she eagerly provided. Feeling her fingers slide through his hair, he gently pushed his lips harder against hers.

Remembering the cautious words carefully spelled out to him by Dr. Solomon, Jadon stopped. "Are you feeling okay? Are you tired?"

"I'm perfect," Meg said, trying to continue the kiss.

Trying not to look into Meg's eyes, Jadon found the strength he needed to restrain himself. "I think you should lie down. It's been a long day. And I don't want anything to happen to you. Sitting next to Bob's grave at Chick's . . . I know that was hard on you. It was hard on me. It was hard on all of us. It had to be unbelievably hard on you."

"I'm good. I'm great," Meg smiled, trying to reassure him, pulling his face closer to hers.

"Dr. Solomon was real serious, Meg. He sat me down . . . and . . . I'm putting you to bed. You need to rest," Jadon said adamantly. Bending down, he scooped Meg into his arms, and carrying her into her bedroom, he carefully set her down on the bed.

"Lie with me," Meg asked.

"Oh . . . well . . . no," Jadon said, taking a deep breath to clear his mind.

"Please. Just stay next to me and . . . we can talk," Meg said, wanting him close to her.

"Talking is good. It's calm," Jadon said, not completely convinced of his ability to keep it at strictly that. "The doctor said nothing but calm, Meg. He was real serious about it. I mean . . . he *really* spelled it out."

Turning onto her side, Meg shifted her head onto the pillow Jadon's head was rested on, bringing her mouth near his.

"I should probably not be here," Jadon said, realizing he didn't possess the resolve needed.

"Here's where I want you."

"My heart is pounding so hard. Meg. I swear it's going to jump right out of my body. Let me take your pulse," he said, reaching for Meg's wrist.

"No. No. I'm very calm. Trust me," Meg lied.

"Really? Because, I can hardly hear myself think, my heart is pounding so hard."

"I'm perfectly calm. I'm in that place that sits right above perfect. That's where I am," Meg said, leaning over to kiss his lips.

"I want to make love to you so much. Oh," Jadon said, pulling his head back slightly. "Meg. He said you could . . . you could die."

"What a wonderful way..."

"No, Meg. Really. You don't understand how much I love you. There's this normal love that I think others feel, then there's what I've got going on . . . and it's . . . it's out there, Meg," he interrupted, terrified by the threat of losing her. "He said not to do this at all. And . . . and then, how do we do it calmly? God, I've been thinking about this . . . I've been picturing this over and over from the moment I first saw you."

"I'm perfect. And I want to feel you. I want to lose myself in you. We'll take it slow . . . and if anything changes we can stop," Meg lied again, knowing that her words sounded convincing.

"Slow? Well . . . we haven't even done anything yet and I feel like my heart is going to burst. How do I know you'll be okay? If anything happened to you, I wouldn't make it, Meg."

Leaning her body against his, Meg ran her mouth softly up and down his neck. "I'll be okay. I'm always okay when I am with you," she said.

Giving in to the forces that removed everything around him, everything except Meg, Jadon began to explore her body. Running his fingers across her skin, he slowly removed her clothes, and slid out of his own. Gazing at her body, he gently kissed her inner thighs, brushing his mouth over her stomach and onto her mouth before bringing his body carefully into hers. He was trying to be as slow as possible in all of his movements, while everything inside of him spiraled out of control.

Studying his sensitive face above hers, Meg watched as Jadon tried to calm himself. Not wanting to calm anything, she lifted her head and gave him a heated kiss, nibbling at his lower lip. Rocking her body beneath his, Meg pulled him closer.

"Meg . . ." Jadon winced from the pain that lives only in the moment of lovemaking. "Kiss me like that again . . . and . . ."

Without hesitating Meg lifted her head and gave him the same kiss.

Wrapping his arms around her, Jadon vanished completely within the beautiful world that is Meg, releasing every captive wish and desire he held within his heart for her. Moving her body onto his, his hands traveled the curves that flowed gracefully over her slender frame.

Bringing her body back onto the bed, he held her tight against him, wanting to absorb her body into his. Opening his eyes, he recorded within his mind every moment while watching Meg draw her head back in pleasure.

Within the short moment of silence that surrounded them, with his heart pounding heavily on Meg's chest, Jadon quickly grabbed Meg's wrist trying to find her pulse.

"No. I'm fine. I'm more than fine. Let's just fall asleep like this. Passed out . . .drunk with love. I just want to hold you then wake and see you . . . I'm good. I'm perfect," Meg promised, trying to hide her heart as it hammered against her chest.

"Promise?"

"Promise."

"Meg?" He asked, looking at her face across the pillow they both shared.

"Hm . . ."

"What would be the right thing to say to a woman who doesn't want to ever get married . . . but you desperately want to spend the rest of your life with?"

Taking a moment to think, Meg smiled contently.

"Will you fly with me?" she answered, turning to look into his eyes.

Pausing for a moment, Jadon searched her face once more before letting his eyes relax onto hers. "Meg, will you fly with me?"

the end

CPSIA information can be obtained at www.ICGtesting.com
Printed in the USA
BVOW071820261211

279116BV00001B/6/P